Daisy Haites thought she'd left everything about her old life in the past: the crime, her family and the man she loves. But when her safety is threatened by an unknown source, not even her policeman boyfriend Tiller can protect her.

Suddenly Daisy finds herself back under the watchful eyes of her gang-lord brother Julian and her ex-boyfriend Christian, both desperate to keep her safe. Daisy's return to the Boroughs is exactly what Christian has been waiting for; finally a chance to prove how much he really loves her and how badly they belong together, boyfriends be damned.

Everything gets more complicated when beautiful, broken-hearted socialite Magnolia Parks enters the scene and Julian finds himself falling for her in a way he swore he never would for anyone. Because for Julian, falling in love isn't just unwelcome – it could be deadly for everyone involved. And just as Daisy and Magnolia finally strike up a peculiar friendship, Julian's past might be about to catch up to them all, with terrible consequences.

By Jessa Hastings

Magnolia Parks
Daisy Haites
Magnolia Parks: The Long Way Home
Daisy Haites: The Great Undoing

Daisy Haites

THE GREAT UNDOING

JESSA HASTINGS

THE EPHEMERAL HAPPINESS OF THE
HOUSE
OF
HASTINGS

For all the people in my DMs saying I need to pay your therapy bills. I won't do that, but I will dedicate this book to you. Stay that dramatic forever. Within reason. In appropriate circumstances. Probably don't be that dramatic in your daily lives. Regardless. Thank you for everything.

And for Christa. Just because.

Daisy

I roll over and rest my chin on his chest.

"Morning." He flashes me a tired smile and tosses his arm around me. "How'd you sleep?"

"Good, I think."[1] I nod. "Did I?"

Killian Tiller shrugs with both his shoulders and his mouth. "You didn't smack the shit out of me when I got into bed last night, so that felt good for me."

I smile up at him proudly and he sniffs a laugh as he stares back. Normal people don't reflexively strike their boyfriends with their elbows when said American boyfriends climb into their beds late at night.

"What time do you want to head to the farmers' markets?" I sit up, shifting into him more.

He pulls an uncomfortable smile. "I've gotta work—"

"It's a Saturday!" I frown.

"I know." He shrugs again. "Just a bit time-sensitive—"

"Tills." My shoulders slump. "Is it about my brother?"

"Dais, you know that they took me off everything to do with him—"[2] He presses his lips together and shakes his head. "Just think — without me there, you can spend as long as you want in the leafy green section…"

I give him a measured look. "You are very annoying in that section."[3]

He sighs, steeling himself for the conversation we've already had 50 times. "A leaf is a leaf, Daisy—"

---

[1] Eventually. A melatonin and four guided meditations later.

[2] A conflict of interests, his boss told him.

[3] Doesn't like leafy greens, my boyfriend.

I shake my head. "It isn't."

"It is." He nods his. "Just a bunch of leaves named by eccentric botanists—"

"A head of romaine looks and functions very differently — to say — kale." I give him a look, and he shakes his head all stubborn, just to get a rise.[4]

"Will you be home for dinner?"

"Should be."

He nods, then leans over, kisses me how I've always wanted him to for so many years, and then rolls out of bed to shower.

He has his own place, but really he lives here with me in my apartment in Kensington Garden Square.[5]

About a month into living by myself I came home one day to find my apartment broken into.

Door smashed in, lock broken, place tipped upside down — nothing missing, not that I could tell, anyway.

I called the police because apparently that's what normal people[6] do if something goes wrong — they don't call their brother[7] or his Lost Boys[8], they just call the police[9]. So I called the police[10].

And then Killian Tiller showed up.

He knocked on my broken-down door and it swung open slowly. I was there, perched up on a bench next to my neighbour, Jago,[11] who eyed the man in the doorway suspiciously.

I jumped to my feet when I saw him and a funny prickle rolled through my body, some sort of relief and sadness all at once. I remember becoming acutely aware that I was in baggy old 501s and a black crop top. Mismatched socks and my hair all shoved up into a little ponytail, barely there because I cut my hair when I cut everyone out of my life.

---

[4] And if Killian Tiller thinks that a rocket leaf is interchangeable with baby spinach, I honestly can't help him.

[5] Bayswater

[6] Which — to reiterate — I am now.

[7] Because he's an idiot.

[8] Because they're all idiots.

[9] Also possibly idiots.

[10] Even though everything in me really just wanted to call my brother.

[11] Yes, Jago Benz. The one from the band. He's only here some of the time, most of the time he's in New York.

"I heard it on the radio—" Tiller told me with a frown as he reached into his back pocket to pull out his badge, flashing it at Jago.

"This is Killian Tiller—" I nodded over at him. "He's a..." I squinted at Tiller and his eyebrows arched in that old, playful way. "Sort of an old friend."

Jago nodded, told me to call him later — that I could stay with him if I wanted to — and then he left.

Tiller glanced around. "Your housekeeping's gone downhill."

I rolled my eyes and he gave me a small smile. Happy to see me, I could tell.

"This how you found the place?" He started poking around with a pen as to not touch anything. "Did you move anything?"

I shook my head and he whipped out his phone, taking a few photos.

"Any ideas?" He looked down at me.

"Was it Julian, do you mean?" My brows arched in defence.[12, 13]

His jaw jutted. "You said it, not me."

"No, it wasn't Julian." I glared over at him and he just nodded, walked around a bit.

"How have you been?" he asked, looking up at me from across the way. Arms folded over his chest, serious brows.

"I mean—" I glanced around my trashed living room. "I've been better."

He squashed a smile. "Before this — how were you?"

"Good." I pursed my lips. "I guess."

"You heard from him?"

I shake my head. "Last I heard, he fled London[14] because he's wanted by Scotland Yard." I gave him a dark look.

"Well..." His American shoulders shrugged. "He's stolen a lot of art."

"I know."

"Evaded a lot of laws."

"I know." I nodded, impatient.

"Kidnapped some kids."

---

[12] I guess because old habits die hard.

[13] Or perhaps because I will defend my brother whether I want to or not and til my death.

[14] Somewhere in South America, Miguel told me without my asking him.

"I know, Killian," I sort of yelled and then my voice went soft. "We don't talk anymore."[15]

He nodded once, eyes dropping from mine. "Sorry." And he was, I could see it on him. "You need a new lock," he told me, pointing at it.

I pursed my lips together, nodding. "So, do I just call a locksmith then?"

"I'll do it—" he said, quickly. His eyes met mine and held steady.

I shook my head at him, flashing him a thankful smile. "That's not really in your job description."[16]

His mouth pulled, like he was amused. "Yeah, but neither is this though, so—" He gestured to my apartment.

"Just in the neighbourhood, then?" I asked, eyebrows up.

"Yeah—" He nodded coolly. "Something like that."[17]

That moment to me, still to this day, were I to put it to pictures: it's a tiny sapling breaking through the dirt.

That night I stayed at Jack's[18] — Tiller drove me there, and then late the next afternoon, he turned up to my apartment with a new lock and a tool box.

As soon as he arrived, Jack, who had been with me all day,[19, 20] his eyes went wide and he mouthed across the room, 'Oh my fuck, he's so hot.'

'Shut. Up.' I mouthed back.

Jack made a circle with his index finger and his thumb, then plunged his other index finger into it repeatedly.[21]

---

[15] I managed to say that without outwardly resembling the cracked egg I feel like inside.

[16] Which, to refresh you, is an investigator with the NCA.

[17] I'd later find out that he'd listen out for things about me and my brother, just in case, because he knew I was alone.

[18] Who was — by the way — very dramatic about the entire thing, saying I should have been living with him, that this would have never happened if I'd had a housemate, he knew we should have gotten a flat together, and I said, "With all due respect, Jack — you had a spider the size of a 1p coin in your laundry room the other day and made me come to get rid of it, so my expectations for how you'd deal with a robber aren't currently sky high."

[19] Which, to refresh you, is an investigator with the NCA.

[20] And because he was hoping to get a look at the Sexy Police Officer.

[21] That absolute child of a man.

"Get out—" I pointed to the door and my best friend cackled as he glided over to me, kissing my cheek. "Call me."

"We're fighting," I called after him.

"What are you fighting about?" Tiller asked, looking up at me from his tool box.

I flashed him a quick smile. "Nothing."

I wandered over and stood by the door he was fixing because — us and doorways, you know? My heart was fucked. I missed my brother, I missed Christian. I was alone and I was afraid, and Tiller was on his knees in my apartment fixing a thing he didn't break.

He knew what he was doing. Which — I mean — of course he did, he offered to do it, but I'd never really watched a man fix something before.

The drilling, the chiselling, the screwing — oh my God — it was torture. I bit down on my thumb because without something to bite on, I would have just been staring at him, mouth fallen open in a permanent way because Tiller was just — he's Tiller, you know? He's heaven with that blonde hair and those blue eyes and those shoulders, with that accent. I've been a puddle around him since I was about sixteen and I was melting all over again there in my own kitchen.

His eyes flicked up to me.

"So—" He coughed, super casually. "You seeing anyone?"

"No." I cracked my back as I stretched my hands up over my head. A bit because my back was sore, a bit because all of the rest of me was sore in a way I couldn't fix alone. I hated being alone. I spent my whole life desperate to be alone and there I was, all alone just how I'd hoped to be and I didn't know what to do with it.

"What about you?" I asked lightly. "Anyone?"

Tiller stared over at me a fraction longer than he probably should have and then shook his head. "Nope."

"Oh." I nodded once. Cleared my throat. "Hey, do you want a drink?" I launched myself off the wall towards the fridge, not waiting for an answer. Tiller glanced back at me with his little serious face that was so sexy to me[22] — his eyes flicked from me to the fridge then back to me. Nodded once, then focused way too intensely on the door.

---

[22] Still is. Concern is so cute on men like him. Endearing somehow, not patronising.

I poured us two well-oversized glasses of wine and I could tell that he knew I'd done it because our eyes caught when I handed him his and it looked like he was bracing himself — like he was on the edge of a cliff, talking himself into jumping off.

Tiller took a big sip then handed it back to me, kept on fiddling with the lock, and I remember so clearly finding his sublime lack of attention on me to be so hot and so sexy, and then I began to wonder whether he was doing it on purpose? The not looking at me. The brows so low with focus he was practically smouldering at the door...

After a little while, he stood. Locked the door and unlocked it again.

"All fixed—" He flashed me a quick smile. He looked flustered. Cute.

I reached past him and locked the door and the sound of the dead-bolt echoed around us and cracked open that old pit inside of me.

"Thank you," I said, quietly.

Tiller's eyes held mine. "You're welcome."

Then he nodded once, knelt back down on the ground and began packing up his tools.

It was around that point in the evening that I began to wonder whether all the sexual tension I thought I was feeling was entirely in my head. Was his drilling really just drilling? Was the want I thought I felt between us all just one sided? I don't know why, but then rippled through me this old feeling I'd get sometimes when my parents first died, that I was a small, helpless girl, all alone in all the world. I only really felt like that for a few months after it happened that day on the beach but I'd have a dream most nights, sometimes I still do: me on the sand, them still dying, but Julian's dying with them and it's just me there — alive — but I really am an orphan and I really am alone. I'm all the things my brother said I am.

That's how I felt when my brother walked out of that hospital room and that's how I started to feel again watching Tiller pack up his tools there in front of me, so as soon as I felt it, I wanted him to leave — needed him to. I didn't want him to see my face, see that I was sad — see that I hadn't changed at all, that I'd sleep with him on the spot as much as I would Jago or the barista across the street, that I'd use their bodies as a plywood board to lay over the pit so I wouldn't fall back into it.

I knelt down next to him to help him pack up faster, picked up a drill and blew the sawdust off it it when—

"Ow! Shit!" My hand flew to my eye.

"Are you okay?" Tiller frowned, concerned.

I stood up precariously, felt my way over to the guest bathroom and he rushed over, and I remember seeing with my good eye that he was more concerned than a speck of sawdust called for.

Splashed some water in my eye, tried my best to flush it out. And then a hand on my waist spun me around.

"Let me see." He took my face in both his hands and carefully, with his thumb, dragged my closed eye open.

Our faces were close enough for me to feel the residual warmth of his body.

When I think back to that night, that's the part I remember best. He made me feel warm.

"I think you got it—" he said but it came out a little croaky.

His eyes flickered down me, pressed his tongue into his bottom lip, eyes glued to mine and then he leant in... slowly... it was such a measured lean in.[23] Him just watching me the whole time to make sure I didn't change my mind.

Like I ever would, that face coming towards me finally how I always wanted it to.

I slipped my hands around his waist and tugged him in towards me, our mouths brushed and then all his measures were cast to the wayside.

Here's the truth: I had daydreamed about sleeping with Killian Tiller an innumerable number of times since I was about 16. So that — there and then — had years of expectations riding on it and Tills did not disappoint.

It never slowed down, it never lulled — he didn't miss a beat. He picked me up on his waist and we did it on my bathroom sink under incredibly terrible lights — the kind that show every flaw you have and I couldn't see a single one on him.

Then afterwards, he sat back against the wall of my tiny bathroom staring up at the ceiling, looking all pensive, back to worried.

"Fuck—" He shook his head.

"What?" I sat up, pulling my shirt back on over my head.

---

[23] Makes me smile when I think about it now. It's so Tiller to be measured.

"Sorry—" He started frowning. "I shouldn't have done that."

"Done what?"

He pointed a finger vaguely at me.

"Me?" I blinked.

He nodded quickly, running his hands over his face, stressed. He tugged his t-shirt back on, standing up. "I didn't mean to like, take advantage of you—"

I looked over at him confused. "Tiller, I poured the equivalent of about three wines into your one glass because I wanted this to happen..."

He flashed me an unimpressed look.

"Been trying to bed you for years, Tills—" I told him, trying to keep it light. I didn't like how strained he looked.

"Tiller!" I laughed, because he was being so cute. "It was just sex."

And then I remember how he eyed me all suspicious, like I was full of it. "There's no such thing."

"Yes, there is!" I shook my head, laughing again. "Of course there is! We just did it!"

He breathed out like he'd been holding it in. "I swear to God, I really did just come here to fix your lock."

I gave him a tiny smile. "I believe you."

He left not long after that, and later on texted me saying he was sorry and if I needed any help with anything else, just to text him.

And would you believe it? A few days later, my drain clogged.

That's how we started. First the lock, then the clogged drain. Then my fridge started leaking and I needed a new one. Then my car ran out of petrol... on purpose.

And then I started doing things like shaking a lightbulb til the tungsten filament broke and then reinstalling the bulb, pretending I didn't know how to change one.

"You know you can just ask me to come over for sex, right?" he told me that night, as he tugged on my hair playfully. Which I did, for about a week. Because when I stopped, I missed... him.[24] And it was a great week. Tiller would come over most nights after work, 'bang one out' as Julian would say. And it was working for me, because I

---

[24] The other him. The one I love but can't love anymore, because I'm normal now.

had school and no friends besides Jack[25] and I was single and alone and being alone reminded me that I was, actually, really, very alone. No family, two friends and a bodyguard who won't quit.[26]

And then there was a knock on my door one night unannounced.

"What are you doing here?" I blinked up at Tiller unceremoniously, glancing at the wine and flowers in his hands.

"It's Valentine's Day." He shrugged.

I shrugged back. "I know."

"I want to take you on a date," he told me, stepping around me to get inside.

I closed the door. "What?"

"What?" He sniffed, amused. "This can't be a huge shock to you — we've slept together most nights the last... two weeks."

"I know." I rolled my eyes. "But all that's — just, sort of perfunctory, is it not?"

Some hurt rolled over his cute face. "Not to me."

"Tills—" I sighed. "I've always... With you, you know I[27]—" I gestured towards him and swallowed because he's so handsome. "You know I have, but I'm still not really like, past—" I couldn't say his name, I still can't. It always stops short in my mouth like saying it out loud might mean I'm letting some part of him leave me,[28] so I waved vaguely towards the ghost of Christian Hemmes that follows me everywhere.

And then Tiller tilted his head, gave me a quarter smile. "I'm not asking you to marry me, Dais. It's just a date."

So we went out. And then the weirdest thing happened — I had a really, genuinely wonderful, happy time. It was the most fun I'd had in months. And we didn't do anything special — we got Nando's because every restaurant in London was booked and he didn't think to book it, because he didn't think I'd actually say yes, so we had Nando's[29] and then we went for a walk and we listened to country

---

[25] And, sort of reluctantly, Taura. I don't really know how she wormed her way in here, but anyway.

[26] Try though I do, daily. I also do not let him in my house, just to be difficult. One time I did let him in to do a wee though.

[27] 'I have always liked you and I've always wanted some version of this.' is what I do not say out loud to him.

[28] And I don't think I will ever.

[29] The dodgy one, on Queensway.

music, which back then in February I thought was shit and I teased him for how much he loved it but now it's nearly November and I can sing you the lyrics to every Thomas Rhett song and don't even get me started on Dan + Shay...

That night he came back to my house and we watched *The Sixth Sense* — I picked a sort of scary one, because I hoped it meant he'd stay, and when we were watching it he put his arm around me and he looked nervous when he did it — he wouldn't look at me, just at the screen, and then he did stay.

Tiller falls asleep easily, I've worked that out by now — I think it's because he is so innately good, he has no worries, he's sort of the human personification of Hakuna Matata — he's just relaxed at all times, and to get a rise I tell him I think that's because he'd spend his summers with his grandfather in Venice and he smoked too much weed and he says to stop saying that so loudly all the time and that he only told me that under duress and I said it was hardly duress and he said handcuffs were involved, so technically... and that's as much of the story as you need to know. Tiller sleeps easy, that's my point.

And on that Valentine's night, as I stared over at him — him, who is arguably one of the most beautiful men I've ever seen at any point of my whole, entire life — then and there, I made myself a deal: I would be done with Christian Hemmes. Done as I could be and I won't ever be fully, I don't think, but Christian was in the corner there, this towering statue like some alter I built of him or for him in my living room and he was always there — casting a shadow on everything, discolouring all the ways I might potentially be happy without him — because I don't want to be without him, I want to be with him. I did before, I still do now, of course I still do, but I can't be. We want different things. He wants to be there and amongst it and I... well, I miss it, actually, if I'm being honest. But that's because it's all entangled with my brother and probably, really, I think I miss it mostly in a Stockholm Syndrome kind of way where it's all I've ever known and I'm scared without it and so it doesn't count. And so it doesn't matter that I love Christian, which I do,[30] because love isn't enough and it's not all you need and we are the proof of that.

So I decided then, that night on Valentine's Day, that I was going to pack Christian away. He couldn't live in my living room anymore.

---

[30] More than anything and painfully so.

I didn't know how to pack him down, I didn't know how to take loving him apart[31] — I don't think I can. I think I accidentally loved him in a way where he'll be my weak knee forever, so maybe he's a statue I can't tear down and I'll always bow to and see in some holy light but maybe he's a statue I could shift onto a trolley and move him out of the main room and away into the guest room — the same room where all my thoughts live, the ones about my brother and how much I miss him and how scared I am without him and how I wish he would just come and get me and make me come home but he won't so I won't either. So what if Christian is just another thing I won't ever be able to disassemble? At least I can put him a room, bolt the door shut and wear the key around my neck. Visit when I need to — if I have to — but then I just close the door. That's what I did that night, I closed the door and I looked straight ahead, and straight ahead was Tiller.

And that was nearly nine months ago.

I buy two coffees from the shop downstairs, but I bring my own muffins because mine are better than theirs, and then I cross the road to the black Escalade that's always parked across from my place.

Tap on the window and it rolls down.

"Stop following me," I tell Miguel as I hand him a coffee and a muffin.

"Stop with the chia seeds, I told you I don't like them."

"No." I shake my head. "You need the potassium."

"So give me a banana—" He frowns as he takes a bite anyway. "And no." He gives me a bright smile and I roll my eyes at him, handing him my coffee wordlessly as I bend down to tie my shoe.

"Where are we off to today?" he asks as I stand up again and he hands me back my coffee.

"We're off to nowhere." I give him a look before gesturing to myself. "I'm off to the farmers' market with Jack."

He nods. "Which route are you taking?"

"Oh, the None of Your Business route — very scenic." I flash him a smile.

"Tell me."

"No."

"Just tell me."

---

[31] I still don't.

"Piss off—" I glare at him as I back away.

"Misty Way?" he calls after me.[32]

I flip him off as I open my car door.

"Is that a yes?" he calls, exasperated.

"Yes," I growl.

~

"Does your brother know he's still with you?" Jack asks a few hours later, nodding at Miguel as he slips into the booth behind us.

"I presume so." I shrug. "Otherwise Julian's just resigned to Miguel suddenly becoming a terrible employee — disappearing for massive chunks of the day."

"It's kind of sweet." Jack shrugs, trying to help.

"It's kind of unnecessary—" I say loudly, loud enough for Miguel to hear. "I don't need a bodyguard, I'm dating someone in law enforcement! I'm normal now!"

"You sound normal! Yelling away in a coffee shop, idiota louco—" Miguel calls back and I pout.

Jack reaches over and squeezes my hand.

"How are you doing today anyway?"

"Today?" I bat my eyes, shrugging like I don't know what he means. Jack rolls his eyes. "What's today?" I keep it going.

He gives me a look, nods at my plate. Breakfast hash.

I push the plate away from me. It's not as good as the ones I used to make anyway.

October 30th. My brother's birthday.[33] Barely thought of him once.

"Are you going to send him something?"

"Of course not." I shake my head.

Jack gives me a gentle shrug. "It might be a nice peace offering..."

"I don't want a peace offering," I lie. And I know it won't work. If there was ever a thing that was going to work for my brother and me to be okay again, it's already happened and it didn't change a thing.[34]

---

[32] Hhhh.

[33] Thirty-One today.

[34] And I don't want to talk about it.

"Come on." I clap my hands together. "I have to go and put dinner on."

○

"She's very good," Tiller announces, pulling me down onto his lap and leaning back into his chair.

"It was a roast chicken—" I roll my eyes at him and he wraps his arms around me tighter.

"How's it going with that guy,[35] Jacko?" Tiller nods his chin at him.

"Yeah, good—" Jack tries not to smile too much. "We've been together a month now, bit more—"

"What's his name again?" Tiller looks between us.

"August Waterhouse," I announce.

"Producer." Tiller nods. "Got it. I remember. Sick, man — I'm glad it's going well."

Jack smiles and opens his mouth to say something before glancing around our apartment. "Why do you have so many roses everywhere?"

I glance around at the six bouquets in the dining room alone.

"Oh—" I shrug. "Tiller sends me flowers all the time."

Tiller sniffs a laugh. "No, I don't."

I turn back to look at him. "What?"

"I don't send you flowers." He gestures to the flowers. "These aren't from me."

"Are you sure?" I frown.

"Am I sure I'm not sending you flowers?" He gives me a look. "Yeah."

"But you come in with them sometimes—"

"Yeah." He shrugs. "They'd just be sitting there at the door—"

I blink. "You've never sent me roses?"

"You thought I was sending you flowers all this time and you've never once said thank you?" He sits up.

"Oh my God." I roll my eyes, shifting in his lap. "They're roses, not the Hope Diamond — you pass them to me, I say thank you, that's a perfectly acceptable exchange."

---

[35] Brace yourself. Big news!

Jack gets up and starts poking through a bouquet.

"No cards—" I tell him. Never cards. I turn back to Tiller. "I just thought they were from you."

Tiller shifts, tensing underneath me a little. Holds me different. His face flicks into worried mode. He looks from me to Jack.

"Hemmes?" he suggests.

I shake my head. "We haven't spoken since—"[36] It catches in my thought so I catch Tiller's eye to steady myself. "Since that night here."

His face pulls — that was a hard night for him — but he nods.

"Romeo?" Jack throws out there.

"Hates me." I flash them both a brave smile.[37]

Tiller's hand rests on the small of my back as he sighs. "Your brother?"

I shake my head. "Also hates me."[38]

A cloud settles over the room that I feel the need to swat away, so I jump to my feet and start clearing the plates.

"It's probably just a mistake—" I shrug.

"What?" Jack and Tiller frown in unison.

"Like, someone's got the address wrong, and they're trying to send flowers to the fit girl upstairs."

Jack rolls his eyes. "Dais, you *are* the fit girl upstairs."

I bend over and touch Tiller's worried face. "It's nothing, Tills. Just some poor dyslexic's dosh down the drain—" I give him a light-hearted shrug. "They're not for me."

---

[36] Since that one night where nothing changed.

[37] Like saying that doesn't make me sick to my stomach.

[38] I force a smile because it'll ward off the crying.

2

Christian

I thought a lot about it, why I did what I did... Why I left her, walked out of that apartment like she wasn't all I'd thought about since we first ended that night at Jules' birthday. Like she's still not all I think about now.

It's too late. She's with someone else.

Seems stupid these days when I think about it, so I try my best not to.

Daisy for me was a complete trip — I accidentally fell in love with her, and I accidentally lost her. I wasn't ready for it. I wasn't ready to love someone how it turns out I love her.

I just never saw her coming, I couldn't have picked loving her out of a lineup until it happened and then it was everything: my first thought, last thought, mid-thought, the name I'd say in my sleep, the body I'd think about when I was with other bodies, the smell I'd try to chase down every time I'd walk through a Selfridges just so I could breathe in something that smelt like her and feel close to her again, but I can never find it.

When she asked me to leave everything with her, all the shit of the life we were born into... I don't know why I didn't — I just wasn't expecting it. That, and I have nothing else? I don't have a life plan. My life plan's been laid out in front of me since I was fifteen.

Me and Jo doing this fucking thing together.

Less 'him one and me two', more equal partnership, but then again, he is getting pretty cocky these days—

I don't really care though, if I'm being honest. It's a business, and I'm in it because I have to be.

I wish a bit that I could be like Uncle Harv, who pissed off to Aus and all to play sports, but it'd kill Mum, and Mum's had enough killing in her lifetime, I reckon.

So I stayed, stayed with the familiar even though it ruined me a bit. Stayed in London, a few streets away from where Daisy lived but not anymore because she made good on what she said. She said she'd leave it all behind and she did. She's done. Out of this life like a light and she's probably better for it. Better how we'd all be if we'd just sort ourselves the fuck out but we can't because it's fucking hard to leave the only thing you've ever known, even when you want to and you can be sure of this: some days, I really want to.

I'm glad for her, that she seems okay. I mean, I'm fucking gutted. I've fucked up a lot since we broke up but I'm happy for her. As long as she's happy.

She seems happy.

Taura says she is.

After everything that's happened, she deserves happy.

And me? I stare at daisies when I see them on the sidewalk, I watch GBBO now to fall asleep at night, I see her face every time I close my eyes even though I'm about two months into sort of dating Vanna Ripley.

It's messy, she's a bit of a punish, and I should know better, but she's hot and complicated in a way that distracts me enough from who I'm actually in love with.

Before that, I kind of bounced around. Almost had a dicey night with a lonely Parks in New York but we didn't do it in the end — it was me who stopped it, if you can believe it — thought of Daisy, how it might crush her if she knew, which she wouldn't. How would she know? Like she'd care anyway, she's with the policeman now who was always popping up around her. But I thought of her anyway; it stopped me in my tracks.

I toss myself down into one of the red velvet seats at The Lecture Room & Library at Sketch; we're late. We got flogged by the paps on the way out of my apartment and again outside the restaurant, and I'd be lying if I didn't admit that I'm pretty sure she called them herself.

Bit of a pain, if I'm honest, old Vanna, but how the fuck else do you pass time in the town you live in when the girl of your dreams won't talk to you and is holed up with someone else?

I have dinner with her brother, that's one way I pass the time these days. I nod my chin over at Jules as we clasp hands.

"Happy birthday for the other day, man—"

Vanna kisses his cheek before sitting down next to me and smiling curtly at the girl across from her who came with Julian.

"This is Josette Balaska," Julian tells me, gesturing to her loosely.

Beautiful girl. Short, almost-white blonde hair, pale skin, eyes that are sort of purple but they don't look like contacts?

"So you're the famous Christian Hemmes." She reaches across the table with a knowing smile. We shake. "I heard you saved his life."

I give her a shrug. "Something like that—"

Julian rolls his eyes at my faux-modesty and Vanna shifts in her seat because she's not used to not being the centre of attention.

"This is Vanna." I nod my head at her.

"Pleasure—" Josette extends her hand to her and Vanna stares at it before reluctantly taking it.

Josette gives her an easygoing smile. "How long have you been together, then?"

"Oh, we're n—" I start but Vanna cuts me off.

"Two months." She flips her hair over her shoulder.

Julian and I catch eyes and he looks away amused, flagging a waitress down and ordering a bottle of their best red.

"I don't drink red wine," Vanna tells Julian, clearly bored.

"So drink something else." He yawns without looking at her.

I toss my arm around her chair. "What do you want?"

"Surprise me," she says, not looking up from her phone.

I order her a bottle of champagne, and she reaches over and kisses me like she has something to prove, then glances at Josette, then Julian and then back to me.

"How'd you save him?"

I lick away a smile as I roll my eyes.

"He helped me find something," Julian offers.

"What?" Vanna asks, putting her phone down.

"A painting," he says, pouring himself more wine.

Vanna breathes out her nose and picks her phone back up again. "Sounds boring."

Josette and I catch eyes. I guess she knows.

"Yeah." I shrug. "No big deal—"

Just a painting worth £45,000,000 that's been missing for the last twelve years that Scotland Yard was willing to trade for Jules' freedom.

A crazy few months, actually.

Jules left in January on the run. Made it down to the Dominican Republic and then camped out til he hatched a plan.

The boys and I went for a surf trip in Hawaii and on my way back I flew through Playa Rincón. Jules told me he wanted to find a Van Gogh, barter his way back into London and have them drop all charges.

I didn't have much else going on, and I missed his sister. Wanted to find a way to feel close to her without dragging her back into what she left behind.

So I tagged along.

Found it in the end, that's how he's back — not a single charge against his name.

At some point, Vanna gets up and goes to the bathroom. Julian waits til she's out of earshot and gives me a look.

"I'm sorry, man — but there's no possible way for the sex to be good enough to put up with her—"

I sniff a laugh. "She goes alright."

Josette shakes her head. "She's the most painful person I've ever had dinner with — and I once accidentally shared a meal with a Neo-Nazi."

I nod my chin over at her. "That sounds like a good story—"

"I'm sure all stories sound good to you at this point, bro." Julian throws me a look. "The precision with which she chose what lip thing to put on just before, holding those two tubes like they weren't the same colour — are you on heavy drugs to cope?"

"If she's holding you against your will..." Josette gives me a look. "Blink twice."

"Alright—" I roll my eyes. "How'd you two meet then?"

"Oh," Julian cocks his head towards her, "we're old friends—"

"Friends is a loose term." Josette's eyes sparkle. "I'm between Berlin and New York, mostly. I fly through London a lot. We try to make the most of it."

She pokes him in the ribs, and he elbows her away. Not massively touchy, even with the girls he's shagging.

The only girl I've ever seen him hug is his sister, so I guess he's hugging no one these days. He misses her — I can tell he does.

And I'll say this, knowing him the way I do — which is well, now, by the way — the more I've gotten to know Julian, the more obvious it's become: He didn't just break Daisy's rules, she broke his.

I can see how he skirts around her name, he leaves the room when I ask about her. Which I do, I check in with Miguel all the time, creep her Instagram, pester Tausie for clues — no one gives me much, just crumbs, really. But it gets me by. It hurts Julian, though. He blinks every time you say her name. Looks away and takes a breath.

I get it. It hurts me too, but mostly, I'm just glad she's okay. I know he is as well, even though he wouldn't say it because he can be shit like that.

He still pays Miguel's salary, even though he turns a blind eye to what his day job is because he can be like that too.

I wonder how Daisy feels about that. Annoyed, probably. Bodyguards aren't normal — she used to say that a lot.

But that's part of the problem I guess. She took herself out of this life to be normal, but she's her. The hottest girl in the world, honeypots for eyes, smartest person in every room. She'll never be normal, even if she tries.

3

Julian

I think about what happened with her in the hospital every day. Wear it around my neck like a yoke that weighs me down and reminds me what the fuck I am — that my stupid sister's wrong, she doesn't know shit, I'm as bad as they say I am — the proof is in every single thing I said to her that day because they weren't just fighting words, I wanted to put her in the ground.

Me and Dais, we know each other too well not to destroy each other. And I knew as I was saying them that they weren't these fucking hapless, blind words — I knew what I was doing. Knew saying it wouldn't just make her feel sad and alone in that moment but would probably strip from her every sense of security I'd spent my whole life building up for her.

So I know she's wrong. There is no good in me, just in her, and I didn't put up a fight when she said she wanted to be normal, whatever the fuck that means—

She wanted out? Fine. Fuck her. She's out, I don't need her. Even if she's my best friend, even if walking away from her that day felt like lopping myself in half.

Had to get out of London pretty quick after that, Scotland Yard breathing down my back and shit.

Probably worked out good in the end. I don't know what sort of shit I'd have gotten up to here without Daisy to keep me in check when I was that angry.

It was on the way home from the hospital that I got the call from Declan telling me not to come back to the Compound, that the police were there and waiting with an arrest warrant.

Koa and I ditched the car, made it on foot to the Bambrillas' hangar out in Clavering.

Flew into the Onasis family's airstrip over in upstate New York.

Thought for a hot minute about paying someone a visit, but it felt too risky. We drove south to Florida. Paid a guy in Key Largo to go Nassau, Nassau to Cayo Romano. Cayo Romano to Baracoa, Baracoa to Haiti — they nearly caught me in Cap-Haïtien but we got away, made it over the border into the Dominican Republic, thank fuck. No extradition with the UK. So we set up shop in Playa Rincón.

And you know what? For all the shit I give my sister about her fucking normal-dream life, it wasn't half bad.

Surfed, caught my own fish. Saved a puppy from being killed. Pretty thing, really. Rhodesian ridgeback born without a ridge. The breeder was going to off him so I said I'd take him. Didn't have much else going on so I trained the shit out of him. Top-notch guard dog now, crazy ferocious, really protective of me — exactly what you want when you're on the run.

Hardest part of the whole thing? Not knowing if Dais was okay.

I hate her, right? I do. But I've spent my whole life looking after her. My whole life was pointed towards keeping her alive, so it doesn't matter — and fuck her for this — it doesn't matter if she's out because I can't be. She's my kid, even if she doesn't want to be anymore. She still is.

But we had no contact — just me and Koa out there, him breaking the hearts of half the girls on the island, me house-breaking the fucking dog. I didn't hear anything about my sister until Christian blew through, told me she was dating that cop.

I acted like it shitted me but actually I was a bit relieved. Without me or Christian there, her in the pursuit of that fucking normal life… I know Miguel still trails her, but it's from more of a distance now. Tiller in her bed should have made me angry, made the betrayal of what she did so much worse, but honestly, I was just glad she was safe.

There's a big story here, but the short version is me, Christian and Koa found the painting — in Rotterdam of all places. A minor hiccup along the way. But I got it. Handed it over to Interpol after arranging a deal to drop every charge against me and voila, I'm back in London. Handed it to Tiller, actually. He's not Interpol, but I knew he'd get it to them. Hoped he'd get the message to my sister that I was back too, but I don't know that he did. She didn't come home to check on me. Not that I needed her to, didn't even want her to, actually.

Anyway, first order of business was to run Ezra fucking Brown out of town, but I guess he heard I was on the way back and he fucked off pretty quick. Dipped off the map. Haven't heard of him since, so there's a pin in that.

Been home just about three months now, and it feels like it's about time to find something to do. I've laid low for a while now. I'm a bit bored.

God knows that Scotland Yard's watching me still, but I don't mind the challenge. Even if they catch me, there's always another priceless painting that needs to be found. Come to think of it, I might even have a few in my basement...

4

Daisy

Third year med school is no joke.

I've been placed at Mary St Angela's for Clinical Placement.

Placements vary in length depending on the field — up first was a six-week psychiatry placement and that was more taxing than I could ever tell you. Then four weeks of Family Medicine — not much better.

Right now I'm five weeks into the six-week Obstetrics and Gynaecology block.

Days are long and the tasks are thankless, but I wear a white coat and have a beeper, so that's pretty cool.

"You had sex—" Eleanor Wells tells me, her bright sapphire eyes flickering up and down me in suspicion.

I roll my eyes and toss my bag down on the bench to find a hair tie. "I have a live-in boyfriend, that can't be that surprising."

"How do you have time to have sex right now?" She breathes out her nose loudly. "When I was a third year I waddled around permanently with a rally pack intravenously attached to me. My only relationship was with my vibrator—" She takes the homemade muesli bar[39] I'm eating from my hands and finishes it in two bites. "How do you have time for sex?"

"How do you not, El?" Says Warner (your classic upper-class WPM.[40] Don't know if Warner is his first name or his last. Great head of hair, eyes like swimming pools, a real smooth talker, and I am positive (though do lack the personal experience to prove it) that his penis is gravely smaller than his ego would imply. "It's the most important part of life. We'd die without it."

---

[39] https://goop.com/gb-en/recipes/homemade-granola-bars/
[40] White Privileged Male

"Are you maybe confusing sex with air?" Alfie Farran[41] offers.

"What about a eunuch, then?" Grace Pal[42] asks, folding her arms over her chest.

These are my colleagues, I suppose. We've all been assigned to shadow the same F2 doctor here, which has worked out well for me because that F2 doctor is Eleanor Wells.

The others don't like me so much because I'm overtly her favourite. I'm fairly sure our relationship would be, on an academic level, deemed inappropriate. I don't know how we became friends, really — I think she saw me fighting with Miguel the first day here in the stairwell and she asked me if he was stalking me and did I need help, and I thought it was so funny and sort of nice, and her relentless love of sweets[43] made her endearing and significantly less threatening than a girl who looks like Olivia Munn should be.

I decided to be forthcoming regarding my family history in my small group. More so with Wells than the others but they catch dribs and drabs because we talk like they're not there.

"We wouldn't literally die without it," Warner huffs. "Obviously."

"Just metaphorically?" I say, tossing Wells a look as I grab my bag to put it away. Open my locker and something falls out.

I look down at my feet.

A bouquet of daisies.

"Oh!" El coos. "Someone gave you flowers! That's so nice—"

I frown down at them. Daisies. That's new.

"What?" she asks. "You don't like them?"

"Are they from you?" I ask, probably too quickly.

"No?" She laughs, picking them up. "No card."

She gives a mindless little shrug, how a normal person would, because to a normal person flowers would just be flowers, but to me, somehow they feel vaguely ominous.

I look up at the rest of them. "Did you see anyone in here?"

They all shake their heads and they're giving me weird looks because they're normal, and I'm worried I won't ever actually be.

---

[41] Very handsome, dark skin, kind eyes, short hair.

[42] A bit annoying, but very clever. Sensible hair, perfectly fine eyes and a hint of a German accent that she inherited from her father.

[43] Haribo, in particular.

I take the flowers from Wells and shove them back into my locker and pull out my phone, dialing Tiller.

It goes to voicemail.

"Hey, it's me. There were daisies in my locker today at the hospital. Did you—I know you said you didn't, but did you? Because — never mind, it's probably a coincidence. It's fine, don't worry. I'm just — bye. Have a good day, I love you, bye."

I flash Wells a smile trying to prove to her that I'm calm[44] and she gives me one back, mouth all stained from the Dib Dab she's eating at nine in the morning.

Her coping mechanism for this life is sugar. No sleep.

Pure sugar and caffeine.

Eleanor grabs the charts from the nurses' station as she checks her phone, clocking over her shoulder that we're all following her.

She'd be late 20s. Well-to-do family, for sure. You can tell that much by how she holds herself. Good upbringing, great parents. She's too confident in herself and her abilities not just as a medical professional but also as a woman and human in general that she must have had great parents. No mother issues there.

"Why are you so weird about flowers?" she asks, taking the coffee Alfie offers her. He's my favourite of the lot. He's sweet and really, honestly very good looking. Brown, warm eyes that swallow his whole face, smart but quiet, sort of a goody-goody always bringing Wells a coffee, but sometimes he brings me one too so I don't care too much. If I was Wells, I'd shag him. That might be illegal though, I'm not sure.

"I'm not weird about flowers — they were just in my locker — how'd they get in my locker?"

"So you have a secret admirer." She shrugs. "Maybe they're from the patient last week, the one who had that boil on her labia and you drained it—"

"Oh, fuck—" Warner shakes his head. "I wanted to give you flowers myself for doing that."

I glare at both of them. "That was fucking disgusting and I deserve more than daisies for that."

"I mean, we technically don't do this for the glory, but — yeah,

---

[44] I am. Why wouldn't I be?

no. I agree on that one." She gives me a sorry glance then snaps her fingers twice. "Grace—"

Grace Pal looks up with her dark chocolate eyes that always look wound up. She has a face that reminds me of a cartoon fox and I can never tell whether that's a nice thing or not.

Wells holds her hand out, waiting. Grace plonks a freshly opened packet of Jelly Tots in her hands.

"Thank you—" Wells pauses in front of the bed of Ms Green, nodding at Grace. "Go."

"Ms Green is a 37-year-old female who presents at 36 weeks for dehydration due to gastroenteritis; her past OB history is significant for a full-term normal spontaneous vaginal delivery in 2015. Her Gynaecological history is significant for....."

The day goes by fairly quickly for a twelve-hour shift. I love the feeling of taking off my scrubs, a bit because they're usually disgusting by the end of the day and I get to put on clean clothes but a lot because it just feels like I've done something good and worthwhile with my time and my day.

I take my bag from my locker, bin the daisies and walk out into the lobby, fishing for my keys, and I bump straight into my boyfriend.

"Tills." I blink up at him. "What are you doing here?"

He's got stress-face. "This was at the door when I got home."

He presents me with a box and lifts off the lid.

A bunch of mulched daisies.

My heart sinks as I nod once.

"Not a coincidence."

Tiller shakes his head.

"Come on." He nods his head towards his car. "We've got to go."

"Where?" I frown, even though I already know.

He gives me a long look. "To your brother."

5

Julian

Dinners have really fallen to the wayside around here since my sister left.

Carry-in every night and it's fine but it's just not the same as a home-cooked meal.

Indian tonight, good enough I suppose.

I've never had to organise meals for anyone before so I tend to over-cater.

"Did you do a headcount before you ordered?" Christian looks over at me and I glance around the room.

Christian pulls out ten containers of butter chicken.

"There are eight of us," he tells me as he unpacks five lamb saag-walas and four chicken kormas.

I roll my eyes, shrugging as I sit down.

And then there's this weird ripple through the room and everyone goes quiet. Romeo kicks me under the table and I look up.

In the doorway of my dining room is my baby sister and her police-man boyfriend.

"Well," I say, pulling my gun out and laying it down on the table. Hope she sees it as a proper threat and not the hollow one it really is. "Look what the cat dragged in."

Daisy's eyes flicker around the room and she frowns at the table. "How much food did you order?"

Annoying.

"The perfect amount." I fold my arms over my chest.

"For what, all of Cambodia?"

Christian licks away a smile.

She walks over to the table — everyone's sort of frozen, like they're watching a ghost.

Rome won't look her in the eyes. Hates her more than I do. Which, I guess, is maybe not at all.

She looks closer at the food on the table. "Is this Karma Marsala?" She sounds horrified.

"Yes." I frown.

"Why wouldn't you order from Khan's?"

"Because Karma Marsala is fine." I shrug.

"Khan's is better, though," Kekoa jumps in.

"Yeah." TK nods.

And I roll my eyes and — fuck — I take it back — I do hate her.

"What are you doing here?" I ask her, standing.

She opens her mouth to say something then notices LJ at my feet. "Did you get a dog?" She rushes towards him.

"Don't—" I shake my head. "He's a guard dog, Daisy. He can be vicious — really not good with stran—"

She drops to the ground to pet him and he — the fucking traitor — rolls over so she can scratch his fucking stomach.

("That's embarrassing for you," Koa whispers.)

"He's so cute!" Daisy coos. "What's his name?"

"LJ," I grunt, glaring down at him.

"Oh, why?" she says, not looking up at me.

"Little Julian."

Now she looks up at me, frowning. "You're such a fucking narcissist."

"I am not—"

"Why wouldn't you give him a proper name?"

"That is a proper name!"

"You don't have to make everything about you—"

"He's my fucking dog!" I yell louder than I need to.

She stands up, walks back over to Tiller and then — can you believe it — the bloody dog follows after her, tail wagging and all.

I once saw him bite off the ear of a crooked cop in Brazil.

"Why the fuck are you here?" I ask loudly — ignoring the look half the room throws me for talking to her like that.

She stands in front of Tiller, shielding him with herself.

Probably smart. I know Rome would kill him in a second if I gave him the chance.

"Are you sending me flowers?" she asks.

I look her up and down and scoff. "You're taking the piss, yeah?"

She folds her arms over her chest. "Are you, yes or no?"

"Why the fuck would I send you flowers?" I spit.

"I don't know—" Tiller steps around her, glaring over at me. "Maybe because she saved your fucking life?"

"Oh." I lift my eyebrows. "Look who found his voice."

Daisy grabs Tiller by the wrist. "Let's just go—" She tugs him away but he doesn't move and locks eyes with me over her head.

"Someone's sending her flowers," Tiller tells me and Christian frowns over at him.

"So?" Declan asks.

"Who gives a shit?" Romeo chimes in and he and Daisy catch eyes. She looks sad, he looks hurt. Soon they'll trade places, it's just the dance they do.

Tiller doesn't give a fuck either way. He doesn't seem phased that he's in a room with London's most wanted — he's just focused on me.

"They leave them on our doorstep," he says.

Christian flinches at the 'our' in that sentence. He hasn't let it go. Noticed that Daisy doesn't even look at him and I can tell that he thinks that means she's past him but he doesn't know her face like I do. I can tell by how she's blinking that she's barely holding it together and if she looks at him she'll lose it.

"Right." I nod. "But they're flowers, not grenades, so..."

"I want to leave—" She stares up at Tiller, her eyes raw as she tugs at his sleeve, and you know that pain you get that shoots through your bones when you're fucking up and you know you're fucking up and you're hurting someone you love but for some reason you can't stop? That happens.

Tiller's gaze doesn't change but he reaches for her and pulls her behind him, holding her hand. Shielding her from me, and about half of the room tenses up.

"They started off as roses—"

"Ooh." I roll my eyes. "Shit, that does sound dangerous."

"Fuck you," Daisy says poking her head out to glare at me.

"It was roses for months — right, Dais?" Tiller looks back at her.

"About three," she tells him. Him not me. I've lost eye contact privileges with her now.

"Today there were daisies in her locker at the hospital—" He continues and a frown breezes over my face. Don't like that.

"And then this was at the front door when I got home."

He tosses a box down on the table in front of me.

I give him a long, unimpressed look before I gruffly knock off the lid.

Mulched daisies.

My stomach lurches. Feel sick. It's definitely a threat. Don't let it show on my face though.

I look back over at my sister. "What's the problem? You love crafts, just use it for potpourri."

She sniffs out this laugh that's all hurt, zero finding anything funny, then turns and walks out.

Tiller juts out his chin and nods a few times. "Just imagine if you were even a quarter of the man she talks about you being…"

He gives me this flash of a smile, like he's disappointed in me — don't know why that stung but it did — and then he walks after her.

I wait for the front door to slam shut and then I look over at Christian.

"Is it you?"

"No." He frowns. He looks worried.

I look over at Rome. "You?"

He shakes his head, swallows nervous. This'll fuck with his head too. In his mind, no one's allowed to hurt Dais but him.

I nod my chin at Decks and he rolls his eyes. "Fuck off—"

"Right then." I nod. "Everything else stops — call every florist, gardener, every botanist, every fucking horticulturalist on the British Isles who's grown or sold roses and daisies in the last three months." I look at Miguel. "How the fuck did you miss this?"

This offends him, I can tell. He frowns at me. "She doesn't let me inside."

"Force yourself in then." I bark.

He rolls his eyes. "Oh yeah, I'm sure that'd go over well."

I give him a look and point to the door, nodding after her. "On your fucking bike, mate. Pip pip."

Miguel glares at me again but stands up and walks out.

"Roses and daisies are pretty common flowers to send," Declan says carefully.

I shake my head at him. "I hella don't give a fuck, bruv—" I flick my eyes around the room. "Find them. Get the Boroughs on the horn — you ask anyone we've ever known if they've sent my fucking sister flowers."

Everyone nods and disperses, but not Christian. He stares over at me, looks annoyed. Leans back in his chair.

"Feels like an overreaction," he tells me, eyebrows up.

I mirror his face. "Does it?"

He shrugs. "Especially when you made her think you don't give a shit…"

"I don't give a shit—" I lie, trying to palm it off with an indifferent smile.

Christian sniffs, amused. "Well, you clearly do…"

I shake my head. "She sold me out—"

He picks something out of his teeth. "You broke her rules."

"I raised her," I counter.

"Yeah—" He stands, annoyed. "And she saved your dying-life on a table in her spare room."

I squint over at him. "What's your point?"

"Just tell her you're sorry!" he says, exasperated.

"Fuck off," I grunt.

"You could have fixed it, Jules — not made her feel like fucking joke when she's scared of something. She might have come home—"

"Don't want her to come home," I lie again.

"Alright." He nods, annoyed. "Give denial another crack then, we'll see how that goes—"

"Just find out who sent them," I tell him.

He shakes his head. "I don't work for you."

"Yeah?" I pull my head back. "You are in love with her though, so probably worth your time either way."

"Yeah, okay." He shrugs, gives me a look as he gestures over at me. "But you love her too, so why don't you grow the fuck up and start acting like it."

6

Daisy

I hadn't seen them in months. Neither seen nor spoken to either of them. I'd heard my brother was on the run, out of London, that Declan was here and in charge in his absence — that Julian had taken Koa with him — that made me feel grateful. At least he wasn't alone — at least he had someone who wouldn't let him be a complete arsehole 100% of the time.

Tiller and I had been together for a while by then, about five months. Even back then he stayed at my house most days of the week. Sometimes we stayed at his place, but he had a roommate and my place was nicer anyway, because as much as he hates to admit it, crime actually really does pay quite well.

It was the middle of the night. July, I think. There was this crazy banging at the door.

I bolted upright.

"Do you hear that?" I looked over at him, frowning.

He jumped out of bed; so did I. He grabbed his gun from the bedside table and I grabbed mine — he stared at it for a few seconds, frowning, and I ignored him, following the sound to the front door.

I went to open it and Tiller shoved me out of the way.

"What are you doing?" he scowled. "I'll open it." He peeked through the peephole and his face froze.

"Oh, shit." He sighed then swung the door open.

My brother, blood pouring out of his stomach, being held up by Koa and Christian Hemmes, Miguel behind them.

"Oh my God." My hand flew to my mouth.

Julian was sort of slumped between the two of them, head flopped forward. So much blood.

My brother rolled his head to look up at me. Our eyes held. Neither of us said a thing.

"We didn't know where else to bring him," Christian said, eyes heavy with an apology I think he thought he owed me, like he thought he'd done the wrong thing by me by bringing him here.

Christian was staring over at me, his eyes looking a bit raw like it was hard for him to see me so undone with another man. I wasn't in much, I guess...[45] I wouldn't have liked to see him like this with any of the girls he'd been sleeping with.[46] But we couldn't be together — him being there, then, with my brother bleeding in his arms, that proved my point.

Forget that my heart was a small boat on a stormy sea with him standing in front of me, never mind that a day hadn't gone by since we stopped talking in January when he hadn't cropped up in my consciousness... He was there with my brother on my doorstep. Dragging me back into the life I've left.

I pulled them inside, shutting the door behind them.

"Do you have a room?" Kekoa glanced around, looking from me to Miguel, but he didn't know because hadn't been in my appartment before.

Tiller frowned, confused, looking between all of us. "For what?"

Koa ignored him, kept his eyes on me.

I shoved my hands through my hair, tying it back with a hair elastic.

"Second door on the right." I gestured towards it and they started dragging my brother that way.

I remember Tiller was staring over at me, jaw ajar, eyes wide and confused.

I looked up at him but could barely meet his eyes. "There's so much you don't know about me."

And then I ran after them.

"What's the pin code?" Kekoa called out.

"Three-zero-one-zero,"[47] I yelled to Koa and our eyes caught—he looked sad for me.

The door swung open and Tiller tensed up behind me.

A surgical table, a couple of IV poles, a cabinet of basic medical

---

[45] A white button-up nightshirt, and Tiller just in CK bed pants.

[46] I hear things.

[47] Julian's birthday. The only pin I remember.

supplies, a medical equipment stand with the tray ready to go.[48] On the other side of the wall, a cabinet of knives, guns and weapons.

"Fuck." Miguel let out a wry laugh. "Old habits die hard, huh Dais?"

All of it was a bit much, I'd imagine, for the middle of the night in general, but I think the real cherry on top for Tiller was what was hanging on the wall directly across from the door: *Vanitas Still Life* by Pieter Claesz.[49]

Tiller's eyes dragged over towards me like I'd betrayed him.

I keep this room locked. I've always told Tiller it's because it's where I keep my guns, which is selectively true. It's actually where I keep all of my past life. It's where I come to mourn them on the days when I wonder whether I've made a mistake.

I haven't, I don't think. I don't think I have. I wanted normal.

Tiller gives me normal.

He comes home every day, he is dependable. He's good, he's kind, he's steady, but with that painting, he was struggling.

But I didn't have time for his struggles then. His breathing got quicker. He pointed to it. "Tell me that's not real."

A clunky pause.

"Okay." I shrugged weakly and Tiller scoffed.

"Daisy—" Koa called me back to focus.

"Put him on the table," I told him but he didn't, pausing instead.

"Are we safe here?" Koa asked and both Miguel and I scowled over at him. I couldn't bear the insinuation. He's known me all my life, he should know me better than to think I'd turn away anyone bleeding how my brother was, let alone him.[50]

"Of course you're fucking safe here—" I spat.

And Koa shook his head, nodding his head towards Tiller, who was pacing the room, shaking his head as he stared at the floor.

I grabbed him by the arm and pulled him out into the hallway.

"What?" I shook my head, impatient.

---

[48] And the Heart Tag Hemmes necklace Christian gave me, but I hope no one finds it because I probably shouldn't have kept it.

[49] 1625. Oil on panel. 29.5 × 34.4 cm. It hangs in the Frans Hals Museum in Haarlem (Netherlands). Or so they think.

[50] Him. My only family, my best friend, my saviour, my protector, my nemesis, who I have loved and will always love, every day of my life. Even if I never speak to him again.

He let out a hollow laugh. "What the fuck is going on?"

I shook my head, annoyed. "What do you mean?"

"Pieter Claesz?" He stared down at me, eyes wide. "That's not even been reported missing—"

"I can't do this right now, Tills — I need to fix him—" Tiller stared back into the room at my brother, unsure.

"You can't tell anyone he's here." I touched my boyfriend's wrist.

Tiller's jaw went tight, shaking his head more.

"He's my brother," I told him loudly.

"He's wanted for kidnapping, extortion — murder! Murder, Dais!"

"I don't care!" I shook my head wildly. "He's my brother, I don't care—"

"But I care!" Tiller thumped his chest. "I'm a federal agent. I care."

I took a step closer to him.

"Do you love me?" I asked, my voice breaking.

He blinked, thrown. "What?"

"Do you love me, yes or no?" I took a staggered breath.

Tiller gave me a look. "Daisy—"

"Yes or no?" I demanded.

He sighed. "Yes."

I swallowed heavy. "Then you won't say a word."

I dashed back inside. "We're fine," I told no one in particular. "Put him on the table and tell me what happened."

I stared down at my brother who hadn't spoken a word to me and our eyes caught and my heart choked.

His eyes looked worried. Julian never worries.

It'd been months. Six maybe? Or thereabouts. The loneliest six months of my life. I'd missed him every day, I'd had so many things I'd wanted to tell him, so many things I wanted to let him know, and I'd told him none of them and maybe I'd never get to now anyway, because he was watching me with dying eyes.

Do you know about dying eyes? There's a hopeless reckoning about them, a resignation to your fate, a lean-in towards the inevitable darkness that's coming for them and I could see it in my brother — he was leaning. I held his face in my hands because I didn't have enough words to tell him how much I loved him when I still hated him as much as I did for breaking our rules.

"GSW to the lower abdomen," Kekoa told me, snapping me out of it.

"Exit wound?" I felt under Julian's body and he groaned in pain. Christian shook his head.

"Dais—" Kekoa gave me a look. "He's lost a lot of blood."

"How much?" I held my hand out. "Scissors."

Koa handed them to me and I cut my brother's shirt off him. He grimaced. "At least a litre. Probably more."

I took a staggered breath, nodded a few times, trying to process.

My brain was swimming[51] in what the world might look like and feel like and be like if I actually lost my brother for good, in the permanent way where he's in the ground, in the way where there's no overarching hope that maybe we'll make up one day, that he'll take back everything he said to me, that I'll stop caring that we are who we are, that we can find a way through the mounds and mounds of shit and garbage we've hurled at each other. Losing him in the way where not just his world would go dark but mine too, because even then, even when I wasn't ready to admit it out loud or in a way where it would move me to change, I knew that I didn't know who I was without my brother.

I turned away from them all, just for a second. I didn't want a single one of them to see on my face the anguish that surfaced.

Tiller because he didn't get it. He's too black and white.

Kekoa and Miguel because they'd tell my brother.

Christian because he's him and he knows me how I've always daydreamed someone would truly know me, and now he did, but it didn't matter anyway because we couldn't be together either, so I muffled the cry that came from my mouth with my hand and took a few breaths.

Then there was a hand on my arm.

"You're shaking," said my favourite voice in the world.[52]

"It's just adrenaline," I told Christian without looking at him.

He nodded and pushed some hair behind my ears without meaning to do it.[53]

"You've got this, Dais. You can do it..." He tilted his head so our eyes caught. "What do you need?"

"Um—" I turned back to face the rest of the room. "Blood."

---

51 Drowning
52 And it's not my boyfriend's.
53 And my boyfriend in the background shifted on his feet.

"You don't have any?" Kekoa stared over at me.

"She's not a fucking hospital, Ko!" Miguel yelled at him.

I shook my head, staring at one of my oldest friends and protectors wildly. "I don't just keep bags of blood in my refrigerator, Kekoa—"

"Fuck!" he yelled and I started to feel panicky again.

"What's wrong?" Tiller frowned.

Julian's blood type is hard to match. A Negative. We both have it. Kekoa is O Positive, so is Miguel. Statistically most people are.

"I can't give him as much as he'll need and still work on him. What blood type are you?" I asked Tiller.

"O Positive," he offered and I shook my head.

"And you?" I asked Christian.

"O Negative," he said, already rolling up his sleeve, and I sighed, relieved.

I couldn't take a litre. I shouldn't really take more than 450mL but I was going to try for 600 and then he could have 400 of mine, and then maybe we were going to be okay—

"You're going to do a whole blood transfusion?" Kekoa stared over at me.

"We don't have a choice." I shrugged. "Koa, hook him up to the monitor[54] — SpO2 Sensor on his left finger, the red lead goes top right, yellow, top left and green—"

"I've done this before, Dais—"

"Tiller—" I looked up at him. "You keep pressure on the wound — once he's connected the machine's going to start beeping, because he'll already be hypertension stage one — maybe two. I want his readings under 160, over 100 and if it rises, you tell me straight away."

"Okay." He nodded obediently.

I pulled Christian over to the side of the room and grabbed a CPD-A1[55] blood bag.[56] He took his jumper off and I took his arm, trying not to think about how touching him, even then in that circumstance, made me feel.

I bent his arm a few times, flicked the vein on the inside of his elbow.

---

[54] Edan iM60 Patient Monitor.

[55] Citrate phosphate dextrose-adenine, which helps the red blood cells last longer.

[56] 600mL blood bag with a pre-attached 16-gauge venipuncture needle pinch clamp.

And Christian, he was just staring down at me with these raw, heavy eyes that I couldn't meet.

I wiped his arm with an alcohol swab and inserted the needle, released the clamp, and that beautiful O Negative blood started filling the bag.

I rolled up my own sleeve, looking for my best vein and I could feel Christian frowning at me. "Take more of mine."

"You'd go into hypovolemic shock."[57]

"That's bad?"

I glanced up at him. "Yes, that's bad."

He nodded once and I kept looking for a vein.

I found one, stuck myself and sat down next to my ex-boyfriend. "Do you feel okay?" I asked him.

"Do you?" he asked, looking worried.

I stared over at him, and all of it, the whole thing felt like a fever dream. I never thought Christian would be one of those people for me, truly. When we first started hooking up — which feels like a lifetime ago now — I never thought that he'd morph into one of those rare people whose presence undoes you, and not only in a bad way, (but yes in a bad way) but also in the good way, where he makes me feel safe when I'm not safe, and brave when I'm not brave, and okay when I'm not okay, and I wish that yoke would break, I wish I didn't feel those things as I stared over at him, but I did.

I very much did,[58] so I looked away from him and back to Tiller who was watching us with that serious face of his and I wondered if he knew.

If he did know, it changed nothing. We've continued dating for months and he's never mentioned it.

I started to feel a bit dizzy so I stopped letting my blood for a minute. Stood up, found a vein for my brother to transfuse with.

"How are his vitals?"

Koa shook his head. "Not good."

"158 over 100," Tiller told me and I nodded.

"I need to get the bullet out." I pulled the needle out of my arm and smacked on a plaster. "Pass me the gloves."

---

[57] When you don't have enough blood for your body to pump around to the rest of your body.

[58] And do.

I sanitised my arms and then put the gloves on.

"Lights up." I nodded to Kekoa. "How many am I looking for?"

"Two," my brother croaked. First thing he said.

The first one was easy. A few centimetres into his abdomen; the light caught the metal right away. It hadn't hit anything. I'm guessing that he was on his way down when they fired the shot again, or he moved slightly or something, but it hadn't knocked anything and it was an easy fish.

The second one...

That was where all the bleeding was coming from.

"He has a perforated bowel," I whispered.

"Oh, fuck—" Koa said under his breath, and I hated it so much because even though I already knew it was dire, something about Kekoa's acknowledgement of that made it insurmountably worse.

"It's still in there — light—" I shook my head. "I — give me a clamp."

I tried to stop the bleeding. Packed him with gauze.

I looked up at Kekoa. "I — I don't think I can—"

Julian started to go pale. More pale than he already was.

I pointed to the drawers. "I have a Maglite in there — get it and shine it in here."

Christian obeyed.

"His stats are dropping, Dais—" Tiller told me.

I shook my head. "I can get it, I can't close the perforation but I can get the bullet out and make the bleeding stop... Hemostatic forceps... Clamp—" I held my hand out and Koa passed them to me.

"Dropping," Tiller said even though I could hear the beeping. I still hear the beeping now, actually.

The monitors were going berserk and my brother's breathing was getting more and more faint and Koa was yelling for me to stop and I was yelling that I could get it and for more gauze and he was yelling there's too much blood — and then I felt that horribly gratifying feeling of metal clamping onto metal and I knew I got it. I got it.

I pulled the bullet out and dropped it on the table next to my brother.

And then he crashed.

Christian stared down at him. "Holy fuck—"

"Julian?" I shook him. "Oh my God—"

39

"Daisy—" Tiller grabbed me and held me by both shoulders. "Do you have a defibrillator?"

"Um — uh — yes?"

"Where is it?" he asked loudly and calmly.

"I — in the—" I pointed to a cupboard. I was shaking. The edges of my vision were blurring — I'm embarrassed. How embarrassing. I should have been better than that. I should have been the one remembering there's a defibrillator in my cupboard, should have been the one getting it, putting electrode gel on his chest.

"Julian?" I knelt down next to him, pushed my hands through his hair.

"Daisy—" Koa said, holding a manual resuscitator. "Move."

Tiller powered up the defibrillator. "Clear?" he yelled, and I didn't let go of my brother, so Christian yanked me away, holding me from behind, not letting me go. Part of me wanted to hold on to how it felt with him on my body again but I lost the moment to the swirling trauma.

And then they shocked him.

And nothing.

My brother's body did that horrible leap off the table, thudded back down.

Koa started pumping the McKesson.

I elbowed my body out of Christian's arms and snatched the paddles from my boyfriend because I am better than I was being in that moment.

"Clear—" I said again then I shocked him.

And it hung there — a little infinity where my brother wasn't alive. I was alone. Unshielded from everything this world might throw at me and I'd shoulder it all myself anyway if he'd just wake up. He is so many things, so many terrible things, and still he's my favourite person on the planet. I don't remember my dad, really. Not any more, and that used to make me feel sad, but now I think it's because Julian did such a good job I don't need to remember this guy who died on a beach because I had my brother instead.

I banged his chest as hard as I could with my fist — twice for good measure — and then, beep.

My brother took a massive, gasping breath and his eyes peeled open and caught mine. I dropped my head on his chest crying, and he weakly dropped his arm on my head and held me how he could.

He fell unconscious again shortly after and I got back to work.

It was imperfect and he'd need to be seen by a proper doctor. All I did was stop the bleeding, clear the wound and transfuse some blood. The perforation was still there.

I looked over at Tiller and he flashed me a quick, tired smile.

"You good?" His breathing was heavy, like he'd been holding it.

I nodded once.

"I'm going to get a shower." He nodded back then left the room.

"Tiller—" I walked after him. He stopped in the hallway and looked back at me.

I ran up to him, held his face in my hands.

I choked. He didn't.

"You saved him."

"No." He shook his head, turning it in my hands and kissed my palms. "You did."

"Hey—" I looked for his eyes and I know the truth whether or not he's willing to admit it. My brother is alive because of him. "I love you too," I told him.

And it was true. Is. As much as I love someone else? No, but I can't love that person anymore, even if I still do. Christian still lived behind that door that I bolted shut[59] and Tiller was still straight ahead. I still wanted to be normal. That night changed nothing. I love normal, so I love Tiller.

He gave me another tired smile and went upstairs.

I walked back into the room and Christian was leaning back against the wall, exhausted.

"Are you okay?" I asked, frowning at him. "You look a bit pale."

"Yeah, fine." He shrugged. "Just a bit dizzy."

"Come on." I nodded my head towards the kitchen. "You need a banana."

He followed me there wordlessly, leant back against the bench.

I peeled him a banana, handed him a glass of milk.

"Blood cell builders." I flashed him a quick smile.

I felt like I might cry, I don't know why — what had just happened aside, seeing him at any point I think would fuck me up a bit.

"You were incredible tonight, Dais—"

---

[59] That tonight was blown wide open.

41

I shook my head at him and sighed. "What are you doing with my brother?"

He thought about it for a few seconds then shrugged. "We're friends now."

"Why?" I blinked and he gave me a look. I sighed. "What happened tonight? Why was someone shooting at him?"

"We're tracking down a missing piece—"

I nodded, staring straight ahead. "Which?"

"A Van Gogh." He swallowed some milk.

I turned to him as I lifted an eyebrow. "He's looking for *Poppies*?"

Christian nodded.

"Oh." I got it. "He's trying to come back."

Christian nodded again.

"And you're helping him." I bit down on my bottom lip.

"I am."

"Why?"

He poked me in the ribs and I sniffed a sad smile.

"Dais—" Koa called, nodding his head. "He needs some morphine."

"Yeah, okay." I nodded. "Coming—"

I looked back at Christian and went to move past him.

He grabbed my hand, held it for a few seconds, squeezing it. I glanced up at him, ran my thumb along his a couple of times and he swallowed heavy.

Lifted my hand up to his mouth and kissed it.

He didn't say anything, just kept his eyes on me, blinked a few times then let me go.

They were gone when I woke the next morning.

I would have nearly thought it was a dream if there wasn't still my brother's blood all over my house.

Tiller and I, we never spoke about it again. About the fact that he saved my brother, about the painting, about the weird little hospital room I have hidden in our house, that I think he knew that I still loved someone else too—

There were too many layers to that night, what it said about me, what it said about us, me in context of him with that painting in the house we both, for the most part, live in. He saved a criminal, he now had incontrovertible proof that he was also dating one —the implications of that alone — he couldn't pull at one thread without pulling at them all and so he pulled at none, and that whole night became a thing we put in a box and hid away under our bed.

7

Christian

"Alright." Jo arches back in his chair at South Kensington Club. "Fill me in—" He gives me a nod. "Why's Jules all of a sudden off his fucking rocker about flowers?"

"What?" laughs BJ, glancing over at me.

"Julian," Jo gives him a look, "suddenly has become the ultimate authority on rose varieties."

My brother gives a baffled shrug and I roll my eyes.

"Someone's been sending Daisy flowers." I sigh.

Henry squints over at me. "Is that someone...you?"

"No—" I roll my eyes. "The whole thing's pretty weird—"

"What?" Jo scoffs. "Someone sending her flowers?"

Beej gives me a look. "She's pretty fit, man — I feel like she'd get hit up a bit?"

"No." I sigh again. Shake my head. "It's — never mind." I can't be bothered to explain it. It sounds like I don't care, which isn't true. I've thought of it non-stop, but they're not going to get it. Jo never takes anything seriously and it's not the sort of thing we'd tell the boys.

"Julian is Julian — mountains out of molehills." I say instead.

Henry stares at me for a few seconds and then blows air out of his mouth.

"Not you here pretending like he's overreacting when you're staking out a different florist every other hour..."

Jonah starts laughing.

I swipe my hand through the air, try to brush it off. They know the CliffsNotes version of me and Daisy. Know that I fell hard and then it didn't work. They don't know that she loved me back. They don't know about her lifelong pursuit for normalcy and they don't know how much it's cost us both. They don't know I still love her.

Because why should they? I come off like an idiot loving some girl who doesn't want me back — or does maybe, or did before and now it's too late because I probably should have picked her over this shit but I didn't and now she's got normal with someone else who can actually give it to her.

Beej nods his chin over at me. "How's Vanna Ripley feel about you visiting florists for your ex?"

"Vanna Ripley's in Mykonos."

Henry shakes his head, rolling his eyes. "She *would* be in Mykonos, that minger."

I roll my eyes. "We go to Mykonos."

"Yeah, not anymore now," he says, tossing back his drink.

Beej flicks his brother an amused look. "Not a massive fan then, Hen?"

"Of the raging bitch narcissist he's shagging?" He points his thumb at me and I roll my eyes again. "Nah, can't say I am."

Jonah looks between us. "Must be awkward around the house?"

Henry and I trade looks and I yawn. "Henry doesn't let her come over."

BJ starts laughing. "How's that one go over?"

I shrug. "Usually I just tell her Henry and Taura have weird sex so we should go to hers—"

And then the table tenses up.

Probably shouldn't have said it. Definitely a sore spot for Jo and Hen.

Henry tosses me a look and Jo sniffs out his nose, looking away.

"Nice." Henry nods, annoyed.

I shrug again. "Maybe you shouldn't shag the same girl, then—"

"Maybe you should shut the fuck up," my brother tells me.

I raise my hands in surrender.

I look over at Beej. "What about you, champ?" Nod my chin at him. "How are you feeling?"

"About?" He pretends like he doesn't know and I give him a look. "Oh, Magnolia flying in? Yeah — fine. Haven't thought about it."

Jo nods his chin at him. "Is that why you got a haircut?"

"Got a haircut because I'm a model—" BJ pours himself some water.

"Ooh," Henry chides. "He's a model!"

Beej rolls his eyes as he shoves his hands through his hair, then shakes his head. "I probably won't even see her."

"At her own father's wedding?" Jonah sniggers. "Okay, then."

"Are you bringing Jordan?" I ask.

Jordan is BJ's new girlfriend. Very new. Beej has never had another girlfriend besides Parks, it's a pretty big deal. I don't mind her. Henry's not her biggest fan, but I don't think that's about her personally, if I'm honest.

BJ shakes his head and I lean back and fold my arms over my chest.

"Interesting."

"Very." Henry nods.

"How does Jordan feel about not being your wedding date?"

"Fine." He shrugs. "Doesn't care."

"Ah." Jonah nods. "Lies. The foundation of every healthy relationship…"

"Oh—" BJ clocks him. "Know a lot about those, do you? All zero girlfriends you've had."

"Alright—" Henry scoffs. "Calm down over there with the whopping total of two that you've had."

"Parks is coming back—" BJ shakes his head. "It's not a big deal. Business as usual."

"Yeah," I snort. "Right."

8

Daisy

Tiller opens my car door and pulls me out onto the street. "Are you okay?"

"Hmm?" I smile up at him, distracted.

"You've been quiet since your brother's place."

"Oh, no — yeah. No—" I nod. "I'm fine."

He pulls me in towards him, rests his chin on top of my head and holds me against him tight.

"You seem sad," he says into my hair and I pull back, glancing up at him.

"No — I'm—"[60]

"Sad." Tiller nods, sniffing a smile.

"My brother—" I shake my head. "There's never a time where — he's never been indifferent towards my safety before."

Tiller turns me around and starts walking down the street, hugging me from behind. I hear him sigh. I feel stupid and embarrassed for all the times I've defended Julian to Tiller, for telling Tills about the kind of person my brother can be when he's not trying to prove something to a room full of idiots I miss every day.

"I'm not indifferent about your safety," he tells me, trying to make me feel better.

He isn't. I know he isn't. That little worried crease in his brow that's been there since we left The Compound tells me he isn't.

"I know." I nod up at him as we stop outside of Tell Your Friends,[61] where I'm meeting Dellina[62] for breakfast.

He turns me around, drops his hands to my waist. "I love you."

"I know." I nod again.

---

[60] Shattered.

[61] 175 New King's Road, SW6 4SW

[62] Bambrillia, in case you've forgotten her, but how could you?

"You love me too," he tells me and I nod a third time.

"Yes."

"You're going to be okay here? Getting to the hospital?"

"I'll be fine." I shrug. "No florists anywhere around here." I flash him a playful look.

It feels easier to just dismiss it now that my brother has. Like I'm an idiot to worry about it if he doesn't.

But then again, I am dead to him, so...

Tiller rolls his eyes — he doesn't like any of this, and he really didn't like how my brother was. He ranted about it for about an hour, which was sweet, actually — how indignant he is about how dismissive Julian was.

They might be two sides of the same coin, Tiller and my brother.

If one wasn't ragingly good and the other possibly quite, quite bad, if he wasn't in law enforcement and my brother wasn't a criminal — if Tiller hadn't been my brother's foil and antagonist for practically the last five years — I think they'd probably be friends.

I can tell Tiller is really in his head about it all — stress-eyes aplenty.[63]

"I can wait for you," he offers, eyebrows up. "I'll just be late for work."

"No—" I wave my hand through the air. "Miguel's bound to be lurking around here somewhere."

Tills frowns. "Are you sure?"

I nod. "I'll be fine."

He nods back, still not sold, then brushes his mouth over mine, kissing me a bit then kissing me more. Which is always how our kisses go. He might be my favourite kisser in the world, actually. Because it always starts out quick, like a habit, and then it's as though he remembers how good we are at it, and he kisses me more and more and his hands go in my hair and on my face, and I feel like I'm the prettiest girl he's ever seen, but that's just how it feels whenever I'm with him. That's how it's always felt with him even before we were together — that he always liked me, mostly by accident — which he's said is true — that he never meant to like me, let alone love me.

---

[63] Cute, but.

Never meant to have sex with me that first night. He hadn't even planned on kissing me, but he couldn't figure out how to... not.

Romeo, he's always loved me but he was never shy about watching another girl in the room. And then Christian, for the vast majority of our relationship, I was an afterthought. Maybe I wouldn't be now, I'll never know anyway — but Tiller...

Kissing me how he is on New King's Road at nine in the morning, like he's forgotten we're in public, like he doesn't care either way — if this is what being loved by him on accident feels like, I can't imagine what it'd feel like to be loved on purpose.

I pull back and my cheeks are all pink.

"Okay," I laugh. "Bye."

He ducks down and peers through the window, waving once at Dellina, and then he walks away. "Call me when you get to the hospital, okay?"

I walk into the restaurant and sit opposite my ex-boyfriend's mum, hands on my cheeks so she doesn't see the pink — she doesn't need to anyway, she knows all my faces.

She gives me an amused smile. "He's very sweet."

I've missed her voice. Mostly British but still faintly trimmed with the hints of her Eritrean accent.

She leans across the table, kissing each of my cheeks.

"You've missed our last few breakfasts." Dellina gives me a look.

I give her one back. "You're my ex-boyfriend's mother."

She breathes out her nose. "I am more than that."[64]

I roll my eyes as I flag down a waiter. "You know what I mean—"[65]

She nods, thoughtfully. "Yes." Purses her mouth. "Romeo said he saw you the other night — that there are some flowers?" She frowns, confused. "He seemed concerned?"

She's right — Romeo did see me the other night, and though not on the spot, he was concerned. That whole sentence is an understatement as well, because the truth is after that night I told my brother about the flowers, I've seen Romeo every day since.

The last four days I've finished work, gone downstairs to the carpark, and he's just waiting there by the elevator.

He doesn't say anything to me. Doesn't even look at me, actually.

---

64 She is so much more than that.
65 I order an oat milk latte and Dellina orders a pot of tea.

Walks about a metre behind me. He walks me to my car, watches til I drive out of the garage and then he leaves.

"I wouldn't know—" I give his mother a polite little look, because I don't know that he'd like anyone knowing he's doing that. "He's still not speaking to me."

"You would know, even if he's still not speaking to you…" she begins. "Which, we all know you deserve—" she tacks on at the end and my eyes drop from hers.

"Of all the people to do that in front of — my son?" She shakes her head. "Daisy."

"Dellina," I sigh. "It was ten months ago."

"And he's still in therapy for it." She nods. My shoulders fall. "Imagine harming yourself in front of a boy who's spent his whole life trying to protect you."

That makes me want to cry, not just that she's disappointed in me (which she is) and not just that he's in therapy because of me (which he is)[66] but that Romeo is what he's always been to me, even when he hates me. My protector.

"But…" She shrugs her shoulders. "You know this. This is why you've been avoiding me."

I pout. "I haven't been avoiding y—"

"Uh uh—" She holds up a finger to silence me like she'd do when I was five. "I wasn't asking, I was telling. You have been avoiding me."

I put my chin in my hand. "Do you think he'll ever forgive me?"

She takes a sip of her tea. "The second you ask."

---

[66] To be fair, he needed it anyway.

9

Christian

"And how's the rumoured-boyfriend of Hollywood's darling Vanna Ripley doing this fine evening?" Taura asks as she flops down next to Henry on the couch.

I lift my brows unimpressed but don't look over at her, just keep playing Halo.

"That good, huh?" Taura gives me a smug smile.

"Yeah, no—" I shrug. "I'm fine, how's my brother?"

Her face goes still and she presses her tongue into her cheek, squinting. "Dick."

"Slut," I fire back.

She shrugs. "Takes one to know one."

Henry fires the remote at me as hard as he can. Hits me in the head. I glare over at him.

"Oi," he growls at me, eyes dark. "Take it back."

"No—" Taura shakes her head. "Don't. I don't care—"

"Well, I care," Henry says, not taking his eyes off me.

"Then stop." Taura smiles at him gently, pushing her hands through his hair. "Christian's always been a child with his emotions, and he lashes out when provoked as a way of grappling with his inner turmoil."

I point at her without looking away from the television. "Not loving this dynamic—"

"Oh no." Taura rolls her eyes. "Whatever will I do."

I breathe out of my nose, flick her an annoyed look, pause my game. "Sorry."

She gives me a little wink.

"Go on then." Henry nods at me. "What's this inner turmoil?"

I look back at the television. "There's no inner turmoil."

"So Daisy, then?" Taura asks brightly.

I look over at her, annoyed. "No. I haven't seen her in months."

"Til a few days ago…" Henry gives me a look.

"What happened a few days ago?" Taus asks, instantly excited.

Henry shrugs. "I don't know, someone gave her some flowers or something—"

I swear under my breath, toss the controller down, get up and go to the kitchen.

Henry follows me a few seconds later, frowning, confused.

"Is this about someone giving Daisy flowers?"

"No — I — fuck—" I shove my hands through my hair, shaking my head. "Can you just put it in the basket of shit that you're not going to understand because you're normal?"

Henry blinks a few times.

"Okay." He scratches his chin, sensing the mood. "Is she okay?"

I shrug. "I don't — yeah. I think."

Henry opens the fridge and tosses me a hazy IPA, gets one for himself. Cracks it open and leans back against the door, watching me for a few seconds.

"Do you love her again?" he asks carefully. We've been friends for too long. He can see the answer on my face but I think about lying anyway, almost want to to save some face but don't really feel like denying her anymore either, not after how we started.

I shrug. "Never stopped."

Henry stares over at me, silent.

"Fuck—" He breathes out. "I didn't — shit. But Vanna—"

I roll my eyes. "Is a shitty distraction."

"Does Daisy — you know—" He doesn't finish the sentence.

I nod. "I think sh— I don't know. I thought, but…"

"She's with the policeman, right?"

I nod.

Henry frowns. "Then…?"

I let out a tired laugh. "There's a lot of the story you don't know, man."

We walk from the kitchen and out onto the patio.

"So tell me." He shrugs, sitting across from me, but I shake my head.

"You won't get it."

"Try me."

I stare over at him a few seconds, thinking about it. What the hell...

"She shot herself in the stomach to fuck up a job her brother was doing—" Henry's eyes go wide but I keep going. "They had a massive fight, don't speak anymore—"

"I know that part." He nods, trying to keep up.

"Last January, when it happened — she asked me to leave London with her."

He blinks a few times. "What?"

"She wants out. She doesn't—" I pause. "What our families do, she doesn't want to do it."

"Right." He nods once.

"She wanted to be normal?" I shrug.

"Okay—"

"And she asked me to go with her and be normal. She said she loved me." He didn't know that til now and his face lights up, but mine doesn't.

"I said I couldn't go."

He frowns. "Why?"

I cover my face, stressed. "I don't know! She put me on the spot—"

"And now—" He squints, doing his best to track it. "Someone's sending her flowers, you're with Vanna, she's with the police, you still love her but we don't know how she feels about you?"

My face falters and he gives me a look, leaning in intrigued. "Do we... know... how she feels about you?"

I shake my head again. "A few months ago there was an — incident." That's the word I go with. "And we held hands... for a couple of seconds."

"Shit." Henry sits back in his chair, blinking, processing it. "I wonder if you got her pregnant..."

I give him a look.

"No, I mean it." He shakes his head. "That is some sexy stuff—"

I kick him under the table as hard as I can and he starts laughing.

"It's cute. This is cute." Henry nods, not even trying to hold his amusement together. "Are you going to do something about it?"

"No." I shake my head. "I want her to be happy. I want her to have her normal life."

10

Julian

Right, so — I would've gone to Christian's launch either way. We're friends and shit — helped me find *Poppies* and cleared my name, didn't ask for a thing, just came along for the ride so I would have come either way.

But when I walked past a newsstand and saw *'Magnolia Parks - Back in Britain!'* on the cover of *The Sun*, did it peak my interest a bit more? Maybe.

I walk into the place with Decks — it's a pretty good vibe — think like, Positano in the summer, even though it's winter here now.

He flits off to the bar, seeing some girl he's on the tune with.

I look around, head towards the loudest table in the whole place, and then she's the first thing I see.

Sounds romantic. It's not. She's just one of those girls with a gravity to them.

Watch her for a few seconds, sitting across from her ex-boyfriend and his new girlfriend and actually, she looks insecure which is wild because... she's her.

The new girlfriend, she's fit enough, wouldn't kick her out of bed— but it's not the same. And Magnolia's sporting this little pout on her mouth that I'm interested in, because with a girl like her, beauty is currency. And she has it in spades, but here, it's doing nothing for her.

I'm good at reading people. Always have been. It's why I'm good at what I do, it's why I have a team who'll do anything I say. I know how to ask the right questions, know what strings to pluck to get the answers I want. It's all just reading people.

And reading her, she looks sad.

I walk over, stop about a metre from her.

"Well, fuck—" I look down at her, pretend I'm just noticing her now. "Here's trouble."

"Julian." Her face lights up a bit.

"Oi." I nod my chin at her. "Get up and give me a squeeze—"

She tosses her arms around my neck and I slip my arms around her waist, don't know why, but I lift her up off the floor and she lifts like a paper bag. Don't hate the feeling of her in my arms, actually. Or her face being this close to mine.

Don't like feeling sentimental about a person though, so I drop my hands down her body, trying to cop a feel and she locks eyes with me, gives me this playful smile, when last time I pulled this shit with her she smacked my hands away.

Interesting...

I stare at her for a couple of seconds; she doesn't look away. I swallow heavy, fucking pull it together and put her back down on the floor.

"How's New York?"

"It has its perks." She blinks up at me.

I look past her to some geezer who's in the chair I want to sit in. Cock my chin, tell him to move without telling him to move.

He does it quickly and Parks' little eyes light up like it's a party trick and she's impressed.

I pull her down next to me. "Like what?"

Her mouth squashes together. "Like New York paparazzi don't give a shit about me—"

"Bullshit—" I shake my head. "They'd follow you in droves."

"No, actually—" She looks down at her nail, back up at me. "They have real celebrities there. They don't care about people like me."

Surprisingly, this seems to make her happy.

"What else, then?"

"Mmm..." She presses her thumb into her mouth as she thinks and I stare at it propped up. Swallow heavy again. "Horse-drawn carriages. My completely ridiculous neighbour, Lucìa. 5th Avenue. Central Park at midnight—"

I give her a look. "Central Park at midnight? You got a death wish?"

She rolls her eyes at me. "You're one to talk, how was your little trip down through South America?"

I chuckle. "Pretty fun, actually—" I look past her, catch eyes with Christian, give him a nod. "He's a good time."

She glances over at him and snaps her head back, scowling.

"Yuck! What's Vanna Ripley doing here?"

I sniff a laugh. "Pretty sure she's doing your mate?"

"Still?" She blinks. "God, this place really has gone to the dogs."

"Oi—" Ballentine leans across the table to get her attention. I stare over at him; we're friends, I guess. Through Jonah. Something about him just shits me though. Today at least, had lunch last week with him and the boys, had a good time. But today I'm off him. Don't know why.

She's always been so hung up on him, it's annoying. Also annoying is that he treats her like shit and she trails him around anyway — I'm not really listening to what they're saying, something about Gwyneth Paltrow, and then I hear something — double take — throw my hat back in the ring.

I lean in. "Did you say 'vagina steams?'"

Magnolia nods.

"With Gwyneth Paltrow?" I clarify.

She rolls her eyes. "Well, who else are you going to do it with?"

I pull my head back. "Who else would I do it with?" I nod my chin at her, lift my eyebrows.

She laughs, practically bursts into flames. I like that. Makes me feel good.

Ballentine shifts in his seat.

"What do you talk about when you're getting your vagina steamed?" I ask.

"I mean—" She shrugs breezily, eating up all the air in the room. "What don't you talk about? It's all already on the table—"

"Are you on a table?" the new girlfriend asks.

Parks flicks her eyes over to BJ and I feel a tug of jealousy. "I'm sorry to say you didn't fare particularly well during the vagina monologues."

"Can't imagine I would have." He shrugs and they start nattering on again. Look away, talk to the girl on my other side.

She's boring, pretty enough. Studying physiotherapy. I don't remember her name. I don't think I asked for it — bit unlike me, if I'm honest. But it's not her I'm interested in talking to.

Feel like a fucking idiot waiting for Magnolia to give me her attention again so I decide just to take it.

"When are you headed back?" I toss my arm around her.

"I fly out December fifth."

I nod, giving her a little smile. "Maybe I'll come visit you—"

She grins. "You should."

My eyes fall down her face, land on her mouth. "I think you could show me a pretty good time."

She holds my eyes, throws back her drink. "Oh, I don't think you could keep up."

Ballentine pushes back loudly from the table. He looks pissed off, watching her watch me. "Let's get out of here," he tells the girlfriend.

"Nice to meet you," she tells Magnolia who just stares over at her for a few seconds. Makes me feel sad for her.

"Yeah, you too," she says, eyes a bit heavy.

Ballentine nods his chin at her. "See you around, Parks."

Walks away, turns back and mouths something to her.

I squint over at Parks. "Did he just mouth that he's going to text you over his girlfriend's head?"

She presses her lips together. "Yes. He did..." She folds her hands in front of her. "How terribly clandestine..."

"Like clandestine now, do you?" I elbow her.

She looks up at me, eyes unflinching. "I might do."

I swallow. "Good to know."

I'm going to pause here to say: I don't get it. I don't. I don't get hung up on people — and to clarify, I'm not hung up on her. I think of her sometimes, that's all.

Text her when I think of her. Which isn't often, but just sometimes.

Just one of those people your head gets stuck on.

"So..." She clears her throat, looking nervous, maybe. "What's this?" Takes my drink from my hand, lifts it to her mouth. Tries it. Tequila, straight and neat.

She coughs and I lick away a smile as she makes a disgusted noise. "We do not have the same taste in drinks."

I take back the glass from her. Take a sip, watching her as I do. "Never have."

She says nothing, just sits there, waiting for me to say more, chin in her hand, blinking slowly. Fuck. She makes me feel uneasy, but I love it. The power scale's tilted in her favour somehow. Never had to work for a conversation a day in my life but she's milking me.

I press my tongue into my bottom lip. "We could have other things in common..."

"Could we?" She picks a piece of lint off my shoulder.

Fuck. Swallow heavy again.

"Mhm." I nod.

She lifts moderately interested eyebrows. "Pray tell..."

I glance around, shrug my shoulders. "We're the best looking people here."

She peers around and then nods thoughtfully. "Well, BJ's left now so that is true..."

I scoff a laugh but I'm annoyed and I fancy her more than I did a second ago.

"What else?" She bites down on her thumb — fuck me.

Deep breaths. Casually lift my shoulders. "Think I'd have to show you."

"Julian." She bats her eyes. "If we were to take our clothes off and we had those same things in common, I'm sorry to tell you, but I'd be terribly disappointed."

I laugh. She smiles.

A waiter hands her another martini and she flashes them a smile.

"How's your sister?" She takes a sip.

The question throws me. "Yeah — I— uh—" Shake my head. Pull it together, don't want to look like an idiot in front of her. "Do you know what happened?"

"No, not really..." Magnolia shakes her head. "I heard you weren't speaking."

I nod.

"I'm sorry—" She touches my arm. "I know what she means to you."

"Meant," I clarify.

Parks rolls her eyes. "Liar."

"She's got a boyfriend," I say, I don't know why.

Toss it into the pile of things I don't understand about Magnolia Parks but I think she's okay to talk to.

She nods. "I've seen them around. He's really handsome."

Scrunch my nose a bit. "Is he?"

"Yes!" She laughs.

"Fuck—" I shake my head. "You and my sister have a lot of overlap with the men you're interested in."

She fishes out the olive from her drink, bites it off. Leaves the stick in her mouth.

"Not exhaustively."

My throat makes a choking sound I don't appreciate, but I shake my head, smiling at her. "Can I take you home?"

"You mean 'drive me home?'"

I laugh. "Uh — yeah." I chuckle again. "Sure."

"Julian." She eyes me.

"Magnolia."

She breathes out her nose. Shakes her head. "I just got out of something."

"Just in time to get into my bed." I give her a grin.

She rolls her eyes again as she shakes her head. "You're an idiot, Julian Haites."

I swallow, concentrate on making sure my face doesn't show I'm disappointed she said no. "One of these days you're going to say yes…"

She pulls a big, apologetic smile. "I don't think I will…"

Put my hands on my head and breathe out. "You are my Everest."

She gives me a little look and shakes her head. "People die trying to climb Mount Everest."

I stare over at her. "Not afraid of dying."

She breathes out a laugh, rolls her eyes like she thinks I'm an idiot again. No one thinks I'm an idiot except for her apparently and it makes me want her more.

She grabs her bag. Stands up. I copy her. Why am I copying her? "I'll come visit you in New York."

She tilts her head. "You already said that."

"Well, I mean it." I shrug.

She kisses Henry Ballentine on the top of his head without a word. Blows Christian a kiss. Glares at Jonah.

Flicks her eyes back to me. "You've said that before too."

"Yeah but…" I roll my head back. "I was in a bit of a pinch."

She squeezes Taura Sax's hand then peers up at me. "A self-inflicted pinch, I presume?"

"Easy, tiger—" I give her a look. "But yeah, I guess."

Magnolia laughs and the sound makes me smile. Which is weird so I stop.

"See you," she says, brushing her mouth against my cheek, and then she walks away.

So how clandestine are we talking here

Hah.

Hotel rendezvous or more like...

I take you out for a bite and cop a feel under the table

Either, possibly.

Perhaps even both!

Right

Right.

Just tell me the time and the place.

11

Daisy

I take the elevator down to the carpark after work with Grace. She's blabbering away about Warner, how she shagged him on the weekend and she shouldn't have, because he's a prick[67] and he's spoilt[68] and he's misogynistic[69] and that she feels like a bad feminist for doing it.

Grace is one of those girls who strikes me as someone who loves buzzwords. She'll be an introvert with a lot of social anxiety who's been gaslit all her life, though she isn't, she doesn't have any and she hasn't been once.

The proof in the pudding is that I haven't said a word since we started walking from our locker room a full four minutes ago, but that works fine for me because I'm tired and I don't feel like dishing out sex advice, though I'm a tiny bit keen to know how Warner goes.

The elevator dings open and there he is, waiting for me like he has every evening for the last two weeks.

Romeo Bambrilla catches my eye. We stare over at each other for a few seconds — too many things to say, I don't even know where I would start[70]—

"Oh, hello." Grace stares over at him, blinking. Not really her fault, he's very beautiful.

I step out of the elevator and start walking.

"Do you know him?" She scurries after me, looking back over her shoulder at Rome as he trails slowly after me.

"Yes." I look for my keys even though I'm not near my car yet.

---

[67] He is.

[68] He is.

[69] He is.

[70] 'I'm sorry, you're my best friend, I love you, please forgive me' might be a good place to start.

"He's very sexy—" she says, looking over her shoulder again and I hear Romeo snort.

I look over my shoulder at him — our eyes hold — I turn back at Grace.

"Yes," I say.

"Is he your boyfriend?"

"Ex." I stop walking, rummaging though my bag.

Where are those ruddy keys?

Rome folds his arms, staring at me. I know his eyes are impatient without me even looking at him, I can feel it.

"Why did you break up?" Grace asks looking from me to him, like I'd answer her in front of him. As though I'd answer her at all?

I stare up at Rome and my heart sinks because he offered me a normal life once when I was too young to know I needed it. He knew though. I said no, I broke his heart. Traded it and that normalcy he was offering me for a couple of extra years with my brother, and where did that get me?

I sigh, open my mouth to say something — what could I say? — And then there's the loud screech of tyres.

"DAISY!" Romeo yells — a van pulls up next to me — two gunshots fire — I look down at myself, try to see where I've been hit, but it's not me — I look over at Rome, he's reaching for his gun — swings it around, pointed towards me, but it's not at me — it'd never be at me? Where's Grace? I look at my feet. I hear a van door swing open.

She's dead at my feet, that's where Grace is. Maybe she's not dead, but she's face down. I can't see.

The pool of blood seeping out of her leads me to believe, medical opinion aside, that she is probably dead, or very quickly dying.

And then I feel these arms grab me from behind.

And it's funny, I don't feel scared, I don't think about who'll save me, if I'll even be here to be saved. I don't worry about dying — I think dying's always been my lot. The first thing I think?

There goes normal.

The man who's grabbed me, he's pulling me backwards towards the van, and Rome's not shooting at him because he can't get a clean shot — but he's still firing as he runs towards the front of the car, shooting at the driver—

I buck in the man's arms but he doesn't let go, so I bring my knees up to my chest, grab my knife[71] out from my Balmain combat boots[72] and start blindly stabbing behind me.

Shoulder, neck, face — I don't care, I hit it all, and he's screaming in pain — lets me go as he falls down and another man emerges from the van with a gun — points it at me, and then I hear a shot. I touch my head — still not me.

The man falls down dead.

I look back at Romeo.

His chest is heaving — that old look back on his face that he's had too many times in our little lives.

I bend down for Grace.

"No!" He grabs me.

"Yes!" I pull away. "She could still be—"

"She's not—" He shakes his head.

I shove him away from me. "You don't know!"

"I do!" he yells back. "It was a head shot, I watched it hit her—"

I put my hands on my cheeks — I think I'm going to be sick.

"We've got to go, Dais—now." Rome grabs my hand and we run towards my car, he snatches my keys from me, unlocks it, shoves me inside.

"Are you hurt?" He doesn't look at me as he asks, just starts the car, peels out.

Drives straight through the arm of the parking gate.

"No." I shake my head, tucking my feet under my legs. "Are you?"

He looks over at me, shakes his head.

He nods, pulling out his phone.

"Miguel?" he says into it. "No, they came for her. In the garage. No, yeah — I'm — she's with me." He glances at me. "They're dead." Pause. "So is a girl who was in the lift."

"Grace Pal," I say.

Romeo doesn't repeat her name.

"Do you have the Escalade?" he asks instead. "We'll meet you out front. Ditch her car."

"No." I smack him and he gives me a sharp look, then hangs up the phone.

"How did you know?" I ask, crossing my arms over my chest.

---

[71] Bear OPS Single-Edge Boot Knife Fixed 3.25" Black Spear Point Blade.
[72] Ranger. Black leather.

He takes a steep breath. "You've pissed off everyone you know, who the fuck is gonna send you flowers?"

12

Julian

I got the call when they were already on their way back to the Compound.

Felt sick to my fucking stomach that I didn't act faster, that I didn't just make her come home the minute they came here.

I had a feeling I should have when she came here the other night — didn't imagine it going down too well. She'd have put up a fight, that would have made me angry—

Also didn't fancy her getting big for her boots, thinking I miss her or some shit, which maybe I did but it's not like she needs to know.

But now this has happened and I don't really give a shit about any of the rest.

She storms through the door of my office and then bolts straight into my arms. Lets out one big sob into my chest, and I hold her tighter — pull back a little to look down at her.

"Any of this yours?" I nod at the blood my sister's covered in.

She shakes her head.

"Are you okay?" I put my hand on her face and she glares up at me, smacking it away.

I stare down at her wide-eyed. "Smack my fucking hand away, are you daft?"

"We're still fighting," she says loudly.

"So?"

("Oh, God." Koa cracks his neck.)

"So—" She smacks my arm. "Don't try to be nice and comforting to me, you fucking psychopath."

"Okay." I give her a dark look and move back behind my desk. "Excuse me for having a moment of concern for the girl I raised."

Daisy glares at me and moves without realising it over towards

Rome, perching on the arm of the chair he's sitting in. These two, I swear to God.

My dog crawls out from under my desk, walks over to my sister, drops his head in her lap. She pets him mindlessly and I roll my eyes.

I put my elbows on my desk, drop my head into my hands and breathe out.

"Takeaways?" I ask the room.

Romeo shakes his head. "Shit show — complete shit show."

I look over at him. "What are you talking about?"

"It wasn't a tight job." He shakes his head. "It was sloppy."

"The girl who died—" I start.

"Grace," Daisy jumps in.

"Grace—" I lock eyes with my sister. "What do we know about her?"

Dais shakes her head. "23, smart, bit annoying. I'm guessing upper-middle class family."

"Could she have been dirty?" You never know.

Daisy shakes her head like I'm an idiot and I can tell by her face she's about to launch into something annoying when Tiller bursts into the room.

"Where is she?" he says, spots me first.

She stands at the same time he turns to see her, all covered in blood.

"Oh my God—" He grabs her, looking all over her for the bleed site.

"It's not mine—" She shakes her head quick.

Puts his hands on her face and kisses her cheek, holds her as tight as I've ever seen her be held. And it's weird watching someone love her so much all of a sudden. This weird thought rattles through my brain that I should have been there to see it. You want to watch someone fall in love with your kid the way they deserve to be loved and I missed it. I've dropped back in now that they're all fully formed and shit — but I guess this is what happens when you turn away from everything you know and everyone you know, you have just one person to invest in and he was hers.

"What happened?" Tiller pulls away from her, looks between us all.

"There was a van waiting for me in the carpark — they shot my friend. They grabbed me—"

Tiller pulls out his phone and Daisy pushes it down. "No police."

"You just said a girl died—"

I shake my head. "I got some boys making it look like she was jumped in the parking lot—"

"Oh." Tiller nods at me sarcastically. "That makes me feel so much better—"

Daisy takes his phone from his hands, puts it back in his pocket, shaking her head at him.

"How are you fine?" He gestures to her.

Daisy looks over at Romeo, who stands. Tiller's eyes flick between them. Thinks for a second. Then steps towards Rome, extending his hand.

A strange peace offering, copper to criminal.

Rome stares Tiller dead in the eye.

"Fanculo," he mutters under his breath and moves past, but not before he pauses in front of Daisy, kissing her forehead. "Welcome back," he tells her before he walks out.

"I'm not back—" she calls after him.

I sniff, amused. "Yeah, you are—"

"No—" She glances quickly between me and her boy. "No, I'm not."

"Yes. You are." I give her a look like she's an idiot. Which she is. "You're not going back there — you're back in the Compound here on out— I already have people packing up your place — I was wondering where my Matisse went—"

I give her a look and she shifts on her feet, ignoring her copper boyfriend's wide eyes.

"You don't even like Impressionism—" I tell her, folding my arms over my chest.

"Well, I like that one." She shrugs.

"Why?" I give her an annoyed face. "It's just 'naked crayon ladies.'" I roll my eyes, quoting her.

"Doesn't even have faces." She growls under her breath.

"So why'd you take it then?"

"Because it reminds me of y—" She presses her mouth shut. Breathes through her nose. I feel shit.

"I'm not moving back in." She shakes her head, glances over at Tiller for back-up, and — here's a surprise — he's got this reluctant look on his face.

"I think you should." He nods.

"What?" She blinks.

Tiller gives her this sort of hopeless shrug, sighs. "Who can protect you like he can?"

No one, is the truth. At least he knows it.

Tiller shakes his head. "Because I can't — I want to, but I can't. Whatever I can do, it's not enough, Dais — you're protected with him."

"I like my place." She shakes her head urgently. The look on her face — it's weird, really desperate. I know all her faces, she's losing something here. Like she's trying to hold on to something and it's slipping through her fingers. I don't know what it is, but I can tell she is. There's some sort of grieving in her eyes.

"Actually," I make an uncomfortable smile, "on that... It's already up on Right Move."

She launches for me immediately. "Fuck you!" She smacks me. "Fuck you!" Hits me again, and again, and then Tiller picks her up, moving her away from me.

Again with the hands on her face. She's crying now. Shaking her head like mad.

"This isn't what I want — it's not what I want—"

"Dais." Tiller looks for her eye. "It's going to be okay—"

She looks at him, and it's strange. Frantic. Like she's trying to tell him something. "It's not what I want — I don't want this—"

Tiller nods, sort of confused. "I know."

She shakes her head. "We can't stay here—"

I stare over at her, confused — Don't know what she's getting at? I wave my hand at Tiller dismissively. "He can stay here, the boys won't touch him—"

"We don't want to stay here!" she yells, more angrily than needed.

I get up close in her face. "Well, do you want to die?"

Tiller tugs her away again, wipes his hands over her face — he's alright at calming her down, actually. "I'll stay with you, Dais — it'll be okay."

She nods, crying a bit still. "Promise me that you'll remember—"

Tiller looks confused now too. "Remember what?"

Dais looks up at him, eyes all glassy. "That none of this is what I wanted."

"Yeah." He shrugs, not getting it. "Okay."

I think he thinks she's just in shock or hysterical or something.
He starts leading her out of my office.

"Take your old room—" I call after her.

Daisy doesn't turn back but Tiller gives me a nod.

I look over at Koa and give him a look. "What the fuck was that?"

"He doesn't know it yet, but she does." He shrugs. "It's quicksand around here."

13

Daisy

When we get into bed that night, Tiller loads his gun and I stare over at him — his face pulls and then he says he's sorry, but then he puts it under his pillow anyway.

I don't say anything, just lay there, staring up at the ceiling.

"It'll only be for a while, Dais." He rolls in towards me.

"Mmm." I nod.

It's not what I want, that's what I said to him. Even if it is sometimes. I spent all my life wanting to be normal, and then I got it, finally — it only cost me everything else. And then once I got it, I'd wait til Tiller would fall asleep at night and creep into a room I kept locked up and sit under a painting my brother and I stole together and wonder whether it was worth it? I don't know if it was.

I love Tiller. We work, when I'm normal — we work. He's good, he's beautiful, he's protective, he's thoughtful, he's kind — and we work in my W2 4BA apartment. We work in the cafe across the road. We work in the Thai restaurant around the corner, at the cinema and the farmers' market, we work when we walk around Kensington Garden Square...

But I don't know if we'll work here.

"We're going to be okay," he tells me, his nose pressed up against mine. But I suspect he knows as well as I do—

I've never been on a sinking ship, but I do think about them a bit... How my life is one, just slow-motion sinking. They'll get me one day... One day, I will die. Someday, someone will take me and the penny will finally drop and my ship will be sunk.

Tiller and I, we're a sinking ship now. We're on the Titanic and they've struck the iceberg but everyone is telling them there's no danger, they're fine, it's an unsinkable ship, keep sleeping.

As I lay my head down next to him I know there is a hole in the ship, and the gun under his pillow says he does too — it's just that neither of us are willing to climb off the boat yet.

"We're going to be fine," I lie back.

~

Tiller wakes up early the next morning — he says he has a work thing and he's got to go.

It might be true, I just think he doesn't want to be here. I get it, I don't hold it against him.

He works with the girl he used to date before me.[73] They're friends still.

I don't think those two things really have anything to do with each other, but I guess your mind does go there because can you ever fully disconnect from a person? I don't know... He goes in to work early, she's there — she says, *you're here early* and he shrugs, says something like, *yeah I just had to get out of the house.* And she's like, *uh oh, trouble in paradise?* And he's like, *I don't want to talk about it,* which he mightn't, maybe that's true, but it's also simultaneously telling her that there's something to talk about — and she'd touch his arm and say, *well, if you change your mind...* and then she'd walk away and he'd watch her walk away, and he'd wonder if it was easier with them than it is with us, and of course — of course — the answer is yes. It's yes. She was a little British country girl who grew up in Bakewell, came down to London to be a big city copper, moved over into the NCA after a few years and fell in love with the American transfer.[74] And him, well — he grew up near Cisco Beach.[75] Middle child, his mum is a dentist[76] and his dad was a police officer — retired now — originally from Ireland.[77]. Two brothers, one's a teacher,[78] one's a lawyer[79] — and him, the police officer-turned-Interpol-turned-NCA-agent. He did well in school, he was popular, well adjusted, completely handsome all his life but it didn't seem to disable him in any of the

---

[73] Michelle is her name.

[74] What? I have a dossier on everyone I know.

[75] Nantucket, MA.

[76] It's why his smile is so perfect.

[77] Hence, Killian.

[78] Marcus

[79] Phelan

ways it sometimes can — two serious girlfriends before me, one in college, and then Michelle.[80]

I know that he brought her home to meet his family at least twice[81, 82] but he's never asked me home. Even though he's been home twice since we've been together. Even though he's going home next month for Christmas.

I've met them on FaceTime. His dad doesn't stay on for long — he's not much of a talker, Tiller says. He pretends like it's not about me. We both know it is.

"How's wee Michelle, then?" his dad asked him once, in front of me.

"Dad—" Tiller gave him a look, nodding his head at me as subtly as he could but his dad just waved his hand through the air and then Tiller slammed shut the computer, pulled me onto his lap, kissed me a lot which lead to more than kissing me a lot. That was the moment I became sure that it actually was about me personally — I'd wondered up until then whether his parents had a problem with me, me being me and Tiller being Tiller. Tiller being the personification of good, me being the sister of the personification of bad, at least to them — I'm not an idiot, so of course, I'd considered that — I just didn't know whether it was completely true until that day when he tried to cover his father's rejection of me with a million tiny kisses and eventually his whole entire body.

It's because Tiller is good that I know he's not going in to work to see Michelle, I know that,[83] I trust that. It is also because Tiller is good that I know that he's left the Compound early because he's trying to get as far away from it as quickly as he can, like he might catch the badness of us all — or worse, he might catch its appeal.

I wander downstairs into the kitchen midmorning the next day, Julian's dog at my heels. I like him. He's such a smooch. As soon as he heard me get up this morning he ran out of my brother's room and over to me. I've always wanted a dog. We had a tiger once, briefly. Julian was trying to steal *Impression, Sunrise*[84] which everyone thinks

---

[80] She's older than me. Born in the early '90s. Tiller doesn't like it when we mention I was born in the year 2000.

[81] I checked their corresponding flight records.

[82] Shut up.

[83] I mean that, I really do.

[84] 48 cm × 63 cm. Oil on canvas.

72

is hanging in the Musée Marmottan Monet,[85] but actually the real one is hanging in the office of the woman Julian stole it for. Allegedly, the man Julian stole it from was her ex husband, the painting really belonged to her, he refused to hand it over in the divorce so she hired my brother to take it for her. When he and the boys got to the house, they found a caged tiger cub— Julian can't stomach a caged animal so he stole the painting, took the cub and banged the ex wife.[86] That's the story anyway. The cub lived with us for a while, he was so gentle and so sweet, but the bigger he got, the more precarious it became, and Julian would never declaw an animal so we had to get rid of him and now he lives on a reserve for Sumatran tigers in Ubud.

It's a strange feeling wandering down the stairs I've wandered down all my life until my life got turned on its head. I love these stairs, they're so theatrical. Everything in our house is palatial. Steps that would easily be at home in a grand museum or a baroque palace somewhere in Austria, but they sit here quietly in South Kensington and have witnessed an array of illegal and smutty things in their time.

I make my way to the kitchen, wondering whether I'll see my brother, and if I do, whether I'll speak to him.

One of us will have to say sorry first and maybe it should be me because I lost him a lot of money but then maybe fuck him because he said the meanest things he could to get back at me — and he did it, it worked — he broke me.

Cried myself into a panic attack, the nurse at the hospital had to give me something to calm down.

I don't want to see him. But the fridge is open when I walk in anyway. A pair of legs.

Not Julian's though.

He sticks his head out. Best head in the world, I'd wager — but I shouldn't think that, so forget I said anything.

"Hey." Christian stares over at me.

"Oh." I swallow. "Hi."

"Hi." He closes the fridge, smiles a bit as his eyes fall down me. Of all the people to see — Christian Hemmes hadn't even crossed my mind as a possibility. I'm in Stella McCartney trackpants and a sports bra.

---

[85] 2 Rue Louis Boilly, 75016 Paris, France

[86] Of course he did.

He nods his head at LJ. "That dog's pretty keen on you, ey?"

I shrug. "I don't know why."

He watches me for a few seconds. "Dogs are a good judge of character."

"What are you doing here?" I blink.

He gestures to himself. Workout gear. Grey track shorts, black muscle t-shirt, trainers. "Best gym in Knightsbridge."

"That is true." I nod once, smiling — but not too much. I don't want him to know how happy I am to see him — and however happy I am, I know it's more than I should be.

He walks towards me, and God he's very, very beautiful. I try to downplay it in my mind when I think of him, which isn't often,[87] that hair of his always pushed back to some kind of perfection and the pink mouth with the smile that could get you pregnant. He stops, tilts his head.

"Is it weird I'm here? Because if it is..." He trails. "I'm still going to come over—"

I start laughing and he grins over at me.

"For the gym." I nod.

"I mean, gym memberships are very expensive—"

"You drive a £180,000 car—"

He shrugs like he's helpless. "You gotta skint somewhere—"

I roll my eyes, brush past him on purpose a little as I walk over to the fridge.

"There's no food in here." I stare at the horrible emptiness of it.

"Yeah, well — didn't you hear?" He gives me a look. "The chef quit about a year ago—"

I give him a look. "Did she?"

He nods.

"Terrible working conditions, I'd imagine — it's a thankless job cooking for a band of boys—"

"I remember personally thanking you—" he tells me and it looks like he's trying not to smile, and I close the fridge.

"Do you?"

He nods coolly. "I thanked you there—" He points to the counter top. "I thanked you there—" He points to the table. "Thanked you up against that window."

---

[87] Even if it's all the time.

"I think with that window you actually just thanked yourself—"

He cracks up and I don't smile back even though I want to.

Is he really flirting with me? I don't say anything, just boost myself up on the bench and stare over at him.

"Your brother went to Waitrose—" Christian nods with his chin. "I think he was hoping to have the kitchen fully stocked before you woke up."

I shake my head. "That doesn't sound like my brother..."

But actually it does.

"Hey—" He stands in front of me. "I'm sorry about what happened to your friend."

My eyes drop from his. "Thanks—" Shake my head a little. "We weren't close, really" — I roll my eyes at myself — "not that that makes it better."

He nods, looking for my eyes. "You're okay though?"

"Yeah—" I give him my brightest look. "Not a scratch."

He breathes out, sounds relieved, actually. "Romeo fucking Bambrilla—" He shakes his head. "What a smooth move..."

I give him a look. "It wasn't a move."

"That's just his schtick, then?" Christian lets out a laugh. "Saving you?"

I sit up tall, eyebrows up, defensively. "So what if it is?"

He throws his hands in the air and turns away. "How the fuck am I meant to compete with that?"

I frown at him curious. Is he—? I can't tell. I feel like I can tell, but I don't know. I've been wrong before.

Also. Boyfriend. I have one.

He looks back over his shoulder, breathes out a smile, shakes his head a little.

"I like seeing you in this house again," he tells me.

I shrug my shoulders.

"I don't know how I feel about seeing you in this house yet—" I squint over at him suspiciously. "You and my brother being friends... who'd have thought?"

"You—" He leans back against the fridge. "Once upon a time, at least."

I give him a small smile, I don't know what it means — but I feel too exposed sitting across from him, all still where he can read me and watch me, so I jump off the bench and start loading the dishwasher.

"So," he says, moving over to the sink, rinsing plates and then handing them to me, "how does that normal life we got for you feel about the developments of the last few days?"

I purse my lips, stare at the plate in my hand, make a conscious decision not to read into the 'we' in that sentence. I peer up at him. "Not that good."

That makes him look a bit sad. "Yeah?"

I nod. "I had to postpone this semester."

"No—?" He frowns and I nod.

"Julian said he'll bring me in a private tutor—" I shrug. "But it's not really the same."

Christian sighs. "I'm sorry, Dais."

I give him a resigned shrug, because what else can I do? All the decisions for my life were taken back out of my hands overnight.

I fought for so long to be the one who got to control my life, and some flowers, one dead girl and a stupid white van usurped all my efforts.

Christian's staring over at me, face as serious as always, watching me with eyes I don't even dare to believe in, and he's frowning.

Moves in closer towards me. Elbows me. "Are you at all happy to be back, then?"[88]

I breathe in through my nose and look up at his face.

"Do you smell different?" I ask, trying not to sound devastated.

His head tilts, not sure what I mean.

"You don't smell like John Varvatos anymore."

"Oh." He nods, getting it. "No— I stopped wearing it."

"Why?" I frown, like I'm not personally offended at the thought.

His face pulls uncomfortably — and holy shit, what a face — that's the first thing I think. It is, for the most part, just as I left it.

A new freckle under his right eye. Eyes are just as much trouble as they've always been, coloured like honey spilt on leaves in autumn.

Cheekbones and a jawline that cuts like glass. Hair's a bit longer, just as golden though.

He feels like I'm looking at a painting.

---

[88] Yes.

"Because Magnolia bought it for me when we were at school, so I always wore it because I thought she'd like me more if I did."

"Oh." I say, turning away.

"I don't want her to like me anymore." He says and I turn back to face him. "So I stopped wearing it."

I cross my arms over my chest. "Well so, what do you wear now then?"

A little smile tugs at the corner of his mouth. "Blanche. Byredo."

"Okay." I shrug. "Why?"

He shrugs back. "Just reminds me of something I love."

14

Christian

I didn't see it coming — which, now that I know, I feel stupid because it's obvious… It's so fucking obvious and it makes everything about them, all their fucking issues, all the ways they couldn't figure out how to let each other go, them disappearing that week at school — all of it, it just makes them make sense, which honestly — and I mean this — they never have until now.

They had a baby. Beej and Parks. In high school, they had a baby.

Truthfully, I've been pretty fucked up about it since I found out.

It makes why Beej was how he was with me and Parks make more sense too.

Makes what me and Parks almost did back in March way worse.

I want to be pissed at her for that, but how can I be, all things considered?

I chew on it for a couple of days, whether I should talk to Beej — feel like it's the right thing to do.

He's been around our place a bit lately. Usually we'd spend more time at their place, but I reckon he's trying to catch a glimpse of her.

He's been quiet since they told us, even in the group.

Hen and Jo are playing *Red Dead Redemption 2* and Beej is out on the balcony, sitting by himself with a scotch.

"Oi." I stand in the doorway.

He cocks his chin towards the boys. "You leaving them alone in there?"

I shrug. "They've gotta figure it out."

"Are they talking?"

I shake my head.

He rolls his head back, looks at the sky and sighs. "I can't work out whether it's better or worse than you and me—"

I fold my arms over my chest. "It's worse. Parks wasn't torn." He flicks his eyes over at me. "For her it was always you. But Taura—" I shrug. "She doesn't know what she wants."

Beej nods, thinking it through, and I sit down in the doorway, sighing.

"I didn't know, man—"

He looks up and shrugs. "Yeah, I know—"

"If I had—" I shake my head. "I never would have — you know—"

"Yeah, alright—" He scoffs, tossing me a dirty look. "Let's just us pretend that's true—"

I roll my head back, blow some air out of my mouth. He can be a little prick when he wants to be. I want to smack him in the face for a second but I fight the urge.

"Are you okay?" I ask instead.

He sinks his drink. Stares at the empty glass. "No, man—" He shakes his head. "Not really." Flashes me a quick look then looks away again.

"It's typical Parks." He breathes out. "She comes home, fucks me up immediately."

"It is." I sniff a laugh, then feel myself frown as I watch him. "Why didn't you tell me about the baby?"

"We didn't tell anyone." He shakes his head.

"But if you'd told me then I wouldn't have—"

"Stop." BJ shakes his head. "It's bullshit. I know it's not true—"

"Bro—" I sigh, ready to defend myself but he locks on to me, staring over darkly.

"You didn't know we had a baby, I know. But like, you knew what she was to me."

I shake my head but I guess it's sort of true.

"Didn't stop you, man. It didn't matter. You just wanted her too."

My eyes drop and a guilt I haven't really felt before for loving her drips through me.

"I'm sorry." I tell him, and I mean it.

He flashes me a quick smile, nodding as he looks away. He looks tired. Stressed, maybe. Then he looks back at me with a crease between his eyebrows that he really only gets when it's about her.

"Did you know?" He asks. "That she was staying?"

"No—" I look at him confused, shaking my head. "How would I know before you?"

He gives me a long look. "Never know with you two."

Parks
9:52AM

I don't want to make this about me, I know it's not—

But I'm pretty pissed

Why?

How could you not tell me?

We never told anyone!

But me?

Christian

No

Shut up. With what we were? And what we did?

And New York?

Like, what the fuck, Parks?

Neither of us knew when we first started
back then that it was anything
more than a few kisses...

Yeah but when it obviously stopped being that?

I couldn't tell you

Why not

Would you have still been with me?

Honestly, probably.

80

Oh.

But you should have told me because he's my best friend and you had a baby with him.

Isn't Henry technically your best friend

Magnolia

Well he had sex with my best friend and he knew he had a baby with me.

You're un fucking believable

Don't be cross!

I am

Don't be!!

This makes New York so much worse

How?

I don't know it just does

Should we tell him?

Oh! Perhaps...!

Tell me, do you feel like dying today?

A bit.

Same, actually :)

Sorry.

Are you ok?

He's not happy I'm staying.

Not true

You didn't see his face

15

Daisy

I can hear them all downstairs, all those Lost Boys who used to be mine, but I don't know how to go down there myself anymore.

They are — just so you know — obnoxiously loud. The kind of loud you'd complain about if they were seated by you in a restaurant. Complete raucous. I try to busy myself with things in my room that I haven't seen in a year that's now all mixed with my stuff from my[89] new[90] place.

No one cleaned out my room after I left. They just left it.

A housekeeper must have come in though, vacuumed and dusted, it's clean. But otherwise, it's just... how I left it.

There's a knock on my door and it opens without me saying anything.

Rome pokes his head around. "Oi."

"Oh, hey." I flash him a quick smile and put a book back on the shelf that I was inspecting for no reason.

"Can I come in?"

I gesture to come in.

"You really hate us all so much you won't even pop downstairs for a minute?"

"I don't hate any of you—" I look up at him quickly, a bit thrown. "I just can't work out how to come downstairs—"

"What—?" He sniffs. "In your own home?"

I blink over at my old friend.[91] "Is this my home?"

"You might have left it..." He looks down at his hands. "But it's never not been."

---

[89] No longer my.
[90] Now old?
[91] Understatement.

I lean over, nudging him with my whole body. "So you're done not speaking to me?"

He purses his mouth. "Depends—" He shrugs. "Are you done being an idiot?"

I sniff a laugh and so does he, and somehow the sounds files down the jagged edges between us.

He gives me a look. "If my girlfriend asks — no, we're still not speaking."

"Girlfriend…!" I look over at him, eyes wide. I'm happy for him.[92, 93] "Who is it? Do I know h—" He gives me a look and I tilt my head in disbelief. "Don't say it—" He presses his tongue into his top lip. "Rome!"

His head rolls back. "Dais—"

I stand up, shaking my head. "Unfuckingbelievable—"

"You have a boyfriend!" He jumps to his feet.

"I just—" Shake my head like mad. "Of all the people!"

"Oh—" He scoffs. "You're one to talk — the cop?" He stares over at me, incredulous. He points at me. "I fucking told you he had a thing for you—" I roll my eyes. "And you over there, always playing it down—"

"Me?" I interrupt. "What about you with Tavie!" I give him a little shove. "Making me think I'm crazy for worrying you'll always go back there—"

"And what do you care if I do, Dais?" He puts his face close to mine, gives me a tight, over-it smile. "It's not me you fancy anyway. You're just shit at sharing—"

I turn away from him, worried that's not true, or worse, that it is. That I've just strung him along for years because I can't bear the idea of someone else having something that was mine first. I cross my arms over my chest. "Why were you following me in the car park?"

He shrugs dismissively. "I had a feeling—"

"A feeling?" I repeat back, frowning.

"A feeling, yeah—" he says louder and a bit defiantly. "Spent my whole life protecting you — like I'm going to let you die now, just because you've spent the last year acting like a bitch—"

"I was hardly a b—"

---

[92] Genuinely.

[93] Mostly.

"Shot yourself in the stomach to—"

"Save some kids!" I jump in.

"In front of me?" His eyes blink, hurt.

"And how does Tavie feel about you saving me?"

He presses his lips together. "Tavie doesn't know—"

"Oh…" I give him a dumb look. "Interesting."

He rolls his eyes and our faces are really close together. "Why don't you just say thank you?"

I stare over at him stubbornly for a few seconds then kick him with my big toe. "Thank you."

"You're welcome." He rolls his eyes, fighting off a smile. "Now come downstairs — we're playing Sticky Fingers."

~

"Right," I hear my brother bellow before we're even in the room. "The game is Sticky Fingers. We know the aim. You have your teams, and—"

He stops talking when Rome and I walk in. He half smiles.

"Oh shit," TK moans. "I don't want to play anymore—"

I stare over at him hurt, blink a few times.

"Why the fuck not?" Rome barks.

"Because you—" TK rushes over to me, picks me off the ground, spinning me around playfully. "Win every fucking time."

I grin up at him, so happy to see him.

I lean in towards him. "Hey, I'm sorry for—" I mime covering his face with a rag.

Booker walks over, slings an arm around me. "Forget about it, I douse him with Propofol all the time."

TK rolls his eyes.

"Only way to shut him up." Happy nods at me and gives me a little wink.

Booker kisses the top of my head and then gives my brother a look. "Teeks is right though, split them up—"

"Oi." Rome nods his head over at both of them. "Fuck off and just play better."

"Nah, it's not fair—" Declan shakes his head, eyeing me down from the other side of the room. "You two invented the game."

It's true, we did. Somewhere between The Floor is Lava, Capture the Flag and stealing.

I stare over at Decks.

'Hi,' I mouth.

'Hey,' he mouths back.

I feel like I could cry, that they're all being so nice to me, treating me like it's not been a year since we last spoke, that I didn't throw our world on its head—

"Alright—" Kekoa walks over to me, hugs me from behind. "Enough chatter. What are we playing for?"

My brother holds up a little box and everyone frowns. "A late 18th-century tablet box. French-made. Pearls, gold and enamel, valued at — conservatively — £20,000."

"Okay." TK nods, impressed. "That tiny box isn't messing—"

"And this." Julian holds up a little gold ring with a navy, heart-shaped stone. Rome squints at it. "Shotgun—" he whispers to me.

"Gold with a sapphire, manufactured in good ol' Blighty in the 15th century, possibly earlier—"

"Worth?" Declan asks, impatient.

My brother tosses him a cocky smile. "About £55,000."

Rome elbows me.

"You know the rules — but I'll say them again for Declan." He gives his friend a sharp look. "No blood drawn, no choke-holds—" He looks over at me. "Daisy, no chloroform." I flip him off. "Me and Koa will be defending the prize." He holds up a paintball gun. "If you get hit, you're frozen for one minute—" Claps his hands together. "Let's go."

This is how it works. The boys will hide the two prizes somewhere in the house, might be together, might not be, and then they hide with their paintball guns and try to shoot us to slow us down. The floor is lava — your feet can't touch it otherwise you are immediately eliminated. It's everyone's favourite game, and not just because the things we're playing for are always good — it's just fun.

Rome and I invented it one Christmas when we were small.

We don't win every game, but we do win most.

People don't like it when we're on the same team because most of them consider me to have an advantage — for one, I'm lighter and smaller — I can contort myself into smaller spaces, you can toss me higher. But that's not why we win. Rome and I just win because we're always on the same wavelength and we don't need to communicate when we communicate. I usually win if I'm teamed with my brother, too.

We've already found the little pill case, which I'm glad we found because I wanted it — actually I wanted both, but Rome already shotgunned the ring,[94] so never mind. It was in the air vent above the kitchen sink.

And we've located the ring — on a little prong on the chandelier that swings above our foyer. And I'm swinging from the said chandelier — one-handedly — with my brother and Miguel yelling at me from the ground as I'm swinging back and forth — Kekoa's brought out a drop mat for me to fall onto — and Rome is trying to grab my ankles to bring me back onto the balcony—

"Just let go!" Julian yells up at me.

"Nah — I've got her—" Rome says, a bit unsure.

"Just drop, Face!" Koa tells me.

"But I want the ring!" I yell at my brother without looking at him.

"You're going to die!" Yells Miguel.[95]

"Whose idea was it to put it on a chandelier, then?" I yell down at them. "That's on you."

"No one made you JUMP ON IT!" Julian yells and it's right then when Tiller walks in.[96]

"What the fuck is going on?" he yells, as I reach, reach, reach with the tippiest of my fingers, and my hand is slipping — I'm going to fall, I can feel it — and I feel my hand close around the ring right as my other one slips off the chandelier and I start falling — what, I don't know — eighteen feet through the air.

"Incoming!" Romeo yells and my brother and Kekoa tighten the slack of the drop mat and I land perfectly, popping my head up like a little meerkat, proud of myself.

"You're fucking ridiculous." My brother lets out a little laugh, shaking his head. "Did you get it?"

I hold up my finger, flashing it to him.

---

[94] And if he's going to give it to Tavie, I will scream.

[95] And that said in his Brazilian accent sends Rome over the edge.

[96] That meme where Danny Glover walks into the room on fire holding a pizza? This is the real life version of that.

He sniffs a laugh, offers me his hand to pull me out, but as soon as he does, Tiller snatches me away from him, glaring between us.

"What are you doing?" he asks, looking around, confused.

"Just playing." I shrug innocently.

"What in the hell are you playing?" he asks loudly.

"Nothing—" I shake my head dismissively. "It's just a game — it's dumb," I say,[97] and my brother frowns.

"Uh oh," Romeo says as he trots down the stairs, coolly. "Playtime's over. Dad's home."

Rome walks over to me.

"Good game," he tells me and I hold out the ring for him. He looks at it then shakes his head. "You keep it."

He leans in, kisses my cheek[98] and walks out the front door.

I swallow, suddenly feeling a bit nervous as Tiller stares after him.

"Come on—" I grab Tiller's hand, pulling him away, up the stairs. My brother watches me go, still frowning.

"We three are going to have dinner this week, yeah?" Julian calls after me.

Tiller looks back at him and I shake my head. "Mmm, no—"

"Wasn't a question, Face," Julian says, walking away.

I pull Tiller into my room and close the door, smiling apologetically. He folds his arms over his chest. "What game was that?"

"Oh…" I swat my hand. "Just a silly one."

"What is it?" he asks again.

I press my lips together. "It's called Sticky Fingers."

"Sticky Fingers." He blinks unimpressed.

I nod.

"And what do you do during Sticky Fingers?" He gives me a look with tall eyebrows.

I fold my arms over my chest defensively. "It's a bit like capture the flag."

He squints a little. "What's the flag, Dais?"

"Oh—" I lick my lips and shrug lightly. "Depends."

---

[97] Even though it's my favourite game in the world.

[98] And I have a surge of missing him and loving him, though I couldn't group specifically in what capacity I feel those things for him. Is it nostalgic and he always makes me feel a hint of that just because he is who he is, or is it past-tense tender where he's just something I'll always be fond of, or is there always more to us than that? I don't know.

"On?" he asks sharply.

I look away because I don't know what to say.

"Show me the ring—" he tells me, holding out his hand, waiting for me.

"No—" I shake my head.

"Show me."

"No!" I shove my hand deep into my pockets. "My brother bought it from an online auction—" I tell him, even though I'm not sure that's completely true. Sometimes that's true.

Tiller looks over at me, shaking his head. "Daisy — I get that you're just trying to make the best out of a bad situation, but I go out for one night and come back here and you're playing a game pretending to be a thief?"

"I am a thief!" I yell and he blinks a bunch of times. He looks scared, actually, so I shake my head quickly. "I mean, I was—"

He breathes out, staring at the ground. "And what are you now?"

"Let's see—" I give him a tight smile. "I did want to be normal, but then I got stalked, I was trying to be a doctor, but a girl died in the carpark because she was standing next to me, and then I used to think I was just — you know — like a good person, but my boyfriend is standing here, looking at me like I'm something on the bottom of his shoe—"

His face softens immediately. "No, I'm not—" He takes a step towards me, pulls me into him, breathes out loudly. "Dais, I can't have dinner with your brother — if anyone sees me—"

I stare up at him. "You're living with him?"

"Yeah—" He gives me a look. "How do you think that one went over?"

"Tiller," I say. "You have to give him a chance—"

He scoffs.

"Please—"

"Daisy—" He sighs.

I bury my face in his chest, breathe him in and feel sad as I do.

He smells like what's been my home for the last year. It's him, he's been my home. He's been the constant, he's been the thing that makes me feel safe. And the iceberg's struck, but they're still telling us to sleep.

I'm still telling us to sleep.

"Please—" I say, all muffled by him. "Please, please — you're going to love him."

He lifts up my chin.

"I don't want to love him," he tells me very seriously.

"For me?" I ask quietly.[99]

"Okay." He sighs, nods a little. "For you."

---

[99] (Manipulatively)

16

Julian

Tiller's not about, seems now's as good a time as any to do the thing I've been avoiding doing but should have done a year ago.

I knock on her door and then my sister screams so I bust in, gun out and cocked.

And there she is, sitting in bed, my fucking dog sitting on her feet, that traitor.

"Are you okay?" I frown, glancing around, gun still out.

She breathes out, clasping her chest. "Fuck—" She sighs. "Put that away — I was watching *Criminal Minds*."

"Why?" I walk over as I put the safety back on, tucking it away.

I frown down at what she's watching. "This show's always given you nightmares."

I close her MacBook. "Where's Tiller?"

Daisy folds her arms over her chest. "Work."

I nod once, watch her for a couple of seconds, trying to read her how I've always done.

"He wasn't a fan of Sticky Fingers?" I ask her.

She looks a bit sad but tries to morph it into a smile. "No, he was not." She looks over at me. "Did you put the ring on the chandelier because you knew I was the only one who'd get it?"

I sniff, trying not to look completely caught out. "Maybe." I shrug. "I was going to steal it for you if anyone else won it anyway."

She stares over at me. "Did you?"

"Did I what?"

"Steal it."

I mash my mouth together and give her a shrug. "Do you like it, at least?"

"Yes." She nods, avoiding my eyes. "Thank you."

"Got you something else—" I toss it into her lap and she picks it up — pretends for a second like she doesn't know what it is... like I don't get her one every time I fuck up or do something I shouldn't or know that I've failed her. I don't know why I give her gold doubloons — it started before mum and dad died, I forgot to get her a birthday present — I didn't have anything that felt like I could give a seven-year old but I remembered I had a piece of gold dad gave me once, so I gave it to her and she lost her shit. She carried it around everywhere for a year. And now it's just what I give her when when I feel shit or I've done something she won't like.

"Where from?" I ask her, testing.

She flips over the eight Escudos, inspecting it. "Peruvian—" She squints. "REX HISPANIRUM ET..." She thinks to herself for a minute and I get this twinge of pride and annoyance that she's this clever. "King of Spain and... Indies?"

I sniff a laugh.

"Good." I think about quizzing her on the value but I don't want her to ask where I got it. She doesn't want to know.

I sit down on the edge of her bed. Pet my traitor-dog's head. "Dais, we need to talk."

She sits up straight, looks nervous. Makes me sad that she looks nervous around me— makes me angry at myself that I tossed away a trust she'd built in me all her life to win a stupid fucking fight.

I lean forward, not looking at her, breathe out — sort of hang my head a bit. "I've done some things I'm not proud of over the course of my life — but what I said to you that day in the hospital — it's probably the thing I regret most."

I peer over at her and I feel sick.

"Really?" she asks, almost hopeful.

I nod.

"Even more than the time Flopsy's head was between the stokes of your bike and you didn't know and you started riding it and you broke his neck?"

I roll my eyes. "Yes."

"Even more than the time you kissed that girl from your school in front of Gia Bambrilla and then the next day they found that girl dead in the Thames?"

Fuck me — I toss her an exasperated look. "What'd you bring that up for?"

"I'm trying to get a gage." She shrugs innocently.

"Fine—" I give her an impatient look. "More than that, then, yes."

"Wow."

I sniff a laugh and then I stare straight ahead. Feel the question bubbling up in me that I don't want to ask because I feel like I shouldn't care but I do.

"Why'd you do it, Dais?" I ask her and she brings her knees up to her chest.

Hope my face doesn't look as sad and hurt as I am about it all. "How could you do that to me?"

She breathes out her nose, chews on her bottom lip the way she's always done when she's thinking.

"Do you remember what Dad said before he died? To me?"

I glance over at her. "You're my keeper."

She stares at a spot in the corner. "You'd kidnapped those kids and you'd worked with the MacMathans, and then, Jules — you worked with Mata Tosell? How could you?"

Wait. I frown. What?

I shake my head. "I've never worked with Mata."

She looks away again, annoyed. "Don't lie to me."

"Dais—" I look for her eye. "I've literally never worked with Mata Tosell—" I'm actually a bit offended. "How could you think I'd work with him?"

"You transferred him £2 million!"

I roll my eyes. "Firstly, how the fuck do you know about that? And secondly..." I give her an exasperated look. "It was a poker game."

She blinks a few times. "What?"

"It was a high-stakes poker game."

"How high?" she asks loudly.

God, she's annoying sometimes. "Very, obviously — I fucking lost two million quid."

She moves in towards me a little, eyes looking a bit brighter. "You promise you've never worked with him?"

I nod once. "Promise."

"And my other rules?" she asks, eyebrows up. "Have you kidnapped anyone since?"

"No." I'm lying, but. "No, definitely not—" I shake my head, flash her a tight smile. "Yes. Fuck."

"Julian!"

"Sorry—" I shove my hands through my hair. "Sorry! I just — it does get it done..."

She lowers her chin, glaring at me. "Julian."

"But I'm done with it now, yeah?" I give her a tall smile. "Promise—" I nod and she's looking at me weird, like she's puzzling something out. "What? What's that look?"

"Nothing—" She shakes her head. "I'm kind of surprised Koa let you—"

"What the fuck do you mean 'let me'?"

"I mean I'm surprised he let you." She shrugs.

"You know, I'm his boss—"

"Yeah—" She rolls her eyes. "But—"

"And you know him. A quick game's a good game."

She gives me a stern look. "It was the wrong thing to do."

"No, I know." I nod, trying to placate her. "But you're the sun, Face! You're the sun that shines on everything and makes it all light and you're the thing makes us know right from wrong — and when you left we got worse, but now you're back." I elbow her gently.

"Kiss arse," she tells me and I say nothing because I am. "And I'm not back back." She looks over at me. "I'm not doing jobs for you or anything, I'm just... living here."

I give her a look. "I never want you to do jobs for me— ever—"

She looks offended.

"It's you— You're the one always trying to worm your way into my jobs—"

She looks more offended and it makes me laugh.

"I'm good at them!" She frowns.

I give her a look like I'm unsure, even though she's better than me at everything.

She smacks me for it and I don't want her to be able to tell from looking at me, so I look away.

"I missed you, Face."

She stares straight ahead and puts her head on my shoulder. Feels like the first deep breath I've taken in a year.

"Same." She says.

17

Daisy

Here's the thing about my brother: You can't not like him.[100] You can try, but you'll bend eventually. He's beyond charismatic, he could be killing you and politely ask you to hand him his other gun and you'd probably do it.

And it's not just women — it's men, too.

He's just the sort of person you just want to be around, whose approval you want.

He has a certain gravitas to him that everyone falls to.

Tonight's the dinner... The dinner Tiller has tried to get out of for the last three days in a row and maybe if I were a better girlfriend I would let him miss it, but I won't let him miss tonight because I can't patch the hole in the side of the ship, but I'm fairly sure I can put out the fire in the boiler room.

I invite Jack for reinforcements on both ends.[101]

"Where are we going?" Jack asks, fixing his shoelace.

Tiller helps me slip into my coat as my brother and I have a Mexican standoff with our eyes about the restaurant we're going to.

I say "The Ledbury" at the same time my brother says "Bar 61."

We stare at one another and then wordlessly on the tacit count of three, we scissors-paper-rock it.

Julian: rock; Me: paper.

Jack rolls his eyes, checks his watch.[102]

Julian: rock; Me: scissors.

"Don't mind them—" Jack tells Tiller. "This is how they decide where to go on vacations too."

---

[100] It's always been this way.
[101] Julian adores him, Tiller loves him.
[102] He's used to our shit.

Julian: paper; Me: scissors.

I give him a smug smile.

My brother sighs. "The Ledbury it is."

~

I knew Jules was going to lay it on thick tonight for Tiller. Knew it, could feel it before he began — Julian needs to be loved by everyone,[103] even my NCA agent boyfriend.

We walk into The Ledbury and we're greeted by the maitre'd[104] and taken to the table Julian and I always sit at.

Tiller watches on in fascination at how people move around my brother.

People part in front of him like Moses' sea, and Julian doesn't bat an eye. He's used to it, doesn't even notice it anymore — and to his defence, he's too busy kissing babies.

It's genuine, too. He clasps the hands and shoulders of the people he's passing by, including several of the staff, remembering all of their names, even asking one waiter how his dad's doing.

Once we're seated, Julian grins up at the waitress. "Zoe, right?" She nods, flushing at him remembering her. Jack and I trade looks.

"A bottle of your best red, a bottle of your best white and all the starters that aren't fishy." Big grin.

Julian looks over at Jack and snaps his finger.

"Where are we at with Waterhouse?"

"It's going okay," Jack says, sounding unsure.

"Okay?" Jules' eyes pinch at my best friend. "Don't you even think about going back to that fucking Hot John — whatever his name is—"

Hot Dom.

Jack looks at me despondently. "For fuck's sake, Dais—"

"What?" I blink, innocently. "I tell him everything! Like a therapist, almost."

Jack flares over at me. "Why don't you just see a therapist?"

"Well—" I frown, glancing between them all. "I did that last year

---

[103] My teachers, the postman, the old lady at the bakery, the old man at the corner store.

[104] Who hugs my brother, and I'd like to re-reference footnote number 103.

— see one, I mean." I look at Tiller for back-up and he nods. "But she kept saying things I didn't love."

"Did she?" My brother frowns, defensively. "Like what?"

"Oh just shit like... that I use sex almost medicinally—"

Julian pulls a face. "Hate that—"

"And as a coping mechanism."

He pulls a face. "Hate that too."

"That I have issues with women because of our mother—"

"I'll say!" Jack scoffs the way only a best friend could but Tiller's nodding away too.

Julian lets out a low whistle then reaches over and covertly squeezes my arm like he's sorry for me, like it's his fault that he stole all our mother's affection, and then he nods his chin at Tiller.

"You close with your family?"

Tiller nods. "Yep."

"Big family?"

Tiller shrugs. "Two brothers, Mom and Dad."

Jules gestures towards him. "American, obviously—"[105] Tills nods. "Where?"

"Nantucket."

I glance over at Jack, making a tight face — the conversation is hardly riveting. Tiller's all walled up.

"Tiller loves surfing—" I tell my brother as I hold my boyfriend's arm, internally trying[106] to coax him out. Jules nods over at him. "Yeah, you look like you would — I caught some monsters at Playa Encuentro—"

My boyfriend's eyes pinch. "Bit of a drive from where you were holed up..."

Julian folds his arms over his chest, unimpressed. "Not like I had much else to do."

I take a breath, smile between them nervously.

"So—" Julian pours Tiller more wine. "How'd you get into what you do?"

My heart twists a little. I was hoping the job thing wouldn't come up — stupid of me, really. Of course it would. A vain thought, but a girl can dream...

---

[105] I love Tiller's accent.
[106] And failing.

A detective at the NCA sitting down with a crime boss for dinner at The Ledbury? It's practically a fucking NATO summit.

"My dad." Tiller nods, carefully. "You?" he adds, playfully.

Jules snorts. "My dad."

Tiller pulls at some bread. Plays with it, doesn't eat it. "Is being a gang lord what you always wanted to do?"

"Not a gang lord." Julian rolls his eyes.[107] "And no—" He cracks a smile. "Not even close, man. I wanted to be an MMA fighter or a fullback for the Harlequins."

Tills sits back in his chair, a little thrown, a confused smile on his face.

"He's very good—" Jack nods his head in my brother's direction.

Julian gives Jack a measured look. "You were very good," my brother reminds him.

"You play?" Tiller asks Jack, brows up.

I kick Jack under the table proudly. "Giles was offered to play for the Saracens out of high school."

Jack could have been anything in the world he wanted to be. A rugby player, a model, the surgeon general, a professional heart-breaker.

"Why didn't you?" Tiller asks.

Jack grimaces a little. "Didn't want to go through life as a gay rugby player…"

"You couldn't have just been a rugby player?" Tiller asks.

Jack shrugs. "You tell me."

Tills thinks on this, looks sad for my friend, and then nods his chin over at my brother. "So if they offered you a place, would you have taken it?"

"They did[108] — and no." My brother shakes his head, and I see a twinge of sadness flash across his face.

Everyone else would have missed it, but not me, because I get it. Jonah would have caught it, so would have Christian.

No matter how you slice it, no matter good our lives are, laced with so many benefits and perks, none of us had a choice.

---

[107] Him and Jonah have never liked that term, but I don't think they've ever offered an alternative.

[108] He was insanely talented at it.

"I've gotta ask, man—" Tiller eyes my brother, flicking me a glance too. "How do you do it?"

Julian cocks a little smile. "Are you being a little meta, Tiller, or are you looking for a literal how-to?"

Tills sniffs a laugh. "The first one."

Julian licks his bottom lip, thinking. "Did you see *Green Street Hooligans?*"

Tills nods.

"*Oceans 11? The Italian Job? Fast* — whatever, there's too many now. Didn't you watch those and think, *fuck, that looks like fun?*" Julian gives Tiller a look and points to him. "And don't lie. Everyone did. Of course they did, it's a fucking blast—"

"But you're doing the wrong thing," Tiller reminds him.

My brother shrugs. "According to who?"

Tiller looks over at me like he can't believe it, like it's obvious. He stares over at Jules. "The law."

Julian swats his hand dismissively. "I don't ascribe to your laws."

"Yeah, bro," Tiller snorts. "I fucking know."

Julian shakes his head, passionately. "I love waking up in the morning not knowing what's gonna happen, or who I'm gonna meet, where I'm gonna wind up—"[109] I take a deep breath through my nose. Jack and I trade looks. He's doing the Jack Dawson speech. He always does the Jack Dawson speech when he wants to deflect. People think it's so charming that someone like Julian would know a Leonardo DiCaprio monologue by heart, and maybe it is. Or maybe it's because I went through a real macabre phase during the tween break-up with Rome and we watched the movie every second night.

Julian shrugs his shoulders innocently. "Just the other night I was sleeping under a bridge[110] and now here I am on the grandest ship in the world having champagne with you fine people—"

Tiller's face pinches, confused. "We're not—?"

I shake my head. "He's quoting *Titanic.*"

Julian does another lighthearted shrug, picking up his wine glass and taking a sip, complete with an 'ahh' as he swallows. "I figure life's a gift and I don't intend on wasting it. You don't know what ha—"

"Alright." I toss a bread roll at his head.

---

[109] Oh, piss it.
[110] Tiller flicks me a look, no longer tracking.

Julian chuckles, and in my peripherals I can see that it's worked.

Quoting that fucking movie has buttered Tiller right up. I can see it in his eyes, he — reluctantly — is finding my brother completely delightful.[111]

"Here's the thing, right—" My brother reaches out and smacks my boyfriend in the arm. "We're all going to die one day. I'm just trying to have fun before I do."

"You know what." I shake my head at him. "I actually don't believe that."

"Why?" Julian nods, loving an argument.

"Because you believe in God—"

Tiller sits back. This surprises him.

"So?" Julian quips, not understanding my confusion.

"So if you believe in God, then it matters how you live. It's not just about fun on earth, it can't be. You have to be good so you can get into Heaven."

"Ah!" My brother grins, eyes like live-wires. "Daisyface, if you think any of us getting into Heaven is predicated on something we have or have not done, you've misunderstood that entire book." He gives me a look. "Detrimentally so," he tacks on at the end.

Tiller blinks, sitting back in his chair. "You think you're saved?"

"Nah, I doubt it—" Julian shrugs and lets out a small laugh as he takes another big gulp of wine. "Probably a bit loved, though."

---

[111] Everyone does.

18

Christian

I'm at the Compound just killing time with Jules, playing FIFA in his media room, when Daisy wanders in, little denim dress, not really done up, but a bit, and I wonder if it's for me? I don't know whether she knew I was here or not, but I want to think that she's showing off for me.

"Hey." I nod my chin at her and she comes and perches on the arm of my chair.

I try not to read into it. There are other chairs about, could have perched on Julian's seat — but she didn't.

He nods his chin at her. "Where are you off to?"

"Oh, I'm just waiting for Tills—" She flashes him a quick smile. "We're going to the National Gallery before he flies home for Christmas—"

"Oh." Julian looks interested. "Casing the joint?"

She crosses her arms, unimpressed, but he keeps going. "You finally going to let me steal *Whistlejacket?*"

Daisy glares over at him and then her phone starts ringing and that suits her brother fine, already bored of their conversation and back into the game.

"Hello?" She plugs her ear. And I'm not trying to listen in, except that I am.

"Oh," she says.

I look over at her; face all fallen. I catch her brother's eye.

"No — that's fine — no, I know. It's — that's fine. Yeah. Okay. Okay, bye."

She hangs up, purses her lips and pockets her phone. She breathes out of her nose.

"You good?" Julian asks, pausing the game.

"Yeah—" She shrugs. "No, yeah — it's fine. He just can't take me anymore."

"Oh—" Julian nods, watching her closely.

She flashes us both a quick smile and she looks sad. "I already sent Miguel home — I thought we — anyway, never mind."

Julian checks his watch, makes a noise with his mouth as he thinks to himself. "I've got a meeting in an hour but I can take you after?" he tells her.

"Oh—" She frowns. "Um, where's your meeting? It's just open til six is all—"

"I'll take you," I say before I even realise I'm saying it.

Both siblings look over at me, surprised. His eyebrows are arched up, well amused, and her eyes are just wide in a way that makes me feel kind of hopeful, kind of sad all at once.

"Really?" She blinks. "You don't have plans?"

I shrug. "Not important ones—"

I ignore the face her brother makes, hope Daisy misses it too.

"Okay—" Her whole face goes bright. "I'll go grab my coat."

I nod at her, hope my face doesn't give me away.

Julian watches her leave then peers over at me, and I'm already rolling my eyes.

"Does Vanna know she's not important?"

"No." I shrug. "Vanna thinks she's the centre of the universe—"

Julian clicks his tongue. "What are you playing at?"

"Nothing—" I give him a look. "Just taking my friend's sister to an art gallery."

"Never mind that you're in love with her, then?" he asks, eyebrows back up.

"Yeah." I sniff. "Never mind that."

We lock eyes, and I think he thinks it's something he has over me, that he knows I love her. But actually, I don't give a shit who knows I love her. Or maybe I do because she loves someone else now and I hate looking stupid.

And then she appears in the doorway, all perfect and shit.

"Ready?" I push past her brother who shoves me as I do, shaking his head.

"Yep." She smiles. She looks nervous, I think.

"Bye, then—" Julian calls after her and she waves without looking back.

She follows me out to the car and I look over at her, offering her the keys.

"You want to drive?"

A proper smile cracks over her and I swallow heavy because I miss her.

"Yes—" She plucks them from me and climbs into my car, peering over at me all happy.

There are so many things I want to say to her — that I miss her, that I love her, that I'm sorry, why is she still with that cop, is she okay? — but I say none of them — mostly because she looks happy and sort of at ease.

I don't know how much peace she gets these days, or space, or silence. I know before she never used to feel like she was alone, so I just look between her and the window. I'm sort of struck that we're here in my car again, and even though it's not how I want it, I'll take it anyway because the sun's behind her and it's lighting her up like she's got a halo, and to me she does.

She flicks her eyes over at me and looks a bit shy. "Are you being quiet out of weirdness or niceness?"

"Niceness." I sniff and she looks over at me with a smile that has soft edges, like she's not all-the-way happy and I want her to be all-the-way happy all the time.

"You're not going home with him for Christmas?" I ask, because I'm nosy.

She glances over, smiles again. Looks a bit sad. "No—"

I frown a bit. "Is that weird?"

She takes a long breath, thinking as she does. "His dad... is a retired policeman."

"Oh, shit—" I laugh.

"I don't think I've been their favourite choice their son has ever made." She flashes me a quick smile like it doesn't hurt her but I know her, so I know it does.

"And he's still going anyway?" I ask, a bit cause I'm a prick and I want him to mean less to her.

She shrugs. "It's his family."

I nod a few times. "You and Tiller are okay, though?" I ask, even though I don't want to know the answer in case they are.

"Yeah, we're—" A brief pause. "No, we're fine," she says with zero conviction. She glances at me quickly and then it's eyes back on the road, and she's holding that wheel so tight at one point I reach over and shake her hands loose, and she says nothing, just laughs like she's embarrassed, but our hands touched, and that's all I think about til we pull up to the gallery.

I open her car door and look down at her. "I didn't realise before," I nod my head back to the old days, "that you liked art. I knew you stole it, I didn't know you liked it."

She purses her lips and looks at me seriously. "There were lots of things you didn't know before."

I stare over at her for a few seconds, sigh a little.

"I know." I nod, wonder if how sorry I am is all over my face. "Are you going to hold it over my head forever, then?"

"What?" She blinks, eyebrows up, eyes sparked and ready to fight. "That you were madly in love with someone else while I was in love with you?" She walks quickly up the stairs ahead of me before turning back to glare at me. "Maybe."

"It was a mistake," I tell her.

Her eyes go a bit dark. "I'm sure it was—"

I shake my head at her. "That's not what I meant, Dais—"

"I know what you meant," she tells me proudly, but I don't think she does.

We're inside now, and I move past her, wordlessly buying our admissions...

Should I feel shit about this conversation we're barely having? I can't tell. She's holding it over my head and she's pushing me away, but there's something about it, that she's still fucked up about it, that she's still angry at me for fucking up how I did, that makes me happy because now I'm fairly sure that her and Tiller aren't actually fine.

I don't speak again until we're standing in front of a painting.

"*Christ Among the Doctors*," she tells me, staring at it. "He's meant to be twelve."

I frown at Jesus. "He's got a beard." I peer closer. "He kind of looks like the *Mona Lisa*."

She laughs a tiny bit — I can't tell if it's because she thinks I'm an idiot or not and then she walks away, shaking her head. Idiot, I guess.

I jog after her, and I like the feeling of wanting her and chasing her. I pass her a map of the gallery and she gives me a look like I'm a dick.

"I don't need it."

"Oh—" I pull my head back, teasing her. "You don't need it!"

She snatches it from me anyway, glaring at me playfully.

"She's back now, you know?" I tell her, watching her close.

Daisy nods slowly. "And how do you feel about that?"

I kind of scowl over at her. "I feel fine."

"Really?" she asks, eyebrows up.

"Why wouldn't I?" I ask, crossing my arms over my chest.

"Because you loved her," she tells me, eyes unflinching.

"Loved." I repeat back. Past tense.

"You must at least be happy?" She peers over at me, asking without asking.

"Sure, yeah—" I shrug. "She's my friend, I'm glad to have her back."

She nods once and moves into the next room.

Four big paintings on a green wall.

She folds her arms, staring at it. *Four Allegories of Love*," she tells me.

"What's your favourite?"

"In here?" she clarifies. I nod once and then she points to one. "*Happy Union*. Obviously."

"Weird." I sniff. "I'd have thought you'd like this one." I nod my chin at *Scorn*, then flick my eyes back over to her.

She does her best not to smile at me and it doesn't matter because I'm still smiling at her either way.

"What about not in this room?" I ask her.

"Ever, you mean?" She arches her eyebrows and I nod.

"Hmmm." She thinks to herself. "*Springtime*. Pierre Auguste Cot. Do you know it?"

I shake my head.

"It's in The Met. It's this young couple in a forest, on a swing—" She's smiling as she thinks of it, makes me want to fly to New York and take it off the wall to give it to her. I would if it'd guarantee I'd get her back.

"They're so in love." She shrugs. "And, I don't know — it's such a simplistic depiction of a complicated thing."

I frown a bit. "You think love is complicated?"

Her face falters. "We both know it is."

I hold her eyes for a few seconds before I sigh, exasperated, walking through a few rooms because I'm tired of feeling stuck.

"Dais—" I start. "Everything that happened — I cocked up, I know I did. I didn't even know I was in l—"

"We don't need to talk about it." She shakes her head quickly.

"Yes, we do—" I take a step towards her, my face all serious.

She keeps shaking her head. "I don't want to—"

"I do." I shrug.

"I have a boyfriend."

I give her a tight smile. "I don't care."

"Christian!" She crosses her arms, face cross and stubborn, kind of stressed. "You're ruining Art Day."

I feel my own stupid face soften. I've ruined enough for her, I never want to ruin anything for her again.

"Sorry," I tell her, following her into the next room.

"This one—" She stares up at it. "Is about five hundred years old."

"Really?" I look at it. It's like — fuck, I don't know? — a satyr and a dead girl and a dog.

"I love this one," she tells me.

"Me too," I say, staring at her. She glances over at me and our eyes catch and my cheeks go hot so then I look quickly at the painting. "Same." I nod coolly.

Sorry I couldn't take you.

A work thing came up.

What was it?

Something about some evidence.

Oh

That's okay

I'll take you after Christmas

Actually, I went anyway.

Did you

Good, I'm glad.

With who?

Christian took me

Christian?

Yes.

Your ex boyfriend?

Julian was going to take me but he had a meeting.

So Christian just swooped in?

He didn't swoop— I was obviously sad

Much better.

He was just being friendly.

How friendly?

Tiller.

I'll be home soon.

Okay, but don't be weird.

I'm not being weird.

19

Daisy

It didn't go over particularly well, Christian taking me to the art gallery, but then there wasn't much Tiller could say, because we both knew he only pretended he couldn't come home. I don't know whether that was because he felt like it was too dicey to go to a museum with me or because he's avoiding my brother, but either way, it wasn't his favourite of all the news I've ever delivered him.

The dinner, however — for better or for worse — went very well. Tiller liked my brother.[112]

He didn't say as much,[113] but I could tell he did. Not his fault, Julian is practically impossible to dislike, even knowing all the shit he pulls and does. He's humanising, my brother — that's where he gets you. He's so obviously flawed, so obviously imperfect and ready and willing to admit it — so much so that it disarms you.

He's not always like this, just when he wants to win you, and he wants to win Tills. A few times I've even caught them watching ESPN Classics.

But tonight after work Tiller comes home and as soon as he walks into my bedroom, I can tell he's in his head.

He can be like that sometimes, I've noticed. He overthinks things. Thinks about how everything might play out, how it might work, how it might not, how it looks, the optics of everything. He needs to be pulled back from the edge of a cliff every now and then, but for the most part I don't mind when he goes serious because I like how his face goes when he is. He has these beautiful eyebrows. Pretty straight across, and he always looks intense, but it's combatted by the lightness of his eyes.

---

[112] Much to his dismay.
[113] I don't think he'll ever admit it out loud.

He walks over to me in my bed, bends down, brushes his lips against mine, smiles down at me tired.

"Good day?" I ask.

He nods, but he looks a bit tired.

"No?" I ask, sitting up straighter.

"Yeah, no—" He shrugs.[114] "It was fine — it was good."

"Okay." I frown, watching him.

"What about yours?" He sits down on the edge of my bed, pulls his shirt off his head they way hot boys do. From the back of the neck and pulling it off forward — I don't know why but it feels like a magic trick.

"It was fine." I shrug. "Boring, really — I'm just around the house a bunch."

"No luck with the tutor yet?"

"Well," I shrug, "Julian's hired a retired military surgeon to come and teach me field tactics, triage and emergency care techniques, you know—" I flash him a little smile. "Things he'd find personally useful."

Tiller sniffs, rolls his eyes a little and then his eyes catch on my bedside table.

Maybe that was stupid of me to leave it out, but I didn't think anything of it.

"What's that?" He frowns, nodding towards my gold doubloon that's sitting on a Moleskine journal.

I have thirty-eight doubloons at this point.

My brother's been giving them to me most of my life. I sketch each one into my journal and write down everything I can find out about the coin and its history and then I[115] put the gold in my safe and daydream about two hundred years from now someone finding my own buried treasure and they'll be confused because there'll be gold doubloons from all over time and the world, and the thought makes me happy.

"This?" I pick it up and toss it to him. "Julian gave it to me." I give him a small smile.

Tiller turns it over in his hands, frowning as he does — then he

---

[114] And I can tell he's lying.
[115] Usually.

peeks up at me, holding the coin between his thumb and his index finger.

"Some coins like these were reported missing yesterday."

I snatch it back quickly. "No there weren't—"

"Oh." He pulls his chin back. "You're monitoring antique thefts now, are you?"

"Are you?" I ask sharply.

"Don't—" He shakes his head. "Don't look at me like I'm the bad guy for doing my fucking job and knowing when shit's been stolen—"

"It hasn't been stolen!" I lie. Maybe. Maybe I'm not lying, I don't know, but it probably hasn't been. "He bought it for me—"

"Your brother, the known art and antiquities thief, just happens to give you a piece of pirate gold the same week some's reported missing—"

I shake my head, dismissively. "This shit is littered all over the seafloor—"

"Really?" He gives me a look. "Peruvian eight Escudos from 1715? What the fuck beaches are you hanging out at?"

I glare at him a bit and he starts shaking his head a lot, standing up, pacing.

"This is bad, Dais — what am I meant to do?"

"Nothing!" I shake my head. "You can't do anything—"

"I'm a fucking detective at the NCA, and my girlfriend is pocketing shit she knows is stolen—" He gives me a look. "Julian's a thief — I know you know he stole that—"

"What are you doing?" I stand up, shaking my head at him. "You like him! I know you like him!"

"You're right!" Tiller nods, stressed, "I do. And I hate that!" He shrugs. "I don't want to like someone like him—"

I glare at him as I fold my hands over my chest, defiant. "You're dating someone like him."

Tiller shoves his hands through his hair and his eyes look heavy. "Yeah, well maybe I shouldn't be—"[116]

My mouth falls open. I blink a few times. "Are you breaking up with me?"

Tiller walks right over to me, hands on my face. "No—" He shakes his head. "But I don't know — I don't know if—"

---

[116] I think he says this by accident.

"I'm not ready—" I bury my face in his chest and he wraps his arms around me straight away, so maybe he isn't yet either. "Please, Tills—" I sniffle into him and his grip tightens. "I'm not—"

I'm not ready yet, that's the bottom line. Because I know what happens soon — I know we're on borrowed time. We have been since the second we walked through the doors here. This isn't what I wanted, God, I hope he remembers that. I don't like the feeling that I need to hide parts of my life from him and I don't like thinking that he has to lie for me, and I know that he has to. And he will, because he loves me. But because I love him I don't want him to have to, and I guess therein lies the iceberg.

We've crashed, I know we have. No way to make it ashore, but maybe we can still pretend we'll make it because I'm not ready. Not ready to let him go, not ready to not see him anymore, not ready for his hands to not be on my waist, not ready to feel alone again, just... not ready to say goodbye to him or the life that he represents.

Tiller shakes his head, nudges my face with his own until I'm looking at him again. "I'm not ready either," he tells me before he kisses me.

He slips his hand under my shirt, keeps it on my waist for a couple of seconds before his hands slip north and take it all the way off.

He lifts me up, carrying me backwards, laying me down, looking at me with eyes I think I'll always be grateful for no matter what happens after or next or later, because those eyes were my lifeline and my safe place when I didn't have anything else.

And his hands slip down my body, his mouth dragging down me with them. There's a sad and desperate urgency to us right now — two people clinging to a life raft, big breaths that feel like last rites.

And I cry a little bit, and I think he sees but he doesn't say anything — a bit because now that we're here, I think the statue I put away in that room in my old house is back out, dead and centre, shadowing everything, distorting light, stealing focus and also a bit because even if that is true, it doesn't mean that I don't love Tiller, which I do — which I tell him, and he says it back. I can tell by the way his eyes go when they look at me that he loves me too but you can ask anyone and they'll tell you for free (even though the lesson itself often comes at great cost) — love isn't enough, and it will hardly ever set you free.

20

Christian

I'm an idiot. I probably should have seen it coming, because she gets like this…

You back Magnolia Parks into a corner and all that upper-crust Kensington shit falls away and she'll come out swinging the best way she knows how to. And if it's BJ who's backing her up — I just should have seen it coming, that's all.

We're at brunch Christmas Eve, a Full Box Set tradition, though some of the founding members are noticeably absent, but for obvious and understandable reasons. Topic of fascination for all of us these last few days has been the revelation that Magnolia was in New York shacking up with Jack-Jack Cavan.

Pretty sure you already know who that is but if you don't, let me try to frame it for you in a way you'll get. What Kelly Slater was to surfing in the early 2000's, Jack-Jack is to skating now. Bit like Dylan Rieder too, crossing over into modelling and shit.

BJ loves him. Or did, anyway.

We've all been pounding Henry with questions but he's been pretty mum about it all — can't believe he knew and he didn't say. A week ago we watched something on VICE about him, Beej was completely frothing. Henry was on his phone most of the time, pretty disinterested.

I can tell Beej is pissed about it, and I guess rightfully so.

Me and Parks drunk, it's not good. It's never really been good at any point of our lives. Before she was with Beej and we were at school, if I'd drink a bit, I'd kiss her even though I didn't really like her, just did it for something to do. Once they were together, if I'd drink, I'd do whatever I could to try to make her jealous — don't even think she noticed half the time, thinking back now in retrospect. If she was drinking, she'd be all over Beej — more than normal — that'd drive me to drink more. And then once they were done and we started — It actually wasn't that alcohol-fuelled, because I wanted to remember it all. But then, once we were done, alcohol became a bit of a gateway to the past. For me and for her, couple of drinks in us and one of us starts whispering something to the other we shouldn't be.

Me and Hen visited her in New York in March. I was on a pretty shit path after Daisy and I wrapped up... I went "Full Beej" as Henry called it. Just something about knowing I loved her and she loved me and our lives were too fucked up to be able to figure it out anyway, that messed me up in the head a bit, tried to drown it out however I could — every party and club London could give me, and then when that failed, Amsterdam, Mykonos, Santorini, Phucket — why not New York?

I didn't go to New York thinking anything would happen with me and her, never even crossed my mind. I thought I'd hook up with Parks' hot, weird neighbour, but Henry locked it in first. He and Lucía hit it off in that annoying way that Henry manages to hit it off with every girl — they were over in the corner of this little booth, and not even drunk, like two wines in, they're hooking up.

Parks looked over at me equal parts irked and annoyed, and it wasn't the plan to go out on the lash but it suddenly felt too bleak for us to just sit there, mostly-sober, watching Henry get to third so I put my hand in the air and ordered a bottle of tequila.

"Oh, God—" She laughed as I poured us each a shot.

"So what happened with you and Tom?" I asked her, sliding it over.

She stared over at me, brows went low, blinked a few times — looked a bit like I smacked her across the face — then she tossed back her shot and snatched mine out of my hand.

"Oh—" I nodded, wide-eyed. "Okay."

"Pour me another." She pointed at the bottle and I obeyed.

You don't not obey her, even if you know better. And probably I did, but I swear to God, I didn't think what happened was where it was going.

I was over her — fully out of love with her — I loved her, she is one of my oldest, dumbest friends — but I was not in love with her.

"Tell me—" I pressed, mostly just because I was more interested now that she was reacting like that.

"Okay," she said, throwing back another shot. "I will once you tell me what happened with you and Daisy?"

I gave her a tight smile. Took a shot.

"You were in love, I know you were — both of you, I saw it on your faces—" she told me, like I didn't already know.

I took another shot.

She does a thing, it's like her drunk tell — where when she gets really bladdered and she drums her fingers on one of her cheeks under her eyes, to see how numb her face is getting. She does it before she realises she does it and it's usually a sign for one of us to wrap shit up — Henry was preoccupied and I was as legless as she was but I knew the wheels would start to fall off soon, so I decided to take her home, tuck her into bed, call it a night.

Told Henry we'd meet him back at the apartment and off we went.

Not a far walk from the bar on Lexington back to her place, and everything was fine — we were fine — completely normal, just friends, I swear to God-

She was walking backwards, showing me how good she could do it in her shoes — absolute monsters, heels like pins — and to her credit, she was doing a solid job. I really mean it, like, she got like twenty yards down the block skipping backwards before she tripped in a grate, twisted her ankle and bloodied her knee.

Now, I've got to say it in case you didn't know — but I guess who didn't see this coming — Magnolia Parks is a fucking toddler when it comes to injuring herself. When she was twelve she got stung by a bee and insisted to her house mistress she had to take the day off to recover because 'it felt personal'. When she got her wisdom teeth taken out she practically wrote herself a fucking obituary and organised herself a Get Well present for all of us to contribute to.

So she was crying, bit of a wanker about blood too, (honestly, in the end it turned out she actually tore a tendon, but anyway) insisted she couldn't walk — so I scooped her up and carried her home.

That was where the trouble began.

We were both too drunk and our faces were too close together, and her eyes went round and her face went serious, and by the time I carried her through the lobby of her building and into the elevator — I kind of knew by then. Knew and I didn't care. Happy for the distraction.

"I can stand—" she told me, even though she couldn't really. I put her down and she balanced on one foot, holding herself steady with my arm.

Like, just inches between us, honestly — and she looked up at me with those eyes I used to love, and bit down on that bottom lip I used to bite on, and I put my hand on her waist and then she pulled the emergency stop in the elevator and then I just pinned her to the wall. She was up on my waist, my hands in her hair, and she took my shirt off without a second thought — it's funny how when you've done this before, sexual muscle memory, how you move around each other's bodies, what each of us do, how to get there faster. I'd already undone the buttons of her cardigan, was kissing down her neck — she undid the top button of my jeans and reached for me and then Daisy flashed through my mind and I froze — thought about how I wouldn't know how to explain this to her if I had to one day. That day felt pretty abstract and mythical back then — still does now — but I thought about her face, how she'd look if I had to tell her Parks and I had sex and suddenly I was off it.

I pulled back, stopped kissing her. Her eyes opened all nervous and sad.

I shook my head. "I can't, Parks — I—" I gave her this stupid shrug. "I'm in love with her. If she knew, it'd kill her."

She nodded, eyes fallen. "I'd quite like this to kill him."

I sniffed a laugh as I leant my head on my old friend's head, kissed her cheek.

"You here kills him every day." I poked her in the side. "You don't need to try."

And then she started crying and then I started crying, and it was weird and fucked up but kind of nice, and it probably pocketed our relationship into a new space — almost and then stopping. She fell asleep on my shoulder on the couch and I didn't move the whole night, not because I'm in love with her but because I love her and she was as fucked up as I was.

"Alright, out with it, Parks." My brother nudges her. "Are you fucking Jack-Jack Cavan, or what?"

"Well." She clears her throat, living for the attention. "Not right now."

"But you are?" my brother clarifies with a smirk.

She leaves it hanging for a few seconds, Beej about ready to neck himself.

"I was. I — we dated." She glances at Henry who nods along like he knew. "Back in New York."

"Bullshit." I frown, staring between the two of them. "And you said nothing?"

Henry just shrugs. It's gotta shit Beej, how they are. It has to. It still shits me and I don't even have a buy-in anymore.

"Jack-Jack Cavan?" I stare over at her, shocked honestly.

My brother shakes his head.

"He's the fucking shit right now!" Jonah says too enthusiastically and it cuts Beej.

Jo scrambles to make it better but can't really.

"So you dated in New York?" Henry says loudly, moving it along.

She nods.

I squint over at her. "How long for?"

"Oh, you know—" She smiles pleasantly, like she's not a Venus flytrap for men. "My usual max— four months? Thereabouts?"

And Beej, he's as bad as her. They're too good at hurting each other. It's the bad part of loving each other as much as they do. They know how to rip each other to pieces without even trying.

BJ stares over at her, glaring. "So why'd you break up?"

She gives him an icy look, not taking the bait. "He was too much for me in the sack."

BJ sniffs, over it.

"Alright—" Jo shakes his head. "So give us a breakdown of your time in New York then—"

"Okay—" She nods. "Well I arrived last December. My family flew over just before Christmas and we went to Whistler with Tom. Then he and I spent New Years in Hawaii with the Foster sisters, and then in January I—"

"—I meant sexually," Jonah interrupts.

Henry tosses him a look as Taura glances at him. BJ goes still.

"Oh." She pulls a face. "A bit pervy from you, but I'll oblige."

He shakes his head. "No, it's just — you and casual sex? It's like watching a dog walk on its hind legs... like, I cannot fathom it. Like, when did you first sleep with Rush?"

"How did you know I slept with Rush?" She asks, eyebrows up.

My brother gives her a shit-eating grin. "I didn't till now—"

"March." She stares at her nails.

"And you slept with Stavros when?" Jo squints.

She shrugs demurely. "Just for a minute."

Beej looks like he's going to be sick, and I should have seen it coming — She loves a kill-shot — but I'm too busy trying to the math in my head from when we hooked up to spot it.

"So Rush, then Stavros, then—"

"No—" she shakes her head. "Rush, then Christian, then St—"

BJ's cutlery falls and he stares over at her like she just cut his fucking heart right out of its chest.

"Parks!" I yell, sinking back into my seat. "What the f—?" I shake my head, furious. "Why the fuck would you—"

Jonah presses his hands into his eyes; Henry looks from me to her, frustrated.

"Thought we decided to keep that one under our hats—"

And Beej? He's just frozen over there—

"Listen, drama queens—" Parks holds up a little hand to silence us both. "Baxter James Ballentine had P in V sex in a bathtub at the height of our relationship with the girl who used to be my best friend."

"Did he really?" Taura asks sarcastically.

"Yeah — but—" I've got my hands on my head, stressing heavy. "He's gonna fucking fr—"

"It's fine—" BJ tells me but I can tell on the spot, it's not.

"Thank you, BJ." Magnolia gestures towards him knowing full well it's not. "I really do feel like Beej fucking Paili and then lying about it for three years gives Christian and I a little bit of wriggle room to have nearly had sex one night in a lift in New York." She flashes BJ a smile that I think is supposed to be the nail in the coffin for him, but somehow it just throws him a bone.

"So why'd you only almost fuck, then?" he asks her, eyebrows up. "What stopped you two from finally going all the way?"

I blow air out of my mouth, tired and over their shit and I can already feel the direction the night is going. They'll fire shots til one of them finally keels over. Knowing him these days, it'll probably be her. I clock Henry, ask without asking who's going to clean up the mess his brother's about to make of her. Could be either of us, but it'll go down better with the group if it's him tonight.

Parks' eyes catch on BJ's and we all know he knows why she

stopped, like there was ever a question — like there ever is with them— and it hangs there, how fucked up it all is, how much she loves him, how much we know he loves her back, and that despite that, despite their history, in love all their lives and a baby between them, how indescribably frustrating it is that they cannot, for the love of God, pull it the fuck together.

She leaves. He stays.

Henry and I catch eyes and I tune out the rest of the conversation before I get up and walk outside, waiting really. I know what's coming. Kind of deserve it, but I sort of think it's pretty fucking rich either way, if I'm completely honest—

BJ follows me out a few minutes after.

"Are you taking the piss?" Got his fight-face on. "Her I get, but you? How could you do that to me?"

I blow air out of my mouth, shaking my head.

"Beej, for fuck's sake—" I shove my hands through my hair. "I don't know how to get this through your fucking head, but you need to understand that not everything is about you." I give him a curt smile and point back to New York. "That wasn't about you."

He lets out this growl. "She—" He shoves me. "—is always about me."

And I just stare over at him for a few seconds — I'm bored, if I'm honest, but I shove his hands off me for good measure, because he's always too big for his boots, not really worth the drama of the fight though.

"Beej—" I shrug. "You're hers, she's yours, I get it— but I wasn't thinking of you—" I poke him in the chest. "You didn't cross my mind once. I was in New York with one of my best friends, and my heart was fucked — I was in love a girl who I couldn't be with because she wanted something that I couldn't give her. I was fucked up and so was Parks, and we got drunk and she fell and I had to carry her home. We kissed and I felt her up and this is the important part, man— I didn't think of you." Lift up my eyebrows, wait for that one to sink in a little for her. ""Believe it or not— it wasn't about you. For me anyway," I add as an afterthought, give him a small shrug. "Everything for her is always about you."

He breathes out loudly then leans back against the wall with me. "You could have told me—"

"Yeah—" I give him a look like he's an idiot. "Because historically you've taken shit about me and Parks so well."

He rolls his eyes as Henry walks out, nodding his chin at us.

"You two sort your shit out?"

"Yep." I pull out my phone, keen to ditch them.

Oi

You out?

Nah, at home.

What doing

Chilling.

I'll come for a drink.

Yeah if you want

But heads up — Daisy and the Cop are naffing. 100%

Fuck. Nope. Not tonight. Text someone else.

Hey

You about?

Yeah, just at my place

Come?

On my way.

21

Daisy

Christmas morning is quiet and I don't like it. It's never quiet around here.

A lot of the boys went home for it, even Kekoa took a few days to fly home which he's done, like, twice my whole entire life.

That's a good sign though, that makes me feel like I must be safer than before, because he'd never leave if I wasn't. Miguel's also taken a well-deserved vacation to Spain for a few days, and Julian's behaving like my shadow now that he's my self-appointed security guy in-lieu.

I don't mind it though, really — besides the house feeling too big for just us. We spend Christmas Eve in the kitchen. My brother is — and I cannot stress this enough — the worst fucking sous chef in the history of time. He eats all the ingredients, he thinks he knows techniques he doesn't, he's very cocky, he burns shit, always thinks adding more salt is always the answer — but still, he's my favourite[117] person to have in a kitchen.

Christmas Day, we watch *Mickey's Twice Upon a Christmas* at 7am in our pyjamas like we always have since I was four. He even wears the matching pyjamas I left for him on his pillow but he said if I took a photo of us in them he'd break my phone.

Usually we'd go to the Bambrilla's after church, but Dellina told me that Tavie was going to be there and even though she said we're still welcome to come, I'd just rather not see it. Maybe that's stupid and childish, maybe it's even technically un-Christmassy of me. But it would feel like losing. Not just face, but losing in general. And I don't want to lose anything on Christmas. Even if I miss my best friend and his mum and his dumb brother and his dad. I never miss Gia though, because she's a bit too nutty for me. She lost her

---

[117] *Second favourite.

virginity to my brother and I only know that because she brings it up in every conversation humanly possibly, even the ones with me. It doesn't matter how I stare at her,[118] how perturbed my face may look[119] whenever she recalls their first tryst[120] that took place in the back of my brothers car[121] — she still tells me.

Did I think it was weird Tiller and I aren't spending Christmas together?[122]

Yes, maybe — but no weirder I suppose than when I know he's doing something with his work friends and he doesn't invite me.

He did invite me once. The ex-girlfriend[123] was there and I wouldn't say that I'm her favourite person.

Not that I give a shit — she reeks of regret and insecurity and I'm fifteen times hotter than her,[124] but she is mean, and she went out of her way to make sure I knew I wasn't really welcome and they were all just obliging Tiller by meeting me.

His partner[125] — Dyson[126] — he's nice enough, if you can get past the incessant chattering, which I'm not really sure I can. He's never been unkind to me though.

I know Tiller gets drinks after work most nights at this bar by their building[127] and I know it because I walked by there once with Jack, not because Tiller invited me.

"Is that Tills?" Jack did a double take.

I glanced over my shoulder. "Oh—" I cleared my throat. "Yes."

"Should we go say hello?" Jack beamed.

"Err—" I hope my frown didn't look like anything other than consternation. "No, let's leave him be — it looks like he's having a boys' night."

"There's a girl there." Jack told me with a frown.

---

[118] Like she's an idiot, is how.

[119] It looks very.

[120] Vomit.

[121] Vomit again.

[122] 'Weird' perhaps isn't the right word.

[123] Michelle.

[124] A conservative estimate, honestly.

[125] At the NCA, not romantically. I am romantically his partner.

[126] Regrettably not immediately related to the vacuum dynasty.

[127] The Lion's Gate

But it wasn't consternation; I didn't want to say hi to him because Tiller told me he was working late, not getting drinks.

And things change, I get that — but then I wondered if he just thought it was better to not have me there — and do you know what, that's totally fine. I don't need us to live in one another's pockets, I don't need to be a part of his every waking moment, but I don't like feeling like I'm being hidden.

And I know he's in a tough position in the real world — it's me who brings the precarious edge to what we are, it's me who brings the baggage, but in my world, with my family, with my friends — Tiller is the problem. For me and my people, it's Tiller who's quite literally caused us many a grievance, and I don't hide him. I'm still proud of him. And I don't know for certain that that's why we're spending Christmas apart — but I know when he said he was going back to Massachusetts for a week over Christmas[128] and I said I thought that probably I should stay here with my brother, he agreed very quickly.

"Yeah—" He swatted his hand through the air. "I know you two are just getting back to normal — probably better not to rock the boat."

"Right." I nodded, and I agreed. I didn't want to not have Christmas with my brother; I love Christmas with my brother. But there was a relief and an eagerness that I'm sure I saw on Tiller that I don't think I was projecting onto him myself.

And it's not like we both don't know what we are.

We can pretend — easier to do so after the other night, but we both know. Just neither of us are ready.

Do I dress for church on Christmas morning thinking that I might see Christian Hemmes? I might do.[129]

Do I see him?

Yes, but I barely let myself look at him. I focus on the Christ-child and the terrible set-up that was his short, little life. Dead at thirty-three? That's Jules in two years. Jesus was born to die. The cruelty of it is astounding. And here we all are, Sunday best to celebrate his slow-burn demise.

---

[128] And that he'd be back in time for New Year's Eve.

[129] Floral crystal-embellished mini dress (Oscar de la Renta); Aveline 100mm bow sandals (Jimmy Choo); Desire cropped jacket (Unreal Fur). I look pretty in it.

Julian says I've missed the point, but I think he has. Jesus died for us, is what my brother says. Which... fine, sure, that's grand, it's not my point though. My point is that he shouldn't have had to.

After, Christian walks over towards us and it's a bit of a bashful walk, almost like he's nervous. He and my brother hug and he looks at me, eyebrows up, asking without asking.

"Merry Christmas." He opens his arms for me and I step into them. He wraps me up and I sink into him, and it's bad for me — I forgot what it was like to be held by him. I put it out of my mind that it's my favourite feeling on the planet, that there are no arms, not even those of my boyfriend — who I'll remind you that I *do* love — there are no arms that feel like Christian's arms. Like he's just pulled a curtain closed around me and blocked out all the bad, and I have this screaming revelation of all I've lost to gain my normal life and *what normal life?*

I don't say anything, I don't want to fracture the moment. If I don't say 'Merry Christmas' back, I can pretend for a second that we're just hugging for no reason at all, that he's just holding me for kicks the way he used to a year ago for that brief moment in time we had where we were working.

He doesn't let go — he holds on to me for a beat longer than I think either of us could argue is normal, and he breathes in. I look up at him, sort of wide eyed, sort of confused, and he gives me this half-smile, and then he lets me go.

"What are you two doing today?" Jonah asks as a man I've never seen before stands wordlessly behind him. I think it might be their dad?

"Oh." I shrug. "No real plans... most of the boys are off—"

"And away," nods my brother. "Just a quiet one—" He looks over at me. "We'll probably watch *Iron Man 3*? Maybe *Die Hard*."

"And I'm going a cook a ham." I give them a smile.

"For the two of you?" their mother asks. She bustles between her sons to give me a kiss on the cheek.

"Come with us," Christian says, staring over at me.

"Oh, no—" I shake my head. "We couldn't impose."

Julian gives me a little peek, asking without asking. I barely move my eyebrows but still he knows it's a yes.

"Of course you could!" Jonah chirps brightly, tossing an arm around me. "Your brother imposes himself on us all the times. At least this way we get a ham out of it."

~

The boys ride with us to show us the way. Jonah in the front with my brother, Christian in the back with me. Julian gave me a lot of things for Christmas, including the Centenary Egg from Fabergé, but the best thing he gave me was when he gruffly told me to sit in the back and up front is for the oldest. Then he gave me a little wink, which means he knows I still love Christian, which isn't necessarily the best thing in general but I was grateful for it in the moment.

I've never been to Christian's house, not the one he grew up in. Obviously I've been to his one in Knightsbridge, but he never took me 'home' home.

Just that one time we had lunch with his mum and brother at the Berkley, otherwise I wasn't much included in the family events with him either. I don't know if that's because he was embarrassed of me, though... I think he's maybe a bit embarrassed of them — I'm not sure. He's weird about his dad.

The house though, it makes things make sense to me. The house makes Christian make more sense somehow.

It's in the St George's Hill estate, and it's massive. A huge, old manor. Kind of dark, but definitely beautiful, a bit like him.

His face goes instantly stoic as soon as we're inside, it's strange. The house rests on his brow all heavy, and he's so handsome when he goes like this, worried about things he won't say, but all I want to do is lift it off him and hold his hand, but his worries are invisible and too high up for me to reach and his hand isn't mine anymore. I don't know if it ever really was.

"Where's the kitchen?" I ask, nodding at the ham he's holding for me. "We should get this going."

There's this funny clash of old and new, modern and ancient.

Tapestries on the wall, fireplaces in every room, even a suit of armour in the foyer, but then the kitchen looks like something from a Swedish Architectural Digest.

"Up to your standard?" he asks playfully.

"An Aga!" I coo, dashing over to it. I love them but Julian won't let me get one. He says it makes the house too hot. It makes sense for a house in the country, though. And they're so beautiful. "Put that down over there—" I tell him, pointing at the bench and he does, then leans back, arms folded, smiling a bit.

"What?" I look at him over my shoulder as I get acquainted in the kitchen.

"Nothing." He shakes his head but he's still smiling. "Just, Christmas—"

For some reason my cheeks go pink so I turn around quickly and open three cupboards to find a chopping board, except that I can't.

He walks up behind me and slides open a drawer, pulling one out and handing it to me even though I didn't ask for it.

Our eyes catch and I swallow heavy — think of my boyfriend and that beautiful face of his, how he was there for me when no one else was, how he gave me normal—

"Did you get any good presents?" I ask, trying to keep it feeling light.

"Yep." He nods.

"Favourite?" I ask, without turning to him.

"My best friend in my kitchen at my mum's house," he says without missing a beat.

I look back. Our eyes catch. There's that noon-sun poking through the window above the sink and right into his eyes — he squints with one eye to block it a little but still he doesn't look away and it brings my inhibitions to their knees, and thank God we're around other people, his family and my brother, because I have a boyfriend and I'm not like this — but something about how the low winter light catches him and warms his face, it jolts me back in time and I remember with full force how badly I loved him, and in an instant, I'm pining for what we were — and I hate it. I hate how out of control loving him feels, I hate that I'm with someone else and so is he, I hate that that doesn't seem to matter because it does matter to me even though it doesn't. I hate that I got used to being without him and then it's not even a month back home with him just hanging around the house with my brother to undo something I spent the last year trying to box up and leave behind. Never mind that I love someone else now too, never mind how Christian hurt me, never mind that I spent months in twisted-heart agony trying and failing to get over loving him, because here I am, a year to the day where I stood on the steps of a church daring him to touch me again so my brother might have a reason to fight him, and right now I have my face pushed against the past peering back at what we were.

I clear my throat, trying not to let it show on my face how dizzy I feel with all our history and the ways I love him lapping at the edge of my concentration.

"How is this the kitchen you grew up with and you didn't even have a vegetable spiralizer?"

He rolls his eyes.

"His mum doesn't cook—" says a voice I don't recognise.

I turn around and it's the man who was behind Jonah.

Definitely their dad, their eyebrows are the same. Christian's hair is blonder and this man's skin is a bit browner, but you can tell.

Christian stiffens up in his presence in a way that makes me want to stand in front of him.

"Oh," I say, because what else could I?

"Dad," Christian almost sighs. "This is Daisy."

"Julian's sister."

I nod with a smile. "That is my God-given name, yes."

Christian chuckles but the dad just turns and leaves.

I wait a few seconds and let out a low whistle. "Dads usually like me." I pull a face.

"That tracks," Christian shrugs. "He's not much of a dad anyway."

It takes a few hours to get the lunch ready, and I tell my brain not to feel the longing it does for this to be my new normal, moving around the kitchen, Christian on the counter,[130] drinking wine, talking about nothing how we used to, his mum coming and leaning back next to him — I love cooking for people I love, and the ones here that I do, they all gravitate to the kitchen. Julian teaches Barnesy how to juggle with oranges, Jonah uses a spoon to sing Christmas songs and Christian stands closer to me than he needs to. It's my favourite Christmas in years.

When we finally sit down to eat, I somehow manage to sit between my brother and my ex-boyfriend, which I guess makes me about the luckiest girl in the world.

I'm also glad for it because their uncle is here. Not the one

---

[130] A worse sous chef than my brother, it turns out.

Christian likes,[131] but the other one. Callum Barnes. The youngest of the three[132] Barnes children.

Now, I have known many men — many. Our family's line of work has afforded me to meet the worst of the worst and the lowest of the lows, and there are markers normally for why I won't like a person. They'll be rude to servers, they'll have guns at the dinner table, they'll look at parts of my body that aren't on display for them, they'll shake my hand and hold it for longer than what anyone would deem normal or okay — but this man... He's handsome, he seems laid back and casual. He's well dressed. He's not too much. We've never spoken at any of the Borough meetings I've seen him at. He's never been too friendly, his eyes have never lingered longer than they should have. He doesn't seem annoyed that we're here, which is nice enough, I suppose?

He is, by all accounts, perfectly acceptable and completely normal — likeable even — and yet, I don't like him at all. He makes me feel uneasy. I don't know why.

He sits at one end of the table, their dad at the other, and I don't think it's in my imagination that they're glaring at each other.

Still, this doesn't bother me. It makes me feel almost like I'm in a movie, heightened family drama at Christmas. We've not had any since our parents died, not since the Christmas my mother refused to sit next to me at the dinner table when I was six and Julian got so angry at her for it that he picked me up and put me in his car and drove me to McDonald's for our own Christmas lunch. When we got back, she told me I ruined Christmas and then Dad started yelling and so did my brother, and Kekoa took me into the laundry room and put the coins in the dryer.

"So," Barnsey says eventually, setting her cutlery down, "you're dating someone new?"

My cheeks flush. I set my fork down. "Yes."

Christian glances at me.

"A police officer," she says. It's not a question.

"What?" Uncle Callum sputters his wine.

"Actually," I look between them, "he's a detective with the NCA."

"Much better." Jonah winks.

The dad leans in, fascinated.

---

[131] Harvey, who's over in Australia.
[132] Living.

"You're joking, right?" Callum says, frowning.

"I wish—" snorts my brother and I give him a little glare. He swats his hand, dismissively. "No, he's a good guy—"

"He's a cop," says Callum.

I give him a stern look. "He can be both."

He shakes his head. "Not in my house, he can't."

"Lucky we're not in your house then, ey?" Christian eyes him.

"What's your deal, then?" the dad asks gruffly from the other end.

"Jud," their mother sighs.

Jud Hemmes. I like that name.

"No deal—" Christian shakes his head.

"You two sleeping together?"

My brother's head pulls back, staring over at him, eyebrows up and daring — Jonah shakes his head, jaw jutted out, staring at the table.

Barnsey takes a sip of wine and Christian's tensed up next to me, but dealing with parents who don't like me is my grace zone.

"We used to date," I tell him, gaze unflinching.

"You dated?" he repeats.

"Yeah." Christian nods.

"But not anymore." The dad squints.

"No." I give him a curt smile.

He nods his chin at me. "Why?"

This throws me, actually. "Pardon?" I blink.

"Why'd you break up?" he asks, eyebrows up. "Did he fuck up, then?"

I frown over at him, sort of stunned at the assumption. Offended on Christian's behalf, hurt even. "No." I shake my head sternly at the same time that Christian says, "Yes."

And then we turn to face each other, and I don't know what to say or do, and I feel stuck and a bit embarrassed and definitely nervous, because I wonder if maybe he loves me still? But then, I've thought he loved me before when he didn't so I don't trust my read on him.

"Actually," my brother says loudly. "It's my fault."

I stare over at my brother, eyes wide and unsure where this is going to go.

"I did something last year that Daisy really struggled with, and so she decided to leave—" He gestures vaguely around himself. "— everything. Took a step back." He glances at me; his eyes look sorry.

"She took a step back from everything that had anything to do with this shit."

"What shit?" Callum frowns.

Julian gives him an impatient smile. "Crime."

It flashes over Uncle Callum's face — he didn't like that. Didn't like that I'd leave it, didn't like that my brother referred to it as 'this shit'.

Christian's dad sits back in his chair, staring over at me in a different way.

"Keep up, Cal, honestly—" Barnesy shakes her head.

And then I feel self-conscious, like everyone's staring at me for all these different reasons — his uncle, I've offended. His mum, I think, is sorry for me. Maybe for us? His dad, I don't know why he's staring at me but all of it make me feel nervous so I look over at Christian.

"Can I see your room?"

"Yep." He pushes back from the table quickly.

"You're not going to ask to be excused?" his dad calls after us.

"Why would I?" Christian stops in his tracks. "You didn't when you excused yourself from our lives."

He turns on his heel, grabs my hand and pulls me up the stairs.

Its only half-way up he realises he's holding it, but I've known he's been holding it all along.

"Sorry—" He snatches it back.

I smile at him, shake my head but barely. "It's fine."

"So." He keeps walking up the stairs slowly. "You tell Tiller about the other day?"

"What about it?" I play dumb.

He looks over his shoulder, rolls his eyes.

"I did," I say, keeping my voice upbeat.

"What'd he say?"

"Nothing much, it came out over text—"

"Oh."

"But when he came home that night he said, 'You aren't spending Christmas with him, right?'"

Christian lets out a single laugh as he leads me down a hall. "What'd you say?"

I grimace. "'Of course not.'" He laughs again and I shrug, helpless. "It was true at the time."

He gives me a strained, half-smile. "I'm glad it wasn't true in the end."

Then he opens his bedroom door and I burst out laughing.

A Pussycat Dolls poster hangs above his bed.

My hand flies to my mouth to suppress it and he's fighting off a smile, shaking his head. I walk in, still laughing, eyes wide.

It's a child's room, really. LEGO on the shelves. Model trains and cars. Every XBox game on the planet.

"I started boarding at Varley when I was eleven." He glances around the room. "I never came back."

"Oh," I say and I feel sad. "And they just kept is as is all these years?"

He shakes his head, glancing around. "This whole house is a fucking mausoleum—"

"Is this the house your sister died in?"

He nods, not looking at me.

"Your family didn't move after?" I tilt my head.

"I think my dad thought if we stayed here he'd be close to Rem still."

"Oh." I nod. "Did it work?"

Christian shrugs. "Maybe. Not close with anyone alive anymore, but..."

I touch his arm. I don't know why, I just want to.

He looks down at it and then back to me. He swallows heavy.

He runs his tongue over his bottom lip and his eyes flicker to my mouth — is he about to kiss me? I think he's about to kiss me — and I'm frozen because I want to kiss him back, of course I do! But — Tiller — and I died last time I let myself love Christian in an out loud way — and my breathing is going anyway and without my permission, I start leaning in towards him too and then my phone rings.

FaceTime.

I pull my phone from my pocket.

It's Tiller.

Christian scoffs a laugh and takes a concerted step away from me right before I slide to answer.

"Hi!" I grin down at him. I wonder if I look weird — do I look weird?

"Merry Christmas!" he sings.

"Happy Christmas, Tills." I smile at him.

He's in a navy, knitted sweater with a collared shirt under it and it's maybe the most dressed up I've ever seen him. He nods his chin at me.

"You look pretty in that colour—" he tells me.

I glance down, feeling self-conscious because I know full well I wore it not for him.

"Thanks—" I say quickly, ready to change that topic. "How's your family? Where are they? Have you had a happy morning?"

"Yeah—" He grins. "It's been great." Then his face falters. "Where are you?"

"Oh—" I flash him a quick smile. "I — um. Well—" He frowns. "We bumped into the Hemmes family at Sunday morning mass—" My boyfriend is already frowning. "And then they invited us back for lunch."

"It's 7pm GMT."

"Right, well—" I shake my head dismissively. "It took a minute for the lunch to cook and then we've just sort of stayed the day..."

His eyes pinch unhappily. "Right."

"It's not a big deal—" I shake my head. "It was just going to me be and Julian — they were just being friendly—"

He shakes his head. "You told me you weren't spending Christmas with him—"

I flick my eyes over at Christian and he's standing there in his own room in his own house looking uncomfortable and maybe a bit sad. Though I suspect that it's not the first time.

"I wasn't—" I insist. "That was true when I said it—"

"Are you with him now?" Tiller asks, jaw tight.

Instinctively my eyes glance back over at Christian who's shaking his head aggressively. 'Say no,' he mouths.

"Yes—" I say, because I don't fancy myself a liar.

Tiller rolls his head backwards.

Christian trots over, glaring at me before he brightens his whole face and leans into frame. "Merry Christmas!"

"Yeah—" Tiller doesn't smile back. "I kind of just want to speak to my girlfriend."

Christian nods once and moves out of the frame.

"Is he still there?" Tiller asks with a frown and I breathe out through my nose and step out into the hall, but I keep Christian in my line of sight because I'm an old addict.

134

Tiller's shaking his head. "I'm going to fly back early."

"No — why?" I frown.

"Because at the rate you're going, you're going to kiss him on New Year's Eve."

Our eyes catch again, me in the hall, him in his room. I wonder if for a second it's true — but of course it's not. He's with Vanna.

"That's not fair—" I glare at my phone, act more offended by that than I really am.

Tiller's head pulls back. "Isn't it?"

My boyfriend's jaw goes tight. "I'll see you tomorrow night."

Then he hangs up.

I stare at my phone for a few seconds then look over at Christian who's cringing.

"Well," I sigh. "That's not going to make his family like me more—" I say as I walk back into his room, perching on the edge of his childhood bed.

I look down at the quilt and then back up at him.

"Is your bedding the Millennium Falcon?"

He shakes his head. "I don't want to talk about it."

I squash a smile because I think that's cuter than I should.

He sits down next to me. "They don't like you?"

I purse my mouth and look at my hands. "His dad's a retired cop, remember?"

"Ah." He nods, then gives me a consolatory shrug. "His son's into it?"

I sniff a laugh. "Skips a generation."

He looks over at me.

"Sorry," he tells me, and I think he means it.

"Yeah." I nod and I feel the water on the boat I'm ignoring lapping around my knees. "Me too."

Christian watches me for a few seconds, thinking, reading me. "Should I take you home...?" he offers.

He also swallows heavy as he offers it and I think about what it might be like, what could happen if he drove me home alone, if there was no one in our house but us and the security outside. What we could do, how we would have filled that time before, in every room, loudly because why not when no one's around, as many times as we could — and I pinch my bottom lip, tense my stomach hoping to squash the butterflies that are going nuts inside of there and shake my head quickly — I know what will happen if he does.

I'm not like that.

I don't want him to be like that either.

"Um—" I shake my head and shrug and pull a dismissive face and wrinkle my nose all at once. I basically just have a big stroke on the spot. "No—" I stick out my bottom lip awkwardly. "No. I — I mean we should be — my brother and I — you know — give you a minute of family time."

He blinks twice as he watches me. "Don't want a minute of family time, Dais."

I take a shallow breath. "Even still."

He breathes out slowly and I think he's disappointed. "Okay."

"Okay?" I sort of frown up at him, annoyed at myself, sorry to have made him sad. Sorry to have made myself sad, actually.

But Tiller. He's cut his family trip short and is flying home three days early.

I can't do that to him, even if I really, really want to.

Hey

Are you out tonight?

Yeah. Club Haus.

Stay there.

Ok.

Why?

you made me a promise once.

22

Christian

A few days after Christmas I head out to one of the clubs with Jules and some of his boys because I know Tiller's back and I feel pretty fucked in my head about Daisy still being with him and not me.

All that shit aside, Jo said that while they were away for Taura's birthday it seemed like Beej and Parks were finally sorting themselves out, proper together and shit. As far as I'm concerned, that's good news. Beej and Parks should be together — they're opposite ends of magnets that destroy everything that drifts into their magnetic field. They'll be together no matter what it is between them, I see that now. Wish I saw it before the top of my heart was lopped clean off by one such magnet, but anyway, fuck it.

I texted Jo for an update just before — because let's be honest — BJ and Magnolia are our own private version of Made in Chelsea, except it's probably called Made in Trauma — all Jo replied was "Shit's fucked."

Don't know what that means. Whatever the fuck's going on, I don't really want to be a part of it at the minute. I'm painfully aware of how fucking single I am. Even though I'm technically not single, I guess. Not according to Vanna or any of the shit tabloids she runs her mouth to. I forgot about her over Christmas — I honestly didn't think of her once. Pretty shit of me, I know. I didn't hear from her til Boxing Day. I said I had plans even though the plans were really just me and Parks being miserable on my couch about how we love people who don't love us back, but now maybe she's flipped teams, that fucking traitor.

So I come out tonight to get drunk with the brother of the girl I love, but he's fucking MIA — no idea where he's gone. We're at one of my brother's clubs, so probably Jo's office.

Julian loves an 'office reprieve' as we call them. Drugs or girls or both, some sort of debauchery always happens in the offices and Jules is usually right in the thick of it.

And then I hear arguing behind me and I look over.

"Magnolia, no—" Henry yells firmly. "Listen to me—" Henry holds her by the shoulders. Gives her a firm look. "No."

"Move—" She tries to push past him as I walk over, frowning. When did they get here?

"Hey—" I nod my chin at them but neither of them say anything back.

"No! Magnolia, stop —" Henry shakes his head. "This isn't the same, it's not Rush or Jack-Jack—"

"Henry," she growls. "Move."

"Magnolia — listen to me—" Henry says in a low voice.

"What's going on?" I frown at her.

"Henry's being controlling," Magnolia says at the same time Henry says, "Magnolia's being insane."

I look between them, confused. I could count on one hand the amount of times in my life I've seen these two fight.

"About what?" I look between them both.

And then from behind me, Kekoa steps forward and peers down at us all.

"There a problem here?"

"No—" Magnolia and me say at the same time, except that she precision-elbows Henry out of the way, pushes past me to stand toe-to-toe with the Pacific Islander giant.

I scrunch my face a bit, trying to work out what's happening.

"I'm here for Julian," she says, her shoulders square, trying to look brave but I know her too well and I can hear the waver in her voice. Spin around to face her, look her in the the eyes and I know mine are bugging out. Henry does this hand motion like he's been vindicated, and all of it means fuck all because she's ignoring us both.

"Are you just?" Koa smirks down at her, amused. "Who's asking for him?"

Magnolia scoffs, annoyed and bored, shaking her head up at this tower of a man who —I'm not joking — when grown men see him, they walk the other way. He's so fucking jacked he looks like he's from a Marvel movie. He's one of the most feared people in the world. My world, anyway— and it occurs to me that me and Jo might have shielded her too much. That she's here, standing toe-to-toe with the

139

bodyguard of a man who, until about four months ago, was wanted for kidnapping, assault, theft and murder.

"Don't be stupid." She crosses her arms impatiently. "I know you know who I am. You made me pancakes."

Henry frowns more.

Kekoa smirks, amused. "I did."

She shrugs, conceding.

"They were good."

He shrugs, conceding to the fact. "They're my speciality."

"Yes, well, as spectacularly fluffy as they were—"

"It's in the buttermilk," he tells her.

"I'm actually not here for your specialty." Magnolia gives him a look. "I need Julian's."

I look over at Henry and my eyes go wide as he shoves his hands through his hair, stressed. BJ's going to fucking murder us.

"He's expecting me," she tells him, eyebrows up.

"Baby girl, I reckon he's been expecting you for about five years—" Kekoa tells her with a look, then nods his head towards the offices. "Come on, I'll take you up."

I take a step towards Henry and whisper-yell, "What the fuck is going on?"

Henry grabs her wrist, shakes his head a tiny bit. "Just... the end of the world as we know it."

She starts following Kekoa through the crowd.

"Text me when you get home," Henry calls to her.

"I'm not going to go home, Hen," she tells him solemnly.

And Henry, that poor bastard — he looks like he's about to pass a fucking stone as he watches his best friend of twenty years disappear into the belly of the club.

I blink a few times. "So what did I miss?"

Henry rubs his temples. "A lot."

23

Julian

I'm sitting at Jonah's desk when there's a knock on the office door — I don't say anything and it opens anyway.

Koa pokes his head in. "You've got a visitor."

'What a fucking understatement,' I think as she walks on in.

I've been staring at her text the last forty-five minutes trying to work out if this is legitimate — and listen — I don't actually have any real expectations of what could happen tonight. We text. Always have, sort of. I think it's cause we're both removed from each other's immediate worlds. An abstract place to debrief and offload, no consequence for doing it. And this has happened before, her coming to me in this capacity — just the one time, I guess, but even still, nothing happened. A girl like her needs to feel like she's not on the track that she is, and a man like me feels like a confined way to explore it. I've been many a toff's rough and tumble night, but if I'm completely honest, it's not really how I'm imagining my night with Magnolia will go. She's not like that.

She steps further into the room and she's holding her right index finger with her left hand, her eyes all big and round, and — fuck, she's beautiful — that's the first thing I think as I stare over at her.

Koa makes a face over her head, eyes wide — knows I've always been a bit keen on her.

I wave my finger towards the door, telling him to leave, and then I stand up, walk around the desk and lean back against it. Cross my arms over my chest and stare over at her.

"Hello," I say, don't let myself smile.

She stands there, feet together, eyes still round, face still nervous. She swallows. "You made me an offer once—"

I nod slowly. "I did."

She squares up a little. "Are you still good for it?"

I push off the desk and walk over to her, tilting my head.

"We're talking about sex, yeah?"

She holds my eyes. "Yes."

"Yeah—" I give her a reluctant smile. "We've tried this before, you and me—"

"Yes." She nods resolutely. "But that was before, and I'm different now."

I look over her face, eyes fall to that mouth of hers I've thought about kissing too many times since the one time I did. Embarrassing, really… for someone like me to think of someone like her as much as I do. Not that she's embarrassing, she's — I don't know. I just don't think of girls if they're not in front of me.

Drag my eyes back up to hers, cross my arms again because it's the only way I'm not going to start feeling her up on the spot.

"Yeah? How are you different now?" I ask, coolly.

"Why don't you take off my clothes and see?" she says and I swear to God, my face almost falters. That line takes me fucking out, enough so that I don't even respond, I just stare at her and her cheeks start to go pink.

She waits for me. "Do you not want to?"

I shake my head, pinching my eyes at her. "That's not it."

She takes a shallow breath. "Then what?"

You know how girls' cheeks go a bit pink after they've been crying? And the rims around their eyes are always more obvious? Their noses kind of go redder from wiping?

"Did something happen?" I ask and I don't move towards her even though I think about it.

"No." She shakes her head quickly.

So yes.

I tilt my head to the other side, not looking away from her face. "Are you okay?"

"Yes." She nods, again quickly — so no.

I walk over to her and wipe under the corner of her right eye with my thumb. "You look like you've been crying."

She takes a breath and a step backwards, frowning up at me. "What, are you a detective now?"

I shake my head a bit. "Just paying attention."

"Well stop—" She stomps a foot before rushing me, grabbing my face with her hands, pressing her mouth up against mine, pushing me back towards the table.

And I'm not a saint, let's not pretend I am. We all know I'm not — I lean back against the desk and she's pressing herself into me, standing between my legs. My hands grip the table and not her because I don't fully trust myself to stop if I were to start. But there's an upside — me not holding her, it means she's holding on to me more. Pressing herself into me, coiling her little body around me.

And kissing her — fuck — it's — I don't know. You ever stand on sinking sand before? When you're by the shore, and your feet just melt into the ground?

That's what kissing her feels like, so I hold the fucking table tighter.

Lose track of time for a bit — don't read into that, she's just a good kisser — and then her hands start to get busy, fumbling around the top button of my jeans—

"Woah, woah—" I pull back a bit, but not too much because I don't really want to stop. "Whats going on?"

"Nothing?" She shakes her head quickly.

I put both my hands on her waist — probably not a good idea because now that I've done it, now that she's in my hands — probably not going to let her go again.

"Magnolia." I'm firm now. "What happened?"

She takes a few shallow breaths — no good, she's about to cry.

"I told BJ I loved him. He told me he loves me back—" Another shallow breath. "He kissed me. He slept with me and told me he was going to break up with his girlfriend. Then we had a fight, and he slept with her instead."

Her eyes are shiny from not crying even though she wants to.

"Shit." I blink over at her. This fucking guy.

"Yes." She holds my eyes, looking defeated. Don't like it on her, it doesn't suit her. A girl like her, she's not made to lose. I lick my bottom lip, thinking it through quickly.

"And now you're here?"

She nods.

Tilt my head at her. "Why here?"

She swallows nervously, gives me a small shrug. "You're Central Park at midnight."

My face falters. I'm her death wish?

I frown at her. "I'm not going to hurt you."

"He wields how much I love him around like it's a play sword," She gives me a hopeless shrug. "And it doesn't matter how he looks at me or how my whole body feels when my arm's pressed against him in the back of a car — there are lots of ways a person can be dangerous and you aren't the most dangerous man I know."

And now I'm in. She's hurt, she wants to hurt back. Happy to help.

"You're out for blood." I stare over at her.

She nods.

"Alright then—" I pull her quickly back in towards me. "Arms up, Tiges. Let's make him bleed."

24

Daisy

Tiller flew home the next day like he said. Boxing Day night. His family was not pleased and I don't suspect I'll be receiving a warm reception from them any time soon. It felt normal enough. He seemed happy to see me, or relieved, maybe? We went for a walk around the park. We didn't talk that much but I thought it was nice, his arms around me and the cold air on my face. He kissed me up against a lamppost, told me he shouldn't have gone away for Christmas anyway, that was his fault, and I feel bad because I had the happiest Christmas I've had in years, and I had it without him.

Two days later, he's back at work — which I don't know why, really. I thought he'd taken the time off, but I think he's finding it hard to be around the house, maybe? The boys are friendly with him. He's friendly with the boys.

Maybe that's the problem, I'm not sure—?

As soon as he walked into my bedroom tonight he was on me, arms wrapped around my waist, walked me backwards, threw me down on the bed, didn't even take off his clothes or mine, just straight in for the kill—

There's something about things not working that makes you try harder. It's the wiliest thing sex does. Tricks you into thinking it's working too — Tiller inside of me, his hand holding my face, foreheads pressed against each other, you do feel like nothing could really come against you that you couldn't figure out.

And he was proving that to himself more than he was to me, I think, that we work. That it's good — and it is. That he wants this, which I think is true still. Or it was — I think you can want two things at the same time, I just think they'll take you on different paths — and he is watching me, eyes on me with a heavy focus, convincing himself that he wants me more than he wants whatever is pulling him away, and I am watching with a dawning revelation that yes, I love him, and yes, I want to be with him, and still maybe, somehow, maybe that's not enough.

It gets closer to enough when he pushes into me more and his breath gets caught on my neck but even then — it's just that fucking oxytocin that we all know I struggle with.

Afterwards, he kissed me and said he was going for a run, and I took a shower because I was feeling guilty about how conscious I had to be during it not to think of Christian.

I haven't thought of Christian when we've done that in months and months and months and my mind kept wandering over to the idea of what we might have done if he drove me home, but he didn't because I didn't let him, so even though I think I'm kind of a shitty person for having to decide not to think of my ex-boyfriend while I'm having sex with my current boyfriend, I tell myself I'm not all the way shitty, because even though old habits die hard and Christian Hemmes is a habit I've never wanted dead in the first place, I still didn't when I think I probably could have.

I don't know what that means though, in the larger context of life, and I don't think I'm ready to figure it out just at the minute, not when Tiller's ruined Christmas for me to prove something which I think if we were our friends on the outside looking in, we'd tell ourselves that it's not the sort of thing you should need to prove, so if we have to, why do we have to?

I head downstairs, eager for the distraction that my brother and his boys always provide.

Haven't seen my brother all that much these last two days because he's been holed up in his room with — kill me please and wait for it — Magnolia fucking Parks.

Her face lit up when she saw me the morning after — so annoying. I think she thinks we're friends. I don't think she knows that she's the thing that tipped my whole life on its head... I don't think she realises she's this little grenade of a person, cute as a fucking button, waltzing on in, blowing shit up. She waved at me brightly from my brother's office this morning while she was perched on his lap, and I rolled my eyes and walked up the stairs—

They're not quiet, either — I don't know if Magnolia Parks is discovering orgasms for the first time or what, but it's disgusting.

Tiller asked who my brother was with and I honestly couldn't even bear to say it — just begging whoever the fuck clearly isn't listening to my damn prayers for it to blow over and her to blow away.

I peek into the dining room, making sure she's not in there before I wander in — the coast is clear.

My brother glances up, nods his chin hello.

"Oh." I give Julian a look. "Look who decided to come up for air." He rolls his eyes. "Where's your little play-thing now?"

He glares over at me a bit, rubs the back of his neck. "She's here still. We needed to have a meeting though—" He gestures to the table of his men all assembled and leaning over what I know to be a plan of sorts.

I frown at him. "What, she's just hanging out here?"

He picks up a piece of paper and squints at it. "I brought her in a masseuse."

I glance around the room, searching for a face of mutual horror, but I don't find it. "Why?"

"For a massage," Julian says as he picks up another piece of paper.

"Why wouldn't she just leave to go get one?" I frown. God, she's so annoying.

"Because—" Julian points to something on Declan's computer screen. "I don't want her to leave."

He glances over at me.

"Why not?" I scowl.

He licks his lips, looking annoyed. "Is there a problem, Dais?"

I shake my head stubbornly. "Nope. Just — don't like her."

"That's okay." My brother shrugs. "I'm the one fucking her, not you."

And a few of the boys laugh and my intolerance for her grows because it's one night with her and suddenly Julian thinks he's a comedian? She ruins everything.

I scowl down at him to make sure he knows how annoyed I really am and he just gives me an indifferent smile.

"What are you doing anyway?" I huff, crossing my arms over my chest.

"Working," he says without looking at me.

I roll my eyes. "On…?"

"A job," Declan says, unhelpfully.

My brother looks over at me. "You don't want to know about this, Dais — go on—" He nods towards the door.

I growl a little under my breath and I'm about to leave when my eye catches on the computer screen.

A painting.

"Is that—?" I start, but I shake my head at myself. *Don't get involved*, I tell myself. Normal life. Do not get involved. I take a few more steps and then I see the picture again on TK's screen. I've seen it before.

I purse my lips. "Are you going to steal that?"

Julian flickers his eyes up at me, eyebrows a little low. "We're going to intercept it."

I nod once. "From where?"

"Through Belgium." Julian glances up, annoyed by the questions. "Why?"

I scratch my neck. "Right."

Julian gives me a weird look.

"Good source?" I ask. "You trust them?"

"Why?" Kekoa frowns.

I lean over Booker, reaching for one of the cookies I'd made for them this afternoon. Dark chocolate and sea salt. Take a bite.

They're very good. I'm very good. I shouldn't be a doctor, I should be a baker.

And also, fuck it. I sit on the arm of Declan's chair and pull his computer in closer towards me.

"Oi," he grunts and I ignore him.

"What are you doing?" Julian looks over, annoyed.

"Nothing!" I squint at the screen as I shake my head, making sure I'm really sure before I say what I say. "It's just —" I glance between all the boys who are now looking at me, waiting, brows up. I clear my throat. "It's a fake?"

Julian snaps his head in my direction. "What?"

"It's fake." I shrug.

"No, it's not." Declan rolls his eyes.

I look between Julian and Kekoa, nodding.

"It is." I'm sure it is.

"How do you know?" Smokeshow squints at me.

I purse my lips, looking back at my brother. "Do you know my friend Taura Sax?"

"Intimately." Julian smirks and I roll my eyes.

"Well, the real one's hanging in her dad's office."

"Bullshit." Book scoffs.

I nod once, annoyed they're not all just believing me instantly. I look over at Miguel to back me up. "Did you see it?" I ask him.

He shakes his head. "You wouldn't let me inside."

"Oh." I let out an awkward laugh. "Sorry."

Miguel rolls his eyes.

Julian leans back in his chair. "It's been missing for—"

"Since 1945—" I interrupt. "I know. The Nazis took it."

"So how did Sax get it, then?" Julian cracks his back, face dubious.

"Her great-grandmother on her father's side was a Nazi."

All the boys scoff.

"Seriously!" I blink. "She was in the National Socialist Women's League, she was really high up—" I shrug. "And then she lost her mind — well deserved, all things considered — and the painting was stored in her daughter's basement, who was Morley's dad's mother, and she only just died a few months ago and then they found it down there—"

Julian frowns. "And he just hung it up?"

I nod, shrugging, indifferent.

"You know the police have been looking for that for about eighty years?"

"Are you really going to yank at that thread when you and your band of Merry Men are sitting around a table plotting how to steal it?"

Julian crosses his arms, thinking as he trades looks with Miguel.

I walk towards the door.

"It's a trap," I tell him, resolutely. "Someone's trying to trap you."

25

Julian

My New Year's Eve parties, they're legendary.

I haven't bought a date to one in about a decade because chances are, it's not who I'll spend the end of the night with anyway, but this year I do.

She actually hasn't left my house since that night I bought her home.

Didn't immediately bring her home though. Jonah's desk is a convenient height and Magnolia Parks was very open to doing things that would wipe that shit-eating grin off her ex-boyfriend's face.

Took her home after that — which I didn't need to. Kind of felt like it though.

Liked how it felt having her wrapped around me, how it feels to move her through a room, up against walls, taking her on tables, etcetera etcetera. Decided to bring her home so I could move her through all the rooms.

She fell asleep before I did, facing in towards me, and maybe I watched her for a couple of seconds — wondered how someone gets a face like that, wondered how much a bottom lip has to weigh for it to part from the top one the way hers does. Thought about how many times over the years I've propositioned her, how many times she laughed it off and said no, but here I am, lying next to Everest herself.

If I'm honest, I always thought that the second I had her the spell would wear off. The fascination with her would dissipate into the oblivion of all my other conquests. I was sure that most of her allure was going to dry up the second we had sex, but we've had it now — three times that first night, I've lost count how many times since — and here is the part I don't know what to do with: I'm still fucking rapt with her. Annoyingly so.

And I know that some boys — like the Hemmes boys, for example

— when they hook up with a girl, they don't like for them to stay the night. Me? I think that's shit — they can sleep in my bed, I don't care, what are they going to do?

Now, I don't like it when they don't know when to leave, but Magnolia — I didn't like it when she looked like she was on her way out.

"Julian—" she said first thing that morning after. Her voice sounded strained.

"What?" I grunted, eyes still closed.

She cleared her throat, politely. "There is a giant dog on me."

Shit. My eyes sprung open and I turned to her. "Okay don't move — he's an attack dog and he can be pretty aggressi—"

And then the dog lunged for her face and licked the shit out of her.

She erupted with laughter and how it sounded, I found disarming and I didn't like it at all — so I shoved him off her so it would stop.

"Oh my gosh!" she cooed, sitting up and chasing after him, and I swallowed heavy because she still didn't have any clothes on. "He is without a doubt the cutest, friendliest dog I've ever met!"

I glared at my dog, roughly pet his dumb head.

"You're a fucking joke you are—" I told him.

Her head pulled back. "Excuse me?"

I squashed a smile. "I was talking to the dog."

"Oh." Her cheeks went a bit pink and she bunched the sheets up around herself. "Well, I should probably go anyway."

Steeled my face. Made sure I didn't show a lick of the disappointment that I felt for a second. "Plans?"

"I was going to get a massage today so I'm all ready for New Year's—"

Tilted my head. "You need a massage to be ready for New Year's?"

She fluttered her eyes, tilted her head back like I was the idiot. "Well, yes — you know — I like to be nimble."

I sniffed a laugh and she pouted a little. Proud little thing.

"What?" She frowned.

I licked my bottom lip. "Don't go."

She looked a bit surprised. "Why?"

I shook my head. "I'll get you a masseuse to the house."

"Well, I was going to go to the gym."

I shrugged. "I have a gym."

She peered at me, suspicious. "I like to work with a trainer."

"I'll train you," I told her, tossing her a crooked smile.

She moved in closer towards me. "Will you just?"

I nodded as I stretched my arms up, leaning back against my bed. "I have a pretty solid plan to work out every muscle you have."

She swallowed, cheeks going pink again. "Do you not want me to go?"

I scoffed at her fishing. I don't know why girls fish. It's fucking annoying, what's a girl like her got to fish for?

"No." I shrugged, looking away from her. Pet my dog's head. "Whatever. I don't care— do what you want."

She watched me for a couple of seconds. Looked a bit rejected — she'd be right.

"Well, so — what are you doing today?"

I leant in towards her, wondered if her mouth was that colour all the time or if she put something on when I wasn't looking.

Licked my bottom lip. "You, hopefully."

This smile cracked over her face that I liked, and then I did.

That was two days ago. It's New Year's now and she still hasn't gone home. Had to nip out to Versace to buy her something to wear for tonight but I'm happy to report that she is, in fact, very nimble.

She also can eye-fuck like you wouldn't believe. It's probably the colour of them, I don't know — might just be her.

The party's started and she's on the other side of the room with Taura and some girl they went to school with, and I know they're talking about me.

I can tell by the way she's looking at me. Head tilted, mouth pouty, eyes heavy.

The other two are looking over at me too, whispering, giggling—

I shake my head, look away because something about it makes me feel like a kid and I'm not one.

I flick a bottle of whisky that I want to be drinking and TK pours me a glass of it.

Have a quick catch up with my mate, Storm.

You get into a jammy situation, he's your guy. He's been my guy plenty of times.

He's a good man, actually. Girls love him, but he's funny about them. More so than I am. He thinks they're too dangerous to have around.

He's probably right. That's why I never keep them around.

Probably why I should keep Parks around less, but then — our eyes catch again and I forget it all.

Koa and Decks are standing there, shaking their heads, smirking at me.

"What?" I frown when I see them.

"Got a bit of a crush there, do we?" Declan grins.

"No." I give him a dirty look.

"Oh—" Koa pulls a face. "Could have fooled me, you've been naffing that girl for the last seventy-two hours."

I shrug.

"You previous record was Josette. Fifty-four hours."

I don't know what he's insinuating but I don't like it. "Bit too observant there, mate—"

Koa rolls his eyes. "I'm your head of security."

"So?"

"So is it serious?" Declan asks me, watching her.

"No." I glance at him, annoyed. "When is it ever?"

I look over at her, still whispering to Taura, biting down on the tip of her thumb — why the fuck is her thumb in her mouth?

She looks over at me and we're back to the eye-fucking.

"You gonna head on back over there?" Koa nods his chin subtly towards her.

"Actually—" I give him a tight smile. "Yeah, I am."

He lifts an eyebrow.

"I feel like you think you're proving something—" I point at him. "But she's just a decent shag."

"If you say so," he calls after me.

That's what she is, because I don't date. Can't date. Besides, she's in love with someone else, which is good. Serves as a nice natural buffer.

I can fuck about with her for a minute, no strings.

I love no strings.

"Oi." I nod my chin at her as I walk over. "Hey Taus—" Kiss her cheek and then look at Parks, keen for a rise. "Is it weird for you that we've fucked?"

Taura rolls her eyes and Magnolia pouts. Doesn't work how I want it to, because the shape her mouth goes just makes me want to kiss her.

"Well, I hadn't considered it until now." She presses her tongue into her top lip. "But yes — I suppose it's not my favourite thought I've ever had in the history of time." She looks away, has a big drink.

And I don't get it — why it makes me feel weird and shit that she's not looking at me anymore, that she looks uncomfortable — I wanted to make her uncomfortable. I think it's fun watching how people tick, but that wasn't fun.

I look for her eye and she doesn't let me have it, so I take her by the wrist anyway and pull her away from her friends.

"Come upstairs with me."

She takes her wrist back, still cross, always milking it. "What for?"

Tilt my head at her. "You know what for."

Her face goes shy for a second before she glances up, frowns. "You have company present."

I shrug, indifferent. "Want me to make them all leave?" Her eyes pinch, amused. She liked that. Loves a power move, this one.

"I will—" I give her half a smile. I might actually if it meant she'd do it.

She sniffs a laugh. I feel relieved.

"Come on." I pick her up off the ground — light as fucking feather — carry her up the stairs.

"This is very uncouth," she tells me on the way up, staring down her nose at me and I laugh.

Kick my bedroom door shut. Lay her down on my bed. "Well, I'm pretty uncouth."

She gives me a look. "Yes, I'm learning that."

"And you—" I toss her further up my bed towards the head. "You're very excitable."

She tilts her head, confused. "That sounds jovial, but I've got a feeling you might not mean it as a compliment?"

"I don't."

"Oh." She frowns and I fight off a smile. God, she's fucking cute. Yuck. I hate thinking someone's cute.

"You come too soon," I tell her. And myself. Need to take some of the sheen of her off.

Her whole face goes pink. "No, I don't—"

"Yes, you do," I tell her calmly.

She sits up, hugging her knees to her chest "Says who?"

"Says me—" I give her a look. "The person you're... not... coming with—"

"Oh." She blinks twice quickly.

There's usually something a bit fun about destabilising the confidence of girls like her — don't know what that means anymore though, because that wasn't fun and I'm not sure there are that many girls like her now.

"Oi." I nod my chin at her. "How many people have you had sex with?"

Her head pulls back a bit, like she's exposed or embarrassed. "Ever?" She blinks.

"Yes."

She blinks more, sits up straighter. "Eight."

"Ever?" My eyes go wide and she frowns defensively.

"Yes."

"I had sex with eight different girls the fortnight before we started hooking up."

"Oh." She nods coolly. "Would you like a merit badge?"

"No." I shrug, giving her a look. "Just an orgasm in sync with the girl I'm shagging."

And it's over to shallow breathing after that — don't like it. Bunches up a bit, like she's scrunched herself up into a ball. She's a fucking mind bend to figure out, this one. She's sharp and playful, but proud and fragile and insecure and gets her feelings hurt too easily, and I'll be straight with you, I don't really usually give a shit, but her — I want to lay her down, stretch her out, make her face look light again.

Most girls I sleep with, they're just happy to be here, but with her, it's me who's happy she's here — I mean, I'm not happy — like, don't read into that. I'm indifferent, right? But, I mean, it's fine she's here, I don't care. But I guess I must care a bit because after I've just said that she looks like I've just kicked her in the stomach.

Sucking on her bottom lip, looking embarrassed — I didn't want to make her embarrassed, maybe just a bit more eager to please me. She doesn't seem like she has much to prove to me. I'm not used to that.

"It just—" She gives a shrug like she doesn't care — stares over at the bottle of tequila by my bed. Pours herself one into my glass from the night before. "Doesn't happen for me like that—"

"Like what?" I squint over at her.

"That — you know—" She waves her hand towards me, like I am the physical embodiment of orgasms. "Just with BJ."

Fuck. Why does that make me feel about two feet tall?

"Makes sense." I nod like that didn't sting. Why the fuck did that sting?

"I get nervous and then — tada." She jazz-hands that. "It doesn't usually — with like, one night stands—"

"It's been three nights," I tell her.

"Eventually I stop being so nervous—" Her nose is in the air now. She can't lose face. "Most boys don't seem to mind it—"

"Most boys are lying because they're just happy to be there."

"Isn't it good that I'm excited?" She frowns. "Why's that bad?"

"It's not bad—" I shake my head at her, give her a shrug. "Just more fun together."

I grab her by the ankle and stretch her out flat against my bed, crawl over her, hover for a second.

"What are you nervous of me for?" I ask, looking down at her, smiling.

"BJ and Jonah, they always said to me if I was in danger and I couldn't find them to come and find you—"

My eyes flicker to her mouth. "Don't think they meant it like this—"

"No." She purses her mouth. "I don't suppose they did."

"You did find me, though," I tell her. Touch her face because I can.

"Mhm." She nods once.

I find her eyes. "You don't have anything to be nervous of."

~

An hour later, she's standing in front of my bathroom mirror in knickers and nothing else.

She's leaning over the sink, pressing some lipstick back into her lips, and it takes a decent bit of my self control not to run my hand up her bare back and try for round two.

"Am I your date to this party?" she asks without looking at me as I pull on my jeans.

Usually I like to shower after I have sex. Don't mind smelling like she's been on me, though.

I shrug. "Guess so."

She blinks then frowns at me. "You guess so?"

"I don't usually bring dates to this—" I grab a t-shirt from my bathroom floor and she stares at it in my hand.

"Not that shirt—" she tells me before darting into my room and coming back a second later with a different one that to me looks like the same white t-shirt.

I glance at them in my hands, give her a look.

"The stitching on the shoulders of this one will make you look broader."

"I am broad," I grunt as I pull it over my head anyway and she tugs at the sleeves of the shirt and I swallow. I don't like it when girls try to dress me or mother me, but I don't move a fucking muscle as she runs her hand down the seams.

"Yes, you are. Very." She nods. "But why not look broader still?"

I say nothing, looking past her in the mirror at myself and I won't say it out loud but yeah, no — hers is better.

She turns back to the mirror. Mascara.

"Why don't you usually bring dates to this party?" she asks her own reflection.

I stand behind her, slip my arms around her waist because no one can see me and I just feel like it. "Makes it harder to sleep with someone else at the end of the night."

"Oh." She bites down on her bottom lip, thinking. "Well, should we perhaps have a code word so I know if you're wanting to bed another woman—"

Shake my head at her in the mirror, still pulling her back closer to me. "No, I'd just tell you to leave."

"Oh." She looks crestfallen for a minute and I sniff back a laugh because she's a fucking rollercoaster of emotions. "That would be rather direct of you—" She purses her mouth. "Though I suppose I should appreciate that considering how indirect my ex-boyfriend is."

"He fucked someone else." I remind her, just because. "I'd say that's pretty direct."

She blinks twice when I say that, swallows once, then stands up straighter, stares at herself, eyes all busy. I think she's looking for something wrong with her face but it doesn't exist and she still glares at herself anyway.

She breathes out, looks down, and I have this urge to move the hair from her neck and kiss it but that's weird, so I don't.

I shift my hand to her waist, stare at her through the mirror.

"I'm not going to sleep with someone else tonight."

"Why?" she asks quietly.

I smirk, eyes falling down her. "Have you seen you?"

And then she turns in my hands, face pulling all upset and I tilt my head confused.

"People say things like that to me quite often — like being beautiful is a personality trait." She glares up at me. I like it when she goes defiant. "Like it's all that I am."

My eyes pinch, interested. "You don't like it?"

She crosses her arms over her bare chest. "I think it makes it easier for people to treat me not like a real person."

Fuck.

"You think BJ doesn't treat you like a real person?"

"I think that he thinks that me being beautiful will absorb the brunt of his repeated rejections but all it's done is show me that beauty is worth nothing in the end."

She moves past me back into my room, over to my bedside table, and finishes her tequila from before. Downs it. She doesn't like spirits. Hates them, actually. And you know what — fuck it, I hate him. I didn't before, but I hate him now.

Cock my head towards my door. "Should we go back downstairs?"

She breathes through her nose as I toss her her dress. "What if he's there?"

"He probably will be." I nod.

Her eyes go bigger, all nervous and shit, and I grab her by the waist again, ducking so we're eye-to-eye.

"Oi. Knives out, remember—" I give her a look. "We're making him bleed."

26

Daisy

My brother went on a coffee run this morning.

Knocked on my door, opened it anyway without a response.

"Oh," I looked over at him, crossing my arms as I sat up, "how kind of you to remove your tongue from Magnolia Parks' mouth long enough to be a functional member of society—"

"Functional might be a bit of a stretch." He smirked.

Handed me an oat cap. Handed Tiller his.

"Americano, right?" My brother smiled at him mindlessly.

Tiller frowned. "Right."

I could see it on him, this weird discomfort in the fact that my brother knows him; knows him enough to know his coffee order, and to think of him in the morning enough to buy him one.

He overthinks, Tiller — I've said that before but I can see the cogs spinning behind his eyes. He thinks Julian buying him a coffee means that he's assimilated too much, that he's too much a part of the furniture, that my brother's too used to him being here, but I don't think any of that's true. My brother's just thoughtful.

People think he's not, but he is. Very much so. He just chooses not to act on it a lot of the time. It's not a far leap from thoughtful to calculated and no one would question me once if I called Julian calculated, but let me be clear: My brother is both.

Tiller put the coffee down, didn't even take a sip.

"Gonna go for a run," he said without looking at me. Swapped his pants, took off his shirt, pulled on his shoes and that was that. Fucked off quick smart.

I sighed, tired, even though we'd just woken up.

I walked over to my brother's room, pushed the door open and groaned when I saw them in bed — even though it's exactly what I thought I'd walk in on.

"Daisy!" Magnolia's dumb face lit up. "Hi!"

She sat up straighter, leant out of my brother's embrace — which was weird, actually — Julian's not much of a cuddler.

"It's great to see you— I'm sorry about last night."

I rolled my eyes again and leant against his wall. "Are you guys trying to break some kind of record?"

Julian tossed me a look as he swallowed his coffee. "You're one to talk, Face — you blocked out your memories of yourself this time last year?"

I flipped him off.

"Do you want me to pick out your outfit for New Year's Eve?" she offered with a big smile.

"No—" I shook my head with a scowl. "I really, really don't."

"Oh." She frowned, looked over at my brother. "Do you want me to pick out your outfit?"

"Nope."

"Strange." Her mouth puckered. "Everyone usually is dying for me to dress them — I'm very good at it," she told us both, glancing between us.

"Still a no from me—" I yawned, walking out of the room.

"Good to see you!" she called.

And I kept shaking my head because I hate her. More than I did a minute ago because before that I hadn't even thought about what I was going to wear tonight and I'd since rejected the assistance of arguably London's most fashionable girl, so I'd had to go all out just to prove to her I don't need the help.

When she'd see me later in the outfit I'd eventually pick,[133] she'd tilt her head and stare down at my feet in their boots and say, "You might want to pair that with a strappy sandal instead."

And I'd say, "Or I might not" before swearing under my breath, because fuck, she's right. A strappy sandal would really tie this together.

God, she's fucking annoying.

More annoying is that an hour later the perfect pair of strappy heels for the outfit is sitting on my bed, new with tags.

When in the actual fuck did that idiot have time to run out to Harrods and back?

---

[133] The black 'Nyoka' dress from Nanushka.

160

I decide I'm not going to wear them until the very last moment when I haven't found anything better and now the outfit feels incomplete, and I almost don't care until I wonder if Christian will be there? And then I feel like shit, because maybe Christian will be there, maybe he won't, but either way, Tiller will and so I should wear the shoes because I want to look good for him. And let me just reiterate, she is unbearably annoying, but God, she's good at clothes.

I put it on, steel myself for the barrage of annoying comments I'm sure I'm about to get from her about being right and knowing everything and having the supreme style of the galaxy but all that happens when she sees me is her eyes fall down my outfit, land on the shoes and she smiles to herself a tiny bit before standing with my brother's friends while she waits for hers to get here.

Tiller comes and stands next to me uncomfortably, surveying the crowd.

"This party is both better and worse than I'd imagined," he concedes.

"Come on Tills—" I poke him. "Loosen up."

"Daisy." He gives me a look. "I'm in a room full of people who I have dedicated the last five years of my professional life to catching. Give me a fucking break."

I sigh big and take a drink before I shake my head at him, sort of feeling as though I'd like a bit of row. "You know I didn't make you come to this..."

"Yeah—" He rolls his eyes. "Like I wasn't going to spend New Year's with my girlfriend—"

"You didn't spend Christmas with me." I remind him, not sure why.

He gives me a look. "And how'd that turn out?"

"We could have spent it with your friends—" I shrug with an innocent face before I swap it to a glare. "Oh no, wait — we couldn't have, because you don't invite me to shit with them."

He swallows, shaking his head. "Let's not do this right now."

"Why?" I ask, sort of liking the friction. Maybe because it's at least something.

"Because I'm not ready, Dais," he tells me with this look that makes me stop.

His eyes look round and sad and I remember that before he was my boyfriend who I fight with constantly because who my family is and maybe even who I am — to him — is fundamentally unacceptable, there was a time when Tiller was the man with the bluest eyes on the planet who for me became a winter coat in the dead of a cold December's night when I was in nothing but a tank top.

"Okay." I nod and take his hand, squeezing it. I nod my head out of the room. "Let's go upstairs…" I pull him out of the room, catching my brother's eye across the room. 'Roof?' I mouth to him.

Julian nods as he slips his hand into Magnolia's, and I watch it kill BJ a bit and I watch my brother see that, scoop up the squashed parts of him[134] and spread them on toast.

Julian's relishing in it. He's such a prick sometimes.

And then I realise Christian's here, on his way up to the roof with us. I feel this burst of excitement and sadness. That he's here, that I can see him, but also that I'm excited and I'm with someone else anyway and somehow I now seem to want different things than what either of them can give me.

Tiller strikes up a conversation with Henry because Henry could strike up a conversation with a mute foreigner in under five seconds — probably heal their muteness and teach them seventeen languages while he's at it.

"Hi," Christian says, siding up next to me. He looks so good.

"Hey." I smile.

"Like your outfit." He nods his head at me. "Sick shoes."

Magnolia Parks looks over her shoulder and gives me a wordless, smug look and I wonder if she knows in this very moment I can think of three legitimate ways to kill her on the spot. Four! I just thought of a fourth.

The roof is a bar that my brother made. Fully stocked and staffed at all times with everything you could possibly think of. There are rumours about it, whether it's even true — stuff of legends up here, the things that have gone down, the deals that've been made.

There's one way up, one way down.[135] There's a secret path through the hollow of the roof to a little nook that's not on any blue plans (not that there are blue plans) that I'm not meant to go to unless I'm hiding but sometimes I use for the view. Not lately, obviously — I haven't been here lately.

---

[134] Him being, BJ, the person he was friends with a week ago.
[135] …that anyone else knows about.

Tiller peers down at me all curious when we step out onto it.

"You've never brought me up here before."

I give him an uncomfortable smile. "It's not really the sort of place you'd usually want to know exists."

He nods once and looks around uneasy but he sits down next to my brother anyway — looking between Julian and Magnolia, who, once again, is on his lap.

"So, how long have you two been hooking up, then?"

"Hmm." Magnolia purses her lips, thinking. "Probably broaching on seventy-four hours now?"[136]

My brother bites on her shoulder because he's disgusting like that. "Non-stop."[137]

I make a sound at the back of my throat.

"And you—" She bats her eyes at Tiller. "You two have been quite together a while then, yes?"

Tiller nods, throwing an arm around me. "Nearly eleven months," he tells her.

Christian shifts in his chair. Looks at his hands.

I feel sick.

Magnolia leans in towards Tiller curiously. "You have such a wonderful smile[138] — your teeth are so clean."

Tiller lets out this little baffled laugh which is one of three possible responses to Magnolia Parks at any given time.

"My mom's a dentist," he tells her.

"Ah." She smiles pleasantly.

"You have good teeth too," Tiller tells her. "What's your story?"

"Oh." She shrugs. "I just have very attractive, albeit rather shitty parents."

"Same—" I say without thinking and Magnolia lights up at the connection point, so quickly I say, "What are doing back here? I thought you moved." Because I don't want her to think we're suddenly friends.

Julian gives me a look, knows what I'm doing — I ignore him.

"I was offered a new role here if I moved back—"

---

[136] Revolting. Please kill me.

[137] Kill me faster.

[138] He does.

163

"Doing what?" my brother asks, interested, and I look over at him, a bit annoyed.

"You've spent how much time together and you don't know that?"

He shakes his head indifferently. "Haven't done a lot of talking, Dais."

Magnolia smacks him quiet — never seen anyone smack him quiet before.

"Just the fashion editor at *Tatler*." She says with a breezy smile before she leans in towards Tiller. "Julian says you're an agent at the NCA?"

Tiller looks past her to my brother for a second, and I think he thinks it's weird, maybe, that Julian talks about him? Tiller nods anyway.

"I am."

"That's such an exciting job." She smiles, takes a drink from my brother's glass. "Who's the craziest person you've ever caught?"[139]

Tiller frowns a bit, catches my brother's eye before he points a bit gingerly towards him.

"Oh." She frowns, purses her lips. Shifting on my brother's lap, turning in to face him. "Was it a misunderstanding?"

Julian stares at her for a few seconds, I think trying to work out whether she's serious.

"Yeah." He nods eventually.

"Oh—" She breathes out, content with that answer. "How won-derful that you sorted it out, otherwise this would have been very awkward."[140]

"Right?" Jules nods as he flicks me an amused look.

Christian's watching me closely, trying to catch my eye, but I won't let him because I don't want Tiller to see that I still look at Christian how I do, because I don't mean to do it, I just do it, and I'm already feel sad because everything about Tiller and I feels so strained right now.

Tills isn't having fun, that much is obvious — which means I'm not having fun, because he's my boyfriend, and I can't leave him. So even though I'm with a bunch of people I really like and Mag-nolia Parks, I'm having a rubbish time because he is. He's stiffened

---

[139] Oh, God.

[140] She's a spectacular idiot.

up, talks a little to the Ballentine boys for a while, probably because they're not criminals — but then TK, Booker and Decks pull up on the roof and his jaw goes tight and his face goes serious.

He clocks me. "I've gotta go, Dais."

"What?" I frown, grabbing his hand and pulling him away from everyone.

"To sleep—" he says, lying. "Early start, you know?"

I shake my head a tiny bit. "I didn't know you were working tomorrow."

"Oh—" He shrugs. "I am."[141]

"It's a public holiday."

"Yeah, it's—" He shakes his head. "I'm trailing someone."[142]

"Right." I nod, and I can't really look at him because I didn't want this. I want him to remember that I didn't want this. Also, I hate being lied to, and I know he's lying. I know it's just that he can't work out how to ring in the new year with all these people who I love who just happen to be criminals and still do what he does for a living. That's what it actually is, it's easier for us both to just pretend he has an early start... that he's not just going to spend tomorrow driving around following a lead that doesn't exist for a case that isn't a priority.

I lead him downstairs, down to my room.

He touches my face. "I love you,"[143] he tells me.

He does. I know. But it's past midnight on that stupid ship and the water's up to our knees now.

"I love you too," I tell him anyway. Sinking ships can pull you under like that.

"I'm not tired," I tell him. "I might head back up."

Something pained darts across his face, like how your face might go before a doctor resets a broken bone.

"Yeah—" He brushes his mouth over mine. "You should."

I nod.

He kisses me again and I feel like I could cry.

"Will you be sad by yourself down here?" I ask, taking a step back.

He shakes his head. "I'll be sleeping." And we're back to lying.

---

[141] Another lie.
[142] Another.
[143] Not a lie.

"I'll come back down soon," I tell him even though we both know it's not true and it frightens me how life can sneak up on you and unravel you and your boyfriend completely, turning you into a pair of liars, making your safe place all of a sudden feel like a house of cards.

I close my door, try not to feel like I'm closing the door on us as I make my way back upstairs, Julian's dog following me for some reason, which I guess is sort of cute. I don't know where Christian is anymore, and that's not why I'm coming back up now anyway, the thoughts aren't connected. But it doesn't bode that well for a boy like him, to not know where he is. Too many nooks in this house for him to use, he knows them all, I've shown them to him. He's with Vanna now probably, I tell myself as I look around on the roof. I don't know — I didn't see her before, but then I wasn't paying too close attention, nor should I have been because I have a boyfriend.

I have a boyfriend but here I am anyway.

And then I see him.

27

Christian

She's standing there by herself. Where'd the boyfriend go? I glance around, looking for him. She stares over at me, holding my eyes. I nod my chin at her, because I'm not sure what else I can do.

She tips her head towards the bar.

I like communicating with her without words. I walk over to it. Makes me feel like we're still connected in the ways I want us to be.

"Where's Tiller?" I ask her as casually as I can, look over my shoulder like I'm hoping he's around.

"He's sleeping."

I pull back a bit. "Wow."

She reaches over the bar and grabs an olive, popping it in her mouth. "He has an early start…"

My face falters. I don't mean for it to. It's just — she has to know it's an excuse. A piss poor one at that — and who's making up excuses not to spend New Year's with her?

"Don't—" She shakes her head.

I give her a look and she rolls her eyes amused.

"Stop—" She shakes her head. "Don't be shit."

"Sorry." I do my best to squash a smile so I look away from her.

Hard to keep your smile in check when you're looking at the girl you — you know, you know?

"What?" she asks, turning in towards me more.

I peer over at her out of the corner of my eye. "Maybe this year won't be so shit after all…"

She smacks me in the arm and turns to the person behind the bar.

"A Sazerac and a greyhound please," she tells them before she turns back to me.

"You didn't bring Vanna."

I shake my head as I crouch down to pet the dog. "I wouldn't do that to you."

"Why?" She smirks, amused. "I'd do it to you..."

"Yeah, but I deserve it more than you—" I tell her with a shrug. Mean it too.

"Yeah?" She frowns a little. "How do you figure?"

"It took me too long to figure out what you are to me..."

Her eyes pinch as she slides me my drink. "What am I to you?"

"Oh, I don't know—" I give her a little shrug, stare straight ahead. Take a long sip before I look over at her. "Like, just — everything."

She looks rattled, head pulled back and blinking a lot. "Why would you say that?"

"I don't know—" I shrug as I shove my hands through my head. "I guess I just thought after all our shit before, and the ways our wires got crossed, that for you and me, honesty would be the best policy—"

Her eyes look wide and worried and I wonder if I've overstepped.

"There is no us," she tells me with this voice that sounds kind of startled and sort of pleased at the same time so I decide to double down.

"For now," I tell her with a smirk.

"No—" She shakes her head, cheeks going pink, looking flustered. "No! I'm with Tiller—"

I like riling her up so I do it some more.

"For now."

She gives me a look. "Christian—"

"Daisy—" I reach over and push some hair behind her ears.

She blinks at me, frozen. "What are you doing?"

"Sorry. You're just—" I shake my head and laugh once even though none of this is funny to me. "So beautiful it hurts."

She blinks a couple of times.

"Are you drunk?"

"A bit." I nod, sliding her drink over to her so we can be on the same page. She tosses it back easily and then gestures for the bartender to make another.

She swallows, cheeks on fire, shaking her head weakly. "You can't say that to me."

I like making her go weak. "I'll say shit like that to you forever if you'll let me—"

"Well I — no—" She blinks a lot, swallows more. "I don't. I won't—"

I take a step towards her, tilt my head, take another drink. "You want me to stop?"

She scoffs at least twice and I start laughing as she frowns, annoyed and rattled.

"Yes!" she says quickly.

"Yes?" I repeat, taking another step towards her, not giving a shit about anyone up here seeing us. I want them to see us, I want the world to. She's not moving back, she's staring up at me, toe-to-toe, a worried face I want to smooth out and kiss all over.

I give her a look, tempering the smile I've got. "Do you want to try that again, Dais? Maybe with a bit more gusto?"

"No!" she breathes out. Hands on her hips. "And there was plenty of gusto!"

I look over her face; I love all of it. I've missed not being able to stare at her how I am now, a bit like she's mine, a bit like I can do things to her that no one else can.

"'No' you don't want me to stop? Or...?"

"No—" she stutters. "No. Yes — I — stop it." She stomps a foot.

I lick away a smile and nod once. "Okay."

"Okay, you'll stop?" she asks, eyebrows up as she straightens her dress that's just fine as is.

"For now," I tell her with a smirk and she squashes one back, and I love her. That's it for me. That's all there is. I love her.

I need to be with her, actually. I need to figure it out.

And I can't tell if she loves me too right now— I think she might? — all those pink cheeks and being up here with me instead of down there with him, but I don't know—?

Daisy looks over her shoulder and her face scrunches up as she looks at Julian with his hand up Magnolia's dress.

This fucking party, man — so rife with drama.

Beej is pretty fucked up at this point. His eyes practically fell out of his head when he saw Parks trot down the stairs with Jules.

Hasn't really spoken to me all night, avoided Henry too. Like it's our fault that he fucked up so bad she's run to the arms of the most dangerous man in England.

He's pissed at Jo too. But he can't leave, because everyone would know why he left, girlfriend included, and he's too proud.

How proud he is could be the death of them one day.

So there's that, and then there's all the shit between my brother and Henry. Taura's here, technically with neither, technically with both.

Seen her kiss them both at certain points throughout the night — which is fucked up and probably makes her sound worse than she is.

Watching Parks and Julian together —that's still weird to say — it's interesting. Because she's doing what she's always done... You know that part in *Jurassic World* where the Indominus Rex escapes its pen and it's chasing Chris Pratt and he hides under a car and cuts the fuel line, covering himself in the smell to throw it off? We've seen this before, she's done it a thousand times. Done it with me, did it with Tom and Rush and Jack-Jack... Julian is the petrol she's covering herself in.

But Jules — I don't know. We've been proper mates a few months now, more than that, probably. I've seen him with a lot of girls. I've never seen him with a girl how he's being now.

All over her. Hands in her hair, her on his lap, chin on her shoulder.

I wonder if it's for show?

Wouldn't put it past her, honestly, to strike up a deal like that — tell him to act a certain way, to touch her a certain way — but if she hasn't told him, if he's doing it himself... Fuck, we're all in trouble, then.

"God, they're hateful," she scowls over at her brother and Magnolia. The sight would have knocked the wind out of me a year ago — Parks leaning back against a wall, Julian hovering over her, nudging her face with his as he kisses her all over — but now? I couldn't give less of a shit.

Actually, that's not entirely true, I'm a bit sad about it, but for her because she's my friend and she's a fucking mess.

"Should we go somewhere else?" I nod my head towards nowhere.

She gives me a look, somewhere between suspicious and hopeful. "Maybe."

"Where?"

She purses her mouth — I love that mouth — I think about that mouth all the time.

"I have a place," she says before she takes my wrist in her hand and pulls me past the bar and through a cool room into what looks like a little dead end room. I give her a confused look, as does this dog of theirs who follows her everywhere. And then I notice the trick wall.

She slips between it and disappears and I follow her, my heart pounding — I don't know why. Because she does this to me, I guess.

She pushes open a window you can't see from the street and climbs out onto a landing on the roof and gestures to London's skyline somewhat pathetically.

"Woah." I blink at it. "I didn't know this place was here."

She stares at me for a few seconds. "No one knows that this place is here."

"No one?"

She shakes her head. "Just me and my brother." She gives me this quick smile that looks sort of sad, sort of tender. "If security's breached, if I'm in danger, I'm meant to come here and he'll find me. It's not on the blueprints. You can't see it from the street."

I stare over at her and feel this weird guilty sadness, because her life is fucked and I can't unfuck it, and even if I want to — which a bit of me does — most of me doesn't because if it's fucked, we can be together, I think.

"No one knows—" she tells me all earnest. "Don't tell anyone."

I shake my head, barely. "Mum's the word."

"So." I sit down on the roof, knees propped up. "What will we do at midnight?"

She sniffs a laugh and sits down next to me, leaving about a foot between us. I'm pretty sure it's on purpose though.

"Nothing."

She gives me a look and I give her one back like she's an idiot.

"We have to do something—" I shake my head at her. "Bad karma for the year otherwise..."

She pats the dog mindlessly. "That's not what they say..."

I elbow her. "What do they say, then?"

She gives me an impatient look that I love because she used to look at me like this all the time when I'd guess the wrong era for a piece of art or call the type of mushroom she was cooking with a 'white one' instead of a 'button'.

"They say that how you spend your New Year's is how you'll spend the rest of the year."

"Is it?" I give her a look, eyebrows up. She nods once. "Right, so what'll we do then?"

"Nothing," she says again.

"So you want to do nothing all year?"

"With you?" She gives me a proud look. "Perhaps..."

"Liar," I tell her, staring her down. Her cheeks go pink. Pink enough I can see them in the dark.

She breathes out her nose. It's more like a huff.

"I will put my head on your shoulder," she says, staring straight ahead. "At midnight." She clarifies for no one but herself.

"I'll take it." I nod, staring straight at her.

And then midnight creeps up on us. We're not checking the time, we're losing it... it's slipping through our fingers as we shoot the shit, talking about nothing and everything, and it's the best night of my life and I realise for the billionth time since that day in her apartment that I should've just said yes, should've just kissed her like crazy, grabbed her hand and followed her wherever she wanted to go.

And maybe it's too late now, or maybe it's not, I can't tell — because she's here with me, not with him, right? That's got to count for something — he gave her the life I said I couldn't, but I think I'd give anything to take it all back and not say no, just say "Okay, where?"

The counting starts, the whole city yelling *10, 9, 8...*

And what would I give to kiss her?

Anything. Literally anything. *7, 6, 5...*

She closes the gap between us, still staring straight ahead.

4, 3, 2...

I shift so my arm behind her back, not around it; it's not around her shoulder on a technicality, but I guess it is.

1.

There's cheering and yelling all around us, muffled by the distance and the bell tower chiming in my mind as she drops her head on my shoulder and my head falls back and I stare at nothing in the sky, take a big breath, breathe in how much I love her.

"Happy New Year," she says, not looking at me.

I don't say anything for a few seconds. Drop my head on top of hers, let it rest there how it always wants to.

"This is the hottest thing that's ever happened to me on a midnight."

She sniffs a laugh. Doesn't move a muscle. "I don't believe that for a second."

I shift a bit, press my mouth into the top of her head.

"Unsanctioned," she says but she doesn't move.

I sniff. "Sorry."

"You didn't say it back..." she tells me, head still where I want it.

I smile but she can't see it, glad she can't, too. I'm smiling like a fucking idiot.

"Happy New Year, Baby."

28

Julian

I'm in the shower when she wanders into my bathroom. She stands at the sink, fishes her toothbrush out of the toothbrush holder — gives me a new feeling.

Never had anyone here long enough for them to put their toothbrush in there with mine.

It's been almost a week now.

I was in my head about it before, how much Magnolia was in my head.

She's barely left my sight so I'll give myself that one. But also, it's not true that I don't get like this with other girls. I do. They're just usually on a canvas. Or wood, or paper — whatever, I'm not particular.

No need to get weird about it — I find Magnolia Parks fascinating the same way I found Klimt's Judith fascinating. For weeks after I got her I'd just stare at her on my wall, wonder a bunch of things about her, what she thought, how she felt, if she was real. Pretty much the same shit I wonder about Parks. It's no different. Beautiful things keep me up at night, what can I say?

That's all she is, just another beautiful thing — won't tell her that though because she doesn't seem to think that's a compliment — but it's what she is. I don't usually go out for a week after I take a painting. Just sort of stay home and stare up at it, proud of the thing I acquired. And all that is a welcome revelation of self because before I was feeling weird and shit, like maybe I — nothing. It was nothing. Stupid. But I realise now that there's nothing special about Magnolia except that she's something I've wanted for a long time. And I've had her now, so if I just lean into the post-had infatuation in a few days I'll be done with her; I'll be the thing she tells her ex about to make him squirm and she'll be another thing I look at on my walls that once I was fixated on and now I look at with an occasional fondness.

Bit of a relief, if I'm honest — because I haven't wanted her to leave. Played on my mind a bit, all the reasons why, but now I understand and it's fine. She doesn't have to leave and I don't need to feel like I should want her to.

"What are you doing today?" I ask, wrapping a towel around my waist.

"It's the Fuck Off Brunch," she tells me, mouth full of toothpaste.

"The what?" I frown.

"It's this thing we do every year. It's actually technically called The Fuck Off New Year's Brunch,"

I squint at her, waiting for more.

"Well, so—" She rolls her eyes, impatient. "New Year's Day brunch, everyone's hungover and gross and nowhere good is open to eat anyway. Plus, you sort of need the 2nd to recover from how terrible the first day of the year usually is, but by January 3rd—" She gives me a look, nose in the air — I brush my mouth up against hers quickly just because I feel like it and because it's not weird now in light of her just being a collection piece to me and nothing else. "—everything's open, no one's hung, everyone's fresh."

"That's cute. Annual brunch..." I give her a look, make it look like I think it's sort of dumb but I kind of like the stupid traditions they all do.

I keep watching her — bit hard not to. She steals your focus, even first thing in the morning. Art does that to you, so does her face.

Best way I can describe it is the first time I saw *The Ninth Wave* — you know the one? By Ivan Aivazovsky, the one in St Petersburg.

First time I saw that, I kind of just stood there, taken aback. How he paints the light, how it breaks through on the horizon and over the water, how it makes the dark darker, how it gives you a visceral feeling in your chest when you see it and the light hits you how it hits the people in the wreck. It's bigger than you think it is, too: 221 cm × 332 cm. It kind of swallows you whole.

So does she, I guess.

She runs her fingers under her eyes, staring at herself, and sighs quietly.

"Nervous?"

"No," she says quickly, standing up straighter. So, yes. "Why would I be nervous?" she asks because she's proud.

"Because you'll be by yourself and he'll be there with her." I tell her and she frowns a bit.

"You'll be the fittest one there." I nudge her with my shoulder from behind.

"Yes." She nods once, pushing some hair behind her ear, doesn't look away from her reflection, doesn't smile at the compliment either. Don't know if it is a compliment for a girl like her anyway as much as it's just fact—

She blinks a couple of time. Breathes out her nose then turns to me.

"And then what?" She gives me a shrug that's meant to be light but it's not. It's the shrug of a girl who's spent her whole life being the most beautiful person in every room just to have woken up one day to discover that ultimately, it means fuck all.

"Do you want me to come to this?"

"No—" She shakes her head quickly.

I pull back. "No?"

She shakes her head more. "Well, I know we're not — I know that you're not like... that."

I tilt my head. "Like what?"

"Like, the sort of boy you bring to brunch." She shrugs, gives me a quick smile.

"First up—" I tap my own chest. "Not a boy. And then, yeah—" I shrug. "I'm not the sort of man—" Flick her a look for that misnomer "—that you bring to brunch."

On principal. Have I been to brunch with girls before? Yes. Have I slept with them after that brunch? Yep. Have I ever been to brunch with a girl who I slept with the night before? Nope.

Oh, except for maybe Josette, if she counts, except it's different because we're mates.

But in general, no. It's too messy.

Brunch after sex is committal. Makes a girl get attached, but now this one — she didn't even ask me. That bodes well. No feelings on her end, which is good. I don't want them there.

Wouldn't mind going to brunch though.

"It's fine—" She gives me a brave smile. "I can go by myself. I'll just drink a lot, it'll be fine."

"I'll come," I tell her.

And then her eyes go bright. "Really?"

"Yeah. I don't have much on today—" That's a lie, but I shrug anyway. "Pretty slow around these parts at the minute." Also a lie.

Why am I lying to spend time with her?

She spins around, facing me, and my eye snags on my favourite freckle she has on her nose and I don't like that I have one.

"Thank you." She gives me a little smile.

I bite down on my bottom lip and grin up at her. "As far as thanks go, Tiges, I'm not really a big words guy…"

She tilts her head. "Is that right?"

I boost her up onto the vanity. "That's right."

~

"Why do your friends go everywhere with you?" she whispers to me quietly, eyeing Declan and Kekoa over her shoulder.

"Security," I tell her.

"Rubbish—" She gives me a little shove as she stares up at me. "Who could hurt you?"

There is something about walking into a room with her — all the eyes that go on you, the heads that turn, how every other male looks instantly fucked off with you — it's a bit addictive.

When we get to the restaurant, the whisper ripple that follows her everywhere happens and I catch myself touching her and I don't know why I do it— to protect her or to just be closer to the shiny thing, let everyone know that she's with me— I can't tell, but Jo spots us first and gets on his feet.

"Oi—" He opens up his arms to hug me. "Brunch?" he says under his breath and I shoot him a dark look.

"Shut it."

He flicks his eyebrows amused.

"We're going to need an extra seat—" BJ tells the waiter as I ruffle his brother's hair.

"Nah—" I wave off the waiter and the chair, pulling Parks down into my lap, pulling her back into me and staring down Ballentine as I do. "We're good."

Magnolia looks back at me, eyes all amused because she knows I'm being antagonistic, so I nudge her with my nose.

Hope no one sees it because it probably looks cuter than I meant it to.

Magnolia leans over the table and grabs Taura Sax's hand. "Miss you."

"Same," she sighs.

Ballentine's girlfriend looks over at her. "Where've you been?"

Parks flicks her eyes over at her, opens her mouth but says nothing—

"With me," I say for her, then look over at Taura, flicking her a look. "I'd tell you to come join us, Tausie, but it sounds like you've got your hands full already—"

Magnolia lets out this little gasp and turns around in my lap, smacking me both accidentally with her hair and also on purpose with her hand.

"So rude—" she scowls. "Say you're sorry."

My mouth falls open a bit, because I've never been scolded in my whole fucking life by anyone before besides my sister.

It's not my favourite thing, but also, I have about fourteen thoughts running through my mind of what I'd like to do with her and I know I won't get to do one of them if she's shitty at me, so I give her a glare then look over at her best friend.

"I'm joking, Taurs. I'm sorry."

Then follows a silence. Christian cocks an eyebrow, Jonah smiles confused and Taura sits back in her chair, arms crossed over her staring at Magnolia.

"Holy shit. How good in bed *are* you?"

I've had better, is the honest to God answer — and still, she's probably my favourite. I catch myself frowning as I think that, turn it into a smile, remind myself she's just Judith on the wall a week after I stole her, that's all. That's all, I tell myself, and I don't think anymore into it, not even when she takes my hand to cover her face when it goes embarrassed.

Magnolia and Ballentine have a passive-aggressive conversation over the table and Christian leans over towards me and mouths, 'What the fuck are you doing here?'

I nod my head subtly towards Parks but that clarifies nothing, he just shakes his head, as though that's not an answer in and of itself.

He tips his head towards her. "What are you doing?"

I toss him a look. "Just having a bit of fun, Dad."

"Yeah, Dad—" Magnolia chimes in. "We're just having a bit of fun."

Christian rolls his eyes and Parks reaches out to poke him in the shoulder.

"I'm glad you didn't bring Vanna here today—"

"Why's that?" Christian asks, even though he knows.

Magnolia looks at him like he's an idiot. He is an idiot. "Because she's very awful."

Such a fucking understatement. Absolute pain in the arse.

"Is she?" Christian says, just to rile her.

"Yes." Parks nods.

"How?"

"She's rude, she's spoilt, she's entitled, she's—"

Christian gives me a goading smile. "If you think she's entitled, Parks — God help us."

Magnolia's chin drops to her chest and she glares up at her friend.

"I'm not entitled," she says and across the table BJ snorts.

I snap my head in his direction, eyebrows up.

"That was a sneeze, yeah?" I stare him down and he says nothing, just glares at me. "Gesundheit." I tell him without looking away, and he doesn't flinch, reaches for his drink, takes a drawn out sip, doesn't look threatened how you'd think he might — don't know who's going to look away first — won't be me.

Then my phone rings and I look down at it. Fuck. He'll take that like he won it, but he didn't.

I dig my chin into Parks' shoulder.

"I gotta take this—" I tell her. "Order me a drink."

She nods brightly. "What do you fancy?"

"Just whatever you're having." I shrug.

She sits up straighter, looking pleased. "Do you like French 75's too!"

"No— Fuck—" I scowl, annoyed. "Jo, can you—"

Jo nods, rolls his eyes and waves me on.

I take a few steps towards Koa and Declan seated at a nearby table — make sure I'm out of earshot from Magnolia when I answer it.

"What?"

It's TK.

"Hello to you too—" he says from the other end.

"I'm at breakfast."

"With Magnolia?" TK asks, merrily.

"Yeah?" I frown.

"Woah! You never get breakfast with girls, this is—"

"We're not having a fucking gab, Teeks. What do you want?"

"Oh — right." He clears his throat. "Don't freak out—"

"Right." I pinch the bridge of my nose in anticipation. "Not my preferred introduction to news, but go on—"

There's a bit of a pause.

"We lost him."

"Which him?" I ask loudly and clearly even though I know which him.

"Brown," TK says. "He was in—"

"Valletta," I interrupt. "I know. And then?"

"And then we tracked him onto a flight to Marrakesh. He boarded the flight — he never got off it."

"Bullshit."

"He's been flying commercial—"

"Why the fuck would he fly commercial?" I respond, annoyed.

"Sloppy, maybe? I don't know. Anyway — I've been watching customs at all the Morrocan airports: Rabat, Fes, Casablanca — nothing so far."

"Fuck!" I say loud enough for Parks to look over with a little, curious frown. Nod my chin at her, mouth to her I'll be one more second.

"I don't like this—" I tell TK.

"I know."

"Fix it."

"Yeah." I can hear him typing away in the background. "I'm on it."

I hang up and Koa stands up, wordlessly asks me about the call with a look.

"We've lost Brown."

Declan crosses his arms over his chest and stares between us. "Well shit."

29

Daisy

A week or two's passed since New Year's and it's been strange between me and Tiller — normal, actually — but even that's strange.

We shouldn't be normal. New Year's Eve wasn't normal.

He went to bed early. I stayed up late with my ex-boyfriend, who maybe gave me the thrill of my life when he spent the night maybe flirting with me. I don't trust it. When I went to bed that night, Tiller was asleep and when I woke up the next morning, he was gone.

Gone for that fake work thing he had to go to to get away from all my favourite people, and I know that we're being stupid, and I know one of us should just make the call, because it needs to be made — but every time I think about doing it, I think about the morning after our Valentine's Day date, when he snuck out of my bed to go downstairs to buy me a coffee and I didn't hear him sneak out but I heard him sneak in, because someone sneaking in to my house are the sorts of sounds I've been trained to listen out for, so I hid behind a wall and hit him over the head with a medical text book, and the coffees went flying everywhere, and he fell to the ground, and I dropped to my knees, half in shock, half laughing, and he had such a big lump, and even still, he laughed and he pulled me into his lap, holding his head with his free hand, and he kissed me and said, "You don't have to do shit like that anymore, Dais." And for some reason, that was one of the most romantic things anyone had ever said to me.

Tonight after work when Tiller gets home, I can tell he's in his head.

He lies down on my bed face-down, climbs up my body, buries his face in my neck and doesn't say anything, just stays there quiet with these breaths that sound like sighs every now and then.

I put my hand on his head, push it through his hair, feel confused how I can feel like I need to end it and how badly I don't want to, even when I do?

Then there's a knock at my bedroom door.

Julian pokes his head in. "Everyone clothed?"

"No, Tiller's naked."

"Daisy—" Tiller growls before rolling over, fully clothed.

Julian rolls his eyes and walks in, nodding at Tiller with his chin.

"You were right." Julian nods once as he sits down on my bed. "About the painting. It was a setup."

I glance up at him, proudly. I love being right. "I know."

"So thanks." He shrugs, uncomfortably. Doesn't really like thanking people, my brother.

"Any ideas who?" I cross my arms and my brother nods cautiously, eyes flicking from me to Tiller.

"Yeah, I've got some ideas."[144]

I frown. "Anyone I've heard of?"

"Nope."[145]

My frown deepens. "Anything I should be worried about?"

My brother gives me a tight smile that he doesn't mean to be tight and ruffles my hair. "No, Face."[146]

My brother stands and walks towards the door. "I'm ducking out for a meeting — you two want anything picked up on my way back?"

Tiller shakes his head, doesn't say anything — and I can already tell by his face that we're about to get into it.

"I'm fine—" I flash my brother a quick smile to rush him along so I can just bloody get this over with.

Maybe tonight's the night?

Tiller shifts, propping himself up next to me. "What's he talking about?"

"Hmm?" I don't glance at him, I keep scrolling my phone, trying to keep this conversation light and vague as long as possible.

"What was he talking about?" he says again, taking my phone out of my hand and tossing it on the bed.

I take a breath. "I just told him something."

"What did you tell him?" His jaw's gone tight.

---

[144] God help them.
[145] He's lying.
[146] Another lie.

I try not to look annoyed and open my face up so the light can enter.

"I just saw something that didn't line up, so I told him." I shrug it off.

"You're being evasive." Him, annoyed.

"And you're being nosy!" I jump off my bed, crossing my arms and staring down at him. "You don't want to know, don't ask—"

"Daisy—" Tiller gives me a steep look as he stands up and glares down at me. "I'm an investigator at the NCA, my girlfriend can't be helping criminals!"

I take a measured breath. "He's my brother!"

"He's a criminal!"

"So what?" I shrug haphazardly. "Would you have me just let him get arrested?"

"Maybe?" he yells exasperated, and it feels like a slap.

"Get out." I point to the door.

"No." He stands firmer.

"He is my family!"

"You ran away from him, Daisy! For eight months!"

And this just tumbles out of my mouth without my coherent permission: "And they were the loneliest eight months of my life."[147]

That's like a slap for Tiller, I can tell with how his face goes. Then he's all silent for a minute, like I've pulled the rug of us out from under him.

"I'm sorry—" I start, and he shakes his head to silence me.

He's making the face men make when they're upset with you, but they're trying to be stoic and hold it together but they really want you to stop talking because if you keep talking a crack will appear and if a crack appears the veneer will chip away and they won't be composed anymore and they'll lose face when they already feel like they're losing.

"He is a wanted criminal," he over-annunciates to make his point.

"He," I point in the direction of the door my brother just walked out of, "is the only family I have!"

"Then why the fuck did you help me sabotage his job last year?" He towers over me. Says it like he thinks I'm a traitor for it too.

"Because I was saving him!" I yell.

---

[147] I shouldn't have said that.

Tiller shakes his head. "From what?"

The room goes quiet, like someone's vacuumed up all the air.

"Himself." I peer up at him.

His face starts to soften how it always seems to eventually when it comes to me.

"Tiller—" I reach for his hand. "I get that for you, raised how you were, there is good and there is bad, and there's nothing in-between. But for me—" I give him a look. "—how I was raised, in my world — which for me, is just as real as yours—" He rolls his eyes. "Yes, governed by different forces but with laws nonetheless, and what my brother did on that job violated the rules we created for ourselves so we could coexist in this life. Julian crossed our line, Julian did wrong by me on that day. But everything else… Everything outside of my forbidden three—" I offer him a hopeless shrug. "I don't know how to care about — not in the way you want me to."

Tiller sits back on the bed, drops his head in his hands and sighs loudly.

I pull his hands from his face and sit myself down on his lap.

"Can you just kiss me and forget about all of it?" I sigh, tired, feeling on the edge of tears and I use this to my advantage — I need this conversation to stop. I let my bottom lip go a little. It trembles and my eyes get a little glassy.

Tiller's face softens how I knew it would because he has a thing he thinks about when he's ready to break up with me too[148]— I know he does — I can see it, whatever it is, whatever he thinks of, play out in front of his eyes, and right when he's about to undo his seat belt, he thinks of me like that and then his face changes and instead of undoing it, he pulls it tighter.

He pulls it tighter. Slips his arms around my waist, pulls me in towards him, and he brushes his lips against mine and it's in the kiss.

A Judas Kiss, that what Jack always calls it.

The kiss before a break up.

I know it's coming. I can feel it like you can feel a sun setting. Everything gets cooler and darker and more shadowy and that's what we've been like since Christmas, and I should have called it already, but I think of him in the coffees on the floor, how it felt to wake up next to him, how he felt like morning light no matter the time of day;

---

[148] I don't know what it is though.

it's hard to walk away from the light. He is light, Killian Tiller. He's very beautiful, very light filled, he sees everything in black and white, I think — or he used to, I think the world is greyer for him now because of me — that's not what I want for him. It's not what I want for him and still I say nothing, I kiss him back, give him a Judas kiss of my own. Then, I guess they're all Judas kisses lately. He tells me he has to work. It's a lie, he just got back from work. He's getting sloppy.

It must be nearly 2am on our sinking ship.

I wander down stairs to the kitchen because my bedroom feels convoluted now, for about a hundred different reasons, and besides, the kitchen is and has always been my safe place.

So imagine my dismay when I walk into it and Magnolia Parks looks up all bright-eyed from the 18th-century Neoclassical white Italian marble table I bought last week.

I let out a groan. "Do you not have your own place?"

She sits up a bit straighter, folding her hands in front of her.

"I do." She nods once.

I lean down on the bench, rest my chin in my hands. "Is it being fumigated?"

She blinks twice. These big, wide-eyed stupid blinks. "No."

I lift an eyebrow up. "Then why aren't you there?"

She breathes out her nose, pushes back from the table and gives me an uncomfortable smile as she walks towards the door. "I'll go."

"Oh no—" I say, in quiet sarcasm. "Don't... stay..."

She stops, turns and looks at me with a tiny frown.

"You know, I didn't know." She crosses her arms over herself defensively.

I stand up, feeling annoyed already. "Know what?"

"That Christian loved me still." Her mouth goes pouty, and I can see more bubbling up to the surface, like she's wrestling with herself. "Sort of."

I give her an unimpressed look. "What?"

"I mean, maybe I did—" She shrugs. "—know. On some level."

"Oh, you mean like the obvious one?"

"No." She scowls at me a little bit, like I'm sinning against her by not following along with her incessant babble. "On the one where acknowledging that he still loved me meant acknowledging that he treated me special, and I didn't want it to stop because when it did I felt alone. And I don't like to be alone."

I stare over at her, confused. I — why did she…?

It throws me a bit, her being honest like that. I don't want to think it, but there's something disarming about her. It's annoying. I want to keep being annoyed by her, so I focus on the negative.

"Is that what my brother is to you?" I ask her, eyebrows up. "Just a thing for you to do so you don't feel alone while your boyfriend's off feeling up other girls?"[149]

I regret it as soon as I say it, to be honest. There's something about the way her face goes with BJ, you don't even need to say his name, just the air of him knocks the wind out of her, and I've got to be missing something… That there's more to it than I know, there has to be. That or she just loves him too much and stupidly, probably like me with Christian, and for whatever reason — and knowing her, it probably is stupid — they just can't be together.

I feel shit though as she turns back to the door.

I let out a little groan.

"Wait," I call to her and her head drops back as she stops. Like she thinks I've asked her to stay just so I can keep being a bitch to her.

She turns on her heel.

"What?" she asks, tiredly.

"I'm going to open a wine," I tell her, though I don't completely know why. Stupid, disarming bitch. "Do you want some?"

She stares at me for a couple of seconds, confused, then she nods quickly.

And then, I don't know what happens, it's an hour later and we're two and half bottles deep, sitting on the kitchen floor and she's telling me with a true and absolute conviction that my brother is definitely not an art thief while she braids my hair.

"Because he's just so sexy, and charming, and sexy with his hands and his mouth and his—"

"Okay." I frown, cutting her off.[150]

"He's just so like, obviously not an art thief.[151] Like probably he's a professional something. Like a, something very sexy and shouldery,[152] like a rower."

---

[149] That was mean of me, but I hate her, so…

[150] Because yuck?

[151] Okay, if you say so.

[152] ?

"A rower?" I repeat back as I roll my eyes, catching at my reflection in a soup spoon. I look quite good.[153]

"You would know how to braid hair." I sigh. "Girls like you always do."

She peers at me, confused. "Girls like me?"

"The popular ones." I shrug, annoyed that she's made me say that out loud.

She purses her lips, thinking about it.

"I have hair that's more like my mother's hair — you know, like, white person Caucasian hair—" She shrugs. "A bit wavy, it kind of — well, no, actually — I haven't done it in a few days, this is what it looks like."

And honestly, fuck her because it looks like a fresh fucking blow out.[154]

"But Bridget's is a bit more afro-textured, from our dad—" She looks confused at herself. "I mean father."

She corrects herself for no reason and I frown, because what?

"And anyway, when she was little, Bridget didn't like her hair in her face so I learned how to braid it for her."

Fuck. What a sweet story.[155]

I give her a bit of a glare. "Why didn't your mum just do it?"

She gives me a pleasant, little bleary-eyed smile. "Not that kind of mother."

"Oh." I nod once. I eye her, looking for something else to dislike. "Why is your posture so good, then?"

She shrugs. "I modelled a bit in high school."

"Oh."[156]

"But probably really, it's because if I slouched my grandmother would whack me in between my shoulders with a rolled up *Argumenty i Fakty.*"

My mouth falls open. "Was your grandma a Soviet?"

"Defector." She shrugs.

"And what's going on here?" my brother says, confused from the

---

[153] Annoying.

[154] I'm not joking, when I first saw her in the kitchen, I thought, *I wonder how long it takes her to make her hair look like that?* Zero time, it turns out.

[155] Ew. She's so annoying!

[156] Annoying.

kitchen doorway. Happy-confused though, maybe? And then Christian's head peers out from behind him and I sit up straighter and instantly Magnolia tugs me back by the shirt so I look less eager, and I don't understand how she can be so acutely aware of some things and painfully oblivious to others.

"You're back." Magnolia smiles over at my brother and truthfully, her face might look like it relaxes a bit in his presence.

Now that the boys are in the room and I have a sober frame of reference, I can tell we both are (but she in particular is) much more drunk than I realised.

My brother nods once, trying not to smile at her how I know he wants to. "I'm back."

"That took a very while longer than you initially said," she tells him as she stands to her feet and immediately stumbles.

Julian lunges for her and catches her before she even has a chance to get close to the ground, then plants her back on her feet, before he peers over at me.

"What the fuck did you give her?"

"Oh, you know — some absinthe, a bit of Flunitrazepam—" I shrug sarcastically and Julian doesn't like the joke. His face goes dark. "A Napa Valley Chardonnay that she didn't like, she said it was too big—"

"It was very big!" she whines.

Christian shakes his head. "Palette of a toddler—"

I smile over at Christian, pleased he's being mean to her too.

Magnolia points right in his face. "You take that back Christian Hemmes, you know I have a very fosiphticated palette!"

I giggle a bit and Christian cocks an eyebrow. "Do I know that?"

"Come on." My brother lifts her up onto his waist[157] and carries her over to the bench. "Let's make you a sandwich."

"No—" She pouts. "I wouldn't like for that."

She brings her knees up to her chest, hugging them. Then Christian takes a step towards her, frowning a bit. "Would you not?"

She shakes her head, eyes closed, stubborn and drunk.

He goes and stands right in front of his old friend, gets closer to her face than I'm comfortable with and then a jealousy that ruined us this time last year rears it ugly head again and I grab Magnolia's

---

[157] Revolting.

wine that she left three quarters full on the bench and throw it back in one go.

Christian stares at Magnolia, eyes pinched as they search over her face looking for something I don't understand. He nods his chin at her.

"Did you eat today?"[158]

Her eyes pinch back at him and she puts her nose in the air. "Yes."

"When?"

"Before."

Julian pauses at the fridge, looking over at them, frowning the same as me.

"When before?" Christian presses.

"Before Daisy came into the kitchen — I was sitting at the table, and I — remember?" She looks at me for back up. "I was sitting at the table?"

I nod along confused. I don't remember her eating though.

Christian flicks his eyes over at me to verify, jaw still tight as he looks back at her. "What was it?"

"What?" She blinks a lot and my brother folds his arms over his chest.

"What did you eat, Magnolia?" Christian asks, over-annunciating every word.

There's this strange, weighty pause as she thinks of the answer. And it could be because she's drunk, or it could be the other thing, I don't know — I feel a bit woozy too now.

"Leftovers," is what she goes with.

"You don't like leftovers," he tells her.

Her eyes pinch. "I like Daisy's."[159]

I'm curious now so I walk over to the sink to check if that's true and then I slip on some wine Magnolia split before they got here that I forgot about and I go down like the ship me and Tiller are on.

Both Christian and my brother reach for me, except unlike Magnolia, I do hit the ground.

"Are you okay?" Christian asks as he dives down on to the floor next to me.

---

[158] What?

[159] I don't honestly know if I had any leftovers in the fridge? I could have. But I'm not sure.

I feel stupid and embarrassed I fell in front of Her Grace the Lord High Empress of Decorum and maybe Blighty herself, so I nod quickly, trying to get up so no one can see my face flushing.

Christian sits back a little and offers me both his hands. "On three, yeah? One, two, three—" He pulls me up but my ankle gives way again — definitely not broken but at the very least, absolutely sprained and possibly a torn tendon — I'll need to look at it in the light.

Christian catches me this time, slipping an arm under my knees and scooping me up.

Magnolia's watching, wide-eyed, gripping my brother's arm like she's watching the exciting part of a movie. Julian's just standing there, watching, hint of a smile on his face, then he and Christian trade looks.

No words, just my ex-boyfriend's eyes saying to my brother, *I've got her*, as he nods towards the stairs.

Julian gives him a small nod and a subtle wink.

"Bring me up some ice," he tells my brother as he carries me out.

He says nothing as he carries me up the stairs and my heart's galloping in my throat because he's carried me up these stairs before for different reasons and him holding me like this makes me think of them even if I shouldn't.

"Christian," I say quietly.[160]

He glances at me, his face all serious. "Mm?"

"I don't think that she did eat."

His mouth pulls tight. "Yeah." He nods, his brow gets more serious. Keeps carrying me up the stairs. "No, I know. She goes like this sometimes when she feels—" He trails, gives me a quick smile. "Don't worry about it. I'll keep an eye on it."

He looks a bit sad and I feel a bit sad, not just because of him but for her because I wonder for the first time if her life is less perfect than I thought.

Christian opens my door, sits me down on the edge my bed, and looks down at me, shaking his head with a tiny smile. "Fuck, Dais, if you wanted my attention this badly all you had to do was—"

---

[160] If I were to be completely honest, and maybe I'm only being that because I'm a bit drunk, I feel nervous for her.

"Fuck you." I glare at him, propping myself up on the bed, despite how much it hurts me to do so.

He gives me a look and gives me a tiny shove that sends me off balance and straight back down. "Don't be stupid."

Happy brings up the ice and I flash him a quick smile, self-conscious of the fuss.

"Thanks, mate." Christian takes it from him before he manoeuvres my ankle and sits down next to me and carefully rests my ankle on him as he begins to inspect it.

"It's swollen," he tells me.

"I know." I say it like he's an idiot because obviously, I have eyes too, and anyway, I go to med school, not him. Or I did until I stopped being normal again.

He pokes the swollen area and I wince. "It's probably not broken though."

"I know."

"You just rolled it. Maybe tore it." He inspects my ankle more than he needs to.

"I know!" I say loudly as I roll my eyes.

He stares at me for a few seconds, jaw a little tight, then he clears his throat, nodding once, and then I see his mouth twitch. He looks at me out of the corner of his eye. "Are we fighting?"

Our eyes catch and my heart's knees buckle. I give him a look, my eyes smiling a tiny bit more than they want to.

"We don't fight."

He shifts the ice on my ankle and then stares at nothing on the other side of the room.

"Where's Tiller?"

I watch Christian a few seconds before I answer because I don't often get to stare at his profile and it's just… everything. He's perfect. Like he's made of marble. Forget David, he is the real masterpiece over there with those angles and that nose that looks like a Disney prince.

I swallow. "He's at work."

Christian nods once. "Oh."

"He doesn't need to be." I tell him.

"Oh." He turns to look at me. "Why then?"

My head drops back and I stare up at the ceiling as I sigh. "Tiller's whole identity is wrapped up in being good. And I'm…" I trail.

"The best?" Christian offers me[161] and I flash him a tiny smile that's probably sad at the edges because I don't know whether he means it.

"Not good... enough," I tell him.

He shakes his head, eyes angry. "Bullshit. He said that?"

I lay down on my bed, legs still draped over my ex-boyfriend.

I flash him a quick, wounded smile. "He didn't have to."

Christian shifts the ice again and looks over at me, cheeks a bit pink.

"Is it a bad vibe that I'm up here?"

I purse my lips. "Maybe?"

"Should I go?"

I cross my arms over myself, feeling self-conscious. "If you want to."

He presses his mouth together, squints a tiny bit. "I don't."

Our eyes hold and my face goes still.

"Then stay for a minute." I shrug.

He leans back on my bed so he's lying down on it too, except it's not bad, not even sort of in the vicinity of cheating because we're lying perpendicular to one another which is the least sexy angle.

He looks over at me, pulling my ankle up onto his chest and settling back into it.

"If it's all the same to you, Baby, I might even stay for five."

---

[161] I miss him so much.

Magnolia
11:43AM

> Not keen on me and your dad being mates?

It's a smidge weird but it's overall a bit cute

> I'm not a cute guy

I beg to differ

> I'm not

"okay"

> I'm not

Right

> Parks

Yes, cutie?

> Fuck you

> And should we have lunch with your dad though

.....

> What?

The cuteness of you

> No

> Your dad is famous and cool. I'm not cute. I'm using you

What ☐

?

Nothing
I guess that's fine

I suppose I'm using you too.

Great. Same page.

Cute of us.

There is no us

You're exhausting

Better than being cute

30

Christian

Nothing happened with me and Daisy the other night. I think maybe, possibly, if I wanted it to, it could have.

'If I wanted it to' — like I fucking want anything else in the world — I just don't want to fuck it up again.

Which is why I'm here.

At Vanna's hotel.

I knock on her door, she opens it and she's in this tight red dress; I know her pretty well at this point.

The colours she wears are indicative of her state of mind and I'll give you three guesses as to what it means when she's wearing red.

She grabs me by the wrist and pulls me inside — closing the door behind me and then pushing me up against it.

"We have some time before dinner—" she tells me, reaching for my top button.

"Actually—" I hold her hands out away from me and give her a quick smile as I walk further into her room.

She's got a residence in one of the penthouses at the Corinthia. It's a nice room. A bit white, cream and gold for me, but then again, Daisy's house is all those colours and that's my favourite place in the world, so take that to mean whatever you want it to.

She's why I'm here. Because I can't get Dais out of my head, because I feel like shit about it, like I'm doing the wrong thing by everyone — by Vanna, definitely, even by myself. And I feel like I'm doing wrong by Daisy too, and that's the one I care about.

I don't ever want to do wrong by her again.

I don't know what she wants or how she feels about me, whether there's anything more than what we are now on the horizon for us, but either way, I'm being shit with Vanna, staying now that I know I want to spend all my time with someone else.

Haven't called her in a week.

Kept her at bay with texts, the promise of a dinner soon.

I can never fully tell what she thinks we are.

Together, depending on the day. Sometimes, the papers say I'm her boyfriend, other times they say we're exclusive. For the most part we have been. I'd be an idiot if I wasn't aware that whenever she's with Rush Evans, she's shagging him, and they're together a lot. They're in the same film franchise. Probably half the reason Magnolia hates her. She's territorial like that. A couple months back Parks saw an article about Vanna and Rush in a shop window we walked by. She went in, picked it up — Henry made a face at me over her head. Funny timing, now that I think of it. She would be been with Jack-Jack. Doesn't matter to Magnolia though, unless she has BJ's, she wants everyone else's attention on the planet to be entirely focused on her. Anyway, the article was photographs of Vanna and Rush on set, not filming, his hand up her dress.

The day I worked that out was the day I realised how fucked all this was. Because I didn't give a shit.

Made me feel fractionally less shit myself for being in love with someone else our whole fucking relationship.

"Vans," I push my hands into my pockets. "Listen — we've gotta talk."

She gives me a bored smile. "Yeah?"

"I can't do this—"

"What?" She looks over at me, confused. "Dinner?"

I shake my head and gesture between us.

Her face shifts a bit and she blinks a couple of times.

"What are you talking about?" she says quickly.

"I don't—" I shrug. Why is breaking up hard even if you're not actually into the person? "I don't know what this is, Vans, but I don't want to do it anymore."

She blinks quickly, like her mind is rejecting what I'm saying. "Sorry, what?"

I don't say anything. Not really sure what to say.

"Is there someone else?" she asks, shaking her head, not under-standing, and my face falters suddenly. I feel like shit because all this time, I thought I was to her what she was to me — a distraction. That she was trying throw Rush Evans by chilling with me and that I was distracting myself with her, but how she's looking at me now, I feel like maybe I misread the situation.

I think she likes me.

I frown a bit and I wonder if how sorry I now actually am shows on my face.

"Vans, there's always been someone else."

There's a lot that you could say about Vanna Ripley, and yep, okay— a lot of it's bad. She's vapid, she's self-involved, she can be rude, she can be selfish — kind of everything you expect from a child star. She can't totally fathom that the entire world isn't just about her. But then, you know how when you spend more time with someone, you get to peek through the shit and they make more sense?

Being famous from five years old, it was crippling for her. Emotionally, relationally, socially. She's got a shit relationship with her dad and a complicated one with her mum. She's been an alcoholic since she was about sixteen. In and out of rehab, though people don't really know about that. Fame isn't easy, it fucks you up. It's fucked her up.

She's probably less fucked up when she's in London, but she's only here some of the time. All those stories you hear about what LA does to a person? They're about her.

Vanna dated a lad from school, Thatcher Hendry, used to knock about with BJ sometimes, so I've known her for a bit, but we were really sort of thrust together at Cannes this year. Parks and Rush were doing whatever the fuck Parks and Rush were doing — in some ways with that whole thing, Parks got on a track she couldn't work out how to get off of. Or she didn't want off it. I don't care what she says, I think she was into Rush. Or as into him as she could be while being completely fucked about Beej still.

I'm pretty sure she thought having me and Henry there with her might have thrown England off the scent of what she was doing with his best friend.

It didn't.

Them on the red carpet of that movie, where his hands were on her body, this one photo of her smiling as he whispered something to her — it would have pulled you apart if you loved her. Beej was shattered. Fully, properly wrecked. Can't even imagine for Tom, not just seeing her like that but with his best mate? Fucked up.

Guess I'm not one to talk.

That was when Rush and Tom had their big blowout. Unfortunate timing for Rush Evan's face that the England Family were on their boat in the Riviera when *The Sun* ran a series of photos of Magnolia and Rush lounging around together on a yacht, kissing and shit.

Total disaster, but anyway, me and Vans were on the same flight back to London after all that and we hooked up on it. And then — bang — we were hooking up. And I thought that's all we were doing until I saw my face with Vanna's on the cover of *The Daily Mirror.* NEW COUPLE ALERT.

Only that no one had alerted me.

I texted it to Vanna for a laugh and she wrote back "we kind of are" with the shrug emoji.

I didn't know what to say so I sent the shrug back and here we are.

Vanna shifts on her feet, pulls her shoulders back then pushes her hair over her shoulders.

"You know some people would kill to be with me."

"I know—" I nod. "This isn't about you, Vans. It's me — I just love someone else, that's all."

"Love?" She scowls.

I nod.

"Doesn't she have a boyfriend?"

"Yes—" I fold my arms over my chest.

"Then—"

"Vanna—" I push my hands through my hair, breathe out of my nose, tired already. "I'm not calling this with you so I can be with her, I'm calling it because I feel like shit."

She reaches out, touches my arm, her face sporting an immaculate display of concern that I can't tell whether is real or not. "Why do you feel like shit?"

"Because I am shit, Vans — I don't call you, I don't think of you, I think of her. All the time, and I don't want to feel guilty for that, but I do, and I don't know how to stop, so something's got to give. And I'm not giving her up again." I shrug, a bit helpless.

I've got both eyebrows of LA's darling up and unimpressed, her jaw's gone tense in a way that means that for the first time in how-ever long we've been whatever we are, I find myself thinking she's unattractive.

She dismissively gestures towards the door and I give her a tight, uncomfortable smile and leave without saying another fucking thing.

31

Julian

Kekoa wanders into my office the morning after a somewhat big and precarious night. Magnolia's at work, left even though I tried to convince her to not. Don't know why I tried to convince her not to. It's been a couple of weeks now, that grace period of post-have infatuation should be wrapping up. Not sure it is quite yet though.

Koa sits down in the chair at my desk opposite me, nods his chin at me.

"Did you let that little girl tell you what to do last night?"

Grind my jaw, annoyed. Two reasons. Little girl? He's a little prick. And also, just fuck off.

"Nah. I mean—" I scoff. "Just because she's such a fucking pain that otherwise I'd never hear the end of it—"

That particular reason doesn't move Kekoa at all. Doesn't bat an eye.

"So?"

I give him a look. "So then I'd never hear the end of it..."

He shrugs. "Then just give her the flick—"

And then I make a weird noise. Half scoff, half laugh, 100% incoherent, non-English garble. In response to my old friend telling me to give Magnolia Parks the flick, were I to type it, I reckon what I said was: Hkdfvvrt.

Kekoa's face pulls back, surprised. "Wow."

"What?" I frown defensively.

"Wow!" He's grinning now.

I shake my head at him, roll my eyes. "Stop."

"This is big—" Koa nods to himself.

"What's big?" Declan asks as he flops on my carved and yellow upholstered chaise lounge from the Regency era. Got delivered yesterday and the only thing I've thought about is doing Magnolia on it.

Decks on it now sort of maims that image out of my head. Probably good though in light of all this fucking shit.

"No, it's not big—" Keep shaking my head. "It's nothing. She's nothing."

"Who's nothing?" Decks asks and I ignore him.

"Right." Koa nods, folding his arms over his chest.

I give him a look, eyebrows up. "Right."

Kekoa leans back in his chair. "What are you doing later? Want to get dinner later at Connaught? I feel like that fig and prosciutto pizza."

"I'd get in on that." Declan sits up.

"Nah, I can't," I tell him. "I'm taking Parks to—" His eyebrows shoot up, amused. "Nowhere. Never mind. Taking her nowhere. Dinner sounds good."

Doesn't sound that good if I'm honest, but I agree to it because he's going to be a thorn in my fucking side otherwise, he and Decks won't let me hear the end of it because honestly, I did let that little girl tell me what to do last night and I have no fucking idea why. I was shitty at her, if I'm honest.

When we got to Jonah's club, she and Ballentine drifted over to each other how they always do. I gave them space for a bit but after a minute it just annoyed me.

It's weird, a couple of weeks ago Ballentine and I were friends. Technically still are, I'spose. Except now I think he's a fucking pain in the arse.

You look at this through the lens of Magnolia — and admittedly, all my lenses are a bit Magnolia-heavy these days — but no matter which way I look at Ballentine at the minute, either he's the lad that the girl I'm naffing keeps running off to see or he's the thing who hurt the person I'm spending all my time with. Can't say I'm that keen on him either way. But me and Parks, we aren't dating, I know what I'm here for — so I gave them a minute when we walked in. Tell her I see a mate of mine, which I did, and she was straight over to Ballentine like she does.

Touched his shirt, he smiled at her like his girlfriend wasn't right there next to him.

After a few minutes of it I got bored of talking to my mate, barely talked to him anyway, spent the majority of the conversation craning my neck to watch Magnolia and trying to eavesdrop and it was when

I think I heard her say "and then I came" that I decided to poke my head into the conversation.

"Are my ears burning, Tiges?" I flicked her a look and Ballentine rolled his eyes, so I reached for Magnolia, pulled her up off Taura's lap and over onto mine. Don't know why I did that, just felt like touching her so I hooked my arm around her neck, held her against my body as I stared Ballentine down.

"Maybe." Magnolia batted her eyes up at me.

I nodded my chin at BJ. "You don't look too happy, mate. Knickers in a bunch?"

Magnolia pinched my arm, gave me a glare she didn't mean. "Be nice."

I pressed my mouth against her ear and said loud enough for BJ to hear. "That's not what you said last night—"

"Okay—" Ballentine rolled his eyes. "We get it, you guys had sex—"

My head pulled back a little. "Are you talking to me?"

And then Ballentine squared up. "Yeah, I am."

Parks tensed up in my body, so I dropped my chin on top of her head to let her know I was still in control. Also to annoy Ballentine, but that was just a nice aside.

"If you've got something to say, big man, say it—"

And then he nodded his head towards the street. "Do you want to take this outside?"

Magnolia shook her head quickly. "BJ—"

I pressed my tongue into my bottom lip. "Love to."

Magnolia spun around in my arms, put her little hand on my chest like that could actually stop shit.

"Julian," she said, calmly.

"Woah, woah—" Jo jogged over. "What's going on?"

He let out a nervous laugh, looked from me to his other best friend.

BJ shrugged, waiting for me . "Go on—"

"Beej—" She whipped her head around at him, scowling, and I could tell she was scared. She should be. I've killed people for less. I pointed over at him.

"You better check your boy, Jo. That didn't not sound like a threat." I didn't break eye contact with Ballentine as I smirked over at him.

And then BJ cocked a smile, shrugged like he had a death wish.

"You know what, I think you're all talk, man—"

"BJ—" Magnolia whispered quietly. I could hear the fear rising in her.

"Do you?" I nodded my chin over at him, a bit amused. "Are you willing to stake your life on that?"

"Easy—" She spun back to face me, that hand back on my chest and another held my face so she could angle me how she wanted to.

I didn't mind the touching... I'd pick fights with that idiot all day if it meant she'd body block me how she was.

"Look at me—" She gave me a look. "In no world, do you understand?"

My jaw went tight at being told what to do, maybe a bit because it shitted me that she was protecting him. He needed it.

Jo came up behind me, drummed his hands on my shoulders. "Oi— bro, let's go to my office—" Jo nodded in its direction then pointed over at Ballentine. "And you, pull your fucking head in, you git."

I looked down at Parks.

She doesn't like drugs. I could tell when she saw me doing some coke the other day. I was at my desk and it was the middle of the day. She walked in, sort of froze in her tracks. Like it scared her or something. Bit weird.

"You mind?" I asked her, nodding my head toward Jonah. I don't know why I asked — why the fuck did I ask? I don't give a shit if she minds, but then, do I?

She did mind, I could see it on her face, but I decided I'd do it anyway because I do what I want.

I held her by the waist and kissed her heavily just to prove a point to Ballentine, and a bit because I didn't want her to be too shitty at me for it. "Be back soon."

I followed Jo there, and he sat in the chair behind his desk and reclined.

"Sorry." He sighed, shaking his head. "He's a fucking wanker with her."

I nodded and sat down across from him. Jo pulled out a little crystal jar.

"How's it going with you two?" he asked.

"Me and Parks?"

He scooped a little out as he nodded, shaping it into a little line.

"Good—" I shrugged. Regretted that immediately, made it sound like I give a fuck. "Fine."

He looked over at me as he cut it up. "You've been spending a bit of time together..."

I shrugged again.

"Yeah, I guess. She just won't leave," I lied as he passed me the straw. His eyes pinched at that, and I wondered for a second if he already knew that I'd been the main instigator in her not leaving. That she says she's going to go and do something and I say she can just do it at the house, pull an embarrassing amount of strings to make it be true.

"That right?" He nodded slowly and I felt like a twit. I took the line. I pinched my nose and nodded. "That's good. Where's it from?"

"Peru." He sniffed.

Jo sat back in his chair, arms behind his head, watching me for a second.

"She's not good with boundaries, you know."

I flashed him a look. "We're having sex, Hemmes... What sort of boundaries do you want her to have?"

"She doesn't know how to be alone." He scratched the back of his neck. "Never has."

I shrugged. "Worse things—"

"Yeah." He nodded again. "Be careful."

I scoffed. "Of?"

"Her." He shrugged as he put the jar back in the drawer.

"Yeah." I chuckled, rolled my eyes. "Right, she's a real little terror."

"I'm serious, Jules—" He gave me a look and I gave him one back. "She'll pull you in til she makes you fall in love with her and — and you know what—" He shrugged. "She might even fall in love with you too but not how she loves him."

I tossed him an unimpressed look and pushed back from the table.

Don't know why that annoyed me but it did.

Headed back in to the club to find her. Felt like I was proving something but I couldn't figure out what.

And then I saw her at the bar with him, standing so close their arms were touching and I don't know why my skin pricked, but it did.

I watched her watch him. My jaw tightened, brows dropped. Fuck her, I thought. Fuck her for looking at him like that. I don't know why, but fuck her.

I looked around the room and spotted a girl I've hooked up with before pretty quick. She had, like, peach-coloured hair or some shit. Bit too plastic for my personal preference, wore too much of that shiny makeup girls love to wear so they look sweaty or sparkly or some shit. Didn't really care though. Just wanted to feel up another body, prove Jonah wrong because I knew I wasn't falling for her — and maybe piss off Magnolia in the process.

"Hey." I ducked into the eye-line of the girl. Chelsea, I think her name was.

"Hi—" Her eyes went a bit wide.

"Remember me?"

She nodded, swallowed.

I slipped my arm around her waist. "I remember you."

I pulled her over towards where Decks and a few of the other boys were sitting, joined them, then pulled her down onto my lap.

Quickest way to get a girl to lean into you? Hand on her lower back. Girls fucking love it. Turns them to mush.

Chatted with Chelsea for a minute, reacquainted myself with her a bit because I'm not a fucking heathen, asked her how she did on that exam she had the morning after the night we hooked up (not well) and then I told her I liked what she did with her hair — I'm telling you, remember one thing, notice one thing and hand on her lower back and boys, you're in.

Don't know how long I'd been feeling Chelsea up on the sofa before Decks started elbowing me like a fucking maniac, and I looked over at him, annoyed before I saw these little hands on hips in front of me and I glanced up at a fucking pissed Magnolia Parks.

In a split-second move, I decided that being apathetic would piss her off more and I was happy that she was angry.

"Oh." I gave her a bleary smile. "Hey."

"Oh, hey?" she repeated back.

I blinked once and her eyes went to slits.

"Alright look, I don't care what you do when I'm not here, which is this, I presume—"

I scoffed and looked away and she ducked her head a little, eyebrows up waiting for me to give her my attention, which I did. Can't not with that face.

"I'm not done talking." She shook her head and my head pulled back, surprised and amused.

"You want to feel up random girls who are substantially less attractive than I am? That's your prerogative. But when I'm in the same room as you, I am all you see."

Probably never wanted her more than I did in that moment. Played it cool though.

"Is that right?" I asked her like I was bored.

"That's right."

I nodded my chin at her. "Or what?"

"Or we're done." She shrugged too easily and I know my face faltered and I know she saw it. "Which is fine with me, by the way. You've wanted me for — hmm..." She pretended to think about it and glanced over at Kekoa. "What would you say, Kekoa — four or so years?"

Koa was biting back a smile, gave her a little nod. "Reckon it's more like five."

Thought about firing him for that.

"You've wanted me for five years and I've sort of wanted you maybe for, like, three and a half weeks, so really, it's no skin off my back..."

I pressed my tongue into the side of my cheek. The fucking mouth on this girl — unbelievable.

"So." She tapped her little impatient foot. "What's it going to be?"

I held her eyes, trying to make her look away first, but she didn't. It was a power struggle and I was losing.

Licked my bottom lip, shook my head and shrugged. "You heard the boss—"

The other girl sort of tumbled off my lap onto the couch as I stood up and stepped towards Magnolia, slipping my arms around her waist.

She gave me a defiant look, chin in the air. "Don't you do that again."

"Fuck, you're demanding..."

"Oh, you have no idea... But you're about to—" She gave me a tight smile as she nodded towards the door. "Let's go. You're going to take me home and put me to bed."

I gripped her a bit tighter, knocked her chin up with my index finger so her eyes were on me. "Am I?"

She swallowed once, finally got a look on her face like she remembered who she was talking to.

"You are," she said anyway, trying to sound brave.

Tilt my head as I stare down at her. "In what way am I putting you to bed?"

"Surprise me." She said, indifferent.

I took her hand and pulled her downstairs to my car, lifted her up into it.

She kicked off her shoes and tucked her feet under her legs.

"You know it's a two way street, Tiges," I told the window a few minutes into the drive because if I knew it I looked at her, I'd get distracted.

"What is?" She looked for my eyes that I wouldn't give her.

"If you're all I see, I'm all you see—"

"Fine." She shrugged, shifting away from me, arms crossed over her chest all huffy, and I wondered if we were having our first fight.

Why would we be having our first fight though? We're not — whatever—

"Is it?" I kept poking, because I felt like it. "You over at the bar with your fucking mate—"

She let out a puff of air all indignant. "If you think you and I were doing the same things, we're in trouble—"

I gave her a tight smile and an indifferent shrug, "Lucky there is no we then, ey—"

Those eyebrows shot up again. "Isn't there?"

Stared her down. "Just fucking."

Her face crumpled, confused. "Who is?"

"We are—?" I frowned, a bit annoyed.

She looked over at me slowly, placing her hands demurely in her lap as she gave me this fucking smug smile, blinking until it landed.

I sniffed, roll my eyes, ran my tongue over my teeth, tried to look like I was over her shit, but you know what? I'm knee deep in it. Might wade a little further in, actually...

~

A couple of hours later, Magnolia bounces into my office.

Kekoa looks up from his phone, glances from her over to me, barely containing his smirk.

"Hi." She skips over to me, plants herself on my lap.

My eyes wander down her face and I feel happy to see her, find my hands make their way to her waist without a second thought.

"Hey." I give her a confused look. "What are you doing here?"

She mirrors my face. "You're taking me to Le Gavroche, remember?"

I see from the corner of my eye Koa sitting up straighter, peeking over, that nosy bastard.

"Oh fuck—" I sigh. "I forgot to call you. I can't do dinner."

"Oh," she says and her face falls, like I've disappointed her, and for some reason my heart drops a foot in my chest.

"Oh, okay. That's fine—" She forces a smile and she bunches up a bit how she does when she feels exposed.

"Sorry—" I shake my head. "I just—"

"No, you're fine!" She stands up quickly, and she physically removes my grip from her waist.

I stare down at my hands that she just displaced from my body and I get this strange flash through me of how much I hate not touching her. Why do I hate not touching her? Her cheeks are going pink so her eyes are getting brighter and I'm fucked because what am I going to do—? Say no to that face?

"Nah, fuck it—" I swipe my hand through the air. "I'll make it work—" I tell her.

"Will you?" Kekoa asks, licking his bottom lip and pocketing his phone.

"No—" Magnolia shakes her head, waving her hands around. "It's okay, I know you're busy. You have a—" She stalls, confused. "Well, am I correct in assuming it's a somewhat illegitimate business that you run?"

Koa starts laughing and I squash a smile.

"I'll go—" She turns and heads towards the door but I grab her hand.

"No you won't," I tell her, ignoring Koa, who's on his feet now, arms crossed, eyebrows fucking tall to really drive home his point.

I pull her back over towards me, put my hands back on her waist where I want them.

"This is telling..." Koa says from the corner.

Magnolia looks over at him. "What is?"

My friend and I catch eyes from opposite sides of the room and he goes to say something annoying but I cut him off. "Nothing."

"Oh, it's something—" He shakes his head, amused.

I nod my chin towards the door. "Ko, get the fuck out—"

"Ooh," he chimes, just to shit me. "You gonna kiss her with that mouth?"

Magnolia looks between us confused and I roll my eyes, make sure she can tell I think he's an idiot.

But yeah, I am.

32

Daisy

They say that at around 2:17 in the morning her lights went out.

Me and Tiller's lights went out a little bit ago. Probably before Christmas I'd say, but definitely and undeniably by New Year's Eve, our lights were out and maybe if we actually listened we might have been able to hear the rumbling start of us bending and creaking and cracking apart down the middle.

It was weird, he doesn't forget things, really. It's very unlike him, but I guess it's forgivable, what with our sinking ship and all. He's just trying not to drown.

I spotted it on my vanity in the bathroom after my mid-afternoon shower, his badge. Just sitting there as out of place as he is here. I sighed when I saw it because I felt like I should bring it to him.

It would be the nice thing to do. The girlfriend-y thing to do. It's not like I'm all that busy. I only have my private lessons with the doctor my brother hired three days a week, and this isn't one of those days. I already did the reading he asked me to do this week in an hour, and I invented an essay topic for myself. Four thousand words on the ethics of pharmaceutical pricing.[162] No one asked me to. It's not even on topic, I just miss learning and my days are unfortunately empty at the moment, thus I don't have a reason to not go and bring it to him other than it's not what I wanted to do with my day. Not because I'm selfish, I'm happy to help him. It's just — you know in romantic comedies, when the girl walks into her boyfriend's office and everyone makes a big deal of her and them and listen, I don't have a silly daydream of me walking into the NCA and him kissing me in front of all his policeman friends, confessing his love for me, announcing how unshakable we are — though that would be nice and

---

[162] Spoiler alert, the ethics for pharmaceutical pricing are there are none.

maybe we'd kick our way through the freezing water to a lifeboat and survive the night. But we are shakable and he's not going to kiss me when I walk in. He hasn't kissed me since we had that fight about my brother a few days ago. That's a bad sign, right?[163] Sometimes he'll hold my face in his hand and just stare at me. His eyes looks sad like he's sorry and he misses me, and I stare back like I am too. He loves me still, I know that, it's not a question. It's just not enough anymore. But love never seems to be enough to coast by on these days.

I wander down to my brother's office looking for Miguel. They're watching Formula One reruns on the TV over his fireplace and they both look over at me.

"That new?" I nod over at a glass sculpture.

My brother glances at it, nodding. "Walter Furlan."

I walk over to it, expecting it.

"Like it?" Julian asks, standing by me.

I don't usually like Abstract Expressionism but this is quite exquisite — the craftsmanship is, at the very least.

I shrug because I don't feel like giving Julian the satisfaction, nor do I want him thinking it would be fine for him to start displaying Impressionist and Expressionist pieces around our home.

"Are you good to drive me somewhere?" I ask Miguel as I turn to him. He stands and nods.

"Where are you going?" my brother asks.

"The NCA."

"Ah." He nods coolly. "Just what every criminal wants to hear his live-in sister say."

I cross my arms, annoyed. "Don't say 'live-in' like I'm here by choice."

"Just trying to keep you alive, Face!" My brother tosses an arm around my shoulder. "And to what does the NCA owe the pleasure?"

I flash him Tiller's badge and he plucks it from my hands.

"Oi, do we really feel like returning this is the right choice?"

"We do." I nod once.

My brother gives me a look. "Are we sure?"

"We are." I nod again. "I don't feel like you stealing my boyfriend's secretive badge is going to help our relationship."

---

[163] You don't need to answer. I already know.

"And they need all the help they can get!" Miguel announces and I give him an unimpressed look.

"You know—" I stare over at my bodyguard. "The older you get the more you become like one of the grumpy men in the balcony on The Muppets."

Miguel sounds the keys on his index finger and wiggles his eyebrows up and down. "That's what I'm going for."

I roll my eyes and walk towards the door.

"While you're there will you check I'm still their number one?" Julian calls after me.

"Even if you are—"

"I am," he interrupts and I ignore him.

"—I don't think they keep your photo on a cork board or anything."

Julian rolls his eyes. "Tell Tills I said hey."

I flash him a thumbs-up and head to Miguel's car.

"You and Tiller are doing okay?" Miguel asks after about a minute of silence.

"Mmhm." I nod, looking out the window.

"So that wasn't you I heard crying the other night when you had a fight and he left?"

I side-step the question. "He didn't leave, he went for a run."

"Til 3am?" Miguel asks, shooting me a look.

Is that what time he was gone til? I didn't know. I cried and put on *The Great British Bake Off*[164] to fall asleep. Tills was there when I woke in the morning. We didn't talk about why we fought and I don't remember why we did now, but we sort of always fight these days, now that our lights are off.

"Want me to come in?" Miguel nods at the door as we pull up outside.

I shake my head. "I'll just be a minute."

I check in with security, tell them who I am. Their eyes pinch at me how you'd imagine they would and they pat my body down even though they don't do it to anyone else who walks in. Luckily I left my gun in the car.

I take the elevator up to Tiller's floor and ask for directions to his

---

[164] Imagined there was someone else in my bed watching it with me which made me cry more.

office. I'm escorted there by a man who makes no effort to conceal his suspicions of me, and when Tiller's nowhere to be found, I just leave the badge on his desk.

I wish for a second that this man wasn't hovering around me like he is, so I could have a moment in here, try to imagine a life where I might fit in, where Tiller and I work without having to compromise the parts of ourselves we each love more than we love each other — but the man doesn't offer me that. He stands there impatiently by the door, glaring over at me for no reason other than my last name, and there aren't many places in the world I feel intimidated in, and it bothers me that I feel so here. I cross my arms over my chest feeling self-conscious and say nothing to the man as I walk past him, making my way back towards the elevator. There's a build-up of agents waiting for it and I get a wave of nervousness, thinking about how it might feel to stand alone with them, without Tiller[165, 166] there to protect me. I don't think they'd hurt me, but you never know and my gun's in the car, so I decide to take the stairs.

"Are you going to come to the bar with us again tonight?" a woman says. I can't see her, she's somewhere in the stairwell.

And that's when I hear his voice. My heart does this little skip of relief, like it thinks for a second it's safe now, but it isn't.

"I should probably go to the Compound — see Daisy, you know?"

"Why?" says the woman, and even though I can't see her, I know it's his ex. "So you can keep putting off breaking up with her?"

I freeze. Listen for the sounds of them. They're not walking either. I hear my boyfriend sigh. "Who said I'm breaking up with her?"

"Oh, come on!" groans the ex. "You volunteering for every possible assignment and staying at the bar til closing every night this week?"

Someone's feet shuffle and I back myself up against the wall so they can't see me but I can keep listening.

"What are you waiting for?" the ex presses.

"It's complicated, Michelle."

"Yeah." She snorts. "She's a criminal and you're not—"

I can't see his face, but I want it to be completely offended or be down and out furious, or at least for him to just frown at her

---

[165] Or Julian.
[166] Or Christian.

defensively. Anything more than what I think it must look like as he sighs defeated. "Don't call her that."

"Why?" She sounds so capricious. Happy to drive wedges between us. Maybe that's fair though, I guess I drove one between them. "It's what she is. It's actually all she is," she tells him, and I wait for him to jump in, tell her I'm so much more than that. That I'm clever and beautiful and funny and nearly a doctor and that I'm so many other things but in particular I am his girlfriend and she should speak about me as such but he says nothing.

Somewhere in the North Atlantic Ocean at 2:20am on April 15th, 1912 the Titanic sank shortly after she broke in half.

"I'm going to be in archives," Tiller tells his ex. "Come grab me before you leave."

"Okay," she says.

Footsteps start making their way towards me and I jog up two flights with the stealthy silent skills a criminal like me would have.

I wait til I hear two different doors close and then I jog down the stairs, my blood boiling and my heart equal parts a bit broken and a bit relieved. I climb back into Miguel's car and put my gun back where it belongs on my body.

Miguel frowns over at me. "All good?"

I stare at him for a few seconds, not saying anything.

"Take me to The Lion's Gate."

"Isn't that a cop bar?"

"Yes."

Miguel's face falters. "Is that where Tiller is?"

"Nope." I pull out my phone to text someone. "But he will be."

Christian
1:35PM

Hey

Hey

Do you have plans later

Not important ones. Why?

Can you meet me somewhere?

The Lion's Gate

Yeah.

When?

5 o clock

Ok

Are you good?

Don't be late.

33

Julian

"Knock, knock," says a voice and I look up from my desk.

Josette Balaska pokes her head around the door of my office and then closes it behind her.

"Jose!" I grin, standing to my feet and walking over to her.

"Hi!" She beams, throwing her long arms around my neck and pressing herself up against me how she usually does.

"What are you doing here?" I ask, confused.

She usually tells me when she's coming into town.

"Wanted to surprise you." She shrugs. "I haven't heard from you in a little while which I know means you've got a lot on your plate — thought I might be able to help distract you..." she tells me as she pushes me backwards towards the chaise. I fall back onto it and stare up at her, eyebrows up. Takes me by surprise, even though it shouldn't. She lowers herself down onto my lap, straddling me like she's done innumerable times before this.

Any time Josette's in town, we do this. Make a point of doing it. She's insanely good in bed. The best way to blow off steam. We've done this for years, and as she bends down to kiss me, I feel myself frowning at her even though I'm trying to smile.

"Are you okay?" She laughs, a bit confused.

"Yeah—" I shake my head. "I'm good, no, yeah—"

I've probably never been more attracted to a person than I am to Josette. A lot of freckles, short, choppy, bleached blonde hair — these almost purple eyes. She's insanely fit. Sexy, funny, down to try anything. Really cool, chill, doesn't overthink shit. She's just a good time. So why then, when Josette is kissing me how she's kissing me, grinding up against my body as I'm leaned back on this couch, am I thinking about Magnolia Parks?

She's all I'm thinking about. How her mouth looks in the morning.

How she looks in the shower. How her hands feel when she slips them into mine without asking.

I don't know why I'm thinking about that — or her, even. I'm not doing anything wrong. We're not exclusive. We're not even a fucking we. She said she doesn't care what I do when she's not here — she's just usually here. Maybe that's the weird part. I haven't had time to hook up with anyone else for a few weeks now and I'm just feeling off about it, but it's Magnolia's fucking fault because she's always about, organising wardrobes no one's asked her to, working from my desk on my lap because Jonah's right, she doesn't know how to be alone. But none of those things answer the question of why the fuck I'm think-ing about how Magnolia fucking Parks can't be alone when Josette has her hands down my pants. Because this is fine. Good, even. It's what I want — because me and Parks, we're not together and and for the fucking one hundredth time, there is no we.

Josette reaches behind her neck and undoes the tie of her dress. It falls down her body, nothing on underneath it, just this body I've touched too many times to count before, so I touch it again. Almost out of habit, I think — because I'm still thinking about Magnolia. Thinking about why I'm thinking about Magnolia, actually.

And it's a lot — Josette all over my body, Magnolia all over my mind, me trying to convince myself all of it means nothing and it's just Jonah's fucking fault, getting in my head, saying I'll fall in love with her and shit. I don't fall in love. Fuck love. I don't need that chink in my armour and maybe if all that shit wasn't weighing me down I would have paid attention to what I'm actually hearing going on around me: a faint "Don't be silly, I go into his office all the time—"

That might have been a sound I'd react to instead of background noise I'm ignoring as I try to fuck my friend so I can prove to myself that I don't give a shit about a girl that I think I might really actually give a bit of a shit about.

"Oh," says the voice of that girl, standing in my doorway.

"Magnolia—" I sit up a bit. She stares over at me eyes a bit wide, a bit glassy, Decks behind her, holding her arm in a residual way of him trying to stop her coming in here.

Her eyes move from my face to the naked torso in front of it, down to where my hands are on Josette's body and then up to her face — Josette doesn't cover up, doesn't reposition herself, just stares over at Magnolia like she's an inconvenience.

"Oh — uh—" Her eyes flick to the ceiling. "I've walked into the wrong room — I was — I'm sorry — I was looking for the exit—" she says like an idiot. Magnolia turns on her heel and scurries out.

I throw Declan a look, and he cringes.

"Sorry, man — she's hard to control."

I roll my eyes at him, but don't I fucking know it.

I shift Josette off me and to the couch as I stand up.

She glares at me. "Who's that?"

"That's Magnolia," I offer, not really sure what else to say.

"Who the fuck is Magnolia?" She crosses her arms over her bare chest.

"I—" I trail. What the fuck is happening? I never don't know what to say. "We're — I mean, we've been—" I shake my head. "Just give me a minute, yeah?"

"For what?" She frowns but I'm already walking away. I look back over my shoulder. Hold up a finger.

"One minute—" I tell her and then I go after Magnolia.

Run after her, if I'm honest. Never ran after a girl a day in my fucking life and I'm running after this one — I hear my front door slam a couple of seconds before I reach it. I swing it back open and stand at the top of the stairs that lead into our courtyard.

"Magnolia—" I call.

She's speed-walking towards her car. It's the white Aston Martin DBS Superleggera, not a town car. She must have been planning to stay.

"Magnolia—" I call louder, jogging down the stairs. "Parks!"

She keeps ignoring me and I catch up to her right when she gets to her car. I'm annoyed now. I don't chase after people — that was fucking embarrassing — running after her, calling her name, her ignoring me in my own house, in front of the men who work for me. Makes me look stupid.

"Oi—" I grab her arm and spin her around so she's facing me. "I'm talking to you."

"Oh!" Her eyes go wide and she tries to look all bright-eyed and fine and shit. She shakes her head. "Sorry — I didn't hear you."

"You didn't hear me?" I repeat. "In this trafficless cul-de-sac? I just heard a bird lay a fucking egg—"

"Really?" She gives me a a tight smile. "However did you manage to hear that over the sound of that girl taking her clothes off on top of you?"

I breathe out of my nose. "You're upset—"

"I'm not upset." She shakes her head.

I give her a look. "Okay..."

"I'm not—" She shrugs lightly.

"Okay." I nod, not buying it. "You seem upset..."

"What would I be upset for, Julian?" she asks loudly, like it proves that she's not except all it does is show that she is. A bit, at least. Don't know what it says about me that her being upset makes me sort of happy — whatever it's saying, I know it's shit.

She waves her little hand between us.

"I know we aren't... a we, and that— you know... that you're like... that."

My eyes pinch.

"I'm like that?" I repeat.

She nods. "With other girls."

"Right." My mouth pulls tight. Nod once.

"So it's fine—" She shrugs like she doesn't care, but I reckon she might.

"Is it?" I ask, head tilted, looking for her eyes.

"Yes." She avoids my eyes.

"Is it really?"

"Yes!" She stomps her foot and I stare down at it amused.

She's wearing this little white dress and a white coat, her legs poking out at the bottom — fancy her in white, kind of.

I frown at her because she's fucking annoying, knock her headband a bit, just to annoy her.

"I'm not sleeping with her."

Magnolia's face softens from full-blown hurt to some kind of confusion.

"Oh," she says as she straightens it.

"I was before but—" I shrug.

She crosses her arms over herself, impatient and annoyed. "Before like — five minutes ago or—?"

"No—" I toss her a look. "Before like November."

The last few Novembers, if I was going to be completely forthcoming but I won't be. Probably not the time to mention it now. And why the fuck would I mention it anyway?

"I might have if you hadn't walked in—" I shrug. Just being honest. Her face swaps back to hurt.

"But you did walk in…" I give her a look. "So now…"

"Now what?" She frowns.

"Now…" I shrug, voice trailing. "Not anymore."

She sucks on her bottom lip and I look for her eyes again because I get the hype. "Why not anymore?"

I ignore the question and hold her face in my hand like I like to do, duck a little so she's forced to look at me.

"You've gone pale," I tell her and that loses me her eyes again. She shakes her head. "I'm fine."

I angle her chin, put her face where I want it. "You don't look fine."

She straightens up and gets this proud look in her eye that's one of my favourite things about her. I don't know when I started to have favourite things about her?

"Well," she says, nose in the air, "Maybe you don't know me as well as you think you do—"

I sniff, indignant. "Is that right?"

"Mmhm—" She shrugs, eyebrows so high they're basically flying off her face.

And then we just stare at each other, both defiant, both waiting for the other to buckle. I don't want to buckle, I don't understand what the fuck is going on because I don't run after people, I don't care if people aren't fine, if they're going pale, I don't care if a girl I've hooked up with sees me with someone else, but I'm already swimming through my brain trying to work out how to get it out of my head — how she looked when she saw me with my hands on Josette. And why the fuck is she looking at me like that anyway, all hurt and betrayed and shit? She's in love with someone else. So what the fuck is going on?

That's what I want to know as I'm staring at her and she's staring back, and I guess I leave it a few seconds too long because she swallows and her eyes go how they do right before the waterworks start.

She shakes her head. "I'm going to go."

She opens her car door and I close it straight away.

"I don't want you to go," I tell her.

She doesn't turn around, doesn't even look at me, just opens it again. Infuriating! She's fucking infuriating! I reach past her, slam it shut, then grab her face with both my hands, bang her backwards against her car and kiss the shit out of her.

Her body relaxes against me and she does that thing girls do when they melt into a kiss, and I kiss her until she takes a staggered little breath and looks at me with the only eyes I'm interested in seeing.

"I want you to stay—" I tell her, slipping my hand around her waist. "Come back inside."

She says nothing. Blinks a few times.

"Please?" I say, like the idiot I am. Begging this girl. Fuck, who have I become?

She nods, finally, eyes all shy.

I take her hand and lead her back into the house, hands on her waist, walking behind her and up the stairs.

About halfway up, I pause and turn her around so we're eye to eye, nod my chin towards my room.

"Will you go wait upstairs for me?"

She frowns. "Why?"

"Because I have to talk to Josette."

Magnolia breathes out of her nose impatiently, arms crossed now. "What about?"

I uncross her arms, put them back at their sides where they belong. Try to show her I'm still the one in control even though I suspect at this point we both know that's not entirely true.

I push my hands through my hair. "Because I'm going to ask her to leave."

"Right." She nods once, not tracking. "But why do I need to go upstairs?"

"Because."

"Because why?" She asks, she stomps her foot when I say nothing back. "Are you hiding me?"

I shake my head. "No."

"Are you going to try to have sex with her quickly and then come back upstairs to me?"

I press the tips of my fingers into my eyes. "What the fuck did BJ do to you to make you ask that?"

Her shoulders slump a little. I shouldn't have said his name. She closes up when I do.

I sigh as I tilt my head, looking for her eyes. "I don't think she's going to take it well, and I don't want her to be embarrassed—"

"Oh." Magnolia's face softens. "Why wouldn't she take it well?"

I press my tongue into my bottom lip. "We've been sleeping together a very long time."

"Oh." Her eyes drop and she goes back to pouting and this time I do smile a bit. Push that hair of hers that needs no pushing behind her ears.

"And I'm about to tell her that we're stopping."

"Oh." Her eyes crawl back up to meet mine, face opening back up. "Why?"

Why am I telling Josette Balaska that we're not having sex anymore? Because when you walked in on it you made a face at me that I never want to see you make again, you fucking pain in the arse.

That's why. Not what I say though.

Instead I roll my eyes.

"Just go the fuck upstairs, alright?" Shake my head at her like I'm annoyed. Maybe I am, I can't tell anymore. "Why the fuck is everything difficult with you?"

And then she's back to sulking like she always does when she's scolded; indignant and confused about the world not going exactly how she wants it to, bottom lip sucked in, nose pinched, brows down, and I grab her face again and kiss her as big as I can because I don't think I can help it.

"That's why," I tell her and she sort of nods — barely — she's all flustered. I like her flustered.

She turns and walks up the stairs, closing my bedroom door behind her.

I cover my face with my hands, blow some air out of my mouth, and then walk back into my office.

Josette looks up at me, now completely naked on that chaise of mine.

I press my hand into my mouth. Close the door behind me.

"Got rid of her?" She smiles.

Shake my head, cringing. "Not exactly."

She looks confused, and I nod my head back in the direction I came from.

"She's upstairs."

Josette sits up a little, chin lowering. "She doesn't strike me as the kind of girl who's into a threesome..."

I sniff a laugh. A solid read.

"She's not... Listen—" I walk towards her, pick up her dress and offer it to her. "I can't do this with you—"

"What?" Her face freezes for a minute — embarrassment, I think, and then instantly anger. She jumps to her feet and points up. "Who the fuck is that?"

"I don't know—" I shake my head. "I don't know how to explain what she is—"

"Is she your girlfriend?" she asks.

I give her a look. "You know I don't do girlfriends."

And we both know Josette would have liked to be mine if I'd let her.

Her jaw goes tight. "You also don't do girls who don't let you do me, so what is this?" She throws her arm towards the door again.

I shrug. "I'm figuring it out."

"Do you like her?" she demands, eyebrows up.

"I don't know—" I shake my head.

I don't know why I said I don't know. I didn't know I didn't know til now.

Josette shrugs with her mouth. "It's a yes or no question, Jules—"

"No, it's not—"

"Just answer it." She shrugs like she doesn't care. Snatching her dress from me.

"No—"

"No, you don't like her?" she clarifies, eyebrows up as she tugs her dress back down her body.

"No—"

"So you do like her?" she asks me, eyes pinched.

"Fuck. I don—" I'm shaking my head a lot. "Yeah — maybe—?"

She stares at me a few seconds, eyes all glassy. It's the worst when girls cry. I can't handle it, and here she is, my old friend, tearing up in front of me, and all I can think about is how Magnolia fucking Parks looked when I kissed her against her car.

"We've been having sex for four years, five seconds ago I was standing here in front of you completely naked and you're telling me you can't do anything about it because you like some slaggy toff?"

My jaw pulls tight.

"Don't call her th—" I say before I'm interrupted by being smacked across the face.

Not a slap, not quite a punch.

I lick my bottom lip. Taste blood.

She stares over at me, staggered breathing, a bit afraid. As she should be.

Nod my chin towards the door. "You might want to leave now..."

"Or what?" she asks, squaring her shoulders up, trying to sound brave.

I lean in close towards her. "You don't want to know."

And then I leave her, walk back upstairs to the fucking twist I've told myself til now is just a post-have infatuation. Might just be a regular infatuation at this point.

Bit embarrassing, me getting a bloody lip from the naked girl downstairs.

I walk into my bedroom, close the door behind me and look over at Magnolia.

It takes her a couple of seconds to register my lip and then she flies over, hands on my face.

"Oh my God!" She goes on her tiptoes. "Did she hit you?"

I nod, watch her move around me a bit, fascinated by how she does it.

You know, in all the fights I've been in, I've never had a girl there on the other side of one. I mean — I've had the scathing bed-side-manner and un-tender hand of my sister, but no one in that sexy Florence Nightingale way...Where they're worried about you, and they want to fix you and tend to you, and you know what? It's not half bad. Her looking at my split lip like it's a knife wound.

"It's quite bad." She peers at it, less scared of blood than you'd think she'd be.

"Is it?" I brush my finger over it. Cringe for a second. More blood than I was expecting. Worse than I thought but probably not quite a stitch.

"Did she punch you because of me?" She frowns, eyes not on me so I duck down for a hit.

"I mean, usually when she's here — yeah, it ends with a different kind of banging."

Magnolia pinches me in the ribs and I squirm, let out a muffled grunt and then she darts to my bathroom and grabs a few tissues.

"Come on—" She passes them to me and then walks out of my bedroom. "Let's get you cleaned up."

I follow her in silence down the stairs and sit down at the table, watching her dart around my sister's kitchen and then I cut the legs out from under the daydreams that are cropping up in my mind about how she fits in here. She doesn't. It's not like that.

Can't be.

She finds a tea towel, wets it, then fills it with crushed ice. She walks over to me, stands over me in my chair, tilts my head back and starts dabbing my lip gently.

"Ow!" I smack her away.

She smacks me back without a second thought. "Don't be stupid."

Don't like being hit or hit back — these fucking girls, man — I grab her by the waist, pull her down on to my lap.

She's tense at first, relaxes after a second, adjusts herself and the ice on my mouth. Pushes her free hand through my hair like it's something she needs to do and not just what she wants to do.

Tilt my head as I watch her. "How's a girl like you know how to fix a busted lip anyway?"

She pulls back the cloth and inspects it, flicks her eyes from my mouth to my eyes, back to my mouth. "BJ gets into l—"

"Oh fuck —I take it back — I don't—" I shake my head, pulling a face. "I don't want to talk about him."

She swallows.

"Okay." She nods.

I touch her face. Don't know why. Lean in to kiss her and realise there's blood on her dress.

"Oh, shit—" I stare at it, pointing at it.

She looks down and then back up at me, gives me a tiny shrug and a shy smile.

"It's fine."

"It's ruined."

She eyes me. "Yes, perhaps."

I stare at the mark. "Sorry."

She shrugs again, shifts so she's closer to me than she was already just being on my lap, hooks her elbow around my neck and looks down at me with a face that might be the end of me. She brushes her mouth over mine, her hand in my hair, then she gives me half a smile.

"I always knew you'd be an expensive fuck."

34

Daisy

The Lion's Gate is this pub in Vauxhall, about two hundred years old — a lot of wood, a lot of stained glass — the kind of place where if you ask for anything but a beer they'll mock you for the rest of the night.

I've never been before. It's the kind of place people like me grow up hearing about — it's legendary. Once when Romeo was sixteen, he came in here on a dare. He had to ask for a pint of Guinness. He did it. Skulled it, nearly got shot in the process.

It took a lot of convincing for Miguel to allow this plan to happen. I told him to go home and he laughed in my face.

I begged him to wait in the car — that was an absolute no-fly zone.

I tried for him to be in the back corner watching over — still no.

So we agreed on him standing about two metres away, pretending to ignore me how he always does.

And now I'm waiting for Christian — the small mercy here is I really dressed to the fucking nines to drop Tiller his badge. In case I had to see that stupid fucking Michelle, I wanted her to feel bad about herself when she saw me so I wore the Virtus Animalier embroidered mini dress[167] with a black cardigan[168] and these chunky bronze-y heels.[169] I didn't buy a single thing I'm wearing other than my earrings and my bag,[170] they just showed up in my wardrobe — so I guess thank you, Magnolia?[171]

---

[167] Versace.

[168] The Scarlet cashmere cardigan; Khaite.

[169] Aura 105mm patent-leather sandals; Gianvito Rossi.

[170] My Heart box bag; Dolce & Gabanna. Chunky chain drop earrings; Federica Tosi.

[171] And also, fuck you and fuck off.

He walks in at about 5:15 pm. Black baggy pants, cons and a black YSL hoodie.

He spots me straight away, over by the bar on a stool by myself.

Maybe his face lights up a bit, maybe it doesn't.

"Hey," he says, his eyes flicking over my face. "You good?"

I flash him a quick smile and nod. He doesn't buy it.

"What are we doing here?"

"Here?" I look around like I don't know what he means.

"Yeah — here." He flicks his eyebrows up and doesn't wait for an answer before he steps towards me, presses half of his body against mine as he orders himself a drink. "Can I have a pale ale, mate? Hoppy. Darker, if you can—" He flashes the bartender a half-smile then looks over at me, still leaning around me even though there's space for him to just stand next to me like a normal person and I hate myself for being like this already — reading into anything I can.

"What do you want?" Christian asks.

"An imperial stout, please."

He gives me a look. "Look at you, with your dark beer — full of surprises."

He hands me my drink and our hands brush and our eyes catch.

"What are we doing here, Dais?" he asks, waiting.

I shrug innocently. "Just having a drink."

He takes a measured sip.

"This is a cop bar."

"Is it?" I blink about seven times.

"Yeah—" Christian presses his tongue into the inside of his cheek, amused. "Who knew?"

I bat my eyes, lift my shoulders up and down.

"Baby—" He tilts his head so I mirror him because I'm on full-flirting with him now.

"Yes, Christian?"

"I'm not an idiot — I knew what The Lion's Gate was before I came. Came anyway—" He gives me a look. "I'm here, Dais — I just want to know what I'm in for."

And right on cue, Tiller walks on in with all his work friends.

Tills doesn't see us but Christian clocks him and frowns. He turns back to me and takes a step closer as he waits for an answer.

"Right. What's going on, Dais?"

I give him a tight smile. "I'm a criminal. That's all I am."

"Bullshit." Christian touches my arm as he shakes his head a bit. "He said that to you?"

"His ex-girlfriend said it—" I shake my head. "He said nothing."

Christian's jaw goes tight.

"Want me to sort him out?" My ex-boyfriend nods his head towards Tiller and I shake my head back.

"No, actually—" I take another step closer towards him. "I want you to kiss me."

Then there's a brief pause. For a half a second I feel stupid and embarrassed and then Christian cocks a smile and nods once. "Yeah, okay. Can do."

He stares at me for a few seconds, gaze dancing between my eyes and mouth, and my heart is Seabiscuit in my throat, and I can't believe I'm about to kiss him again. I've tried my best to be faithful to Tiller, even when it cost me. As much as I could, I didn't think about Christian Hemmes. Thoughts creep in, comparisons happen, but I did my daily best not to meditate on the way the sun would hit his cheekbones and the colour his mouth goes after I've pressed mine against his.

"Ready?" he asks, brows very serious.

I nod once.

He pushes my hair behind my ear like he always has, then keeps his hand at the back of my neck and slips his other hand around my waist and pushes my body up against the bar behind me.

He's slow to kiss me — careful almost? — and I wonder if he doesn't want to do it? Then he swallows heavy, brushes his mouth over mine and my eyes close without a second thought, because even considering all the circumstances, I just want to swim in this for a second. Bask in the glory of his mouth against mine. And I remember in this split second the first time we did this — that night forever ago, when he kissed me, I felt like this. This stupid floaty feeling, like how those NASA pictures look of the galaxies with the space dust all pink and purple and stars and planets — that's kissing Christian Hemmes. Even if none of it's real.

And then I feel someone saddle up next to us.

Showtime.

I open one eye, my mouth still pressed up against Christian's. Turn my head ever so slightly so Christian and I are still technically kissing.

"What the fuck, Dais?" Tiller asks, teeth clenched.

Christian pulls away, wiping his mouth with his hand and stands tall. Smirks over at him.

"Oh, hi." I beam up at him.

"What are you doing?" he asks loudly.

"Me?" I touch my chest. "Oh, nothing, I'm just here with my fellow criminal—"

Our eyes catch and Tiller's shoulders slump.

"Daisy—"

"Doing criminal things, because that's all I am, actually, did you know—?"

His head rolls back a bit. "Dais—"

"Fuck you, Tills—" I yell loud enough for the people around us to stop talking and look over. "That's all I am?"

He says nothing, just stares down at me with this pained look on his face.

"Yep," says Michelle and Christian gives her a sharp look.

"What's your deal?" I nod my chin at her. "Is your thing with me rooted in the fact that throughout your relationship with Tiller, he was obsessed with me? Or more because—" Michelle's eyes go to slits and Tiller, once again, says nothing, so I keep talking.

"—he'd blow off actual dates with you to stand in my doorway for five minutes and pretend like he was looking for my brother?"

"Actually, my thing with you is just because you're dirt."

Christian squares up and stares her down.

And then what happens next happens quickly. My hand has been on my gun since the second Tiller walked in. I know where he keeps his too. Shoulder holster.[172] So Hollywood... so American... so easy to reach into the lefthand side of his jacket, pull it out and point it at him.

Tiller's eyes instantly go dark and jagged. Like it's me who betrayed us, not him with his silence in that stairwell.

And here we are, both barely alive in that icy ocean water. Only room for one on this floating door, and fuck you, Tiller, I'm not going down with the ship.

The magic of this moment is that Christian knew. Somehow he knew. His gun is out and it's pointed at Michelle whose eyes are wide

---

[172] Galco's Miami Classic II in the brown leather.

and sparky, like someone who enjoys confrontation for confrontation's sake.

"Oh—" I glance at it out of the corner of my eye. "You got a new one."

"Yep." Christian nods. "Just upgraded to the P220 Legion Full-Size."

"Nine millimetre?" I ask.

"Ten." He nods.

Tiller glances between us.

Christian shrugs. "I just wanted something weightier in the hand, you know?"

I nod. "What's the finish on that?"

"Stainless steel."

"Nice." I nod as I stare Tiller down.

Miguel's guns are drawn too, skimming the surface of everyone around us and I won't lie — there are, in turn, about eighty guns pointed at us.

Tiller glances around, eyebrows up, like he thinks it's funny in front of his friends but I know he loves me[173] because I can still see it hiding under the fear in his eyes he's trying not to let me see.

"You three are going to take on the whole of London PD?"

"Nope. Wouldn't be a fair fight..." I jut my jaw out, shake my head. "We'd fucking cream you—"

Christian sniffs a laugh.

"Daisy—" Tiller starts, brows low like they always are around me and I shake my head at him, gun pointed square at his face.

"We're done," I tell him.

"Yeah." He rolls his eyes. "No shit."

I shrug like this is easy, holding a weapon at the head of a man I have loved the better half of a year, a man who's protected me and fought for me, who I've killed for. I press the barrel against his forehead over my favourite scar he has, as though I'd ever blow a bullet through the part of his face I've touched every night like a lamp I rub to get to sleep. Like us ending what we were isn't something I've wrestled with for the last two months, even when I knew it was the right thing to do, even when I knew I still loved someone else, letting Tiller go has felt impossible. I mightn't have done it if he didn't do

---

[173] It's just not enough anymore.

it for me today in the stairwell. And now here we are. Fighting in a bar, me hurling my ex-boyfriend at him and a literal gun in his face just to hurt him, and Tiller's there looking at me the way I've always been afraid he might. Like I am really nothing more than a criminal.

"Put the gun down, Dais—" he tells me.

I nod broadly towards the room. "Them first."

Our eyes lock again, a stand off between us that's the final nail in the coffin of what we were.

Tiller waves his hands downward. "Just a misunderstanding guys, lower your weapons."

Slowly, they do, about a hundred eyes pinched and suspicious.

"I'm going to keep this—" I pocket Tills gun. Christian lowers his but doesn't holster it.

"I'll come pick up my things tomorrow," Tiller tells me.

"Don't bother—" I shake my head. "I'll have one of the boys bring it to Dyson's. Or—" I gesture towards his ex-girlfriend. "Would you rather they drop it at Michelle's?"

He scoffs. "You're one to talk."

"Yeah, well — I figured you weren't saying enough for the both of us." I give him another dismissive shrug and his face falls. I wave my hand vaguely towards Michelle again. "Have fun in the... archives." I give him a fake, unimpressed smile.

"Fuck you—"

"You already have—" I poke him in the chest and he looks down at my finger like it's a foreign object. "On duty, what's more... out of your jurisdiction and everything—" I cringe.

He breathes out his nose calmly. "Actually Dais, I never told you this but my boss told me to come that day—"

That actually does feels like the slap he wanted it to and Christian glances at me like he's sorry for me but I'm a goddamn Haites, raised by my brother, I can't back down from a fight, not even if someone hurts me.

"Yeah—" I shrug again with a grimace. "But did they mean it like that?"

Christian's mouth purses into the shape of an O and it makes me feel clever.

Tiller drops my eyes and looks away.

"Hey, just so you know, Tills—" I duck down to meet him. "I

know that the reason we're actually done is less because I'm a criminal, and more because you're intrigued by it all and you're afraid of it."

His face freezes. It's just for a second but I see this quick-as-a-flash tumbleweed of fear and acknowledgment roll past his eyes.

"Piss off," he tells me like he hates me.

"Gladly—" I nod once and salute him as I back away. "Inspector..."

Christian grabs my hand and pulls me to the street. We run a hundred or so metres down and into a crowd so they can't come after us.

He checks over his shoulder and Miguel pushes me further into the crowd.

"That's you not doing anything?" Miguel asks, eyebrows up. "Get your fucking head blown off to flip off your boyfriend?"

He's angry, shaking his head, brows down.

I don't really have an excuse so I give him a weak shrug.

"Ex." I clarify unhelpfully, and Miguel just gives me a look.

"Don't tell Jules—"

"Oh—" He gives me a different look, steeped in anger. "I'm going to send him a fucking singing telegram about this one, Daisy, you twat—"

Christian tilts his head, staring at me. "Are you okay?"

I nod, looking back over my shoulder.

"He's a prick," Christian tells me and I flash him a sad smile. "You were together a bit though..."

"Yeah." I nod.

Christian notices my hand still in his, lets it go. My hand falls to my side and the moment feels clunky.

He clears his throat. "How long for?"

I purse my mouth thinking. "Ten... maybe nearly eleven months?"

"Oh, shit—" He sniffs, annoyed.

"What?" I frown and he shakes his head like he's stupid.

"I kind of hate that he beat me out—"

I roll my eyes like I think he's stupid too but the honest to God truth is that no one ever could.

I swallow and stare up at him. "Thanks for kissing me."

He laughs, shaking his head. "Anytime."

We smile at each other in a way I don't know that I fully understand. I might hope to understand it but that's not been my lot with Christian so far.

He takes a step back from me then pauses — brows go low and he takes two closer towards me.

"It was just a kiss, right?" he asks with a frown.

No. It never just an anything with you.

But I say "yes."

"Cool." He nods a bunch. "I'll see you later, then—" He turns and walks away and I watch him go and then he stops. Turns around and squints over at me.

"Can I drive you home?"

I look over at Miguel who sighs and rolls his eyes. He points at Christian threateningly.

"No stops along the way."

He nods.

"Get off Vauxhall Bridge as soon as you can. Take Lupus Street, through Pimlico, understood?"

"Yes, sir." Christian nods obediently. "Do you think I'll have a minute to drive her through Ebury Square Gardens and murder her quickly—" Miguel glares over at him, unimpressed, and Christian makes an uncomfortable noise. "Not in a joking mood today? Got it. Home in a jiff."

Miguel exaggeratively rolls his eyes and walks away.

Christian turns and gives me a triumphant smile then nods his head down the street. "Car's this way."

We spend that drive home mostly just debriefing about the night, about all the guns that were pointed at us, how he knew to pull his gun out too, what we might have done if it escalated more than that, how much my brother will never let me out of his sight again.

The car ride is so easy and sweet and mindless and it goes so quick. It should take about fifteen but this time I think it might only take ten, and I feel like the universe is cheating me and so when he pulls into our courtyard I stay sitting in his car, in silent protest.

I clear my throat and don't look over at him.

"Do you want to come in?" I ask my hands.

He opens his mouth to say something and then frowns a bit. Breathes out his nose. "I shouldn't."

I look over at him. "Why?"

He frowns more. "I just... shouldn't."

I cross my arms over my chest, sort of annoyed. "I just broke up with my boyfriend—"

"Exactly—" He gestures at me. "You *just* broke up with your boy-friend—"

"Are you joking?" I ask loudly, unclipping my seatbelt.

"What?"

"You're fucking unbelievable—" I shake my head. "I couldn't get rid of you a week ago, you turned up everywhere — and now I'm available and—"

He shakes his head at me. "What are you talking about?"

"You only want me when you can't have me." I shake my head at him.

His face falters. "That's not true—"

My eyebrows shoot up. "Is it not?"

"No," he tells me.

"Then what is it then?" I shrug. "Now that you're my brother's friend you won't touch me?"

His head falls back like he's tired and he pushes his hand through his hair how I wish he was pushing it through mine.

"Whatever—" I roll my eyes, kick open his car door and throw myself out of it.

I hear Christian growl under his breath and he jumps out of his car, jogging over and standing toe-to-toe with me.

"Can you stop?" He shakes his head. "What the fuck is the matter with you—?"

"Nothing." I try to move past him but he blocks me.

He scowls down at me. "Why have you suddenly gone mental?"

"Get out of my way—" I shove him and his eyebrows shoot up, pissed off and a bit vindictive. He raises his hands in the air, takes a step back, like he's rid of me.

I stare at him for a second or two, hate that we're here again — one kiss? That's what I get? One kiss to remember how good it was, how much I love him and want him and we're back to fucking here? Where he wants me when he can't have me and he's done with me after one fight?

I move past him, hope he can't tell how crushed I am as I do and our shoulders brush then he says, "Actually — no. Fuck it."

He grabs me by the waist and bangs me backwards into his car, pressing his mouth up against mine in this perfect, rushy way.

He kisses me for what feels like ages — a new age — or an old one? If me and Tiller were the Titanic, Christian is New York City on the horizon. He's the tea and blankets that wrap me up on the Carpathia. He's the Statue of Liberty — I'll give him my tired, my poor, my yearning to breathe free—

I love the feeling of his hands on me, one still in my hair, the other firmly on my lower back, pulling me into him.

I pull back a tiny bit, tracing my finger just under the band of his Calvins. "Will you come inside now?"

"After," is all he says before he boosts me up onto his waist, his hands sliding up my dress and then — you know—

Every loud and perfect symphony, every immaculate clash of pastel colours in every sky that this stupid, beautiful world has ever given us — he is all of it. He is the drug. Every high I've ever chased, every good feeling, every momentarily filled void. His hands on my body, his mouth on my mouth, him inside of me — everyone else is Vicodin, morphine and fentanyl, but Christian — he's the good stuff.[174]

He's heroin.

And that sounds bad, I get it — but it's not. It's just — him. I think he's rewired my brain. My dopamine reward system? I know nothing more rewarding than his hand pushing hair that isn't out of place behind my ear. There's not a thing on the planet I love more than that except for maybe him, and I don't know if I can — if I'll have that again, but I'm having this again at least.

I'll take what I can get.

---

[174] To clarify, I am not a drug addict.

35

Christian

It's about 2am, we've taken things inside and I can't believe my fucking lucky stars.

Me and Daisy — I don't know how. I don't even really know what but I'm down for the ride.

We've been at it a good few hours now and Dais goes to the bathroom for a minute so I sneak out of her room to grab some wine from the cellar. I don't want the night to stop.

I want her back.

It doesn't seem like the time, really — her and her ex just calling it and shit. I'll give it a bit, but I'm just glad to be here.

So I sneak down, grab her favourite bottle of red and creep back up. I don't turn the lights on; I know these hallways even in the dark like the back of my hand. I've thought about them since the day I stopped being welcome in them.

I'm midway down the hall back towards the bedrooms when I hear a noise.

I turn around to spot the source, keep walking and bump straight into someone who starts screaming straight away.

I know who it is half a second into the first scream and clamp my hand over her fucking dumb-arse mouth.

Magnolia's practically thrashing in my arms, freaking out in the darkness, smacking the shit out of me.

I turn her around and stare at her a few seconds, wait for her to realise it's me.

"Motherfucker—" She covers her face, exhausted. "It's you—! Oh—" She breathes out, relieved. "Oh my—you scared the shit ou—"

I look at my old friend, baffled. "I can't believe you just said 'motherfucker' — Honestly didn't think you had it in you—"

"I know." She says, her hand on her chest, catching her breath.

"You fuck a gang lord for a couple weeks, Parks, and you get a real mouth on you."

"I thought I was about to die — oh my God! Phewf—" She shakes her head, bending over, trying to catch her breath and then she pauses. "Hold on—" She stares at my lower body for a few seconds.

Worth noting that I am just in boxer briefs.

"Wait. Are you in—" She — Magnolia Parks — my boundary-less childhood friend, reaches down and plucks the band of my Calvins before gasping dramatically.

"J'accuse!!" She points at me like the idiot she is.

"Shut up—" I growl.

"Oh my God!" She whispers.

I give her a steep look. "Magnoli—"

"OH MY GOD!" she whisper-yells.

And then there's this exchange of dialogue between us that's maybe, in context of everything that happened before, miraculous. Also, it's probably because of what happened before, because of the different ways we've known each other and the length of time our relationship has stretched that we can communicate at the rapid (and admittedly, ridiculous) speed that we do.

"You love her—" She pokes me in the chest.

"Shut up!" I poke her back.

"Just tell her!" She shoves me.

"Fucking stay out of it!" I shove her back.

"You're being so stupi—" she tells me, smacking me in the chest a bunch of times and I shake my head at her wildly, right up in her face.

"Well, you're always stupid and I never say anything."

Her eyes go to slits. "Then you're a terrible friend!"

"You're a terrible friend!"

She smacks me in the arm about forty-five times. "I was voted the best friend in the whole grade when—"

I smack her back in both her arms. "We were nine!"

"You act like you're nine!" She's just hitting me now, all over, nowhere targeted or specific.

"What the fuck nine-year-olds are you hanging out with?" I ask, eyes pinched as I try to hold her by her head away from my body.

"I don't hang out with nine-year-olds you stupid idiot!"

She tries kicking me. "I'm not a idiot, you're an idiot—"

Then someone clears their throat and Magnolia and I freeze.

I have her in a headlock and she's trying to backwards-kick me and has fish-hooked my mouth—

Both Haites siblings are standing there, frowning over at us.

Daisy's in a t-shirt (mine) and knickers and Julian's in a towel.

He squints over at us for a few seconds then says, "You two good, or...?"

Magnolia laughs nervously. "This isn't what it looks like—"

"What does it look like?" Daisy asks, not smiling at all.

Magnolia does an over-exaggerated, dramatic shrug and I shake my head a lot. "I'm not still in love with her. At all," I clarify.

"Right—" Daisy nods, not totally buying it.

"No, he's right. He's not. At all—" She clocks Julian, eyes big and earnest. Like she wants him to know that part. "Like, at all."

Interesting.

She clears her throat.

"I just think Christian's being a bit of a—" She cranes her neck to stare at me for a few seconds. "...ninny—" I glare at her, she glares back.

Jules tilts his head. "Why's that?"

"Because he won't just tell Dai—"

And I clamp my hand over her mouth again and laugh loudly to muffle her.

"She's drunk—" I say.

"No, I'm not!" She says, but it's all muffled from under my hand. "I'm sober!"

Julian flicks her a look.

"Well, not sober." She concedes, mostly to herself. "But not drunk. Sober enough to know—"

"Don't listen to her—" I say loudly, then I realise I'm still holding her — our bodies practically tangled from fighting how we were. I make an uncomfortable sound and shove her away from me and into Julian's arms who catches her without looking.

Magnolia gives me a stern look, pointing over at me. "I can't say that I cared too deeply for that, Christian—"

"Oh no." I roll my eyes.

Julian rests his chin on top of Parks' head and pulls a face that's both confused and probably amused.

And I reckon he knows because he glances over at his sister, one eyebrow up.

"What's this, then?" He nods his chin at her. "Where the fuck are your trousers?"

"I took them off her." I grin over at him, proud of myself.

He blows some air out of his mouth, uncomfortable, and Daisy rolls her eyes, turning on her heel and walking back into her room.

"We're good, yeah? Parks? We're fine?" I stumble to say to her, my eyes wide and pleading and I think she goes to say something, call me a name, tell me I'm weak and an idiot, but then she gives her eyes a little flick and breathes out of her nose.

She purses her mouth. "We're going to have a little talk about that shove—"

"Right, okay—" I toss her a look. "Shaking in my boots."

"Fine." She stomps her foot. "Julian's going to talk to you about that shove—"

He turns her around and leads her back to his room.

"I'm not," I hear him tell her and she lets out a frustrated growl.

I go after Daisy, closing the door behind me. She's sitting on her bed, eyebrows up and I laugh a bit nervously — I don't know why.

Nod my head back at the door.

"Is he into her?"

"I don't know — it's hard to tell." She purses her mouth, thinking on it. "He's never had a girl around this long before, so maybe?"

"Never?" I blink and she shakes her head.

"Josette, when she flies in. Soleil when he's in Paris — they never stay, though."

"It's been a few weeks now, hasn't it?" I try to count backwards in my head, thinking back to when they started up. Daisy nods.

"But my brother doesn't fall for girls—" She shrugs. "He doesn't let himself."

"I think he's starting to..." I give her a look. "Magnolia—" I shrug like she's a hopeless absolute. Maybe she is. Not that Daisy's going to like that, and she doesn't — she scrunches her face up and I feel like I need to tell her, even though I don't want to.

"So, look—" I rub my mouth. "While we're talking about her..."

Daisy looks up at me with these round, nervous eyes I hate to see on her.

"I kissed Magnolia."

Her whole face folds in half, looks crumpled and I feel like shit. "What?"

"Not yesterday—" I shake my head quickly, and I think she breathes out, relieved. "In New York. Like, six months ago or something."

"Oh." She keeps frowning so I keep talking.

"I was sad. She was sad—" Shrug again, like Daisy's going to give a shit that Magnolia fucking Parks was sad.

Daisy's face has gone all pinched; she frowns uncomfortable and folds her arms over her.

"Did you sleep with her?"

My jaw goes tense.

"Almost."

That looks like it winds her, shoulders slump a bit, the bend in her eyebrow goes deeper and I feel like shit.

"But you didn't?" She swallows, eyes staring at me big and round.

I give her a look, confused. "We never have."

Her face changes. "Never?"

"Nope."

"Ever?"

My mouth pulls and I shake my head. "Never."

"Oh." Her mouth makes the same shape as the sound and her eyes drop.

"Yeah—" I duck so we're eye-to-eye even though she doesn't want to be. "I probably could have just clarified a bunch of shit for you if you'd just asked me—"

That doesn't go down well as she glares over at me.

"Or you could have told me—"

"I'm trying to now!" I tell her, annoyed.

"Right." She nods. Her mouth pulls as she flicks her eyes up at me. "Sorry. So what happened?"

I sit down on the bed next to her.

"Well, nothing, in the end—" I shrug. "A kiss in an elevator and some clothes coming off."

"What clothes?" she asks without any hesitation.

I look at her, confused. "Like, literally what clothes?"

She stares at me and nods.

Fucking girls, man — they're so dumb and weird.

"Uh — okay—" I toss Dais a face to let her know I think this is a

239

weird exercise but whatever, I'll oblige her stupid girl questions if it helps me win her back. I'd lop off my fucking arm if it'd help me win her back. "Her top... my shirt... buttons of my jeans."

She's staring at the corner of her room. "And then you stopped."

"Then we stopped, yeah." I nod.

She flicks her eyes over at me. "Why?"

I give her a big, dumb shrug. "Because of you— I love—" Fuck. I clear my throat. "I was — at the time—I was..." My voice trails off because I'm chicken shit.

Because I was in love with her then just how I'm in love with her now. I flash her an uncomfortable smile and she doesn't give me one back. Shocker. She loves a good grump, this one.

"And I said that, and then Parks said she still loved Beej, and then it just felt...fucked—" I shrug again. "So we stopped."

"Oh," she says quietly. "Okay."

I watch her, cringing a bit. "Are you... okay?"

She nods, not looking at me, and then she smiles quickly. "Yeah."

"Yeah?" I lift up my eyebrows.

She lies back down on her bed, staring up at the ceiling.

She looks over at me,

"Thanks for telling me."

I lie back down next to her.

"Just... happy to be here," I tell her, trying to sound casual about it but I'm not. Only place on the planet I'd want to be and she looks over at me, best face I ever saw, with those honeypots for eyes and I don't know what I'm doing, whatever just happened, what we've just started up again. I don't care. Whatever it is, I'm in.

36

Daisy

"Oh my God." Jack blinks, hands on his face as I regale him with the story of me and Tiller, our demise, and perhaps more importantly,[175] what happened after it.

He sits back in his chair at the coffee shop we're at. "I can't believe it. What does it mean."

"Nothing—" I shrug, petting Julian's dog's head mindlessly. I don't know why I brought him with me, he just followed me out the door. "It's Christian — it means nothing—"

"It's Christian—" He gives me a look. "It means everything."

I frown over at him and sigh a little.

"I'm sorry about Tiller though, Dais—" He takes a sip of his beer. "Are you alright?"

Am I alright? Yes is the short answer, but I don't like saying that. Saying that I'm alright combined with the fact that the very night Tiller and I broke up I had sex with Christian from sundown til sun-up makes it sound like everything Tiller and I had meant nothing to me, and that's fundamentally not true.

For a long while it was everything to me — it was literally all I had. And then my old life invaded our normal space like a parasite invades its host, and, I mean, the minute I moved back in here I knew.

I could feel it, like a shift in the tides, change coming whether I wanted it or not.[176] You know how they say a lot of the time, the family of cancer patients are okay sooner rather than later? Because they grieve the person in the process? A slow-motion kind of losing

---

[175] Not more importantly, but sort of more importantly. Do you know what I mean?

[176] And I didn't want it. Even if sometimes I did.

a person. I'd been grieving us since that night. We both had been, I think.

Do I wish he'd defended me more? Yes. Do I feel a tiny bit bad about kissing Christian in front of him like that? Also yes, but I was raised by my brother, what do you expect?

I haven't heard from him, before you ask. Nor do I expect to... I can't imagine that him seeing me with Christian's tongue down my throat would have propelled us into civil territory. Before Christian left the next morning he asked whether I thought Tiller might have used anything he saw when we were together against my brother, and I honestly never even thought that — it never even crossed my mind as a possibility. Tiller's not like that. He's not spiteful. Maybe he might be now, though.

"Well—" Jack gives me a look. "How was it?"

I look over and my eyes must turn to mush because Jack sits back in his chair.

"That good?"

All I can muster without bursting into flames on the spot is a small nod.

"Don't be shy, Dais — spill!"

"We had sex outside," I tell my greyhound. "Against his car?"

"The car?" Jack asks. "The driving lesson car? He still has it?"

I nod. I hope he never gets rid of it.

"Wow." He nods, pleased. "Full circle. I love it."

I roll my eyes at him as though I think he's being stupid, but I'd be lying if I said I hadn't thought it myself. I toss the dog[177] a french fry.

"As good as you remember?"

"Better," I say, solemnly.

His eyebrows flick up. "Better than Tiller?"

"Better than anyone."

Jack swats his hand through the air. "That's just the love talking."

"I don't love him!" I sigh, indignant.

Jack stares at me for a couple of seconds before he cracks up and I frown at him.

"I don't—" I shake my head with my pants on fire. "I've been in a relationship with someone else for nearly a year—"

---

[177] I refuse to call him LJ. I also don't know why he's here. He just followed me out the door and into the car.

"So?" Jack butts in. "You can love two people at once — you know that." He shrugs. "You've done it the last 365 days…"

I stare over at Jack and the rims of my eyes feel heavy.

"I can't love him again," I tell him quietly.

He leans across the table and takes my hand. "Well, therein lies the problem, Dais — you never stopped."

I drop my head back, and stare at the ceiling.

"You just put it away—" Jack tells me. "Pretended like you didn't, but you know what happens when you love someone how you love him — when you don't get over them or past them, it's like, he's a compressed little coil under your foot, but take the pressure off, it just springs right back to size."

My shoulders slump and I sigh, feeling hopeless. I hate how loving him makes me go.

"And the coil might even grow back thicker than before—"

I shake my head at him. "Well, now you're just mixing metaphors and I hate it—"

"Don't lash out at me and my metaphors because you're stuck in love," Jack says, looking down his nose at me as he throws back his beer. "Besides, things might be different now—" He adds with a shrug. "He loved you in the end, didn't he?"

I go to answer and then I see him breeze through the cafe doors. Always late, that Romeo Bambrilla.

"Shh—" I shoot Jack a look. "I don't want Rome to know."

Jack gives me a quick nod of solidarity.

"Hey—" Romeo drums his hands on Jack's shoulders, kissing him on the top of his head. He leans over the table to kiss me dangerously close to the edge of my mouth but he's always like this.

He sits opposite me, puts his feet in my lap. I push them off and he puts them straight back up, grinning over at me.

I roll my eyes at him.

"Don't want Rome to know what?" Rome asks, eyebrows up. Jack chuckles as I frown in protest and go to say something but he cuts me off. "I learnt your lips a long time ago, Face—"

He flicks me a look like he's impressed with himself then nods his chin over at me. "Tell me."

I purse my mouth. "I broke up with Tiller."

He nods, smiling like he's proud of me.

"I heard you held him at gunpoint?" I grimace a little and Romeo gives me a tiny wink. "My girl."

"And…" Jack says, annoyingly.

"And." I give him a glare. "I slept with Christian."

Romeo's face pulls ever so slightly, if I hadn't spent every day of my youth gazing at it I'd likely have missed it, but I didn't miss it, I catch it. A flicker of hurt.

"But!" I add quickly.[178] "You wouldn't care about that, because you're fucking Tavi!" I remind him merrily.[179]

His jaw goes tight and he licks his bottom lip.

"Dating," he clarifies, just to hurt me back and it works.

It'll always work. I can be not in love with Romeo anymore and still love him. I can be past him, and still find it completely unnatural to think of him dating anyone else besides me.

He's just a bit of a trick knee for me. Always will be.

"Dating." I eye him down with a nod. "Old habits, hmm?"

He flicks his eyes, annoyed. "You're one to talk—"

I scoff, annoyed. "I never ch—"

"I slept with Taj Owen," Jack interrupts, trying to stop us before we really get going.

"What?" I blink over at him. I shake my head, processing. "What happened to Gus?"

Jack covers his face, a bit stressed. "He broke up with me."

Rome frowns. "Why?"

"Because I slept with Taj Owen," Jack says into his hands.

Rome and I stare over at each other.

Taj went to school with us — Jack's first love, though it was fairly unrequited. Taj really led him on. He likes boys and girls see? And he plays both of them like fiddles.

To Jack, he's the one who got away.

To me, he's the one I'd drop a piano on, any time, any place.

I reach over and touch Jack's wrist. "How did Gus find out?"

---

[178] A bit because I don't want to start something, and as well a bit because I hate to hurt him ever at all and somehow reminding him he's with Tavi makes it seem less bad. Not that it's bad, I'm not saying it's bad. Just, if it was— you know? Never mind.

[179] But not really merrily.

"Um—" Jack flicks me a quick look before staring at his thumbs. "He saw us."

"Oh." I nod, wide eyed at the same time Rome sighs.

"Shit."

"Yeah." Jack nods. "I forgot I gave Gus a key. He never used it before—" He tells us, shaking his head. "He's so measured and calm. Sometimes that's boring, right—"

"Sure?" I say, but I'm not really sure because Gus is great and Taj is a cyclone.

"So Gus just came over?" Rome asks. "And you were—"

Jack nods. "Yep."

I grimace. "Was Gus angry?"

Jack's face shifts, it goes from pinched and stressed to a kind of sorry you don't want to see people you love sporting.

Romeo's face pulls, eyebrows lifting into a grimace. "Don't say he was disappointed…"

"And hurt." Jack nods, ashamed of himself. "He didn't yell, didn't cause a scene. He stared at us for a few seconds. Said 'okay, then,' left my key on the coffee table and—"

"Where were you?" Rome interjects.

"His apartment." I growl. "Pay attention."

"Where in the apartment?" Romeo gives me a look.

"Oh, uh—" Jack thinks for a second. "The couch."

Romeo nods, appreciatively. "That's a good couch for sex."

Jack tosses him a weird look. "Thanks?"

Rome gives me a covert wink no one else was supposed to catch but Jack does, and he points dramatically between us.

"No!" He shakes his head. "No, no!"

Rome shrugs, laughing and I shake my head, annoyed at him but also a tiny bit of me thinks he's funny.

"It's already been done, mate." My ex-boyfriend beams. "Cracker of a sex couch."

"All things considered, Rome, it sounds like he's aware." I give him a curt smile and Jack gives the two of us a despondent look.

"And Taj is, by the way, still based in New York, and I've since found out is dating—"

"Iona Evans."[180] Rome interjects.

---

[180] Rush Evans' little model sister.

Jack stares at him for a second. "How did you know?"

"Oh." Rome shrugs uncomfortably and I know where this is going. "We, like — you know—"

I roll my eyes out of habit.

He throws his arm at me, exasperated. "You were fucking a police officer!"

And I silence him with a point of my finger and a sharp look, nodding my head towards Jack, who's just staring at his empty glass.

"Jacky—" I reach over and squeeze his hand. Are you sad because you miss Gus or because Taj is Taj?"

He looks at me, barely. "Both."

Rome smacks Jack on the back, affectionately. "It'll come good in the end, Jacko."

"He's right." I squeeze Jack's hand. "We'll drag you to good ourselves, if I have to."

Baby

Christian.

Hey

Hi

I had fun the other night

I bet ...

You didn't?

I did.

Good.

Can I see you again?

In what capacity?

Any.

All.

Haha

Okay...

When?

Whenever.

Actually whenever?

I'm housebound, remember?

I'm just here.

I'm on my way.

37

Christian

I'm late to breakfast with the boys. Late because Daisy jumped in the shower with me when I was getting ready to leave and I got a bit sidetracked.

I'd sidetrack my whole fucking year for five minutes alone with her, but by way of miracle, I'm getting a lot of her five minutes these days — and I'm not going to fuck it up this time.

If there even is something to fuck up. Maybe there is, it's so hard to tell with her because she does just enjoy sex. So maybe that's what it is, maybe that's all it is, or maybe — please God — we're sorting our shit out.

"Well." My brother leans back in his chair, smacking me on the back as I sit down next to him at the table. "Look who decided to show up…"

"Busy morning?" BJ asks, eyes up over the menu.

"Yeah, actually—" I nod, coolly.

"Doing what?" Henry asks, eyes pinched.

I leave it hanging for a couple of seconds.

"Daisy." I give him a proud smile and Henry chokes on his drink.

"Shut the fuck up." He grins over at me. "Actually?"

I nod, trying to play it cool.

"How long for?" Jonah asks, smacking me in the arm.

I shrug like I'm not 100% sure, like I don't know off the top of my head that it's been nine days and seventeen hours — give or take — since we first hooked up at my car.

That fucking car, man. I love it. I'll never get rid of it. It belongs in one of her museums.

"And you're just telling me?" Henry scowls.

"Believe it or not, Hen—" I shake my head. "I don't have sex with a girl and immediately think to call you."

"Yeah, but it's not just a girl—" He tosses me a look. "It's Daisy."

"Who is a girl..." BJ tells him gently.

Henry shakes his head. "Not to him—"

I wave my hand through the air like I haven't been missing her for the last year, like there's not a parade sounding off in my chest cavity right now that this morning I had her pressed up against a bathroom wall and afterwards we sat on the shower floor and she explained to me who the Pre-Raphaelites were and how they changed the course of art-history, and she was so happy as she was doing it, completely engrossed in her own little story, I feel sad that she had to hide this part of who she was for a year with that cop, and I wanted to kiss her again to make sure she knows it's a part of her that I love, but I didn't want her to think I'm just around her for the sex — but once she started listing their doctrines off her fingers I couldn't help it — I just leant over and kissed her and she laughed like it confused her why I did it, but she kissed me back and started things up again.

I pulled back from her, wiped some water from her face.

"You didn't tell me the fourth one—?" I told her.

And she stared at me for a few seconds, then kissed me more.

"You been around the house a lot, then?" BJ asks, face looking a bit strained, and I know where this is going.

I nod casually, trying to keep the drama at bay as long as I can.

"Is she okay?" he asks, crossing his arms over his chest.

"Who?" I ask, as if I don't know.

"Who the fuck do you think?" BJ shakes his head annoyed and Jonah sighs like we're up to our old shit again.

The question annoys me.

Everything about whatever the fuck he's doing annoys me — not because I love Parks still, not because I'm blindly on her side, but because whatever the fuck he's doing — it's fucked.

I give him a little shrug. "I don't know what you're asking—"

Beej sort of scowls at me. "I'm asking if she's okay."

"Yeah?" I pull a face. "I guess. As good as she'll be while you have a girlfriend—"

Jonah rolls his eyes and Henry lets out a sigh.

"But how is she?" BJ asks like him repeating the same fucking thing brings any clarity.

"How is she like—" I shrug, waiting for more. "I don't know what you want me to say? How is she in general? How is she health-wise—"

BJ's brows dip. "What's wrong with her health?"

I shake my head. "How is she with him? Is that what you mean?" I stare over at him, waiting for BJ to answer me but he doesn't. He's breathing heavy. I think he wants me to say it's shit and weird and whatever, but I won't.

"She's good," I tell him, unflinching.

"Christian—" My brother sighs.

"What?" I give him a look. "You can lie to him if you want, I'm not gonna to — they're good together, man."

BJ's face goes a funny kind of still.

Jo shakes his head in this dismissive, apologetic way. "They're not together—"

"They're literally always together."

Jonah shoots me a look. "You know that's not what he means."

"I don't know…" I shrug. "Jules blew off Balaska for her—"

Jo looks surprised at that. "Piss off — Josette? He did not."

I nod over at him. "He told her to leave. Parks walked in on her straddling him."

"Oh, yeah—" Henry grimaces. "That one didn't go down too well."

"They sound like they're going good…" BJ says sarcastically.

Henry stares over at his brother, annoyed at him the same way we all are, really, in that 'just fucking pull it together' kind of way, where none of us get what the fuck they're doing or why they're doing it. Parks, I kind of get — just because she's an absolute fucking twist — but Beej? I don't know. It's a mess.

"They're better together than you'd want them to be, mate." Henry says, just to make a jab. "And you're not as good with Jordan as you want everyone to think you are. No one thinks that." he adds, flashing his brother a shit-eating grin.

BJ flips him off and tries to shake it all off but I can see floating barely under the surface that he's stressed.

"It's nothing, Beej—" Jo says with a sigh. "You know Parks, she's just a handful. You can't juggle when you're with her—"

BJ gives him a little glare. "Thought you said they weren't with each other—"

"They're not, but I mean—" Jonah rolls his eyes. "You know Parks. She's bloody Snow White with the songs and the birds on her fingers and deer running after her, but instead of animals, it's men."

I sniff a laugh.

"Jules is just a bird on her finger." Jonah shrugs to placate him but I don't know that it's completely true.

BJ shakes his head thinking, then scratches the back of his neck. "What am I then?"

Henry drains his drink and stares over at his brother.

"The huntsman."

Daisy
1:01PM

You still never told me the fourth doctrine.

4. "And most indispensable of all — to produce thoroughly good pictures and statues."

Did they?

Yes.

Yes, very much so.

Show me sometime?

Okay.

38

Julian

Carmelo opened a little Italian restaurant in Notting Hill. A dream of his for as long as I can remember. Life's been fairly relaxed in the Boroughs lately, and Santino isn't going anywhere — so Carms has a minute to indulge in what his life might have been like if we weren't all what we are.

He's always been a decent cook, in spite of his mother and taught by my sister, mostly. But he can make cocktails like no other, they're his real specialty. Italian cocktails and aperitifs we've all forgotten about.

I get that feeling still, when I walk into a room with Magnolia and everyone looks, such a weird high. Never really had a conscious thought about who I turned up at places with, but with her I like the the stares. I like that she doesn't even notice either.

"What?" She flashes me a confused look once she feels my eyes on her. It's been more than a month of this now — Am I in my head about it a bit? Yeah.

I know I'm well out of that post-have afterglow I was hiding behind before and I'm still here — still annoyed whenever she leaves, still annoyed if that fucking ex-boyfriend of hers flashes up on her phone, still finding myself watching her in my bed at night with a morbid fascination like she's a hand-painted time-bomb.

Grab her by the waist and push her in front of me, walking towards Carmelo who's standing in the centre of the restaurant, grinning.

"Ey!" I give him a quick hug and he turns to Magnolia, picks up her hand and kisses her cheeks. She bats her eyes like she's not used to the whole world swooning after her and honestly, those fucking Italians — so smooth all the time.

"This is amazing—" Magnolia glances around. "The interior is gorgeous. Who did it?"

"My sister." Carmelo gives her a little smile.

"Gia?" I blink, surprised. "Really? She's done well."

She has. It's Cistercian, arches and marble — classic and dramatic. The lighting is impressive for the space.

"You've done good too, man." I nod at him.

He stands a bit taller, pleased with himself, and then points to Magnolia. "And you have done well with him — never looked sharper," he tells her, giving her a playful look.

"A.P.C Wool Mathieu Bomber Jacket, Han Kjobenhavn Grey Distressed T-Shirt, Double Knee black cargos from Stone Island Shadow Project, and some Timberlands." She shrugs. "Easy peasy."

"Can you easy peasy me?" he asks her with a smirk.

I toss him a look and he laughs it off. Can't say I love him flirting with her even if it's just for fun so it pleases me when she scrunches her nose up as politely as she can. "I'm sorry, I'm only interested in easy peasy-ing him."

That made me happier than it should have, but not Carms...He gives her a reluctant, kind of annoyed smile.

"Just my luck—"

Magnolia shrugs like she can't help it. "I mean, have you seen him? So tall — what are you, six foot three?"

"Four." I tell her.

"Four!" She announces, proud. Like she grew me herself. "Six foot four, and look at that face. My God, those eyes. So angry all the time—" I roll them at her and she keeps going like I want her to. "so handsome, every piece of clothing's just begging to be worn by him—"

Carmelo takes a steep breath in through his nose and tosses me a look. "I gather she's helping you keep your ego in check?"

"What ego?" I give him a grin.

Carms rolls his eyes and looks back at Magnolia. "Can I get you a drink?"

"Yes!" She beams up at him. "Whatever you recommend! Nothing with Campari in it though—" Carmelo nods. "Or Cointreau," she adds as an afterthought. Carmelo nods again. "Actually, nothing bitter at all. Except, not overly sweet either— perhaps like a — well, just something rather balanced on the palette, semi-sweet but a little bit tart—"

"Fuck—" I roll my eyes. "Just get her a French 75."

I shake my head at her and she frowns up at me, like I've hurt her feelings but I know I haven't.

"I, though, will have whatever you recommend," I tell him.

Carmelo laughs and walks away.

A server takes us to our table and Magnolia turns to Kekoa and Declan, looking at them over her shoulder.

"Are you not joining us?"

Declan shakes his head and Kekoa gives her a quarter of a smile. He likes her. Thinks she's sweet. "We're going to sit at the bar."

She nods once, a bit confused.

"They don't want to join us?" she asks, almost offended as she takes her seat.

I shake my head. "It's not their job to join us."

I reach around the table and pull her chair over towards me. Too far away. I like her close.

The sound is obnoxious and loud, I probably scuff my friend's marble as I'm doing it, but I don't really give a shit.

She gives me a look as I pull her closer to me. Somewhere between her finding it sexy and stupid, where she likes how strong I am and is scared of it at the same time. Her and me — we're a juxtaposition. We don't work, but I guess we sort of do, even though there is no 'we', and I have this strange moment of clarity — unwelcome, if I'm honest — the thought fucks me up, I don't let the sentence fully form in my mind, wouldn't let myself say it out loud anyway. Don't even really want to think it.

She rests her chin in her hand, crosses her legs and they brush against mine as they do.

"Are you proud of your friend?" she asks, looking up at me.

"I am." I nod once, then look around the restaurant again. "It's good, I like it."

"Do you know his sister?"

I flick her a look.

"Intimately," I tell her, just to get a rise. Her brows dip a little, a tiny bit jealous. "We slept together once about fifteen years ago," I clarify for her.

"Fifteen years ago I was... nine," she tells me, doing the math in her head.

I pull a face. "We were sixteen."

"Did you lose your virginity to her?" she asks, taking a sip of her water.

I shake my head. "I lost my virginity to a girl in Porquerolles."

"What was her name?" She asks, leaning in again. Loves story time, this one.

I let out a small laugh. "I don't know — it wasn't planned." I shrug. "We were just on a boat all day, a bunch of us, she didn't speak English, I didn't really know French at the time, and when the boat pulled in we went for a walk and it just happened."

"It just happened?" Magnolia rolls her eyes. "You just happened to lose your virginity on a beach with a perfect French stranger whose name you don't know?"

"Yep."

She folds her arms over her chest, sits up a little straighter. "Are you going to ask me about my first time?"

I shake my head. "I don't want to know about your first time."

"Why not?" She pouts.

Because it wasn't with me.

"How's Bridget?" I ask, changing the subject.

"Oh." She brightens up. "She's quite well. She's doing tremendously in school, she's midway through her thesis on the globalisation of International Relations—"

"Does she like me yet?"

Magnolia purses her mouth, squinting. "Not quite yet."

I give her a resigned smile. Don't pull at the thread of why that bothers me a bit.

"It's not you — it's—" She rolls her eyes. "She doesn't like our 'arrangement,'" she says delicately.

"What about you?" I lift my chin a bit and look over at her. "Do you like our arrangement, Tiges?" I ask her and her mouth falls open.

She blinks. Pauses. Caught off guard.

I like catching her off guard.

She goes to say something when suddenly the room goes dark.

Music cuts, lights out, all sounds come to a halt.

And I know before I hear a thing what's happening, so I pull her to the floor, down under the table.

"What are you doing?" she asks urgently and I shush her. Listen as intently as I can. I don't hear anything — but I don't trust it. I can't see Carmelo as I look around for him.

Magnolia's eyes are big and confused, maybe a bit nervous.

Kekoa's by my side a second later. The sound of the room starts to rise again as people wonder what's going on—

"Take her—" I shove Magnolia into Kekoa's arms.

"What?" Kekoa shakes his head, I can barely see him in the dark.

"Take her, I said." I stare him down. "Now—" I push her towards him again.

Declan pulls me up off the floor. "I've got him," he tells Koa, who fucking finally hustles Magnolia out of the building via the back way, into the waiting cars.

"Split?" Kekoa asks as he tosses her into the back seat.

I shake my head and shove him out of the way, jumping in after her.

The door closes and Kekoa jumps into the front seat next to Happy, who's driving.

I stare over at Magnolia, who's sitting there confused and maybe a bit nervous in the corner of my Escalade.

"Are you okay?" I grab her face as I slide over next to her.

"I'm — yeah." She nods, a bit confused. She glances around. "What was that?"

I say nothing.

"What happened?" she asks and from the front seat, Kekoa turns around and hangs up the phone. He shakes his head.

"False alarm. Just a power outage—" Nods his head in the direction of the restaurant. "Want to go back?"

I hold my face and sigh. Shit.

No, I don't want to go back. The back of my neck feels hot. Shit. I feel like a fucking idiot.

Magnolia watches me carefully, then touches my arm gently. "Are you okay?"

I move my arm away from her, feeling embarrassed. "Yep."

"Really?" She tilts her head, watching me closer than I want her to.

I say nothing, just stare ahead.

"Are you sure you're okay?"

I snap my head over at her. "Why would I not be okay?"

"I don't know—" She clears her throat delicately. "That was a slight overreaction to a power-outage, was it not?"

I stare over at her a bit incredulous. "What?"

"Do you not think?" she asks sweetly, eyebrows up in a curious sort of way. I hate that she's asking it sweetly. Hate that she sounds worried about me, hate that my hearts pounding in my chest so hard it might blow out through my ribs; the thought of something happening to her there—

I just shake my head at her, look out the window.

And then I notice at the same time she does that my hands are trembling.

She reaches out and takes one.

"Julian—" She says my name too gently.

I snatch it away. "I'm fine, I said."

She watches me carefully before she speaks.

"Do you have PTSD?" she asks in a small voice and I snap my head in her direction.

"Fuck you." I point at her and her head pulls back immediately. Kekoa looks over his shoulder and I ignore him.

She blinks twice.

"I beg your pardon?" she says quietly.

"I said fuck you."

Her face falls in a way that reminds me of the glaciers you see on the Discovery Channel, the crumbly confusion where she doesn't know what she's done or how she's done it.

Me either, actually.

But here's what I do know.

I don't want some nosy toff asking me if I have PTSD. I don't need her touching my hand when she does, I don't need her thinking I'm overreacting because she has no idea what the fuck I've seen, I don't need her to be the face that flashes through my mind when I think someone's trying to kill me. I don't need her at all.

She frowns over at me, wounded. "What are you—"

But I cut her off. "Sorry I worried about you for a half a second—"

"Julian—" I can't pick her tone. Not just confused, not just hurt, something else too.

I shrug like I don't give a shit. "It's gone now, it wont happen again—" I look her square in the eye. "We're done."

She's not moving as she stares over at me, like she's never been dumped before. Probably hasn't, so fuck her for that too.

I turn away from her, look straight ahead.

"Drop her home," I tell Kekoa.

Magnolia shifts her whole body away from me.

Moves as far as she can to another corner of the car and my heart pulls in a way it never has before. I feel a bit sick about the way she looks. Balled up in a corner like it's a winter night and I've thrown a bucket of water over her.

Need to get rid of her though — all of it's bad news.

The lights go off in a restaurant and I cover her with my body like someone's shooting at us? Do I have PTSD? Fuck her.

She hasn't moved since I spoke to her. Wordlessly twisting a ring I didn't buy her around her finger.

We pull up outside her place at Grosvenor Square and I reach over and fling the door open. She looks at me, waiting for me to say something but I don't. Don't say a word.

She grabs her bag and climbs out. I slam the car door as soon as she's on the street and tell Happy to drive. I don't look at her, I don't look back. Cover my face with my hands and breathe out. Try to convince myself it's a sigh of relief not regret, but I know better.

We peel out and Kekoa turns around looking at me like I'm insane.

"You're an idiot." He tells me.

I square up. I feel like fighting. Never fought him before — I'd probably lose — wouldn't hate being smacked in the face right now though.

"Say that again." I stare over at him.

Koa shakes his head all bored, not taking the bait. "I feel like you're going to regret that—"

"I feel like you should shut up."

"You do have PTSD," Kekoa tells me, unflinching.

I glare over at him. Don't like it when he talks to me like this. The only one who might dare to try because he's a bit like a dad. Except he's not my dad.

"I said shut the fuck up."

My old friend stares over at me, unimpressed. "Do we need to talk about what happened?"

My jaw goes tight and I look out the window. "What are you talking about?"

Koa shakes his head, breathes out. He's annoyed, jaw all tense. "You said to take her. Forced her into my hands—"

"So?"

"So my job is to protect you."

I shake my head. "Your job is whatever the fuck I tell you it is."

"No," He gives me a look. "It isn't. My job is to keep you safe and any extension of you. Now, if you're saying that's her then fine, that's a hill I'll die on — happily, Jules. But you've gotta tell me, man — like, what is this? Do I need to get her a—"

"We're done." I pick a piece of thread off my sleeve and flick it away.

Kekoa frowns. "What?"

"We're nothing." I shrug. "You heard me. I dropped her home—"

"I dropped her home, actually…" Happy interjects. Doesn't sound like he's on board either.

"Alright?" I look between them, annoyed. "Want a prize for that? A pat on the back for doing what I pay you to do?"

"Cor blimey—" Happy scoffs and takes a corner extra sharp on purpose.

"She's a fucking pain in the arse—" She's nosy, she's high-maintenance, she's just a distraction "—and I'm done with her," I tell them both again. I tell myself, actually.

"Funny," Kekoa says, facing the front again. "You don't sound all that done, man."

Julian
12:13AM

Where are you?

Upstairs

Why?

Is it true?

Is what

You and magnolia

?

Did you break up

Weren't together.

So yes?

We weren't together???

...

Fuck.

Yeah, sure. We broke up.

Are you ok?

Yep

Do you want me to come up?

Nope

Ok.

I left some cookies at your door.

39

Christian

So Parks and Jules canned it the other night and it's been strange vibes ever since.

Tonight's shaping up to be weird as fuck because Jo's throwing his annual Wet Feb party tonight at Math Club.

Magnolia insists on me and Henry coming to her house to get ready but both of us arrive ready, and I guess this is what happens when you can't be alone and your friendship group is as incestuous as ours and I make a mental note to buy everyone a group therapy session for Christmas this year.

Parks says she's fine but I know her face too well, after years of studying it when I shouldn't have. How her face looks tonight, she looks lost.

Can't do alone.

That's why Henry and I are forced to stand in her bathroom while she asks us both if her mouth is the right colour.

Her mouth couldn't be the wrong colour, it's the second best mouth in the world and I don't even want to kiss it anymore — but I can see it in how she's fussing, this has thrown her. Whatever happened with her and Jules, it's done a number on her.

I go to her kitchen to grab myself a drink, take the edge off and her sister's in there, sitting on the kitchen bench.

"Hiding?" I ask her.

Bridget nods. "She slept in my bed last night."

I give her a bit of a shrug. "You know her and alone."

"Can't do it even for a second." She sighs as her eyebrows lift. "It's getting worse."

I pour myself some wine. Red. Top up Bridget's glass.

"I think she fancied him," I tell her, crossing my arms.

"Yeah, no shit, Sherlock—" Bridge rolls her eyes. "Though, she'd fancy a fucking door knob if it made her stop thinking about BJ."

I shake my head. "I don't know — I don't know if this is about Beej."

And Bridget gives me a look. "Everything about her — God, Christian, you of all people should—" She gives me an exasperated look, and she doesn't need to finish that sentence. "Everything about my sister is about BJ."

Henry speed-walks into the kitchen and rounds the corner gesticulating to us wildly, bolstering arms, thumbs up, jazz hands around his face, mouths the word 'pretty' and then she walks in to the kitchen to a chorus of "wow" and "ooh" from the three of us, and she puts her hands on her hips.

"That felt rehearsed..." She looks down at herself in her little white dress. "Do you not like it? It's Philosophy di Lorenzo Serafini— Should I change?"

"He'll die when he sees you," I tell her, trying to be helpful because it sounds like something she'd want to hear.

"Who will?"she asks, hands on her hips.

"Um... either?" I offer and she frowns so I try again. "N-neither? Both?"

("Oh, fuck." Henry sighs.)

"Magnolia—" Bridget boosts herself off the table. "BJ is — boys, back me up — in a perennial state of obsessing over you."

"Yes," Henry says and we both nod emphatically.

"Bane of my existence for a long time." I give Parks a look as I nudge her and she smiles a bit.

"And Julian," Bridget squares her shoulders, "is a fuckwit for how he treated you the other night—"

"How'd he treat you the other night?" Henry squares up.

"It was nothing, Hen—" She shakes her head dismissively. "It's fine. Are these shoes okay?"

We all stare at them and Bridget is the only one dumb enough to say anything more than 'Yes, they're great.'

"They're just black. They're a black shoe."

"Yes, right, I know, but the tie on my dress is velvet, so maybe I should — oh!" She darts out of the kitchen. "I got a velvet pair from Gianvito Rossi last week."

She comes back in.

"Wonderful!" / "Excellent!" Henry and I say, and Bridget frowns again.

"They look the same."

"For the love of God, shut up," Henry says through clenched teeth and Bridget groans and bangs her head on the bench.

I throw back some more wine and clap my hands twice, because Daisy's going to be there and I want to see her sooner rather than later.

Magnolia breezes back into the kitchen with a purse and a jacket over her arm.

"Ready."

"Great—" I walk towards the door.

"Magnolia—" Bridget calls for her.

("No!" I growl under my breath.)

"What?" She pauses, waiting.

"Do you think that perhaps instead of going out tonight and seeking validation from different men because you feel rejected by the two boys you're romantically interested in, you could stay at home and work on processing those emotions?"

Magnolia stares over at her sister for a few seconds, blinks twice then erupts into laughter.

"You're so funny, Bridge. I needed that! Thank you." She bounces out the door and Henry and Bridget exchange weary glances.

As soon as we walk in to the club she spots Julian. Their eyes catch and she throws the first dagger with hers before Henry throws an arm around her and takes her to the bar.

Julian looks pissed off immediately and starts talking to Bianca Harrington, one of Jo's close friends. Dead hot. American. Dad's a diplomat. Pretty sure Jo's declared her off limits to all of us but Julian doesn't look like he cares about that tonight.

What the fuck happened?

Daisy's chatting to some of the boys. I don't want to seem to eager so I just follow Parks and Henry to the bar. I regret it immediately because Jordan's there with a friend of hers who's so annoying and so keen on me, so aggressively flirty — I don't want a bar of it, don't want Daisy to see and read into it, so I go find my brother, tell him it looks sick and good job — give Tausie a peck and make a crack about it being Jo's night and then Jonah gets shitty and walks off and then I make a beeline over to Daisy.

"Hey—" I kick Daisy in the ankle so she looks up at me.

She looks up and moves over in her seat, making room for me. "Hi."

I kiss her on her cheek and she sort of looks surprised that I do.

Happy-surprised, but surprised.

"Good day?" I squeeze her knee.

"Yeah." She shrugs. "Fine. Normal, you know — what did you do?"

"Nothing." I pour myself some champagne from the table.

"You were with Magnolia?" she asks, I think trying to sound breezy — except that she doesn't, so I hand her my champagne and pour myself another.

"Yeah." I scrunch my face up a bit. "Hen and I went over to hers before—" I lower my voice. "I think she's sad."

"About my brother?"

I nod, looking over my shoulder to check on Parks and lo and behold, there's BJ standing there at the bar with his girlfriend and some girl that was trying to chat my ear off a second ago.

"She looks sad…" Daisy says sarcastically as she eyes her down, unimpressed with my friend as Parks reaches over and touches the hem of BJ's shirt while his girlfriend's not looking.

"Oi," I reach over and smack Jules on the leg. "Are you good?"

He looks instantly annoyed, like immediately and disproportionately shitty.

"Why wouldn't I be?" He scowls, but his eyes drag over to Magnolia and BJ before he glares back at me.

I toss Daisy a look and then give Jules a vague look. "Why wouldn't you be, I don't know—?"

Julian rolls his eyes.

"I've got to say—" Daisy leans forward. "You do seem great — like, mentally, you seem in a really, good, happy place."

Julian glares over at her and points one finger.

"You shut up."

"And you—" I point at him. "Don't talk to her like that."

"Ey!" Julian's eyes light up in a dim way. "We got a big man here today—"

"Oh, ignore him—" Daisy grabs me by the arm, pulling me backwards into the chair we're on and I love it, it's such a casual, mindless grab how she's touching me. I want her to always be touching me. "He's been in a bad mood ever since... you know—"

Carmelo leans in over Bianca (who pushes him off her and goes to find Jonah) to insert himself into the the conversation.

"What happened?"

"Nothing—" Julian rolls his eyes.

Kekoa clears his throat and pulls a face. Something, obviously.

"What?" Carmelo asks, looking up at him confused.

"Julian and Magnolia are done," Declan says as he pours Julian a shot and slides it over to him.

Julian glares at the vodka for a few seconds, like drinking it might be a tacit admission to something he doesn't want to say.

Carmelo, though, he lights up a bit at the news. "Really? What happened?"

"Nothing happened—" Julian says, then takes the shot.

"Something obviously happened—" Miguel says under his breath to Declan but loud enough for Jules to hear.

"Can everyone just shut the fuck up?" Julian growls.

"You're very in your feelings, Julian.," Daisy tells him.

And he glares over at at his sister. "I told you already — there's no feelings. We were just naffing—"

"Really?" Carmelo sits back in his chair.

"Yeah," Julian shrugs. "Really."

Carmelo looks over at him. "And you're done?"

"Yeah."

"Oi—" He smacks Jules playfully in the arm. "Then do you mind if I take her out for a spin?"

Julian turns to look at his friend, brows down, instantly frowning. "What did you say?"

("Shit," Kekoa sighs under his breath.)

"Well, if you're done with her, just flick her my number, yeah?" Carmelo shrugs.

"What?" Julian says, brows low, processing.

"She's like, stupid hot." Carmelo says —I don't know how he's not sensing the tone — "I want a turn."

Julian's staring at Carmelo, shaking his head confused. "A turn?"

"I mean, she's got a tiny rack but she'd be a decent smash—" He laughs and I'm about to say something myself when Julian jumps to his feet, towering over his friend.

"Fucking say that to me again, bruv—"

Daisy goes tense next to me.

Carmelo jumps to his feet, ready to fight on a reflex.

Loving someone is weird. First thing I think is how I need to get Daisy the fuck out of here.

"Say it again," Julian barks as he shoves Carmelo.

("Feelings have entered the chat," Declan whispers to no one in particular.)

Carmelo shoves him back, and there's not a lot of room for anything to go down here — we're in a tight space, there's a table with a bunch of bottles on it, couches, too many people for them to fight how they would if no one was watching, but then, Jules' eyes have gone savage.

"What's your problem, man?" Carmelo shakes his head, smiling but it's strained. "You said you were done—"

Jules shoves him again. "You're my problem."

"You afraid she might fancy some Italian sausage?" Carmelo says with a laugh, but I don't like it.

Julian's face shifts and I glance around, taking stock of the room. This could get dicey pretty fast.

"Jules—" Daisy stands and Julian looks back at her for a second, holds his arm out to keep her away.

"I can't deal with your shit right now, Face, sit down—"

"Julian—" She reaches for her brother and he jerks away from her.

"Daisy, I said sit the fuck down." He growls at her and I don't like that either so I stand up, and pull her behind me.

"Do you want to talk about her again?" Julian asks Carmelo, chin jutted.

"Maybe I do, yeah." Carmelo nods, and I don't know what he's playing at.

Egos, man. They'll kill you.

Julian face pulls. "Go on then."

Carmelo nods towards Parks. "Maybe I'll just go chat to her myself, actually — how's that?"

He goes to move past Julian and then — I don't know how, it's pretty fast — Julian grabs Carmelo by the neck of his shirt and twists it so it's almost choking him, then yanks him close to his face. "Will you—?"

The room seems like it goes silent, like everyone's holding their breath —

And then suddenly Magnolia's in front of him, standing on the table of drinks so she's taller than him. It's the live-time manifestation of why our youth was so fucking dramatic, this idiot-girl here on the table.

She doesn't see dangerous situations and run from them, she runs right to them. And I reckon a huge part of that has to be because BJ always just charges straight in after her. Chaotic childhoods, nothing really sure about her life until him, so she runs to the chaos and finds him in it — but BJ, he's standing here now on the sidelines of this, his face like a fucking cracked egg as he watches her duck a bit so she's eye-level with a man who isn't him, puts her hand on his chest to steady him. I look away. It's hard to watch your friends get hurt and I've got a front row seat.

"Julian, stop—" Magnolia tells him, staring at his eyes, waiting for him to look back at her. "What are you doing? He's your best friend—"

Julian takes the hand he's not choking Carmelo with and puts it on top of Parks', holding it to his chest.

I glance back to see how BJ's doing, but he's already gone.

"Stop," Magnolia tells him again, and he listens. Lets his friend go with a shove, then turns to Parks, lifting her down off the table.

"Come home with me?" he tells her. "Now?"

Magnolia's eyes flicker quickly over to where BJ was but he's not there anymore.

She looks back at Julian and nods.

He nods his head towards the door and Kekoa leads them out.

I look down at Daisy, who I'm holding from behind — didn't even realise.

She looks at my arm and back up at me, then sniffs an embarrassed laugh.

"Sorry." I remove my arm, awkwardly.

She laughs again, her cheeks pink. "It's okay—"

"I didn't realise—" I babble.

"It's fine—" She shakes. "I didn't mind — it's—"

And I feel sort of stupid about myself for a second, not really sure how she'll react to something as overt as that.

Then she purses her lips, eyebrows up, tossing me a look. "So, do you still have a key to your brother's office?"

Jules, I didn't know

Yeah me either

I wouldn't have said shit if I knew

Its cool man

The whole thing snuck up on me

Does she know

Nope

She might now

Nah, she's a bit of a twat.

Thankfully

Alright well it's in the vault.

x

xx

40

Julian

Bit embarrassing how I got the other night.

I don't know what got into me.

Just, freaked myself out a bit, I guess.

Magnolia Parks on a table, her hand on my chest to calm me down — it was a good feeling, though I can't wrap the words around why.

Actually, if I'm honest, I didn't really like those couple of days when she wasn't around.

And I know what that means — she's climbed over the wall and into my fucking heart somehow, but it's fine. Because I know what I am to her.

I'm the buoy she's clinging onto while she waits for the ship she fell off to come back and get her.

Happy to be clung to, I s'pose.

She's out tonight, with all her friends for Ballentine's birthday. I wasn't invited — not a huge surprise. I'm a bit too aware of her absence though, so I do my best to get through a pile of work I've been ignoring to feel her up.

I make a tiny bit of headway but then my office door swings open.

Declan looks up from the corner of the room where he's watching football.

Magnolia's standing in my doorway — I can tell instantly she's been crying.

"Hey—" I frown, standing up. "Thought you'd be at the birthday."

She walks around my desk quickly, stands toe-to-toe with me.

"He didn't invite me."

She's crushed.

"Fuck."

I feel probably an irrational wave of anger over that, like someone's done her a great injustice — I'd hit him if he were here. Kill him, maybe.

Tilt my head.

"Are you okay?" I ask her, and do you know what she does?

Silently lifts her arms in the air, waiting for me to take her clothes off. I swallow heavy.

"Decks—" I call to him without looking over. "Leave. Now."

Declan sniffs, a bit dirty he's got to leave the game, like I don't have fourteen other TV's about the place, and closes the door behind him. As soon as he does, I have her off the floor, moving her backwards and into the wall.

Reach behind her and unzip her and her dress falls off her body. Slide my hand up her back and into her hair, and she's at the buttons of my jeans now, so up she goes on my waist, pulling my jumper up over my head. I walk her backwards into a priceless artefact that crashes on to the floor. My mouth's up against hers as I grimace.

She peers down at the ground. "Should we pick that up?"

I don't look down at it, just at her. It's bronze. Survived nearly two thousand years, it can survive another bump or two.

I kiss her again, feel her smile against my mouth.

"Wasn't that a Chinese Ritual Wine Vessel from the Fanghu Han Dynasty?"

I pull back, surprised.

"Look at you — yep." Shift her on my waist so I can get a better look at her. "From when?"

Her little shoulders go square.

"Approximately 200AD." She gives me a proud smile.

Holy shit. Probably the sexiest thing anyone's ever said to me. I grab her face and kiss her harder than I ever have before.

I press her up against a cabinet where then — unfortunately — my 1919 jade green vase from René Lalique smashes onto the floor and I start laughing and swearing at the same time.

She's grinning at me, pulls away a bit, looking down at it ruefully.

"That's all rather expensive, is it not?"

I shrug a bit. "£100,000 for the pair, give or take—"

"Oh no—" She pulls a sorry face.

I shake my head and kiss her more, make my way up to her ear and whisper, "Expensive fucks, yeah?" She shifts her face into my neck, smiling, and I knock her chin up with my finger. "I'd pay that twice to be here with you."

I carry her backwards and pop her down on my desk.

Pull my shirt off over my head, and she stares at me curious, like she always does.

Reaches out and touches the one on my stomach, the one I nearly died from. The one Daisy saved me from.

"How?"

I don't want to tell her the truth, so I lie.

"Cage fighting—" I say, hoping it might impress her.

She looks annoyed. "Why?"

"It's fun."

"To get hurt?"

I give her a look. "Tiges, I don't get hurt." I push some hair from her face. God, it's a fucking good face. "Sorry he didn't invite you."

"I don't want to talk about him." She shakes her head and I poke her in the ribs. "You always want to talk about him."

"Julian—" She takes my face in both her hands. "Do you think I'm lying here, half-naked on your desk, to talk to you about BJ? Shut up—" She shakes her head at me, annoyed. "And have sex with me."

Don't need to tell me twice.

I lay her out on my desk, arms up over her head — I like her when she's all stretched out. Like when a cat trusts you and it shows you its stomach.

"What are you smiling at?" she asks, sounding amused.

Didn't realise I was smiling, honestly. I am, but drop it quick as I can and turn it into a squint.

"Don't you go soft on me..." she tells me playfully and I give her a look, pin her down at her wrists and then it's happening. Fire behind us. "Wait for Me," Kings of Leon. Most beautiful girl in the world under me.

I love doing this with her, she so blindly trusts me, her body just seems to go with mine, move her where I want her, how I want her — off my desk and onto my lap. Slide my hands down her body, kiss her neck til her back arches.

Her breathing's getting faster, and I know what it sounds like with her now, I know her tells and her cues — push some hair from her face. She touches my face with her hand and it's fucked, I know it is. Because I say her name, and she's looking at me, thinking about someone else.

Do you know what's more fucked? I don't even care.

After, we're on the floor behind my desk — she's got her head resting on my chest, rug over us and I'm playing with her hair, thinking more than I want to.

"You think of him when you're with me," I tell her. It's not a question. I already know it's true.

"Just sometimes." She peers up at me, looking embarrassed. "I try not to."

I give her a small shrug. "I can tell when you do."

"Oh." Her eyes sort of go glassy, and I don't know why. "Sorry—"

I say nothing — don't know what to say. She clears her throat.

"Who do you think of?" she asks as I stretch out a bit, arms behind my head.

"I try to stay in the moment these days—"

She looks chuffed. "You think of me?"

I nod.

"All the time?" She blinks, surprised.

I sniff a laugh, side-stepping the question even though the answer is yes. All the time.

"Have you ever been in love?" she asks and fuck you, no I do not count her blinks.

"Can't—" I give her a tiny shrug. "It's why you're here. I'm no strings."

Her face pulls like she doesn't like that, and I feel confused about her for the billionth time today. She's not even thinking about it as she runs her mouth back and forth over my cheek. Not kissing me, just touching me because.

She bites down playfully on my mouth. "There are some strings."

I sniff, give her a tiny smile as I push her hair behind her ears.

"In another life I reckon I could have loved you," I tell her.

She gives me a little smile back.

"In another life I would have let you—"

Never you mind that I already love her in this one.

I sit up, lean back against my desk, pull her with me and into my lap.

"What's it like loving someone how you two love each other?" I ask her, a bit because I genuinely don't know and a bit because I can't tell her how I feel, and talking around it might be the closest I can get.

She flashes me a sad smile. "Bad."

"Bad?" I frown. "Really?"

"I think so—" She shrugs. "I don't really belong to myself anymore."

"How?" I frown.

"I mean he's in everything… I'm always thinking about him, all the time. I want to know what he thinks, I want to know what he wants. I worry about how he feels and whether he's safe and what he's doing." She picks at the skin around her nail all nervous. "With BJ, I wonder about all the hands that have been on his body that aren't mine— who's were they, where did they go, what did they touch—"

"Fuck." I swallow back a wave of nausea as I think about anyone who's touched her before me.

"He's not my every second thought — he's my every thought." Her voice cracks a bit, and I might throw up. "He infiltrates all of them. All my decisions, all my feelings—"

I shake my head, mostly just to get her to stop talking. I can't handle it.

"I would hate that, you're right," I tell her like I don't know firsthand.

"Yes." She flicks me a look. "You would. Don't ever fall in love."

I kiss the top of her head.

"Deal."

41

Daisy

Christian took me to BJ's birthday dinner.

Or, we went there together — is that the same thing?

He asked me to go, so I went with him.

And we sat together, and he put his arm around my chair, and he talked about my university course, told everyone how smart I am, what a good cook I am, that my Panna Cotta is better than theirs,[181] he talked to me about how he's been reading a book on the Pre-Raphaelites, and I wonder if there's a chance that maybe — maybe — he likes me how I want him to.

And then I think about the last time, and it feels like a rug's pulled out from under me. I thought it before, I thought it before it was true — it doesn't matter that eventually it did become true, I thought it before it was there so I can't trust anything I think I see in his feelings for me — I can't read him, even if he's the only thing I ever want to read for the rest of my life.

He likes sex, you know? He's one of those guys. Loves a fuck. So, maybe we're just back there again — I don't know. He's being sweet and attentive, and in some ways tonight felt like we were together but then midway through dinner he asked me what I was doing later.

And I gave him a confused look and poked him.

And he nodded once, pleased.

So I don't know where his head's at.

The dinner was weird anyway. BJ's birthday is Valentine's Day, so it's already weird — like 8 people at a dinner on Valentine's Day together? I'm sort of grateful for it though, because at least it meant I got to spend it with Christian. I'm not sure I would have gotten to otherwise. Maybe I would have? It's hard to tell. I dressed for it, in

---

[181] It is.

case. Actually — Magnolia dressed me[182] for it.[183] She bought it all, hung it up in my room while I was making dinner one night. Wrote a note on it saying 'wear me on Valentine's Day.'

The dinner itself felt tense. That girl BJ's dating seems to get on everyone's nerves — and my brother and Magnolia weren't there. Which I guess makes sense. Julian, anyway.

Magnolia not being there seemed weird — her and BJ, whatever they are and whatever they're going to be, they're going to be in each other's lives for good. I hope that the girlfriend knows that.

I hope my brother knows that.

Christian and I walk in through my front door later that night and I call out hello.

No one says anything so I open my brother's office door and—

Scream. Cover my eyes.

Christian starts laughing as a mostly-naked Magnolia Park squeaks and hides behind a mostly-naked brother of mine.

"Everyone calm down—" He rolls his eyes.

Christian looks over at me, one of his eyes shut to avoid seeing anything — and he peeks over at them first. Whacks me in my arm.

"Safe," he tells me.

I look over at my brother who's wrapped a bear skin rug around him and Magnolia, staring over at us unaffected.

"I so badly want there to be clothes underneath that rug."

"Well, there aren't." He gives me a tight smile.

I roll my eyes at him and my eyes land on a broken green thing in the corner.

"Is that — did you—"

Julian cringes. "Yeah. I broke the Lalique vase."

"Julian!" I cry.

"It broke." He shrugs.

"And this!" I reach for another priceless artefact dented and on the floor.

"The Fanghu Vase?" I stare at him, horrified.

---

[182] Sequin Embellished Silk Bustier (Oscar De La Renta); leather skinny trousers (Saint Laurent); Tulle and gros-grain sandals with bejeweled buckle (D&G); cherries pendant earring (E.M); Lexington 18-karat gold diamond necklace (David Yurman).

[183] When I thought she was going, and I presume she thought she was going too.

His cringe deepens.

I pick it up, inspecting it. "That's nearly two thousand years old!"

"I know—" He sighs. "It was an accident."

I stand, my hands on my hips. "How did this happen?"

Magnolia shakes her head. "You wouldn't like the answer, I don't think."

I make a growl at her and she buries her face in my brother's chest before she peers over at Christian. "How was tonight?"

Christian's face strains like he's sad for her or something. "Fine."

Their eyes catch before hers fall to the floor and my brother tightens his grip around her and I feel worried for him.

"And your night?" I ask, just to be snippy. "How was that?"

"Highly pleasurable, Face. Thanks for asking."

"Magnolia?" I glance at her. "Do you concur?"

"I do." She nods, nose in the air, and my brother puts his chin on top of her head.

"Wait, are you using the Judith Leiber Chocolate Box Clutch Bag I got you for Valentine's Day?" Magnolia asks me, bright eyes.

"Yes—" I scowl at her. "And why'd you get me a Valentine's Day present?"

She shrugs. "I love gifts." She turns to my brother. "Did you get me anything?"

Julian eyes her. "We aren't together."

"Right, no — of course." Magnolia nods, eyes on the ground, frowning.

My brother groans. "I did get you some earrings the other day, that I saw, that I thought you'd like, I just got them — like in general, not for fucking Valentine's Day though, yeah?"

And then her face lights up and — get this — so does his.

"Alright—" I turn on my heel. "Well, you two are — yuck. Get out of that rug and we're going to—" I gesture behind me to leave.

"Head upstairs to have some more casual sex?" Magnolia calls after me brightly and I stop dead in my tracks.

"Oh my God," my brother groans as he clamps his hand over her mouth.

Christian shakes his head, staring over at her.

"What is the matter with you?" he asks her loudly.

"What's the matter with me!" she yells. "What's the matter with you! What are you doing?"

"None of your business!" he over-annunciates.

"How is it not my business?" She stomps her foot. "You're one of my oldest friends in the world and you're behaving like an absolute buffoon—"

"And why is that?" I snap. "Because he's sleeping with me?"

"Yes!" She nods, then shakes her head. "Well, no — but yes!"

My brother nudges her head with his chin. "Might want to unpack that one a little more before she kills you, Tiges..."[184]

Christian stares over at her. "Don't." Points a threatening finger. "Don't you say a fucking word—" [185]

"Well to be entirely honest, Christian,[186] you're not saying enough words for the both of us, so[187] — he's being completely emotionally reckless."

"Stop talking—" He points over at her. "Cover her mouth — make her s—"

"How's that now?" I cut in, glaring at her.

"Magnolia, I swear to God—"

"Well, Daisy—" Magnolia shifts in my brothers arms, makes herself look taller somehow. "You're sleeping together incredibly casually meanwhile Christian's over here, with very strong feelings of affection for you."

Christian freezes.

I stare over at her, eyes wide. I don't even dare look at him. "How do you know?"

Magnolia's face scrunches up and looks back at my brother, nodding her head in my direction, tapping her forehead tacitly asking if I'm all there, I think. Julian shrugs a bit like his guess is as good as any, and Christian — he's standing there, staring at me, brows crooked, face pinched.

"How do you not know?" His head pulls back, confused. "I literally told you — I said it right to your face on New Year's—"

---

[184] "Would you let her kill me?" She bats her eyes at my brother.

"If you deserved it," I tell her and the same time he says, "No."

[185] "Are you really going to let him talk to me like that?" She stares up at my brother and I roll my eyes.

"Yes." He nods but tosses Christian a warning look. "But watch it."

[186] "Don't be entirely honest, Parks—" he says, covering his eyes. I start to feel sick.

[187] "Shut up—" he interrupts. She ignores him.

I shake my head at him. "You didn't say you liked me — you said I was—"

"Everything to me." He nods once.[188] "Yeah. Was that not obvious — to you? You, with the double doctorate and the—?"

I keep shaking my head. "Jumping to conclusions didn't work out too well for me last time."

Christian takes a step towards me. "There was nothing to conclude, Dais. I was pretty clear."

I square my shoulders a bit, straightening up. "Not that clear."

"Okay." He nods once then ducks a little so we're eye-to-eye. "Let me be clear now then, Daisy—" Gives me a tall look. "I am fucked up in love with you.[189] Have never stopped loving you, since the second I realised I did, and I admit it, it took me too long to know it but I know it now, and I can't unknow it. I don't want to unknow it, I want to be with you." He tells me, not looking away once. "And I'll do whatever I need to to make us work. You want me to leave London with you? Great. I'm in—"

I don't know what to say so I just stare at him, mouth fallen open, heart hammering away in my throat.

"You want me to quit, not have anything to do with this shit—" He gestures around us. "—fine. That's fine, I don't care, whatever it is, I'll do it."

Magnolia leans in ever so slightly towards him and whispers, "Perhaps you should start by kissing her."[190]

His mouth pulls tight as he flicks his eyes over at her. "Perhaps you could help by getting the fuck out."

Magnolia's mouth drops open, horrified. [191]

My brother's staring over at me, smiling and happy for me. Soft like your face might go when you see someone you love get everything they've ever wanted.

---

[188] "God," Magnolia whispers, elbowing my brother. "She's not so good at reading between the lines, is she?"

[189] Magnolia squeals, hands fly to her mouth in excitement.

[190] Damn it, now I love her.

[191] She spins around in my brother's arms, staring up at him. "The gall! Telling me to get out—" She shakes her head, dismayed. "The audacity! The nerve of that boy — can you believe it? Julian, did you hear that?"

"That was so rude." She pouts.[192]

I'm staring over at Christian and he's staring over at me, eyes wide, biting down on his lip and I'm laughing.[193] My brother starts shuffling her out the door, shaking his head at the ridiculousness of her.[194] Closes the door behind him.

Christian and I stand there, facing each other — the weirdest feeling of my life to date — and then I let out a bewildered laugh and he starts shaking his head, smiling and frowning at once.

"She's so annoying—"

I breathe out, concede with a little shrug. "She's kind of grown on me."[195]

Christian reaches out for me, grabs my waist and tugs me towards him. "I love you." Then he gives me a look, quick shake of the head. "Fuck, you're stupid—"

"I am not!" I stare up at him, indignant, slip my arms around his neck. "You just spent all night telling people how clever I am—"

"Yeah, well — I'm retracting it now because you have the deduction skills of a toddler—"

---

[192] Jules holds her face with his hands, gives her a sympathetic look. "I know…"

"In *your* office!"

"I know—" He nods again. "Very rude, Tiges." Tilts his head at her. "We will give them the office though—"

"Oh." She frowns. "Will we?"

[193] "Just for a minute," my brother tells her.

She frowns more.

"I shouldn't much like to after his outburst. It sends a bit of a mixed message, no?"

"Sure, yeah—" my brother concedes. "We're going to anyway—"

"Oh." She folds her arms.

[194] "I did that—" She points back at me and Christian. "I bet he thinks he did that but he didn't do that, I did that, it's because I'm good at matchmaking—"

Julian gives her a look, before saying gently. "I think they were already in love though."

She lifts her eyebrows. "Thanks to…"

Jules gives her a rueful look. "Hate to break it to you Tiges, but honestly probably in spite of you. At least to begin with."

Her mouth falls open again. "Well, we're not having sex tonight."

Julian scoops her up in his arms. "We already did."

[195] Don't tell her.

"In a tertiary sense, I've always done incredibly well with critical thinking, thank you—"

He squints at me. "What about in the normal, useful way?"

I roll my eyes at him. "Just kiss me already."

"Just say you love me back first," he says very loudly.

I stare up at him, can't believe that this is real life. I swallow once. "I love you back."

His face cracks into the best smile I've ever seen and will ever see, because his face is … fuck *The Mona Lisa*, screw *The Last Supper*, never think of Michelangelo's *David* again — they all pale compared to him in front of me.

Rebecca Barnes and Jud Hemmes, they're the real grandmasters of art in this world, that face of his that they made… it's never stopped being the most perfect thing I've ever seen.

And how his eyes are right now, looking at me, they're clouding over with want — I love it when they go like that. He licks his bottom lip, waiting for me.

Wordlessly, I peel his jacket from him and he doesn't move a muscle, he just lets me.

It takes longer than seems natural for the jacket to fall from his body to the floor, like time is suspended, which actually now that I'm thinking of it, it's how all time behaves in the presence of Christian Hemmes.

I glance up at him, and he's still watching me, waiting.

I take the edge of his t-shirt between my finger and my thumb and I fiddle with the hem, biding my time, trying to wring this moment of all it's worth, every part of it. His plain grey t-shirt, the fire behind us, the music my brother left playing in the background,[196] the room barely lit and the smell of John Varvatos on the boy I love.

Christian Hemmes gives me the tiniest smile and I swallow nervously, even though I don't know why I'm nervous, except that I hope I never stop feeling like this — like I'm floating and flying and falling at once.

I slide my hand under his shirt, and then up and over his head, throwing it to the side.

He presses his mouth together, eyes flickering around the room and suddenly, for the first time possibly ever in the history of time

---

[196] "Beautiful War." Kings of Leon.

— he appears self-conscious. Trying his hardest not to smile when finally his eyes meet mine and he bites down on his bottom lip which sounds like he's being sexy but really, he's trying not to laugh which is also sexy, for some reason.

I reach for the button on top of his black jeans and his stomach tenses up and mine goes to knots thinking about what comes next.

He swallows, like he's timid but he couldn't possibly be but I can hear him breathing now, less steady, more ragged.

I reach for the zip — and peer up at him — a hint of a frown present.

"You still haven't kissed me."

He smiles again, big and broad and touching all corners. He hooks his arm around my neck and drives me towards him, our mouths crashing together.

Christian reaches down and starts undoing my top as he walks me backwards towards the couch.

He kicks his shoes off and as I fall backwards, I tug off his jeans and he stares down at me for seconds that drip by like hours on a rainy Sunday as I wait for him to touch me.

And then he does.

He kisses me again, but this time it's all heavy with the weight of how he loves me pressing in against me.

All my old favourite things about doing this with him rush to the surface — things I haven't let myself think about these last few weeks because I was scared of what we were doing, that it might kill me like before if he didn't want me the way he does[197] — like how I love where he rests his cheek on mine; how his hand always sits in the dip of the small of my back; how he gets instant sex hair about a minute in; how he pulls back to look down at me — before he'd lick his bottom lip and give me a look that would make me breathless but tonight he pulls back and looks at me — I mean, really looks at me, all over my face, sees through me like crystal — and then the corners of his mouth turn up because he loves me now.

And our bodies twist all rigid as we get closer to the end, and I love the end because the end is the part where he collapses on me all spent with his thudding heart and sweaty palms and it's the closet I'll ever feel to another human, I think, and the music that isn't even playing

---

[197] He does!

anymore swells around us, every high note and perfect melody —
loving him will be my magnum opus.

He pulls me in closer to him — I don't know how much closer we
could get — then he pushes my hair behind my ear like he always
does.

"I can't believe this is for real," he tells me, holding my face.

I shake my head a tiny bit. "Me either."

And then he kisses me again.

42

Christian

When me and Daisy walk into Harry's on Basil Street hand-in-hand, Henry jumps to his feet and crows at the ceiling. He runs over, takes my face in both his hands and kisses my head.

"Fuck, yes." He grabs Daisy by the shoulders and shakes her excitedly in the kind of way where if she was a baby, he'd be in prison now. "Look at this! What a time!"

Daisy's cheeks go pink from the fuss and I can tell she likes it but she tries to look annoyed.

"Calm down," she says as she kisses Taura on the cheek.

Henry claps his hands as he sits back in his seat, and he's such a fucking idiot but a pretty good friend, being this excited for me.

"It's been a long time coming, this—" He nods over at us, flags down a waiter. "I want your best bottle of champagne—" he tells him.

"Stop." I roll my eyes.

Daisy's sitting there shaking her head, but happy. I love it when she's happy. She has been these last few days.

Suits her.

The champagne comes and Henry holds his glass in the air and I roll my eyes at him.

"To my sanity returning." He beams.

Daisy flicks Taura a look and they clink glasses.

Henry leans over and says to me quietly, "Happy for you, bro."

I give him a small wink because I'm shit at the mushy stuff.

"So," Henry leans back in his chair, "are you two official, or—?"

I sigh, shaking my head. "Henry loves a label—"

Taura coughs awkwardly and Henry pulls a face.

Daisy eyes me, looking down her nose as she clears her throat.

"Nice side-step there—"

"No side-step." I shake my head.

She lifts an eyebrow.

I keep shaking my head.

"You and me are 100% together, Dais." I give her a look. "Boyfriend/girlfriend, life partners, mi familia es tu familia—" I shrug like she's an idiot. "Call it whatever the fuck you want, Dais — I don't care."

That pleases her. She hugs my arm, puts her head on my shoulder and I stare over at my shit-stirring best friend.

"What about you two then, ey?" Flick Henry a look. "Any labels?"

Henry glares at me. Maybe that one was a bit mean on my part.

Taura folds her arms in front of herself. "Not yet."

"Oh good." Daisy nods dimly. "I'm sure this won't be an uncomfortable trip at all."

Henry throws her a look.

We're all going to Italy. I don't know why.

Jordan planned it for Beej and I don't think he knew how to say no, because he told us all to come — it took a particularly weird turn when Julian suggested everyone stay at their place on Lake Como. So now we're all coming, because we're all fucking suckers for a vacation and what doesn't sound relaxing about being in a foreign country with an incestuous friend group who love each other but are fucking other people to teach each other lessons? Sounds great, can't wait.

"Who's coming, anyway?" Daisy asks, leaning into me.

"Us all—" Henry gestures between us. "Magnolia, your brother—" Looks over at Taura. "I think Banksy's coming?"

"Oh—" Daisy nods. "Right, who is that?"

"Just a friend of Jonah's," Taura says, not looking up from her menu. "She's nice."

Daisy looks at me for more information and I give her a shrug. "She's a girl he hooked up with once in high school and they just stayed, like, weird friends."

Daisy looks over at them curiously, purses her mouth as she thinks. "Sorry if this is an uncomfortable question—" Henry looks over at her, frowning in anticipation. "But how are you three going to—" Daisy's face pulls as she tries to word what she's asking. "Are... are you—"

"I don't know," Henry jumps in, gives her a shrug.

"With the rooms, even," Daisy says. "There are only ten, and three of them will be used by security for me and Julian." She gives us all an unimpressed look.

Taura flashes Henry a quick smile. "Me and Gus will share."

And it hangs there, all shimmery above us, how obvious it is that whatever the fuck those three have been playing at is on the wind down. They can't keep functioning like they are. Honestly, they're barely functioning as it is.

43

Daisy

One time when I was small, we all came here. My parents were still alive. I can't remember exactly how old I was but I'd imagine I was about 6.

A few days into the trip Dad said he wanted some father and son time with Julian and said he thought it would be nice if Mum and I had some time together too.

So off they went first thing in the morning, him and Julian, Kekoa and the few boys we had at the time[198] with them, left Mum, me and her security guy.[199]

I woke up early how kids do, bounced into my mum's room — excited for the day with her.

She said she needed to sleep more and she'd be up soon.

A bit past eleven, she swanned downstairs dressed and ready for the day.

"What are we going to do?" I smiled up at her.

"I'm going to go shopping—" She gave me a tight smile.

"Oh." I gave her another smile anyway, because I didn't really care what we did, I was just happy to be there. "Okay — where are we going?"

"Er—" She gave me an apologetic smile. "I'm going to go in by myself with Ankers. It's just easier, Dais, you know? You wouldn't like shopping — you don't like shopping." She gave me a curt smile. "You'd be so bored."

"Oh." I swallowed. "But there's no one else here?"

---

[198] Security was less of a thing for us then.

[199] A Dutch guy called Ankers, who I think she might have been sleeping with, but I can't prove that as they're both dead.

"Oh." My mother looked around, annoyed. And then a gardener walked past.

"He's here—" She pointed at him. "Excuse me—" she called to him, beckoning him over. "Would you mind watching her for an hour of two?"

He glanced over at me, frowning. "Scusa?"

Mum rolled her eyes, checked her watch. "Ti prenderai cura di mia figlia?" She waved in my general direction. "She's very easy. Buono. Brava ragazza."

The man watched me for a few moments[200] and then he nodded.

Mum clapped once, happy with the outcome.

"Have fun!" She gave me a vacant smile and her and Ankers left.

The gardener stared over at me. There are some faces you just don't like immediately, do you know what I mean?

I didn't have a reason[201] but I could feel one brewing underneath the surface.

He moved towards the kitchen and opened the cupboard. Honestly, he seemed more confused than me. He'd look over his shoulder every now and then, make sure I was there, make sure he hadn't imagined the whole thing.

He walked back over, carrying an armful of snacks.

"Caramella?" He offered with a shrug. "Vuoi guardare un film?"

I said nothing.

"TV," he said.

I nodded, following him to one of the rooms.

It started out okay, but about half way through *Pinocchio* he was sitting too close to me, taking every chance he had to tickle me.

Subtle at first, friendly at first, but the weathervane that sits inside of me could sense a change in the wind afoot.

I jumped up to my feet. "Possiamo giocare a nascondino?"

"Sì." He stood.

I pointed to myself. "Me first."

He nodded.

And then I ran.

Dad and Julian had been training me all my life for things like this. They made it sound fun, like a game.

---

[200] And my stomach did an uneasy flip.
[201] Not yet, anyway.

"How good are you at hiding, Dais?" they'd say at least once a week.

"I'm the best one!" I'd say.

"Show me," Julian would say.

Places like closets, a trunk at the end of a bed, obvious ones that you'd hide in naturally as a kid, they wouldn't humour me, they'd find me straight away.

"I heard you run up those stairs—" my dad would say. "It made you easy to find."

"Do you know what I would do if I wanted to win at hiding, Dais?" my brother said. "I'd run up the stairs as loud as I could, and then slide down the banister as quiet as a mouse."

If I ever picked a hiding spot that was terrible, behind a curtain, underneath something with an open back that wasn't up against a wall, they'd find me and tell me why they could.

"I can see your toes, Face," Julian told me once, as he stepped on them.

"Lost that one, angel," Dad would say. "Let's try again."

I like to be the best at everything I do, so I learned quickly that sometimes you have to be uncomfortable to win the hiding game, and that's when I became good at it.

I ran up the stairs loudly, like my brother taught me, and then once I heard the feet coming up the stairs, I slid down the laundry shoot.

A laundry room might be a place someone would look for me though, I remember thinking that. There was a door that opened onto the main courtyard and a tiny window that dropped out near the lake's edge. The window was tight but I could squeeze and I love winning hiding games and this one felt important to win.

I slipped out the window, landed and froze. Got down on the ground and crawled to the dock where one of Dad's Rivamares were. I lay down on the floor of the boat for a minute of two, but it felt like my dad and my brother would find me too quickly if we were playing. I went to put pillows on myself, but when I'd done that before, Julian had sat on me and found me straight away. I went to place to cushions back on the transom when I saw a hidden little handle that leads to the hold.

As soon as I was inside, I crawled in as deep as I could into the hull and buried myself in some life jackets.

I don't know how long I was in there. You know how time is different when you're small? Twenty minutes can feel like eight hours.

It also might have actually been eight hours.

I didn't wake when they started calling my name. They were looking for me for hours, apparently.

It was my brother who found me.

"Daisy?" he called into the hold.

I didn't say anything for a second.

"Is the game over?" I asked after a few seconds.

Julian breathed out all relieved. "Yeah, Dais — the game's over."

He offered me his hand and pulled me out, onto his lap where he hugged me so tight, I could tell something was wrong.

"Why were you hiding, Dais?" he asked me as he carried me back towards the house.

"The man mum left me with kept wanting to play tickles but I didn't like it."

Julian said nothing, just kissed my cheek, nodded and brought me inside.

The second he brought me inside there was this collective sigh of relief from everyone.

"Ah!" my mother sighed, merrily. "See, she's fine."

"Leesh[202]—" Dad pointed at her. "You shut your fucking mouth—"

He rushed over, plucked me from my brother's arms, hugged me so tight that he hurt me a bit, and as soon as I was out of my brother's arms, Julian had the gardener pinned against a wall, his arm pressed on his throat.

"You fucking touched my baby sister?" he growled. He would have been sixteen or seventeen at the time, something like that.

"Julian—" our dad said, pointing at my brother, gesturing for him to let him go and move away.

"Baby girl." My dad shifted me in his arms so he could see my face. He was handsome, my dad. Heavy brow, dark eyebrows. Brown eyes. The sort of facial hair you might see on a well-kept farmer. His jaw was always tense, eyes were always serious.

"Tell me what happened," he said to me calmly.

"When I woke up you and Julian were gone so I went to find mum

---

[202] Laoise, was my mother's full name, in case you didn't know. Everyone called her Leesha.

but she said she was still tired, so for me to go downstairs and so I did—" He nodded once. "And then when she came downstairs—"

"How long were you downstairs by yourself, Dais?" he asked.

"Mmm." I wiggled my mouth around, thinking about it. "I don't know. Do you mean before or after Mum left?"

My dad flicked a look over at my mum and her eyes went wide, nervous.

"Before."

"I don't know still."

"Did you watch TV?" he asked with a smile. I nodded.

"How much?"

My mouth tugged.

"There's no such thing as too much TV on holidays, is there?" My dad gave me a warm smile. "What did you watch?"

I shrugged. "I just watched two movies and then a bit of one more—"

My dad's jaw went tighter.

"And then Mum came down?"

"Yeah, she wanted to go shopping with Ankers."

Dad looked over at her with threadbare eyes.

"And then what happened?"

"Well—" I rubbed my eye. "She said I wouldn't like to come so she asked that man to play with me."

I pointed to the gardener.

Dad nodded. "And why were you hiding, my angel?"

"Just because he wanted to play tickles all the time and I didn't like it."

My dad's nostrils flared. "Where did he tickle you, sweetheart?"

I shrugged again. "Just everywhere."

"Where your swimsuit goes?"

"A bit." I nodded. "But I didn't have my swimsuit on, just my normal clothes."

My dad nodded once, shifted me a little in his arms and then pulled out his gun[203] and shot the gardener dead on the spot. Two shots, straight in the head. He only needed the one.

And then, without hesitation, he swung his gun around and planted it square on my mum's forehead.

---

[203] Smith & Wesson Model 648 22Mag Revolver.

"You're going to leave my daughter with a fucking paedophile?"

I was frozen, squeezing my dad's neck so tight I was probably choking him.

Julian was eyes wide, still. "Dad—"

"Hadrian—" Kekoa moved towards him.

"Fuck off—" Dad said without looking back at him, as he knocked the gun into her head again, pressing it further in.

"I — I didn't kn—" she stammered.

"Dad—" Julian edged closer to him. "Put the gun away—"

"Julian, you stay the fuck out of it—"

My mum's eyes, they weren't on my dad, but on me, like it was me holding the gun to her head, me doing it to her.

"Let my daughter be touched by some fucking pedo so you can go shopping with your boytoy?" my dad roared, knocking her head with his gun.

"Just give me Daisy, Dad—" Julian said quietly from the side of us.

He looked over at my brother then down to me, like he forgot I was there in his arms.

He passed me off to Julian and in a way that was a mistake because as soon as Jules had me, Dad grabbed her throat and pushed her against a wall, gun to her head.

Her eyed filled with reluctant tears and she stared over at me, glaring, saying without saying it was all my fault—

Julian ran me out of the room and up the stairs, closed the door behind him, turned the TV on loud. *Jingle All The Way* even though it was the summertime.

I sigh, chin in my hand, sitting in the room all that happened in however many years ago.

In case you were wondering, it has been as weird a trip as you'd imagine it to be,[204] maybe this house just brings out the weird in people?

"You're wearing the cardigan," Magnolia says, smiling as she watches me. I've lost count of how many new clothes I get on a weekly

---

[204] Too many conflicting agendas, too much tension, etc.

basis because she just puts them in my room. With the exception of my bra from La Perla,[205] this whole outfit[206] is from her, I think.

"Are you okay?" she asks, watching me from the doorway.

"Yeah—" I shrug dismissively. "Fine."

She doesn't buy it and takes a step further into the room. "Are you sure?"

"Just — a weird memory—" I shake my head.

"Tell me it." She takes another step towards me and gives me a kind smile.

I give her a curt one. "No—"

She sort of sighs, flashes me a tired smile and turns to walk away.

"My dad shot a man there once." I point to where she's standing.

She goes still. "Oh." Shuffles to the left a little bit. "Why?"

I think of what to say. "Just a bad man, I think."

"To you?" she asks, delicately.

I nod.

She sits down opposite me, her chin in her hand. "I'm sorry."

"I got away—" I shake my head. "Hid."

She shrugs. "I'm still sorry."

"My mum left me with him," I say, I don't know why.

"Oh, fuck—" She blinks twice.

"When our dad found out, he went ballistic."

Magnolia just nods.

"Gun to her head and shit." She frowns, sad, and I shake my head. "They weren't really the same after that."

"Oh." She bites down on her bottom lip. "Did she leave him?"

"No—" I shake my head. "You couldn't. She wouldn't. She loved him and my brother—"

"And you," she reminds me because it's the normal thing to do, but I shake my head.

"No."

"I'm sure—" She nods.

"No, I don't know—" I shake my head. I'm not fishing. "When they died — do you know how they died—?"

---

205 Logo-trim U-neck bra (La Perla).

206 Cropped embellished mohair-blend cardigan (Alessandra Rich); Open Ankle Loungewear Trousers; BV Lido 90mm quilted mules (Bottega Veneta).

"I know they were killed, I know," she offers. "I'm afraid your brother hasn't gone too more much into it—"

Can't really believe he went into it at all.

"They were shot on the beach." I chew on the inside of my cheek. "The shooter — he tried to kill us too."

Her face falls, devastated.

"Oh my God." She blinks.

"Julian fought him off," I tell her and I think I see some pride in the smile she flashes me.

"How?"

I tilt my head at her. Give her a look — tell her without telling her — I don't want to entirely shatter whatever illusion she has about whoever she thinks my brother is, but I think I still do anyway.

"Oh," is all she says and the pride dissipates, and maybe some fear starts to seed.

"When the shooter pulled the gun out, my dad dove in front of me, not my mum—"

"A father's instinct." Parks nods, then thinks to herself for a second and shrugs. "I wouldn't know, my father has none—"

"It always felt like my fault that she died—"

"Well—" She gives me a look. "It's not."

I give her one back. "Except it is, a bit."

"No." She shakes her head firmly. "That's your mind playing tricks on you, but it's not true. It wasn't your fault."

I sigh, roll my eyes at her dismissively for trying to talk to me about something she couldn't possibly understand.[207]

She purses her mouth, brows knitted into a frown. She swallows.

"BJ and I... well — I got pregnant in high school."[208]

I freeze and stare over at her. "What?"

"We lost the baby."[209] She shrugs with her body like it's casual but her eyes look crushed.

"—Oh my God." I blink over at her.

"And.... I'm twenty-four—" She touches her chest, squeezing her eyes tight shut. "And I know — I know — that I didn't kill her—"

---

[207] How can she be so annoying?

[208] Oh my God.

[209] Holy shit. They instantly make so much more sense.

then her eyes open nervously as she stares over at me. "But sometimes it feels like I did, though."

I tilt my head. "Magnolia—"

"I was... very thin back then." Back then? I stare at her a bit blankly. I can't imagine her being much thinner now. She gives me a sad smile as she shrugs. "I don't know that I was all that healthy—"

I don't know what to say so I shrug a bit. "You were in high school..."

"I know." She nods. "I know that and you know that, and when you hear that, you know that I obviously—" she pauses. Composes herself. "—that I didn't. But sometimes if I were listen to the wrong parts of my mind, it can feel like I did—" she gives me a look. "So even if it feels like what happened with your mum was your fault, I know that it wasn't... okay?"

My eyes feel heavy[210] but I nod anyway. "Okay."

She turns to walk away and then pauses.

"Christian knows," she says.

"Okay."

Purses her lips. "But Julian doesn't."[211]

"Okay." I nod.

Her eyes go to pleading. "Don't tell him?"[212]

I shake my head a little. "I won't."[213]

She pinches her lip in absentminded nervousness. "I just have this awful feeling that if he were to know, that secret decency he has that just you and I know about might activate and he'll do the right thing and end things with me."

"Right." I swallow, feel myself frown a little bit. "But should he?"

Magnolia's mouth pulls. "Probably—" She nods, giving me a sad smile. "Um — probably. But I don't really want him to." I think saying that sentence out loud catches her off guard. She shakes her head quickly. "Not yet."

And I get it, I get a 'not yet'. And I know what she means about my brother... What it's like to be with him or under his protection. He's like the ozone layer, like without him she'd just be scorched earth.

---

[210] But I'd legitimately probably rather die than cry in front of her, so...

[211] Shit.

[212] Double shit.

[213] Triple.

298

"Okay," I tell her with a small nod.

She flashes me a quick smile and goes to leave.

"I'm sorry—" I call after her. "That that happened to you..."

She gives me a small, grateful smile. "I'm sorry that that happened to you too."

44

Julian

Being away with Magnolia and BJ has been a mental clusterfuck. But every time I see them together, which is about as often as you'd think and more often than I'd want, I think I start to understand them more. He's put her so high on a pedestal that he's convinced he'll never be good enough for her, and he's so fucked up in love with her that he doesn't even realise that she doesn't give a shit, she'd take him how he is. But I don't want to know that, I don't want to give a shit and feel sorry for him, I just want to put me and her in a vacuum where there's no one else and nothing can touch us.

Busy myself with trying to work out where to hang Matisse's *Open Window*. A piece I recently 'acquired'. It's a big deal, figuring out where to display a piece. The space has to be right, the lighting has to be right, the height from the ground, the pieces around it. I'm pretty pedantic about every piece I hang but this one — I don't know — I'm struggling to place it. Something about the piece... It makes me think of her in a way that's stupid and I'd rather I didn't. Longing for a life I've never longed for til now. Barless windows, easy breaths, skies that break your heart. I look at it and all I see is aimless walks down cobblestone streets in an old French village with nothing but her in my hands, and I hate the thought because it's not just a thought, it's a tease. Loving her is a tease.

She's been distracted this whole trip. Bit annoying, watching her eyes flit off to Ballentine every time he walks into a room. Bit of an understatement — 'annoyed', put my fist through a wall in the closet last night when I saw them on the balcony.

It was loud enough, the bang, because she came upstairs to check on me.

"Are you okay?" She frowned over at me, standing in the doorway. I nodded. "Yep."

Held my hand behind her back. She noticed that. Don't know how she noticed that but misses so many other fucking things, but she marched on over, pulled my hand out from behind me, inspecting it. A bit roughed up. Tiny bit of blood. Probably a broken knuckle.

"What did you do?" She stared at it.

"Nothing—" I shrugged.

"You punched something." She eyed me.

"Just a wall."

She stared up at me, frowning. "Why?"

Shrugged again.

She rolled her eyes at me like I was the annoying one and walked out of the room. That annoyed me more than the balcony itself. Her just turning on her heel and running back to Ballentine.

Or that's what I thought, til she came back five minutes later with a champagne bucket full of ice, some towels and a first aid kit.

She sighed out of her nose, telling me without her words me she was angry at me.

Pushed me backwards into one of the Bas Van Pelt arm chairs I picked up in the Netherlands last time I was there. Pretty hard to find these days. Not a bad deal. About £15,000 for two.

She knelt down beside me, tossed me another unimpressed look.

"We need to work on your temper," she told me.

"There is no 'we'," I told her, because I want there to be.

She breathed out loudly and rolled her eyes as she dabbed at my hand. "So you keep saying."

"Am I wrong?" I looked for her eyes.

She gave me a tight smile. "Frequently, yes."

I tilted me head. "About that?"

She looked away, inspecting my hand, avoiding my eyes.

She stayed with me for the rest of that night. Felt a bit shit about it because I know it's not me she loves — but then, fuck it, I'm selfish and I like it better when she's with me, and she hasn't been much this trip.

Don't even know if they know they do it — all these stolen moments and glances — how they gravitate to the same places at the same time. It's a fucking punish.

I hate loving her. It's a disaster.

I got a call after she fell asleep.

Told her there was something I needed to pick up in town.

"Shall I come?" she offered in the morning.

Wish I could say yes, but no.

Shook my head and kissed her on top of hers, walked away knowing she'll find a way to spend the day with that ex-boyfriend of hers who used to be my friend but now I feel like killing all the time.

Casa L'acqua is one of the places people like me would frequent in Lake Como.

Us and the braver celebrities about. Right on the water. Only thing more insane than the view are the prices.

I sit down at a table for two, look out at the lake. Wait.

Got the boys with me.

Order a Barbera. Pick at some olives.

Don't have much of an appetite.

I have a feeling.

"Julian—" She stands over me, smiling curtly. I stand because I'm a gentleman, at all times, even with her.

She gives me a weird hug and I gesture for her to sit.

"Surprised you called." I nod over at her.

She tucks some of that dark brown hair of hers behind an ear.

"Felt like time." Roisin MacMathan leans back in her chair. "And where is my niece?"

She stares over at me, eyebrows up.

"Don't call her that—" I shake my head.

"Sure, but it's the truth, is it not?"

"Not in any way that counts."

She shrugs. "Truth is truth, Julian."

"Bullshit." I take some wine. "It's objective."

She lifts her eyebrows. "How's that?"

"Because the truth is coloured and made full by semantics. Absolute truth doesn't exist." I shrug. "Literal truth is that Daisy and I had the same mother. The truth also is — even though she was the same woman — we all know we did not."

"I know you're not speaking ill of my wee dead sister." She crosses her arms.

I flick her a look. "Just speaking the... truth."

Daisy doesn't know. Our mum's name? Everyone around here called her Leesh. But her name was Laoise MacMathan.

I wondered whether I should tell her.

Never really figured how it'd serve her to know it. Her and Mum were so fucked up anyway, she never met any of Mum's family, never knew that side even existed — I've always had the suspicions that Mum poisoned the town water supply when it came to Daisy over there anyway. She could be convincing about it, that Dad forced her to have her (he did), that she never wanted another baby (she just didn't want a girl), that Daisy was difficult and insolent and impossible to control (bullshit), that Daisy wedged herself between their marriage (she did ultimately come between them, but she didn't wedge herself there), that Daisy ruined them — and that's partially true. All Dad ever really wanted was Daisy, he was obsessed with her the second Mum popped her out. And his love for Daisy, it did cloud everything else — Mum nearly died on the table after having Dais — PPH.

Dad didn't even know; she had Dais, Dad took her, sat in a chair gazing at this baby girl, forgot his then-dying wife on the table.

She recovered fine in the end, but her relationship with Daisy was over before it began.

She went home to them for a bit after that… recover and recoup, that's what Kekoa said. Dad didn't say much about it. She went back to The Docklands for about six months. I visited her a few times, Daisy never did. I heard Dad fighting with her on the phone about it. He didn't like it, didn't like how she was treating Dais — that she went straight back to The Docklands as soon as she was out of hospital.

I remember hearing Dad and Roisin going at it on the phone.

"Because she's her mother," Dad yelled. He shook his head angrily, staring over at baby-Daisy asleep in the rocker in his office. "I can, because she's my wife!" he yelled, and then he saw me, gave me a smile that he meant to be brave, but actually it was just sad, then he closed the door.

"That sister of yours has been trouble since the day she was born." Roisin flicks me a look with eyes that look like my mum's. Miss her for a second. It's quick and sudden. Like a drop of water you weren't expecting on your face.

"How would you know?" I yawn. "You've never met her."

Dad made sure of it. He didn't like the MacMathans, he kept his distance too. I think when Mum and Dad first got together, he'd probably hoped for her family and his to fuse — his was bigger, more powerful, further reach. Mum's was prouder.

By the time Daisy came around, the MacMathan clan was well-established in people trading, and you know my sister's rules — they were my dad's rules too, mine now. Don't have the stomach for it, feels beneath us all.

Dais would be crushed if she knew.

"Oh!" coos Roisin. "I'd love to meet her, bring her on down anytime. Cian Gilpatrick would love to say a quick hello."

I lean back in my chair, cross my arms over my chest. "I know that wasn't a threat."

She leans back as well. Too relaxed.

"Do you know that?" She smiles, eyebrows up.

"For your sake, I hope not," I tell her, unflinching.

"Hm." She gives me a small smile. "Threats are so funny, aren't they? They're empty if your life is—" Her eyes pinch. "Tell me, Julian, is your life empty these days?"

I scratch my neck as I stare her down. Wonder if she's inferring what I think she might be.

"You have a wee dog now, do you not?" She asks with a strange smile. "I had a dog once. I loved him very much," He nods solemnly. "So me da' drowned him."

She reaches over and pops an olive in her mouth.

"Hateful at the time, but at the end of the day, I'm grateful. It made me weak."

I give her a little shrug, ignore the sick feeling she's giving me.

"Might have softened your character a bit."

She chuckles at that. Shakes her head as she leans back in her seat.

"I hear you've got yerself a wee girlfriend as well."

My stomach tenses. Fuck. I don't react. Don't let it show on my face at all.

She takes me saying nothing as a sign to keep going. She gestures around her vaguely. "Eyes everywhere—"

I shake my head a bit, run my tongue along my bottom lip. Do my best to look bored. "Well, your eyes are shit—"

"—Is that so?" she asks, eyebrows up.

I give her a look like she's an idiot.

"She has a boyfriend—" I tell her, rolling my eyes. Grateful for

Ballentine for the first time in my fucking life. "They're on the cover of every fucking magazine in the country."

Her face flickers, confused, and I pray a quick prayer that wherever those eyes of hers are, they're watching Magnolia straddle Ballentine at this very moment.

She pinches her bottom lip, looking annoyed.

I sniff. "We're just naffing, Ro."

"How does the boyfriend feel about that?"

"Not good." I give her a hallow laugh, then shrug. "If you saw her, you'd give it a crack too."

She gives me an unpleasant smile. "Maybe I will."

I'm going to be sick, I think.

I nod my head like I don't give a shit about any of what she's saying. Like I'm not going to call Jonah the second I'm in my car to keep Magnolia away from all the windows, as though I'm not about to pull up the video footage of the Compound to check in on LJ.

I stand and her eyes follow me up, glaring.

"I think we're done here." I tell her as I start to walk away.

Then she calls after me, "We'll talk soon."

Magnolia
4:45PM

You good?

Yes! You?

Where are you?

Just in the room

Why?

Nothing

All good

Okay

I was about to go swimming, want to come?

Yeah. Wait for me?

Okay.

Is everything okay?

Yep, grand

Be home soon x

45

Christian

Since word got out that we're back together, my mum has been been biting my arm off to have Daisy over.

Italy was good, but I'm glad to be back. Too many weird vibes there, and me and Dais don't need any of them.

And then, honestly, we were together properly again all of forty seconds before we went off to Italy — have you ever moved into a house, and you can be properly moved in, all unpacked, but then you go away on holidays, and you've only spent a night or two in the place before you left? It still doesn't really feel like yours yet. It doesn't start to feel like yours til you're back in your own bed, learning to use the washing machine, burning yourself in the new shower... living in it. You know?

I just want to be living in it with Daisy.

Sunday brunch with Mum, a thing she's been trying to push on us this last year. They haven't always gone over well.

Sometimes they're at home, sometimes they're out — when they were out, sometimes I'd bring Vanna. Usually lived to regret it.

Mum wasn't a fan.

Daisy looks nervous on the way over. I've got my hand in her lap as I drive and she's holding it with both of hers, pinching my fingers without knowing she's doing it.

"Mum loves you—" I tell her with a little frown.

"Yeah?" She looks over at me.

"Yeah." I nod.

"Who else will be there?"

"Jo?" I shrug. "Callum, maybe—"

"Not your dad?" she asks my hand.

I shrug. "I'm sure he'll be on the property... I doubt he'll be at the table."

I pull in up the driveway and breathe out, feeling some kind of relief to have her with me. I did my best not to imagine her here, in my life how I wanted her to be — because I wanted her to be happy more than I wanted me to be happy. Love fucks you up. I wasn't like that before. I wanted me happy more than anyone, and now I'd probably stick my hand in a blender if it'd make her smile.

"Daisy!" Mum throws her arms around her neck and squeezes the shit out of her. "Sweetheart, it's such a pleasure to see you—" Mum kisses my cheek quickly. "Hello, my darling—"

She whisks Daisy away towards the dining room.

"Now, I'm not nearly the chef you are, Daisy, so I've had this morning catered—"

"Mum—" I roll my eyes.

"You didn't have to do that—" Daisy shakes her head, looking back at me, embarrassed. "I'd eat Cornflakes if you gave them to me."

"Mum, we could have just gone out—" I follow after them.

"Oh, rubbish — I love having my boys home." She ushers Daisy to her seat. I sit down next to her as enough food to feed Papua New Guinea is is carried out to us.

"Who else is coming?" I frown at it all.

"Me," says Uncle Callum, sitting down across from me. He gives me a tight smile.

"Cal," I nod at him. "Been a minute — how are you?"

He eyes my arm around Daisy.

"Well." He smiles and I don't honestly care for it. I've never liked him much. "Look at this—"

His eyes dance from me to Daisy and he opens his mouth to say something when Jonah bursts in.

"Sorry!" he bellows. "Sorry, sorry — I'm late. Came from Tottenham."

"Why?" Daisy frowns.

Jonah ignores her question, gruffly hooks his arm around her neck and kisses the top of her head, then walks around and sits next to Uncle Callum.

Jo doesn't mind him.

"For the love of God, Jonah—" their mother sighs, walking in carrying a platter of croissants. I don't know why, there's five of us and I think twelve croissants. "Is that lipstick on your neck?"

Jonah touches his neck, thinking. "What colour is it?"

"Red," I tell him.

Callum turns to Jo and squints. "I'd say it's more of a burgundy?"

"You have one on the other side of your neck that's decidedly hot pink." Daisy points at it.

"Jonah!" Mum cries. She waves her hands carelessly at the food. "Eat, everyone — eat— except for you—" She smacks a danish out of Jo's hand.

"Are both those lipstick marks from Taura?"

Jonah's face pulls and then he glances over at me. "Is it better or worse if I say yes?"

I shrug.

Daisy frowns a bit. "Who are they from, then?"

My brother stares over at her, saying nothing. I can see it resting on his face somewhere that he feels shit about it, but he doesn't know what else to do.

This shit with Taura, it's been going on too long. And I think he doesn't know what else to do. Jo's locked it down for months — which is weird for him — and all it does is show me that we're fucked. No matter what way that sword falls, we're fucked.

And then my mum, my brother and Callum all freeze, staring at something behind me.

Daisy looks over her shoulder, curious.

"Oh." She smiles. "Hello."

My dad says nothing as he sits down at the head of the table.

"Dad," I say. Not a question, but not a statement either.

He glances over at me, like he's surprised to see me.

"Christian," he says, blinking a few times. Drunk, I wonder?

Then he looks past me to Daisy, blinking. I shift in front of her because I don't want him staring at her — then he shifts his gaze over to Jonah.

"And Jonah." Long pause. "To what do we owe the pleasure?"

"No!" Mum says, swatting her hand in the direction of her eldest. "He's off pleasure—" She points a finger at him. "Do you hear me? Enough! You're twenty-five. Pick one."

Jonah presses his lips together and stares at his plate. Stops one of the butlers. "Bloody Mary, mate." Jo catches my eye. "Three of them—" he calls after him.

"So, what happened with you and that bloody police officer in the end then, ey?" Uncle Callum asks, sipping his tea.

I squint over at him, pissed off, open my mouth to say something but Daisy beats me to the punch.

"He asked me too many questions that weren't his business." She gives him a curt smile and Uncle Callum did not like that one.

His head pulls back. "Do you know who you're talking to?"

Daisy Haites, love of my fucking life, cocks an eyebrow. "Do you?"

That'd hurt his ego, I know it would. Because no matter how you slice it, she's higher on the food chain.

Callum's in no direct line of succession. Mum and Jo and me would all have to take a bullet for him to get a seat at the table, and even then, our family in London doesn't hold power how hers does.

She's a fucking Haites.

"What happened to the blonde one, then?" Dad asks suddenly, waving his hand in Daisy's direction.

Barnesy drops her cutlery on her plate and glares over at the man she married.

Daisy's little body goes tense next to mine so I hook my arm around her.

"Jud." Mum stares him down, then looks over at Daisy apologetically. "She's never even been here. He's never met her. I don't know why he'd—"

Me and Jo stare over at each other, tired of his shit.

"What?" Dad shrugs. "I can't Google the girl my son's knocking about with?"

Uncle Callum scoffs.

"What the fuck, Dad—" Jonah growls. "She's right fucking there."

"Who?" He blinks, and Daisy sits up a little straighter, not as fazed as you'd think.

"My girlfriend, Dad." I give him a glare. "Daisy."

Dad's eyes pinch as he stares over at her. "Was the other one your girlfriend?"

"No." I breathe out loudly through my nose.

"And how old are you, Daphne?"

"Daisy," I say loudly, my hands balling up into fists.

"Daisy," Dad says, over-annunciating her name on purpose. "How old are you?"

She scratches the tip of her nose. "I'm twenty-one."

Dad stares over her, properly seeing her for the first time.

"What do you do, Daisy?" he asks, not looking away from her.

She picks at her croissant. "I'm in third year med."

"You're a doctor—" He blinks, intrigued, glancing between the rest of us.

She gives his a gracious smile he doesn't deserve. "Not quite yet."

I lift her hand to my mouth and kiss the back of it, steady her, even though she doesn't need it.

"What's your specialty going to be?" he asks, reaching for his orange juice.

Me and Jo trade confused looks — our Dad hasn't spoken this much in about fourteen years — and Mum, she's sitting at the other end of the table, watching on curiously.

"Hmm—" Daisy purses her lips. "I think I'd like it to be paeds, but I think it'll probably be triage, in the end."

He frowns a little. "Why's that?"

Daisy shrugs like she can't help it. "I guess triage is probably more beneficial in my family's line of work…"

He tilts his head. "And what is your family's line of work?"

She nods her chin over at him. "Same as yours."

"Ah." He nods, flicking his eyes between me and Jo, then back to her. "Did you get into medicine because of that?"

"Um." She frowns, considering it. "Probably to combat it more than anything?"

"Combat it?" repeats Uncle Callum, instantly offended. "You don't like what your family does?"

Daisy's eyes flicker from mine to Jo's to my mum's, like her foot's caught in a trap.

"I mean—" She forces a polite smile at Callum. "Does anyone? No one grows up wanting to be a criminal, do they?"

I stare over at her, love her more than I did a second ago, I don't know why. Just do. Then she points at me. "—Rugby captain." She nods over at Jo. "Party Cruise director, I presume—" And Mum sniffs a laugh.

Then Dais looks at Mum. "What did you want to be growing up?"

Mum's face falters a little, like she hadn't thought of it in so long that she'd forgotten that once upon a time, before Uncle Beau died, and before Harvey left, she used to have a life that wasn't like this. The question stumps her. She just blinks a few times.

"An English teacher," my dad says from the other end of the table, staring at his wife, brows low, jaw tight.

They hold eyes and the air goes thick with words they refuse to speak, and then Dad turns to Daisy, giving her a wisp of a smile. "She wanted to be an English teacher."

Hey

Hey!

When are you going to tell him.

Tell who

Jonah.

Tell him what?

That's it's not him.

I know it's not him

How do you know?

Taura.

What the fuck?

How do you not know?

46

Julian

Italy fucked me up a bit. The casual little threat Roisin threw Magnolia's way — my natural instinct is to not let her out of my sight. But we're just naffing, that's what I told her.

If I send her to work with my security team, they'll know.

If I drop her myself — like, why the fuck would I drop a girl I'm just shagging to work? I'm not Prince fucking Charming — they'll know.

Best I can do is act like she means nothing to me. Pretty hard to do when she means it all.

That, and she's like a dog with a fucking bone.

I said I'd get dinner with her family before we went to Italy, because before we went to Italy, I wasn't trying to throw someone off the scent of how much I love her — myself, just. Kept putting it off, because why would I get dinner with the family of a girl I was 'just naffing'?

The only redeeming thing here is Magnolia's dad is Harley fucking Parks. And he's not crooked, all his business dealings are above board. But he's an internationally renowned partier.

Well, he was, before he married the maid.

Walk in to Julie's over in Notting Hill, Bridget and their dad already at the table.

Give Bridget a kiss on the cheek, hug Harley as familiarly as I can, make a bit of a show of it.

I hate acting for a camera I don't even know is there — better than the other method of dousing this fire, which is sending Magnolia off into the arms of her ex-boyfriend, which I also did the other day.

Organised a dinner at Carmelo's for all of them, then told her I was running late and didn't show.

Met up with her later at one of the clubs, brought her to Jonah's office — we didn't have sex, she gave me a little PowerPoint presentation on the evolution of sleeves — hated it. Even if I loved it. Kissed her a lot.

Asked Jonah to drop her home. He asked why, I told him not to ask questions.

Then I hooked up with another girl there — kissed her in a corner, felt her up, felt sick while I did it.

Doing it because I love her? To keep her safe? Fuck, what a life.

The stepmother arrives, Arrie Parks, and Magnolia's grandmother with her. They weren't invited.

Interesting decision on the stepmother's behalf, and I watch her throughout the night trying to work out whether it was a guilt move or a power play… Having an affair with and marrying your boss is one thing, but to drag around the woman he left you for — it's fucked up either way, and I can tell quickly that Magnolia's attachment issues are a cross-generational problem.

The grandma is a great time, and I'd — I'm being completely serious — have her at any party of mine.

She offers me her hand and points to herself with her free one. "Bushka."

I shake hers, point to myself with my other one too. "Julian."

She points to herself again.

"Captain of Neighbourhood Watch." Bushka tells me proudly.

"Well—" Magnolia starts.

Bridget shakes her head. "She's not."

Parks grimaces. "It's more of a 'binoculars and hole in the wall' situation."

"I watch." Bushka nods.

"So," Magnolia tilts her head. "It's actually really more in the ball park of questionable legality."

Bridget whacks me in the arm, beaming. "Which you know all about!"

I toss her sister a look. I like her a lot. She reminds me of my own sister.

And then their mum — met her a few times — she's beautiful. Would have given Carla Bruni a run for her money. Pretty sure she did, actually. Honestly, if she wasn't Magnolia's mum, I'd probably have a crack. She's a fucking smoke-show. Like mother, like daughter, I guess — with the eyes and the body and the sadness.

Kind of reminds me of my mum. Regret saying I'd have a crack now — they don't physically look the same. Mum was blonde. It's the lost thing.

And the drunk thing.

Arrie grabbed me by the face and kissed me. Slipped me a bit of tongue, actually.

Magnolia was mortified, flashed me an apologetic look. "Every family has one…"

"God, if I was a few years younger…" Arrie says, chin in hand and staring over at me a bit into the dinner.

Magnolia face twists up. "Or perhaps, I don't know— were he and I not together…"

Bridget's mouth falls open and I glance over at her. I'm surprised. Into it, but surprised.

Her cheeks go pink. "You know what I mean—" She shakes her head. I don't, actually. Do want to figure it out though.

"Anyway," the nanny says, clearing her throat, tossing Magnolia a conversational life raft.

After, I go back to her place with her. Pretty in my head about everything she said. Ignoring the last few weeks, that was exactly what I want to hear. In context of Roisin, it's a fucking spanner.

I sit on the edge of a bed she bought in an antique showroom I took her to. It looks good in here… does something to me, seeing her liking the things I like. Buy things I like, want things I want. Like I'm rubbing off on her.

I stare over at her, pinch my mouth trying to figure out what to say.

"Together, huh?" I eye her, suspicious. And the suspicion is valid. I reckon Jo was right. She'll set any heart she has to on fire just so she can stay warm.

"No, sorry—" She shakes her head, instantly embarrassed. "I know, that just came out— I know that you don't date—"

Nod once. "I don't."

She shakes her head more, hands on her cheek — that's Magnolia for peak embarrassed. "I really didn't mean it like that."

"How'd you mean it then?" I ask, jaw jutted out.

"Sorry." Her eyes fall, staring at her hands.

I stand up, look for her eyes. "You're in love with someone else."

"I know." She frowns.

That annoyed me, can't tell you why. I wanted her to refute me or to hesitate or something... Anything to tell me I'm not completely out here in love with her on my own, but she doesn't throw me a fucking bone.

"So then how the fuck might we be together?" I glare over at her.

She takes a step towards me, eyes big, bottom lip out.

"Don't be cross at me." She frowns.

Shake my head at her. "I am a bit—"

Then she gets annoyed at me. "Why?"

"I don't know—" I scowl. "Because you're so fucking annoying. You don't know what you want. You want everything, you want nothing, you're a fucking pain in the arse."

She stares over at me, nose in the air, crossing her arms over her chest.

"That was a bit mean..."

I know what I want, it's selfish to want it now, but I'll take it for a minute while I can, so I grab her face, knock her backwards and lift her on top of her chest of drawers.

"What are you doing?" she asks without slowing down.

I take off her dress. "This."

She looks confused. "Now?"

"Yes." I unbutton my shirt.

She blinks, confused. "Why?"

I stare down at her, holding her face. "Because this is what we do."

And then I kiss her again. "And don't you dare fucking think of me—"

She sniffs, confused as I lay her down on her bed. "I'll do my best..."

"We're not together."

"This feels like a mixed message," she responds.

I give her a look, make sure she knows I'm serious. "You love him. I love no one. Yeah?"

I'm lying through my fucking teeth, but I am serious.

"Okay?" She shrugs, confused.

I wrap my arms around her.

"Okay."

47

Daisy

I stand in my brother's office doorway, watching him.

He's different these days, beyond just being distracted. I think he's softer. Can't say that to him, though. That'd be the ultimate insult. But he is, softer and more aware. She's thawing him.

"Hey," I say.

He looks up, puts his pen down. "Hey."

"Can we talk?" I ask, shifting into the room anyway.

He frowns: instant concern. "Yeah?"

He tracks me as I walk across the room, watches me as I sit. "Are you good?"

"Yeah," I nod, watching him closely. "Are you?"

He sniffs, amused.

"Yeah, I'm fine." He crosses his arms over his chest. "What's going on?"

I mirror him. "I have something to tell you."

"Okay." He nods, back to frowning now.

It's been on my mind ever since she told me. It makes so much sense. It gives context for their entire relationship, it explains away why they are how they are, and perhaps most pressingly and worst of all: why they will always be what they are.

I didn't plan on telling him, honestly. I don't like telling other people's secrets — I think Magnolia and I are friends now[214] — it's just, it's Julian.

I'd throw anyone[215] under the bus for him.

"In high school, Magnolia and BJ had a baby."

He stares over at me, brows low, blinks once.

---

[214] But for fuck's sake, don't tell her I said that.
[215] Everyone.

"It died," I clarify.

Then he runs his tongue over his front teeth. "I know."

"You know?" I blink, pulling my head back.

He nods. "Yeah, I know — how do you know?" He frowns. "Christian tell you?"

"No—" I scowl defensively at the accusation that my boyfriend might be bad at secrets. "She told me."

That surprises him. "She told you?"

I nod, proudly. "I mean, she asked me not to tell you, but—"

He rolls his eyes.

"How do you know?" I wave my hand at him.

"I know everything about her." He shrugs.[216] "I know she was pregnant when she was sixteen, I know it was his. I know the baby died, I know it was a girl. I know she was in a car accident when she was at school because her dad's friend was driving and he was drunk. I know she was an inpatient and an outpatient at Bloxham House for an eating disorder on and off from fifteen to seventeen— I know it it all, Dais—"[217] He glares over at me a bit. "Doesn't change shit."

"Because you love her."

His jaw juts out, pushes the tip of his tongue into his top lip. Says nothing.

"I'm sorry—" I tell him and I mean it.[218]

"Don't be—" He shakes his head. "I got to fall in love with her for a minute. Tick that off the bucket list—"

I roll my eyes at him.

"You know we can't be together." He gives me a look.

"But why not?" I shake my head. "She likes you, I know she does — I can tell in how she looks at you, how she is around you—"

"I know." He nods quickly. "I think I know, anyway. But even if she does, she loves him more—" He gives me a little shrug. "It's better that way."

"Is it?" I frown.

"Course it is—" He rolls his eyes, like I'm an idiot.

"I think you could be quite happy together."

---

[216] "Bit weird—" I eyeball him and he ignores me.

[217] He hired an investigator, he'd tell me later. Got a little dossier on her. "You think I don't know who I'm getting into bed with? Come on."

[218] This would be his nightmare.

I regret saying that as soon as I say it, even though I believe it, even though I'm convinced it's true, it hurts him to hear it. I see it happen on his face, how it pulls, almost like a wince.

"Yeah—" He stares at his hands and sighs, then he looks back over at me. "But would she be safe?"

"I'm sorry, Jules—" I reach over and squeeze his hand. "You deserve to be loved."

"No, I don't, Dais — I'm a gang lord." His mouth shrugs as he shakes his head. "This dies with me, remember?"

I give him a quick, sad smile. "Or me."

"Nah." He gives me a tired smile. "You're going to live forever."

48

Christian

We all to go dinner at Nobu, except for BJ and Jordan. Don't know why they didn't come, but we head back to Jo and BJ's house after. And the night's looking to be fairly chill.

Everyone's behaving. Neither Henry or Jo are being particularly territorial of Taura — don't know what that means really on a larger scale, but for this evening, I'm taking it as the win it is.

Magnolia and BJ are their regular, weird selves. Stolen glances and all-round inappropriate behaviour for two people who are not dating each other.

I watch it crush my friend.

I know the feeling, I lived with it myself for a long time and I feel for him. But his hands are tied because what can he do?

Daisy and I talked about it, she's pretty wound up about it all.

She's convinced Magnolia likes Julian back, and I said that she might be right, but then you look at her and BJ and it just doesn't size up. Nothing ever does.

And she said maybe it could if Julian told her and they gave it a proper shot, and I said, "How proper could the shot be? He doesn't want to be in love."

"But he's already in it." She frowned up at me.

I pushed some hair behind her ear. "I think you're just going to have to leave it, Baby."

Her chin sunk in. "But his heart's going to break."

I nodded and squeezed her hand. "Probably, yeah."

The novelty of being with Daisy like this, it's still real shiny.

She sits on my lap instead of a seat every chance she gets. Whenever we're standing, whether she's facing me or her back's to me, her hands are in my pockets. Front pockets, back pockets, the big one at the front of a hoodie, her and her little ice-lollie hands always find mine, and we're probably annoying and I definitely don't give a shit.

A bit into the night, Julian's phone rings.

"Teeks—" he says into it. "What's up?" His face falters. "What?" He stands, pressing his finger into his ear, moving away from us all.

Daisy doesn't catch it, misses the whole thing. She's laughing too much at a story Henry's telling about when their dad was detained because they thought he was smuggling children into Britain because we got separated from each other in customs at the Austrian border. The girls were taking too long in Duty Free and Lily went ahead with the rest of us but Hamish stayed trying to wrangle Magnolia, Allie, Madie and Paili, and Magnolia started crying because she said she felt misunderstood when people rushed her in the cosmetics section, and the customs official thought she was being trafficked.

So Daisy misses it, but I don't miss it.

I'm watching Julian closely and so is Jo.

When Julian leaves the room, phone still pressed against his ear I stand up casually, stretch and kiss Daisy on top of her head.

"Want another wine?" I ask her.

She gives me a quick nod and keeps laughing at Henry.

Jonah ducks away, following him and a minute later I slip in behind him.

Julian's standing in the corner of Jonah's room, staring at his phone screen.

"What?" I ask, closing the door behind me.

Julian shakes his head a tiny bit. "Gilpatrick."

"What?" Jo frowns but I know.

I go still.

"Cian Gilpatrick—" Julian stares over at me. "TK just flagged him flying through Heathrow."

"Okay?" Jo frowns a bit more.

Julian licks his bottom lip. "Daisy killed his brother last year."

"Accidentally—" I tack on at the end, like that fucking matters now.

"Oh, shit." Jonah blinks. "He's one of Roisin's boys, yeah?"

Julian nods.

"Jules, it might be nothing—" I shrug, trying my best to believe that.

Julian tosses me a look. "It's never nothing with them."

He sighs, shakes his head a bit. Shoves his hands through his hair. Then he looks from me to Jo, his eyes all pinched. "Roisin was in Italy."

"What?" I blink.

Jonah shakes his head. "What are you talking about?"

"She called me." Julian shrugged.

"Roisin?" I blinked.

Jules nodded.

"Did you see her?"

He nods again.

"Why?" Jonah asks carefully.

Julian presses his tongue into his cheek. "Because she's my mum's sister." He grimaces, then looks straight at me. "Daisy doesn't know—"

"What?" I blink.

"Don't tell her—" He shakes his head.

"Julian—" My head rolls back. "Why the fuck wouldn't you tell her?"

He gets a look on his face, as dark as it is protective. "They've never been and won't ever be any kind of family to her, you can trust me on that."

I stare over at him, not completely sure what he's actually getting at.

"Are you saying you think Cian Gilpatrick is here to k—" I can't even say it. Shake my head. "Here for Daisy?"

Julian presses his hand into his mouth. "Or Magnolia."

"What?" Jonah's entire body swivels.

Julian shakes his head. "Ro said something about Parks when I was there—"

"Julian—" Jonah warns.

"I know—" He shakes his head. "It's fine. I'm going to — I told her it was nothing. She believed me, I think—"

I watch Julian's face. I can't tell if that's true. I can tell he wants it to be, whether it is or not though, I don't know…

"What exactly did she say?" Jonah asks him very clearly.

"She just made a comment about me having a girlfriend—"

"Shit." My brother growls.

"I told her it was bullshit—" Jules shakes his head, but he looks worried. "That she's on the cover of every magazine about with her actual boyfriend."

Jo glares over at him a bit, and I know what's going through his head is the same thing that's going through mine. We should have never let this happen.

"So, what the fuck do we do?" I ask, shaking my head, looking between them.

Julian points at me.

"You're going to take Daisy home to the Compound, she's not going to know anything is wrong, it'll be business as usual for her—"

I frown at him but he shakes his head.

"I've tripled the security, everyone in the house knows that they are to save her at all costs or die trying—" I feel sick.

I'm going to be sick thinking about something happening to her.

Julian sees it on my face, catches my eye as he grabs my shoulder.

"Christian, you just need to keep her calm. Take her home, tell her you have a craving for — something complicated someone you loved used to make—"

"Mum doesn't cook—"

"Then a grandma — you had a grandma who made a fucking ace éclair—"

"We had a grandma who loved a drop—" Jo offers unhelpfully.

Her brother gives mine a look that shuts him up before he turns back to me.

"Just keep her busy."

"And Parks?" Jonah asks, eyebrows up. He's worried. He's keeping it cool on the surface, but he's freaking out. He loves her like the sister we lost.

"And herein lies the problem—" Julian starts pacing. "If I react, pull Magnolia somewhere to keep her safe, then she's my girlfriend and she's a target. If I leave her, she's open, she's a target."

I look between them. "We should tell Beej—"

Jonah looks over at me sharply. "Are you fucking daft?"

"Yeah?" Julian says, eyebrows up. "What's he going to do, smoulder down the barrel of a gun?"

"Yeah—" I glare at him, give him a shrug. "Or just not put her in front of a gun in the first place."

Julian points at me. "Not the fucking time, Christian—"

324

"I'll stay with Taura tonight." Jo nods. "I'll stay at Taura's, get Mum to send some men out for patrol… it'll be fine."

"Yeah and if they get through?" I stare over at him. "Then it's just you and the two most unequipped girls in Britain."

Julian presses his hands into his eyes and Jonah gives me a look. "Not helping."

49

Julian

Jonah stayed with the girls in the end. I thought about trying to sneak over to Magnolia's because that's what you want to do. When you love someone, if they're in danger, you want to be with them, you want to protect them. I'm the only person who can protect her how I want her to be protected and I can't, because if I do, it becomes obvious that she needs it.

The whole thing's fucked. I've got the boys bringing home girls from bars, and then I walk them out of my place a few hours later, kissing them and sending them on their way, hoping whatever eyes of Roisin's are looking, that they're thrown by it.

I don't want to be kissing other girls.

Managed to keep it off Magnolia's radar, managed to make her stay over at the Compound the last few nights, too.

But the whole thing shits me — sneaking around my own city — locking away the girl I love to keep her safe? Fuck it, no—

So I called a Boroughs meeting a few days later. We have these once in a blue moon.

The heads of all the crime families all in one place? Recipe for disaster. We all get along fine — just all of us in a room is an invitation for trouble...

The Boroughs is what my dad oversaw, now me.

Six families, six cities.

London is the epicentre of the Isle's Underworld; with me at London's helm, I sit at the top and everything that flies in, floats in or tunnels into the Isles comes through me — with the exception of Dublin.

The Irish run their own outfit. Three guesses who runs that one, but you're only going to need one.

Could count on one hand the amount of times we've had one of these meetings…

I see them all myself individually all the time. See the Bambrillas every other day but the Boroughs mean business. Barnsey should be here, but she always sends the boys. Calls it a sausage fest.

Daisy's not a fan of the Boroughs either, if I'm honest. Told Rome to distract her so she's in the kitchen making him an Easter pie.

Magnolia's upstairs working — seems like a risk, maybe, but find me a more secure building in London than this one right now.

"So she threatened you?" Santino (Bambrilla, Liverpool) sits back in his chair.

I nod.

"Not good," Hughie McCracken says in his thick Glasgow accent, banging his fist into his mouth, thinking.

"How serious a situation are we talking here?" James Devlin (Belfast) asks.

"Serious." I nod once. "Daisy killed one of Roisin's boys last year."

"What?" Danny Jukes (Birmingham) blinks.

Hughie shakes his head. "Tell me you're joking—"

"It was an an accident," Christian pipes up and Jukes points over at him.

"Let's not hear from the lad who's shagging her right now."

"It was an accident." Santino says loudly over the rest of them. He loves my sister like she's his own daughter.

"I hired them for a job and—" I start.

"I thought you didn't work with the MacMathans." Jukes' eyes pinch.

"Right." I nod. "I forgot I answer to you—"

I run my tongue across my bottom lip, daring him to keep going.

"They went rogue—" Christian shakes his head. "Started shooting people—"

"So?" Hughie shrugs.

"So, Daisy's never been down for shit like that." Jonah shrugs.

"She didn't know I hired them—" I tell the room. "She didn't know who she was shooting when she shot them—"

"She was defending someone," Christian says and our eyes catch.

I like Tiller, like to think I'm a better man these days than I was before Parks found me — but I do find myself thinking for a second how much easier the last year of all our lives might have been if Daisy had just let him die.

Jukes' nods coolly. "And now we're paying for it—"

"Cut the shit, Danny—" Carmelo nods his chin over at him. "How many times has one of us had to come and bail your fucking dumbarse out of a gulag?"

"That happened one time, and it wasn't even you, it was Storm, so—" Danny yells, standing to his feet, so Carmelo gets up on his.

I breathe out my nose and rolls my eyes. "Yeah, and who do you think Anatole Storm is answering to? The tooth fairy?"

I get some chuckles for that.

Danny shakes his head. "If I'm putting my boys on the line for this, I want to know what I'm getting out of it," He yells, looking from me to Santino, ignoring Carmelo completely.

"My protection," I tell him.

Jukes shakes his head. "Doesn't sound like that's worth all that much, ma—"

And then the boardroom door opens and Magnolia Parks barely fills the frame.

"Oh, hello!" She beams at the men and I freeze.

I glance over at Christian whose eyes are wide, sprung, like he's in trouble.

"Hello?" Devlin frowns at her, confused.

Jonah's mouthing over at her, 'get out. Get the fuck out', but she's too busy glancing around, eyes all bright and excited to have an entire room's attention.

"Hi." She smiles politely, ever the picture of London's aristocratic society.

"And who are you?" Jukes stares over at her.

Magnolia walks deeper into the room and Christian's as subtly as possible trying to tell her to stop but she's not paying attention.

"Oh, I'm Magnolia Parks—" She touches her chest. "I'm one of Daisy's closest friends—" And with that, Christian and I catch eyes, and he bites down on his thumb to stop from laughing. "And Julian's current..." She trails, finger pressed into her mouth, thinking.

"Lover?" Carmelo offers unhelpfully and Magnolia shrugs, happily accepting it.

"Sure." She grins.

The tension in the room shifts some.

"Lover!" coos Jukes.

"Ay! Lover boy!" Hugh jeers.

Magnolia looks unfazed at their teasing, almost like she doesn't hear it. It's actually pretty spectacular to watch her conscious denial in action. Legendary stuff.

"Sorry. I — I was upstairs working, and I got lonely—" Her eyes catch mine, but I look away because I don't want my cheeks to go hot in front of everyone.

"I didn't realise you were having a boys lunch—"

"We do love a boys lunch," Devlin interjects.

She smiles apologetically and turns to leave.

"Where are you going!" Devlin calls after her.

"Come in!" Hughie tells her, grinning. "Join us."

"Oh." She shakes her head demurely. "I shouldn't like to intrude."

Santino gives her an unimpressed look — immune to her charm, apparently — what a fucking gift. "You already have."

"Come on—" I beckon her over, eye Santino to let him know that fucked me off a bit.

She perches down on my lap, settles in, then looks around the men. "So, what are you talking about?"

"Oh—" Jonah shrugs dismissively. Nothing much, just plotting the demise of our rival. "Uh — football." He gives her a reassuring smile.

She glances around the room apologetically. "I'm not a sports girl."

Christian rolls his eyes. "You don't say?"

"What kind of girl are you then?" Hughie asks.

"The best kind." She beams and Christian rolls his eyes.

"What do you do?" Devlin asks, leaning in.

"Well." She flattens her skirt. "I'm the style editor for *Tatler*."

Santino looks over at her, maybe mildly impressed. "Are you?"

"Yes," she tells him, nose in the air. "And I have to say, I love that Camp-Collar Printed Silk Shirt from Valentino you're sporting. It's chic. Fresh, very age appropriate — you look great."

Santino stares over at her blankly for about four long seconds and I wonder if she's offended him, if I'll be shielding her from two gang lords now instead of one — and then his face cracks wide with a laugh.

He leans back in his chair, howling.

Magnolia glances at me, confused and delighted.

"So Tatler." Devlin nods at her. "Who would you say is the best dressed?"

"Here?" Her eyes flicker around the table of Britain's most notorious men.

She purses her lips for a second. "Christian, probably. Then Julian, then Jonah—" He tosses her an unimpressed look.

"You wear too much black, I've begged you to stop." she tells him, before she eyes Carmelo. "Then you, I suppose." Tosses a glance at Santino. "Well, perhaps you two tie for fourth."

"Then you—" She points to Jukes. "Then you—" She points to Devlin. "Then—" She stops talking but smiles politely at McCracken.

The room erupts in laughter.

"Are you from Scotland?" she asks gently.

"Yes?"

"I can tell — it's the jeans." She nods like she already knew. "In Ireland and Scotland people tend to wear denim that is, in my opinion, somewhat ill-fitting—" Oh fuck. I'm going have to fight one of my oldest friends, aren't I? This fucking girl, such a motherfucking headache.

"Instead of a skinny jean—"

"I like skinny jeans." He frowns. Holy shit.

"Perhaps we could try a slim fit pant." She shrugs her shoulders. Holy shit.

"Like a boot cut?" McCracken asks and I double take.

"No—" She shakes her head. "My God, no. Kelly Clarkson's stylist from 2003 called, she'd like her jeans back—" Magnolia sniffles at her own joke but literally not another soul laughs and no one knows what she means.

That alone is enough to put Jonah in stitches. Doubled over.

"What are you doing now—?" Magnolia asks McCracken bright. "Shall I take you shopping?"

He blinks a bunch. "I—"

I pull her backwards in to me. "Were in the middle of a meeting, Tiges."

"Oh—" She laughs airily. "Of course. Well, what time will you be done?" She checks her wristwatch.

"In a few hours?" I shrug.

"Oh." Her face scrunches up, and the stares over at him. "How about I just take your sizes down and run out and buy a few pieces?"

"Um—" McCracken looks over at me.

"It's no trouble," Magnolia tells him brightly.

He shrugs, worn down. "Okay."

"Great!" She jumps to her feet and launches over to him, fishing out of her pocket a little Métier leather-clad measuring tape and she spreads it out across his shoulders.

Hughie freezes.

"What sizes are you?" she asks, looking at him.

"I'm 6'0. A 38" in the chest—" he tells her and she measures him anyway.

Carmelo licks away a smile.

"43 for shoes."

"Okay." Magnolia nods. "Suit?"

"38L."

"Right." She makes a note on her phone. "Waist?"

"32"."

"I'll just measure your inseam—" She smiles up at him and he looks over at me panicked as she goes to bend down and Christian and I both yell, "No!"

I shake my head. "No — that's — just — we can guess."

"Oh." She frowns, not really tracking.

Christian and Jonah are cry-laughing at this point.

"Okay." She bounces back over to me, kisses me on my cheek.

"Koa will take you," I tell her and she nods. "You'll come back after?"

"Well, yes." Her face falters. "I'll be styling your friend."

She walks to the door. "Okay, bye!" she sings to them all. "Such a pleasure!" And then she walks out.

There's silence for all of three seconds before laughter breaks in the room like a burst damn.

"Lover!" Jonah crows.

"He's a lover!" Hughie jeers.

I roll my eyes.

"Does she measure your inseam a lot?" Jukes asks and I toss him a look.

"Alright, everyone—" I roll my eyes.

"Yeah, shut up!" Carmelo yells. "Lover's got something to say—"

Santino whacks his son in the chest and our eyes catch.

Feel like he can tell from my face alone that I love her.

Hate feeling see-through but here I am, and I need his help to keep the two girls I love safe.

~

Later that night, the meeting's done and everyone's gone home.

Magnolia's having a steam and I'm just about to join her when there's a knock at the door as I'm walking past it.

Frown at it, annoyed to be opening the door like a fucking servant, and there's someone I'm not expecting to see.

"Tiller." I frown.

"Hey." He nods his chin at me.

"What are you—" I frown more. "Are you here for my sister?"

"No, not — not really." He shakes his head, licks his bottom lip. "Is she…"

I shake my head a bit. "Her and Christian are—"

"I know." He nods.

That strings him a bit, you can tell. Haven't seen him since they ended. I kind of liked him in the end.

I scrunch my nose up a bit. "Sorry."

He shakes his head.

"Cian Gilpatrick flew in to London a few days ago." He crosses his arms over his chest.

I look over at him, surprised. "I know."

"Daisy killed his brother."

"Yeah—" I give him a look. "I know."

His face goes serious, the way it does when you've properly loved a person. "Are they coming for her?"

I cross my arms. Nod. "It looks like it."

His brows lower. "Because she saved me?"

I don't say anything, just shake my head and shrug.

He breathes in, face all pinched like the thought hurts him. "If you need anything, you tell me — I'll do it."

50

Daisy

Christian's in the papers sometimes because of Britain's stupid fascination with the Box Set... Not the same way they are about Magnolia and BJ, but he'd get it a bit.

When he was with Vanna though — everywhere. He was everywhere. I didn't go on Instagram for months because they saturated my feed. It was horrible to watch.

He didn't love her, I know that now, but still, it does something to you as a person, watching the person you love love someone else. I guess he watched me love someone too.

Christian and I arrive at one of Jonah's clubs with my brother and Magnolia. They've just come from BJ's little sister's 21st, and the thought of Julian voluntarily going to a stranger's birthday party is the most overt way of declaring he's in love without actually declaring it.

Christian takes my hand, pulls me through the crowd as the paparazzi goes berserk for Magnolia — my brother breaks a camera when it gets too close to her — she apologises, the picture of grace always,[219] gives the photographer her card and promises to buy them a new camera, but would he please mind leaving her alone for the evening, she's just having some time with his friends.

The photographer looks after her sort of dazed, like he's been touched by an angel, then clears everyone off because I guess Magnolia Parks isn't the kind of girl you make a promise to and then break it.

She pulls my brother inside, scolding him for his temper and he takes it. Rolls his eyes at her, looks like he's bored, but doesn't talk

---

[219] Annoying.

back, just kisses her and I watch on nervous about what life might look like when they inevitably combust into flames.

"Do you want to come to the bathroom with me?" Magnolia asks me sweetly.

"No." I yawn.

"Oh, come on—" She swats her hand then takes mine. "You can stop pretending you don't like me now, we all know you do—"

"I don't—" I shake my head.

"Of course you do." She pulls me away from Christian and Julian. "Your brother told me."

"Julian!" I growl, staring back at that traitor.

He shrugs like he can't help it and I trot after her.

"I didn't actually say that I like you now, by the way—" I call to her through the bathroom cubicle. "I said I don't want to have you killed anymore."

She swings over the door and gives me an unimpressed look. "Well, coming from you that's practically a hug."

She walks over to the bathroom sink, washes her hands delicately as she stares at herself almost emotionlessly, and I think to myself how much we mustn't see our true reflections in a mirror, so used to our own faces that we become disenfranchised no matter how beautiful what's staring back at us is.

"What's it like having that face?" I nod my chin towards her.

"Oh." Her mouth falls open in thought as she glances over at me, giving me a sad smile. "It's not all it's cracked up to be."

Then she peeks at me out of the corner of her eye. "You're as pretty as I am."

I roll my eyes, instantly embarrassed and annoyed.

"No, you are — it's just my eyes, the colour tricks people into thinking I'm more beautiful than I am." Then she leans in towards me and whispers. "Don't tell anyone, it's my biggest secret."

"That you have nice eyes?" I frown at her. "That's not a secret — *Vanity Fair* did a cover story on you titled 'The Girl With The Eyes.'"

"No, Daisy—" She gives me a look like I'm the idiot. "The secret is that I am less pretty without them."

"When are you ever without them?"

"Look—" She closes her eyes and turns her head to face me. "I'm much blander now. Zero wow factor."

"Sure." I nod as I frown over at her. "How often do you wander around with your eyes closed, though?"

"Oh." She shakes her head. "Not all that often."

"Right."

"There is a reason you'll never see me wearing sunglasses though—" She gives me a look before she skips out of the bathroom.

She bounces ahead of me and freezes to a holt. I peer around her and standing way too close to my boyfriend over at the bar is Vanna Ripley.

Christian's not doing anything wrong — actually, his body language screams uncomfortable. My brother's next to him, frowning on as Vanna leans in as close to Christian as she can without pressing herself up against him.

Magnolia makes a sound at the back of her throat.

"Come on," she growls and yanks me over towards them.

Christian catches my eye as we walk over and his eyebrows go up — the tacit international call-sign for 'help'.

Magnolia practically shoves me into Christian's arms, and he pulls me backwards into him, holds me from behind.

"Vans." He gives her a smile. "You remember Daisy?"

Vanna stares at me for a few seconds — eyes me like a bug. I feel insecure for a second, run through my mind what I'm wearing,[220] if it holds a candle to how sexy Vanna fucking Ripley is in that tight black dress. I'm not sure that it does.

Vanna forces a smile eventually. "I don't think we've met."

"Right." Christian nods. "Well, this is my girlfriend. Daisy."

Vanna's jaw goes tight on the G word and I give her a curt smile.

My brother slings an arm around Magnolia as Vanna looks over at her.

"Magnolia." She straightens up a bit, like she's talking to royalty. She kind of is. "So good to see you — how's BJ? How's Rush?" Then adds with a chuckle. "How's Jack-Jack?"

Christian scoffs, surprised, at the same time Magnolia pulls back a tiny bit. Julian gives Vanna a little look, glances down at his arms around Magnolia, raises his eyebrows.

---

[220] Clara belted distressed denim mini shirt dress (Retrofête); Laylis suede knee boots (Isabel Marant); Lennon shearling coat (Nili Lotan); Loulou Puffer small quilted shearling shoulder bag (Saint Laurent) — Thank you, Magnolia.

"I know—" I look over at Vanna, shaking my head as I stare her down. "I know that you weren't just implying something untoward about her."

She gives me a bored smile. "Was I not?"

My brother gives her a look. "You better not have."

Magnolia quiets my brother with that hand on his chest how she does and glares over at Vanna. "Did the Jack-Jack one upset you particularly? He said you always liked him."

Vanna gives her a bit of a dark look. "Not as much as it would have upset Daisy when Christian chose you over her."

I feel sick. Christian's grip tightens around me.

"Oh — you're confused—" Magnolia shakes her head, giving her a polite smile. "That never happened. But he did choose Daisy over you, that happened—"

My brother squashes a smile and Christian sniffs a laugh.

Christian tips his head away from us. "Probably time for you to sod off now, ey Vans?"

"I love it when you tell me what to do," she says, voice dripping all sultry.

"How do you feel when I tell you what to do?" I ask. "Because I'm going to tell you to fuck yourself."

"I'd rather be fucked by someone else." She stares over at Christian, and he shakes his head at her uncomfortably.

"I'm sorry—" he tells me before turning back to her. "You need to stop."

Vanna stares up at him, like she's baffled. "What are you doing with her?"

"What am I doing with her?" He blinks. "I'm in love with her." Shrugs like it's simple. "I love her."

Vanna stares at him for a few long seconds and Magnolia makes a little squeal. "Sorry — this is so uncomfortable." She squirms in my brother's arms. "Vanna, would it help if we were to all close our eyes so that you could slink back away to the hell-mouth from whence you came?"

Vanna stares at her, furious.

"I'll start—" Magnolia claps her hands over her eyes. "Daisy, look at all I'm doing for you, covering my eyes and everything — has she gone yet?"

My brother picks Magnolia up and throws her over his shoulder laughing, carrying her away. "You're so weird."

Christian pulls me past and away from a frozen Vanna, following my brother down a hallway. He stops walking and pushes some hair behind my ears.

"Baby, I'm so sorry—" He shakes his head. "She's fucking rancid."

"I hate her," I tell him.

"Yeah." He nods.

"Julian, have you slept with her?"

"Fuck off!" My brother stares over, offended. "I have some standards—" He looks at Christian. "No offence."

Christian shrugs.

"Nor have I slept with her, to clarify," Magnolia tells me.

"Good." Christian nods. "Just me then."

"You know—" Magnolia leans around my brother. "While we're talking about this…"

"Oh God." Christian sighs, cracking his back.

"Did you know that when you kiss someone you have their saliva in your system for seven years. So—" We all stare at her. "—if you think about it… I hooked up with Julian once when I was nineteen, and then Christian not long after. And then you hooked up with Christian—" She points at me. "And then I hooked up with him again in New York. And then I hooked up with your brother — so if you think about it…"

"I don't want to." Christian shakes his head. "Let's not— think— nope—"

Julian makes a revolted sound.

"I—" I point over at her. "Right, back to hating you. Like, want you dead, hate you."

"Oh!" Magnolia claps her hands together. "There's an idea. Why don't you just kill her?" Magnolia offers loudly, smiling and nodding.

All three of us slowly stare over at her, blinking.

"What?" My brother's face scrunches up.

"I just—" Her shoulders slump. "I don't understand your lives."

There's this awkward silence where none of us can tell whether she's joking or not.

In what other circle in the world could she not have been joking?

Julian howls laughing, as he grabs her, kissing her again.[221]

I stare after them and over at my boyfriend and wonder if this is the normal I've wanted all along. Maybe this is everything I've ever wanted right in front of me. And I pray to that god who I'm sure doesn't listen to us that it'll stay like this forever.

---

[221] I feel worried again.

51

Julian

A week or so passes and everything starts to feel more relaxed.

A coincidence, I'm pretty sure — Cian turning up like that. Or just Ro trying to power move me, so fuck her, I'll take Magnolia out if I want to.

Murano on Queen Street is where we go. Get the charred mackerel, you'll die for it.

I find myself staring over at her, half annoyed, half fucking enamoured — those are my default settings for her — it's a shit feeling, loving someone who doesn't love you back. Sometimes I wonder if she might — if she could — if she knew it was on the table, whether she might be open to it.

She stares back at me from across the table, her chin in her hand. "What?"

"Just thinking how fun it was watching you tear Vanna Ripley a new one."

She rolls her eyes. "She deserves it."

I nod once. "She does."

She takes a long sip of her martini. Likes them wet and dirty, and I'm 90% sure it's just because she likes the way the bartenders look at her when she says it. "Was Daisy okay?"

"Yeah." I nod. "I mean — he's hardly withholding when it comes to — what did you call it?" My eyes pinch. "His strong feelings of affection?" I laugh, shake my head and she smiles at me.

"They're happy." She tilts her head, happy for them, and shit — I love her. Fuck. As she bites down on her thumbnail smiling over at me as she picks at a piece of focaccia, she's the most beautiful thing I've ever seen, and I've seen it all. Her happy for my baby sister, leaning over a table to undo a button on the checked shirt she picked out for me that I wore because I don't care anymore — I'll do whatever the fuck she says. I love everything about her— how she listens to the same song on repeat for about two and a half hours, how she fusses over clothes, how she looks in my bathroom when she's cleaning her teeth, how she sits on my lap no matter what I'm doing, how pink her mouth is with nothing even on it.

She is the goddess in the Botticelli clam shell, her eyes are the waterlilies in Monet's pond, she is the hand of God reaching down to mankind. Klimt's kiss is a portrait of us and I'm gonna steal it. Take it, make it mine, make her mine too. Maybe do that one first.

I'm going to tell her. We can do this.

We'll figure it out.

I push back from the table, standing quickly.

She looks up at me, frowning. "Are you okay?"

"Yeah." I nod quickly. "Bathroom."

"Oh." She flashes me a quick smile.

She grabs her phone from the table and flips it over in her hand.

Kekoa and Declan walk me over and I push open the door, stand at the sink.

Run the water over my hands, my wrists.

I can do this.

Never done it before, but I can do it. Do I just say it?

How do I say it? She could love me too. She might say it back.

Do I say her name at the end — I don't fucking know? I—

"You good?" Kekoa asks, sticking his head around the door.

"Yeah." I nod.

"Yeah?" He doesn't quite buy it. He points at me. "You got a face?"

"No face—" I shake my head.

He shrugs with his mouth. Still doesn't buy it.

I push past him and walk back to my table.

She's sitting there, phone face-down on the table again, her chin back in her hand, grinning away at someone who's sat in my seat.

I don't recognise them from behind and I look back at Koa then over at Decks—

We left her by herself.

I don't run — I don't want to scare her — I walk over to her.

"Julian—" she says, smiling up at me as as I walk fast as I can towards her. "Your friend's just introduced himself."

I turn to look at the stranger and I'm staring straight down at the face of Ezra Brown.

"Julian!" He beams up at me.

I put both my hands on Magnolia's shoulders.

He's more tan than the last time I saw him. Open buttoned shirt, linen vacation kind of pants, drinking my drink.

"It's so good to see you — it's been — God — How long has it been?"

I say nothing, just stare at him.

"How do you know each other?" Magnolia asks, looking between us.

"Oh—" Brown swats his hands as he eyes me down. "Julian used to do some... babysitting for me."

"Did he?" She sits back in her chair, delighted. She looks up at me. "Aren't you sweet?"

Ezra stares at me. "The sweetest."

"I didn't mean to intrude—" Ezra takes a bite of my meal. Fucking cocky bastard. If Magnolia wasn't here I'd kill him on the spot. Club him over the head with that bottle of Malbec, drag him out by the ankles and hang him off the roof of my house for everyone in this fucking city to know that you can't mess with me. Except you can mess with me because I'm in love with someone, and they keep fucking using it against me without lifting a finger.

"I was just getting to know your—" Brown looks at Magnolia, giving her an inquisitive smile. "Where did we land with the label again?"

"Well—" She shakes her head like it's a ridiculous question. "We're certainly not dating, he's been very clear on that—" She tosses me a look, amused, maybe a bit annoyed — I want her to see my face, feel something's amiss, I don't want her to know what's amiss, just to know enough to feel like she should pull back from the conversation but she doesn't. Instead she trades an amused glance with Brown.

"I think the general consensus is lover."

"Lover." Ezra's face pulls into a smile that makes me feel sick. Fuck. He stares up at me and licks his lips. "She is... lovely."

"Get up," I tell her, pulling her gruffly to her feet and then behind me.

"What are you — ow!" She frowns as I yank her behind me.

"He's not my friend—"

She frowns, confused. "What?"

"He turns on a dime, Magnolia—" Ezra shakes his head at her, still eyeing me. He stands, tossing my napkin down on the food I hadn't even started yet. "It was such a pleasure to meet you, darling—" He peeks around, looking for Magnolia's eyes but I shield her.

"A real pleasure," he says, staring at me. "I'm sure I'll see you soon." He turns and walks away.

"Paid your bill," he calls on his way out, and Kekoa and Declan stare after him, their hands covertly on their weapons, just in case.

We don't shoot people in the middle of Mayfair if we can help it.

Watch him til he leaves and then I spin around to face her, holding her face in my hands.

"What did he say to you?"

"What?" She frowns. "Nothing — what's going on? What do you mean he's not your friend?"

I don't know what to say — and I don't have to answer anything either because we're immediately ushered out the back exit, through the kitchen, down some stairs into one of my cars.

I boost her up into the back of the car, and she's scowling away, angry that she doesn't understand.

"Middle seat," Kekoa tells me.

I put her in the middle, and he gives me a steep look.

"Julian—" she says, voice sounds like she's stomping her foot even though she isn't. "What's going on?"

"Someone call Daisy."

"Already have." Declan nods. "She's fine. At the Compound with Miguel."

"Christian?" I ask.

He flicks me an annoyed look. "He's there too."

"Julian!" Magnolia tugs on my arm.

It races through my head what I could say — what I could possibly say to her — it has to be a lie.

What's going on? Just someone levelling a threat against you for the second time in a month because you're with me.

"Who was that?" She shakes her head, eyes starting to look worried — I hate her looking worried.

"An old friend of the family," Kekoa offers without turning around.

"Oh." Magnolia frowns, still confused.

"He's a bit weird—" He glances back, giving her an assuring look. "We don't like him hanging around."

"Oh." She nods like she gets it even though she doesn't. She can't, won't ever. I toss my old friend a grateful look.

I take her home that night to the Compound just to be safe and to be selfish, because I know what this means. This is what it means to love someone.

We have sex, twice for good measure. Once in my bed, once on the bathroom sink. She slips into the shower with me for no reason that I can tell other than to be by me, wraps her arms around me and then nothing. I feel it bursting through my chest even though I haven't done it yet, how much I'll feel her absence once I do. How big this stupid fucking house is going to be without all the clothes she brings thrown about everywhere. How useless my bed's going to feel without her in it. How empty my lap's going to be this time next week.

"What are you doing?" I ask after five seconds of her little head pressed up against my chest in the shower.

"Nothing—" She frowns up at me, offended. "You can bend me over your vanity but I can't give you a cuddle?"

I sit down on the mosaic tile bench built into my shower, pull her down on top of my lap, push some hair from her face.

Fuck. I hate loving her.

It's the great undoing of my heart as I know it. She's made herself at home, kicked off those fucking cerulean heels, put her feet up on my left rib. Over the mantelpiece she hung her own portrait up herself, that little minx. Best painting I've ever seen, too. Better than any woman anyone has ever painted in the history of time, a face I'd win battles for. A face I'd lose anything for. Even her.

It's time.

I love her more than I've ever loved anything and I thought I might have been able to angle it, find a way for us to work. A life between where I can be who I am and love her how I do and it not be the death of her, but it's not in the cards. I'd be the death of her, and I won't be.

So it's time.

52

Christian

Smokeshow pulls up Daisy's car outside De Vere Grand at the Connaught, and I open her door.

Mum throws an annual gala for one of the children's hospitals here, she says it's important to give back to the community. I know she's just easing a guilty conscience.

Magnolia dressed me and Daisy for tonight. Me, I'm in the Slim-Fit Worsted Wool-Garbine suit jacket with the matching trousers, a white button shirt from Tom Ford, and some Oxfords from a brand that starts with B.

I duck my head a little to catch eyes with Daisy as I offer her my hand to pull her from the car.

As soon as she hits the door path, I'm floored.

I laugh some air out and she frowns, offended.

"What?" I glances down at the lime green dress Magnolia laid out for her. It came with a very specific set of instructions and a pre-approved bevy of accessories for Daisy to 'make the outfit her own'.

"I just—" I shake my head at her. "I'm in love with you."

"Oh." She smiles, pleased with herself.

"Alright, no—" Jonah says walking up behind us, standing between. "I'm going to need all of this eye-batting love-bullshit to simmer down for the evening."

"Where's Taura?" Daisy glances around.

Jonah scoffs. Which is Hemmes for 'I don't want to talk about it'.

"Ménage à trois hiccups?" I ask him.

Daisy stares over at him, surprised.

"Are you dateless?" She asks.

"Course not." He gives me a sly smile as he tosses an arm around my girlfriend, leading her over to our mum.

I give my mum a proud smile as I give her a hug.

"Barnesy." I grin. "What a dress!"

She swats her hand at me, glancing down at the red and white dress she's wearing. "Do you think? Magnolia sent it to me."

I roll my eyes. "Of course she did."

"You look good, Barnsey," says a voice from behind and I freeze.

Jo and I catch eyes. Mum looks up, startled, then turns around to face her husband.

"What are you doing here?" she asks, quietly.

Dad shrugs a little vaguely. "This is the thing you talked about at breakfast the other day, isn't it?"

She nods but says nothing.

"I came." He shrugs again.

Her face falters a little. "But you never come to things."

It hangs there, that statement, what it implies, what it's meant for those of us he left behind when he couldn't let go of the dead.

No one says anything, not me, not Jo.

"I like your suit!" Daisy says loudly.

Dad glances down at it, a little amused. "Thanks. It's pretty old now."

"Is that the Tom Ford?" Rebecca peers around at it. "I can't believe it still fits—"

Dad looks down at himself, a bit self-conscious.

"Well, it does—" Daisy gestures to him. "And wow."

She elbows me to say something but I say nothing. I don't know what I'd say.

"Rebecca was just going to grab us all a drink—" Dais starts.

Jonah butts in. "There are waiters everywhere walkin—" Daisy shoots him a look.

"Maybe you could go help her!" She snatches Mum's bag from her hands.

Mum gives her a despondent look as she cottons on and saunters off to the bar, Dad trailing behind her.

But then, here's the thing... once they get to the bar, they face each other. They talk uncomfortably, like you do when you bump into an ex — in a way, they have. The didn't break up, but I can tell you this, they sure as shit didn't stay together.

"What are you playing at?" I ask my girlfriend, eyes pinched.

"Nothing!" she sings, craning her neck to watch them.

I eye her suspiciously. "Mmhmm."

I stare over at them then shake my head. "Dais, it's not going to work — there's nothing left there."

She flashes me a quick smile that I suspect will cause me a lot of grief over the course of my lifetime. "We'll see."

Eventually we all take our seats at our table.

Jonah's pretty fucked and has some leggy Italian girl in a really sparkly dress sitting on his lap. He's doing an Instagram live and she's biting his ear, and Daisy's trying to covertly wrestle the phone off him — I feel sad watching him, because he's wrecked. Jo doesn't get wrecked over girls. I've never seen it before. Best I feel I can do is lean into the live frame and kill the mood before it turns into a soft porn.

Uncle Callum joins our table with a young, blonde heiress who looks Daisy's age. This impresses no one, least of all Daisy (who throws me a horrified face and I fight off a smile).

The heiress, she checks me out how she shouldn't do to someone who clearly has a girlfriend, and how she shouldn't when she's with my uncle. Callum doesn't share. If he'd seen that, he wouldn't have taken it well.

I drape my arm over Daisy's shoulders and kiss her cheek.

"Love you," I tell her just because I can, and she flicks me eyes that say it without saying it.

Dad sits down next to Mum and Uncle Callum looks over at him, confused. "Jud."

"Cal." He nods.

Neither is pleased to see the other.

"What are you doing here?" Cal asks, taking a deep sip of his martini, eyeing him, making sure he doesn't feel welcome.

They've always been tense.

Callum thinks Dad's held Mum back. Dad thinks Callum's a fuckwit, and I hate to say it but I think I'm on Dad's side with this one.

"He decided to come!" Daisy jumps in. "Isn't that wonderful?"

I squeeze her knee, pressing my mouth against her ear. "Relax."

"Yes." Callum nods without a smile. "Wonderful."

They bring around our appetisers and the conversation is shit — everyone is wading through it and Daisy is carrying all the heavy weight.

Uncle Callum has his hands up the dress of the girl he's with, so does Jo — to be honest, so do I, but at least me and Dais can keep up a conversation with other people while I'm feeling her up.

Daisy keeps ordering my parents drinks and all her attention goes into making sure Mum and Dad stay conversationally afloat.

"How did you two meet, then?" she asks, leaning in towards them chin in her hand, subtly smacking my hand away because it's gone too far north to be appropriate.

I smirk and pull her onto my lap as the waiters clear our plates.

Mum and Dad hold eyes, thinking.

"We met at a pub," Dad tells her, with a distant smile.

"Were you alone?" Daisy asks, waiting for more. ("It's like making a stone bleed!" she whispered to me earlier about him) "Were you with friends—?"

"He was on a date, actually," Mum says, barely smiling. But smiling. "I was there with my brother —" She glances over at Callum who's whispering into the ear of his blonde, and he looks hungry.

"My other brother. Harvey—" She clarifies for me. "We were at the Covent Garden and we—"

"No, we weren't," Dad interrupts.

She gives him a look. "Yes, we were."

He shakes his head.

Here we go. I shift uncomfortably, waiting for them to go back and forth for a bit and my Dad to just get up and walk away without another word for a decade.

"We weren't," Dad insists. "I know we weren't."

"You haven't remembered anything for the last fifteen years, Jud. What makes you think you've got this?" Mum asks in this way that leaks our years of hurt and neglect and I feel this surge of anger towards him for treating her like that. She's the best mum in the world, and when Rem died she didn't only lose her daughter, she lost her husband too.

Dad gives her a long look. Like he's confused and maybe a bit hurt.

"Barnsey, I couldn't forget when I met you," he tells her with a frown before looking over at Daisy. "We were at the Lamb and Flag—"

"Oh," Mum says, her face going blank and I can tell immediately that she knows he was right. Her cheeks go pink.

She's happy to be wrong.

It hangs there again, that silence.

347

"So you were on another date?" I ask and ignore the surprised look Daisy is giving me because relationships are like that and sometimes you just don't need your girlfriend to be right about your age-old family feud.

"Yeah." Dad glances over at me. "We'd been on a few dates, by then—"

"She was your girlfriend," Mum interjects.

"She was." Dad laughs. "And thank God she was, because it made for the perfect opener."

My mum and dad stare at each other in a way they haven't in fifteen years.

"What'd you say?" Daisy asks, smiling as she watches them.

"'Hi, my name's Jud and I just dumped my girlfriend for you,'" Mum says, not looking away from him.

Dad swallows heavy.

The servers place our mains down in front of us, these fancy little ribeye medallions, but unfortunately Dad eats his in two bites.

"That was delicious." He nods, heartily. "When's dinner?"

Mum eyes him, annoyed. "That was dinner."

"Bit small—" He pulls a face, glancing at me for back-up, but I shake my head. I don't want to be on Mum's bad side.

"I mean—" Dad pauses when Daisy shoots him her 'shut up' look. "Perfectly portioned. Loved it."

And do you know what, I can't help but notice that Mum, who's pretending to be pissed at Dad for the steak comment, still parades him about to all her friends. She looks happier than I've seen her in years—

"Odd if they're not in love anymore, no?" Daisy elbows me conspicuously in the side, proud of herself.

"Calm down, Parent Trap." I roll my eyes.

Once it's over, we all trot down the steps at the venue, some of the last to leave but Dad ahead of us all. He spins on his heel, staring back up at us. "Who's hungry?"

I take a peek over at Mum, weighing up how angry she'll be if I'm honest.

"Starving." I grimace over at her apologetically.

"Fucking famished," Jonah crows, still pretty pissed.

"Who wants McDonald's?" Dad asks and all of us, Daisy included, peer over at Mum.

"Oh," she groans. "Fine—"

Jonah throws his arms around both me and Daisy, pulling us back a little, letting our parents walk ahead to the golden arches down the street.

He grins down at Daisy with bleary eyes. "You're a little bit magic, aren't you, Daisy Haites?"

Julian

Thought about how to do it for the next few days.

It was a hard one to puzzle out, a bit because I don't want to do it and also because there are some logistics to it all. I want to make it count, for her — if I'm giving her up, I want it to count. And then for me, I need it to be a little announcement to those eyes Roisin has on me, that me and Parks are done.

So I take her to dinner.

Maison Francois in St James. Booked out an entire section. Brought the whole fucking cavalry, just in case.

Had most of them meet us there so she didn't feel uneasy. Maybe I shouldn't have done that. Maybe I should have had her feeling uneasy all this time, maybe she'd have left by herself then instead of it being like it is now. Me in love and fucking shooing her off back to someone who's safer and honestly fuck him for that.

We get in and I sit her down, order one of everything.

She looks at me in this cute, little baffled way.

"What?" I shrug.

Chin in her hand, she smiles over at me. "I like French food."

"I know." I nod, take a thousand pictures in my mind because this is the last time I'll take her for dinner.

The last time she'll reach over and try my drink and her face will scrunch up because she doesn't like new things.

"How's your mum doing?"

She shrugs. "Bridget says she's got a new Boyfriend of the Month." I nod.

She purses her mouth. "*The Mirror* isn't saying very nice things about her—"

"Yeah, but *The Mirror*'s shit."

She nods. Looks sad about it so I try to change the subject.

"Talked to BJ?" I ask and her face falters. I cock an eyebrow. "You trying to tell me you haven't spoken to him?"

"Why are you asking?" She folds her hands in front of her.

Because I'm just making sure you're going to be okay.

"Can I not?" is what I say instead with a shrug.

She breathes out her nose. "We've spoken no more than normal."

"So constantly, then?" I sniff and she gives me a little glare.

"I liked your friends the other day," she tells me, as she reaches over to my plate and pokes an anchovy.

She scrunches her face up.

"Yeah?" I flash her a smile, like it doesn't kill me to hear.

There's not much I wouldn't give to just have her next to me in it all, anything, really. Just not her life, and I'm pretty sure that's the going rate.

"They liked you too, Tiges," I tell her, but she already knows because she's nodding away.

"I assumed as much."

I roll my eyes.

Going to miss rolling my eyes at her.

After dinner, we're about to get in the car and head to one of Jo's clubs, but I don't feel like it yet. I'm not ready.

I nod my head away from the car. "You wanna take a walk?"

"A walk?" She's confused by that.

"A walk, you know—" I poke her legs. "With these things. They move."

She frowns at me like I'm inconveniencing her.

"Come on—" I nod my head in the direction of Green Park. "Humour me."

She groans as I take her hand in mine, but she holds it tight and I memorise how it feels to have her gripping me the way she is.

We walk for a bit. I don't say much and she says a lot. She doesn't do quiet that well. I kind of like it, how she fills spaces and silence with pop culture and fashion shit, talking about the inner politics of it like New Bond Street and Fifth Avenue are countries these people rule.

And it occurs to me that my sister was onto something. That normal life she goes on about. How good it feels to pretend there aren't six men surrounding us as we take a stroll in the park, how good it feels to be talked to about things that don't involve bloodshed and theft and revenge and it feels for a second like someone has driven a knife down through the middle of me.

I want both. I want normal, I want power.

I love what I do. I love her.

I've never had a question about it til now, never felt like the cost might be too high to do this shit and now — really, no matter which way I slice it, the cost is her.

When we arrive at Jonah's club, I pull her up the stairs, kiss her stupid heavy on the way.

Up against the wall, one hand in her hair, the other on her waist, all of me pressed against her. I kiss her like that til I hear her lose her breath and then I pocket the sound so I can think of it when I miss her later on.

"Come on—" I nod my head towards the bar.

Ballentine's standing there the way I knew he would be.

Told Jonah to bring him out tonight.

"Why?" he asked.

I didn't tell him why. I don't answer to him.

"Just do it," I told him, so he did.

He stares over at her as we walk towards him.

His eyes go big and he swallows — and fuck him. I mean, I get it. Same page. But fuck him because he'll have it forever and I'll have her to myself for about twenty more seconds and let's be honest, I've never had her to myself for a minute, not even when I have.

She mouths to him *hi* — thinks I don't see it but I see everything. I don't miss a trick when it comes to her.

I'll try to use how her mouth goes when she sees him as fuel for what I'm about to do; try to hate her a bit for loving him a lot but I can't. I won't ever hate her. Even if I resent her a bit. She undid me.

"Oi." I nod my chin at Ballentine. "I've got some shit to do — can you grab her a drink?"

Magnolia looks over at me, confused. I stare over at her, try to look as indifferent as I can.

BJ shrugs, nods his head towards the bar and she follows him.

"What was that?" Jonah asks as we walk away.

I shrug. "Just needed some space — she's doing my head in."

Something flickers over his face. Doesn't understand what's changed.

We go to his office, do some lines. I do more than I need to because

Magnolia hates it and I want to fuck her off. No, I don't, but you know what I mean.

Then there's a knock at the door.

"Yeah?" Jo calls, and it opens.

Two ridiculously hot girls peer around his door.

"Cleo. Alexis." Jonah sits up. "Hey."

He waves them in. Gestures to the cocaine on his table.

They do a bump, and the one with the brown hair is pretty. She's got eyes that feel like she's down for whatever.

I don't need her to do whatever, just need her to do me.

She tucks her chin but flicks up her eyes. Her short hair falls over her face and I convince myself for the 50th time in the last twenty-four hours that this is the right thing to do.

"What's your name again?" I ask her.

"Cleo. Harrington."

I offer her my hand. "Hi Cleo Harrington, I'm Julian Haites."

She stares at my hand for a few seconds. "Aren't you with Magnolia Parks?" She shakes it anyway.

I don't flinch when she says her name but I might swallow heavy. Still I don't look away from her as I say, "Do you see her here?"

Cleo shakes her head.

Tilt my head at her. "I see you here, though."

A smile twitches over her face.

That Alexis Blau girl, she's sitting on Jonah's desk, eye-fucking the shit out of him, so I catch Cleo's eye and nod my head towards the door.

Take her hand and pull her out into the hallway, bang her up against a wall and kiss her like I mean it.

I hear Kekoa sigh and move away.

I ignore him. We move fast and I hate it.

Try to focus on the parts of a woman's body I like no matter who I'm touching.

Boobs. Magnolia's are pretty small. I like necks and shoulders. Kissing girls in the space between their jaw and the ear drives them all mad and the second I do it to Cleo, she's got both hands in my hair, hands under my shirt, grabbing at my chest.

I boost her up around my waist. She goes for the buttons.

I feel sick.

I'm not fucked up enough to want to do this — I don't want to. But

I just need Magnolia to be cut loose, I need people to see me hooking up with someone else, see us ending in an obvious and indisputable way.

I close my eyes. Think of Magnolia. That makes it a bit better, it doesn't feel the same and this girl's more sexually aggressive, so I know it's all in my head. Power through anyway.

We're well in the throes when I hear a little laugh come from a couple of metres away.

I look over at Magnolia standing there, mouth open, eyes big. She looks sad. That feels gratifying in some way but only quickly and for a second.

For the most part, I just want to die.

Thoughts start flying at me — did I make a mistake? Should I have done this? Can I take it back? Will she ever forgive me? What am I going to do without her? — and then BJ grabs me by the shoulders and slams me into a wall.

Cleo tumbles off my waist but lands on her feet.

I stare over at Magnolia, looking her in the eye as I zip the fly of my pants. I lick my bottom lip.

"What the fuck?" Magnolia asks.

I shove BJ but he shoves me back.

"Yeah, what the fuck—" BJ asks and I turn to look at him, chin down, eyes up.

I roll my eyes at him. "Stay out of this."

"What the fuck are you doing—" He gestures to Magnolia.

I shake my head at him. "Don't see how that's any of your fucking business."

His jaw juts. "She's always my business."

"Do you want to go, mate?" I push him.

He nods once. "Yep."

I give him a half a smile. "I've wanted to do this the last three months—"

Then I crack my fist into his jaw and he doubles over.

It's just for a second because BJ punches me back.

"BJ — stop!" Magnolia yells, rushing towards us at the same time as my boys do.

I'm bent over for a couple seconds before I straighten up, wipe my bloody mouth with the back of my hand and sniff a laugh.

I can see in my peripheral vision that Magnolia is scared.

Wish I could tell her it'll all be over soon but I can't, she's not mine anymore, not mine to make feel better. That's official now.

I spit some blood out on the floor and then catch Koa's eyes and point over at Parks. He comes and grabs her from behind, pulling her away, and she's bucking in his arms. Sick rolls through me, watching her crying how she is, someone dragging her away — like I'll ever let anyone harm her in this lifetime. She doesn't know that though, and she looks scared. So does Ballentine as he goes to lunge for her, ducking one of my swings. "Don't fucking touch h—" he starts but then I uppercut him and he falls backwards.

"Julian—!" she screams as BJ tackles me to the floor.

He's a good fighter, by the way. Better than I would have thought.

I thought I was probably going to have to go easy on him but fending him off isn't nothing. He doesn't give a shit if he takes a hit if it means he'll gets a good one in, and he'll break a bone to get one.

I can't look at Magnolia swinging around in Kekoa's arms trying to get away from him, like he'd hurt her — it's funny how quickly trust can break. Just took a second of her seeing me fuck someone else to undercut all the ways I used to make her feel safe. Trying to get away from Koa or trying to get to BJ? I can't tell. Neither is good, but one of them might kill me. I decide it's the latter and it's a kick in the chest, everything about them is and it makes me angry so I hit him hard for it.

She's crying now — screaming for Henry, for Jonah, for Christian— and then Jo comes barrelling out of his office, shirt half on his body around the same time Christian appears somewhere from inside the club.

Jonah shoves Kekoa — hard. Ballsy. Something comforting in it though, seeing him defend her like that. He plucks Magnolia from Kekoa's arms and gives him a warning look before he tosses her into Christian's arms and dives between Ballentine and I.

He pulls us apart and I stand there — chest heaving, glaring over at BJ, pointing.

"You better get him the fuck out of here—"

Jonah shoves BJ down the hallway, past Magnolia, and their eyes catch. Tells her without telling her that he did it all for her, but fuck him — because same. And then Jonah shoves him away and it's just me and her and Christian in a hallway.

"What are you doing?" she yells at me from a few metres away, so I cross the distance and get up right in her face.

"How many times do I have to tell you?" Christian's grip on her shifts and tightens. He's not happy with me. Actually, he's looking at me like he might punch me himself. "We're not fucking dating! We've only ever been fucking."

She lets out a little choked cry and it's enough to knock the wind out of me. I'll take a punch any day.

I wave my hand in her direction, looking away from her.

"Take her home," I say, turning away. Christian hooks an arm around her and leads her away.

"Come on."

As soon as they're gone I lock myself in Jonah's office.

Punch a mirror, tip a bookcase over, scream into my hands because I miss her and I already don't want this.

But it's done now. She's safe.

I stare at my bloody hands, trembling again. Find Jonah's coke. Do too much. Then I walk back out to find that girl.

54

Julian

I brought both those girls home that night.

Don't remember much about it.

When I wake up this morning both girls are still asleep either side of me and I survey my room.

Bottles everywhere, clothes thrown about, a torn curtain, actually — that's weird.

Rub my eyes. See Magnolia's little devastated face from last night.

Had Decks follow her home to make sure she was okay. She was. Ballentine turned up pretty soon after.

Hard not letting it show on my face how much that stung. But my plan worked — of course it did — that's all the matters.

I stare up at the ceiling, convince myself that that's true. It's all that matters.

It's not magical or grand, love is fucked.

There's a knock on my door.

"What?" I call.

Magnolia pokes her head in and I sit up straighter. Don't mean to. Just old habits and shit, yeah?

Her eyes fall to the girls beside me — Cleo and Alexis — both of whom are now just stirring awake.

"Leave," I tell them as I crack my back.

Both girls roll out of my bed, grab their things and scatter.

I climb out of bed — fully naked. Like I care, like she hasn't seen me naked 12,000 times before. I want her to miss me too — I pull on some sweatpants and she stands there, arms crossed over her chest, nose a bit in the air. Solid glare.

"Nice." She spits.

"You were fucking a gang lord—" I roll my eyes. "What'd you expect?"

"More from you." She gives me a disappointed shrug and I sniff, annoyed.

"Yeah but you got what you wanted, Parks."

She pulls back. "What did I get that I wanted?"

I squint over at her. "You think I don't know Ballentine went to your house last night?"

She blinks over at me, surprised.

"I see everything," I tell her as I shake my head.

She walks towards me, arms still folded, still glaring.

And I roll my eyes again, give her a dismissive wave of the hand.

"You got him back. You're welcome."

Her eyes pinch. "What?"

"What?" I scoff. "You think I didn't know he'd defend your honour if he saw me fucking another girl in a club?" I scoff as I shake my head like I'm not sick over it. "It's sweet— How much he loves you—"

Magnolia's blinking a lot, processing.

She squints over at me. "Did you really do that for me or is this just a merry coincidence?"

"You know what, Tiges, I'm embarrassed to say that I've fallen into the ranks of men who find that there's very little that they wouldn't do for you."

Her face softens how I wish it wouldn't. "Are you telling the truth?"

"Why would I lie?"

"I don't know?" She shakes her head. "Why would you do what you did?"

And I shrug, uncomfortable with how wide-eyed she's getting. I've only got so much willpower. "Ballentine needed to feel good enough for you. Nothing ups a lad's confidence like fighting for the girl he loves—"

"Oh." She says. Takes a breath as she takes my hand and maybe her eyes go teary — I don't know. I'm trying not to look. "Thank you."

I lift her hand to my mouth and kiss it. Weak of me, but fuck it. I'm only human.

"You're welcome—" I tell her and then I drop her hand, ready to lie through my fucking teeth. "And I'm relieved."

She frowns at me but I shake my head at her.

"I thought Daisy was a handful, but fuck me, you're an absolute headache."

358

She frowns more and I laugh because I love her and I'm going to miss offending her.

"But worth it though," I tell her just to keep her a bit sweet.

"So this is it?" she asks, straightening up. "We're done now?"

"Yep." I nod. "We're done."

"I'll miss you," she tells me.

"I'm sure you will—" I nod. "No way is Ballentine as good in bed as I am."

She rolls her eyes and I toss her a smile. Try not to cry as I say it. "I'm happy for you—"

"Yeah?" She smiles up at me, hopeful for my approval.

I can't really give it out loud at the second because I'm on edge so I just nod.

"Hey." She pokes me, catching my eye. "Would you do me a grand favour and not put out a hit on the man I love?"

I purse my lips, pretending to think about it for a second before I roll my eyes.

"He's a Hemmes for all intents and purposes. Under their protection. So are you, so you don't need mine." I take her chin between my finger and thumb. "But you have it. You need anything ever, I'm your man."

She leans in towards me, presses her mouth against mine, light and gentle, wind-in-a-field, sun-on-your-cheek kind of kiss.

"Yes, you are."

She turns and walks away, pausing at my door to turn back at stare at me.

"You are a very dangerous man, Julian. I know that. But I do hope that you know that above that and before that, you really are actually quite a good man."

Fuck me dead and write that on my tombstone, then.

I flick her an edge of a smile. "See ya, Tiges."

~

A few hours later there's a knock on my door again. I'm face-down in my bed, drinking and drunk all at once.

"No," I call to the door.

"COMING IN," my sister yells and I groan.

"Hi." she says from the other side of the room.

I say nothing, so she walks over towards me gingerly and kneels down beside my bed.

"Hey," she says gently, running her hand over my hair and I smack her away.

"Don't." I roll over, glaring at her. "I'm fine."

She watches me closely. "Yeah?"

"Yeah," I tell her.

She glances around my room. "Well, it smells fine in here—"

"Fuck off, Dais!" I snap. "I said I'm fine."

"You're clearly not." She shakes her head, watching me sadly.

"I said fuck off!" I yell at her like I never would otherwise.

She nods once. "I'm here if you need me."

Out. Just saw Magnolia and BJ holding hands.

Seemed romantic.

What did I miss?

Jules and her are done

What!

No?

Why??

Just time.

Do we hate her now?

No more than usual.

Is he okay?

I don't think so.

55

Daisy

I wander downstairs one afternoon a few days later and into the kitchen to start prepping for dinner. Julian's flying off the handle. Fucking for gold at the sexual Olympics. I haven't really seen him and I feel like he needs a hug but he won't let me near him. It's nothing fancy, just his favourites; roast chicken, roasties and veg. I do make sensational gravy from the drippings though, mixed with my own homemade bone broth.[222]

When I walk into the kitchen, all the boys freeze.

TK, Booker, Declan and Carmelo.

"Hey." Declan nods mostly with his chin.

"Hi?" I give him a confused look, walking further in and they all sort of shuffle in unison.

I glance around at them. "What's going on...?" I sing song.

"Nothing—" They all shake their heads.

"Is Julian doing something disgusting and you don't want me to see?"

"Yeah." TK nods. "Yep, that's it."

I try to peer past him. "Is he behind you?"

"No—" Carmelo shakes his head. "You look great today though—"

"What?" I frown.

"Doesn't she?" Carms looks at the boys for back up.

"Yes." Book nods emphatically. "So great."

I cross my arms over my chest. They're being weird. I eye them all suspiciously. "Tell me what's going on."

Declan's face scrunches up. "Nah."

"Declan." I stare over at him. "What the fuck is going on?"

---

[222] Don't buy it, just make it, it's so easy.

"Have you been on the internet today?" Teeks asks carefully and Books elbows him to shut up.

"No—?" I shake my head.

"Good." Carms shrugs. "Keep it that way."

I reach for my phone from my pocket and then realise I left my phone upstairs.

"Just tell me—" I look between them.

"There's a sex tape of Christian and Vanna Ripley on the internet," TK says quickly.

"What the fuck, man!" Declan stares at him. "That is not what we practiced—"

I blink twice. "What!"

My face goes blank and still. I'm just a giant pair of eyes.

Carmelo and Decks move towards me.

"It's old," Carms says. "You can tell it's old—"

"How can you tell?" I frown.

I think my breathing's starting to go a bit funny.

"I mean, I've seen him with you—" Carmelo shrugs. "He wouldn't do that—"

"How do you know!" I yell louder, clearer.

Carmelo starts shaking his head. "I didn't do it, don't yell at me!"

"His hair looks different?" TK offers quickly.

"You've seen it?" I stare over at him.

"Oh—" He shrugs. "Yeah, but, like— it's everywhere."

I press my hands into my cheeks. "Everywhere everywhere?"

He shrugs but it's a passive nod. "Not like, everywhere, just like — Instagram, Facebook, BBC, Loose Lips, TMZ, Tell Me Lore..."[223]

My jaw drops and I glance between the others. "Have you seen it?"

The all nod a bit apologetically.

"Give me your phone," I tell Declan, holding my hand out to him.

"Oh—" He shakes his head with an uncomfortable smile. "I had a feeling you'd say that and that I'd find it hard not to give it to you, so I left mine in my car—"

"Why?" I glare.

"Oi, Dais—" He gives me a firm look. "Trust me on this. You don't want to see it."

"Why?" I ask, my heart racing, palms sweaty, definitely dizzy.

---

[223] So actually, literally everywhere.

Early signs of an anxiety attack.[224] "Is it very bad?" I press.

Declan nods cautiously at the same time that Booker cries out passionately, "Fuck no! He's a master!"

"Get out—" Declan points to the door.

"No!" I yell at Books. "Come back! Give me your phone!"

Booker freezes like a deer in headlights.

"Booker—" Decks starts. "Walk away right now. Do not give her your phone, or I swear to God I'll beat y—"

"Books!" I talk over Declan. "Give me your phone—"

Booker glances back and forth between us, unsure. His head like a ping pong ball.

"Don't," Declan warns.

"Give it to me—" Me, through clenched teeth.

Declan shakes his head. "Do. Not."

"Give me the fucking phone—" I growl.

Declan turns back to me. "You cannot look at this."

"Says who?" I yell.

"Me!" He says, eyes wide. "Consider me Julian's stand in."

I shake my head. "I will not—"[225]

Declan gives me the most serious face he's ever given me in my life.

"Trust me?"

I stare at him for a few seconds, blinking as I say slowly, "Give me a phone."

And then Romeo walks in and wordlessly hands me his.

Declan and Carmelo stare over at him like he's fucking insane but all I have is a surge of affection for him as he glares over at his brother and the boys.

"It's her boyfriend." He gives them all a filthy look. "She's the only one here who has a right to see it and she's the only one who hasn't." He shrugs.

I open Google as quickly as I can and frown at the search bar. "What do I type?"

"'Vanna Christian Sextape' should do it…" Booker tells me with a smile and I glare over at him.

---

[224] I don't usually have those. Not my style.

[225] "Gross, man." TK scrunches his face up.

"Didn't they naff?" Carmelo whispers to Booker.

Decks wasn't exaggerating. It's literally everywhere.

About a thousand hits come up immediately.

Everything from *The Daily Mail* to *Just Jared* to *Cosmopolitan* to *People* to — genuinely — fucking BBC.

I navigate over to some porn website that says FULL VIDEO!!!![226]

"Are you sure?" asks Rome with a frown. I stare over at him for a few seconds and then I press play on the video.

I wring my hands together as it starts streaming.

It's a bedroom I don't recognise — thank God.

Vanna sets up the camera. I think it's an iPhone. Who records with anything but an iPhone these days? And if they recorded it on an iPhone, that stupid cloud gets broken into all the time.

She walks away from the camera and Christian walks into the room,[227] sitting down on the bed. He's already shirtless.

His Calvins are popping out the top of his black track pants and I feel a punch in my gut because those same pants are laying on my bedroom floor at the moment — there's some chit chat between them, I can't hear — she points to the camera, smiling coyly. He glances over, sees it, snorts a laugh, then takes her hand, pulling her in towards him, takes her wrist up to his mouth and kisses up.

Up her wrist, up her arm, she arches back, lengthening herself, and one of the straps from the little silky slip she's wearing slips from her shoulders and Christian smiles up at her in a way that never in my life, as long as I live, will I be able to clear from my memory.

I press my fingertips into my lips to steady myself, and Rome puts his hand on my lower back to help.

Vanna climbs on top of Christian, stays there like that for a while, kissing. The silk dress is soon a puddle on the floor[228] and she's naked now[229], sitting on my boyfriend who, if we're to be counting small mercies, is still in his sweats. He's kissing the same parts of her body that he kisses on my body[230], and a terrible realisation dawns on me: what he likes in sex is not me-specific. It's female specific.

Something happens — I don't know what exactly, my eyes are a

---

[226] Worth noting, the capital letters and exclamation points are not my own personal embellishments.

[227] I feel sick.

[228] I hate silk now.

[229] I hate naked now.

[230] This is a big unmercy.

little blurry with tears I don't even realise I'm crying — and he flips it. Her on the bottom, him on top.

She kicks his track pants off him as fast as she can, pulling down his briefs, and there's my boyfriend — standing extremely tall for all the world to see.

I'm pinching my lip between my nails so hard I start to bleed a bit.[231]

Have you ever watched the person you love having sex with someone else?

Watched it?

I don't mean thought about it — we've all thought about it.

Most people have more than one sexual partner over the course of their lives so at one point or another it has to cross your mind, the person you love with someone else, but that's not what I mean.

Have you seen it?

Have you seen their body move in sync with someone else's?

Have you seen them pin someone else's wrists down in the corner of a bed? Have you seen them lick up the body of someone else? Bury their face in their neck, move up to their ear and watch the person you love make someone else cry out in a pained pleasure?

I watch his hands skim her all over, pausing and taking time on all his[232, 233] favourite parts.

I watch his tongue go places on her I don't think I'll let it go on me again. I watch her claw at his back. I watch him make her toes curl. I watch him eyes-closed, craning his neck back with deep gratification before winding up for what I can only assume (and from personal experience would imply) is the grand finale — and then it goes to black.

I grab the nearby bin and throw up into it.

Rome walks over to me, pulls my hair away from my face, frowning.

"I told you not to watch it—" Declan says from the other side of the room.

I throw up again.

"You should talk to him, Daisy," Romeo tells me once I stop.

---

[231] Rome glances at me, nervous.

[232] Her?

[233] Our?

I shake my head quickly, looking at him like he's crazy. "I can't—"

"Face—" Rome starts. "This isn't his fault. He didn't—"

"I don't care." I shake my head quickly, looking past him to the boy. "Where's my brother?"

Carmelo shrugs like he's a stray dog. "MIA."

"He's fucked, Dais." Declan grimaces.[234]

I cover my eyes with my hands and feel another wave of nausea coming on.

"Come on." Rome nudges me. "I'll take you to Christian's."

"No, Rome — I can't see him." I shake my head.

"I'll take you to him—" my brother says from behind us both.

I turn around and as soon as I see him, my bottom lip starts to shake, and I run over to him.

Julian's face is a bag of liquorice all-sorts. Angry, sad, annoyed, worried—

He hugs me in a way that blocks out the whole world for a second and for one tiny moment, I feel a bit better. Isn't it funny how pain and sadness can be forgotten for fleeting moments? Your brain gets a tiny bit distracted and it offers you the briefest moment of reprieve. The problem with those reprieves is that they aren't real, and reality comes hurtling back. And then you have to remember all over again that your dad is dead or your childhood sweetheart had sex in your bed or the love of your life has a sex tape with his ex-girlfriend.

The walls my brother has spent his whole life building around me can't protect me from this one. It blasts right through in four seconds flat.

I pull back, looking up at Jules. "I don't want to see him."

"Sorry, Face." He shakes his head, giving me a gentle look. "You have to see him anyway."

~

I don't mean to look as pathetic as I know do when I ring Christian's doorbell. I begged Julian to take me home.

I cried the whole drive here — and I mean cried — deep sobs.

---

[234] It's been a handful of days since he and Magnolia ended and it's just been one big string of drugs and girls with him.

I honestly can't believe Julian didn't give in and drive me home and through a McDonald's on the way to placate me.

In a way, it makes me feel better.

I don't think my brother would bring me here if he thought being here would hurt me. But maybe my brother is batshit insane after his break-up because as I stand on the front door step of Christian Hemmes' home, waiting for him to answer the door, my whole self is hurting. My body from crying so much, my heart from seeing so much and my brain from replaying so much.

Christian opens the door with a sheepish smile.

A smile? I purse my lips, confused.

"Hey—" He cringes as he surveys the damage but he can only see surface level.

The main damage is underground. A bunch of burst pipes erupting and flooding and drowning me alive.

He pulls me in towards him, holding me tightly against him. I thought it would feel weird, touching him after seeing that. But it doesn't — as soon as he's touching me it feels like pressure on a wound.

He pulls me upstairs to his room and he closes the door, tilting his head.

"Are you okay?" I ask him softly.

He must be so embarrassed.

"Yeah—" He gives a funny chuckle. "Yeah, I'm fine—" He shrugs his shoulders.

My brows pinch together.

"You're fine?" I give him a confused look. "There's a video of you on the internet having sex with your ex-girlfr—"

"Not my ex-girlfriend," he reminds me. "We were never, you know, like—"

I look at him, a weird feeling settling in my stomach because it doesn't make sense to me that he's being so casual. "That was your takeaway from what I just—?"

He looks at me, quizzically. "It's just sex, Baby!" he says with a laugh. "I mean — obviously she and I had sex, you know that—"

"Yeah! But I never wanted to see it!"

"Then why would you watch it!" he shoots back.

I stare over at him for a few seconds, assessing. "Is it old?"

He scoffs, face looking like I just slapped him. "Really?"

"Is it?" I repeat, arching my brows.

To be completely honest, this conversation isn't going how I imagined—

I thought he'd be sad and I'd be sad, and I'd cry and maybe he would too and we'd present this brilliant united front and it'd prove to the whole world but especially to us that come what may — sex scandals and family shit aplenty — we can make it through whatever is thrown at us if we're together, but now I don't know.

He shakes his head the tiniest bit, looking offended and defensive. "I wouldn't do that to you."

"No, of course not—" I shake my head sarcastically. "You'd just make a sex tape of you and another girl, never mention it and then act like it's no big deal when it comes out—"

"It's not a big deal!" He gives me a look.

"Well, it is to me!"

He eyes me a little carefully. "Don't you think you're overreacting a bit, Dais?"

I let out a dry laugh, but he shakes his head at me.

"You're acting like I cheated on you! But was like four or five months ago! You were still fucking Tiller—"

I squeeze my fists together. "And would you want that on the internet?"

"No — of course not." He breathes out. "But I wouldn't be angry at you if it was."

"I'm not angry at you because it's on the internet, Christian! I'm angry at you because you don't give a fuck that it is!"

"You'd rather me be upset, then?" he quips, raising his eyebrows. "Healthy, Dais—" He shakes his head, looking away, and I just stare over at him in disbelief.

"Daisy, I'm sorry — I just don't give a shit about this sort of thing. It was something I did before, while we were broken up. I was trying to get over you, for fuck's sake—"

I pull out my phone and start scrolling upward, furiously. "What are you doing?" He rolls his eyes.

His phone pings and he looks down at it.

A photo of me sitting on a sunbed with Romeo wrapped around me from behind. We're somewhere in Europe. I'm in swimmers, so is Romeo.

Christian glares up at me. "Why?"

His phone pings again. He eyes me, warningly, then looks down.

It's a photo Jack took of me and Tiller when we weren't looking. We're in a doorway. I'm in tiny pyjamas and he's in just his boxers, his arms are draped around my arms lazily, thoughtlessly, even, and in my guts something pangs like I miss that policeman who I used to love who'd never be cavalier about making a sex tape with someone else, and here I am, fully in love with someone who's made one and doesn't give a fucking shit about it.

The photo I sent to Christian's phone, I'm gazing up at Tiller in it and I love it even now, because somehow Jack caught the most intimate moment. It's so human.

Christian glares over at me, teeth gritted. "Why do you still have these?"

I breathe in and out of my nose.

"Do you still have a copy of your sex tape?" I ask, calmly.

His jaw juts out.

"Fuck yourself," I tell him and then I leave.

56

Julian

It's been a week — could be two, I don't know — since Magnolia and me. I'm not tracking time. I don't care either. It's good. It's all good.

Haven't looked at my phone, don't want to see the fucking parade all of England will have rolled out for her and Ballentine's reunion. I'm not ready for it but I am good.

I've been having a sick time since we called it. Haven't been that checked in though, if I'm honest. Wouldn't have known about Christian fucking Hemmes' little sex tape if Koa hadn't told me. Ran Face over to his house because that was the right thing to do but it didn't go to plan —

There are things I could do for her, to make her feel better. I could take her out for dinner, take her shopping, ask her to cook me something maybe — but I don't want to stop what I'm doing.

I had to stop for a minute when Miguel and me drove her over, but I just felt like shit. Like this kind of missing a person that feels like a screaming I can't turn off in my head. Never had that before.

How the silences go stupid loud now and drag on for too long, how empty my bathroom sink looks without all her shit clogging it up.

I don't know how much time it's been, I don't know how many girls I've seen since. A lot. No repeats. I'm done with repeats, won't get familiar with a girl again.

That's what I keep referring to what happened with me and Magnolia.

"I just got too familiar."

Not sure anyone believes it. Hurts less though.

There's a different girl in my bed now than the one who was there this morning, and you can say whatever the fuck you want about Tinder but it's good for a fuck in a pinch. Haven't had to leave the house since the break-up and girls have been here back-to-back.

There has been one downfall though. Every single fucking girl has said at one point or another, "Aren't you with Magnolia Parks?"

"No." I hope they take the wince I make when they say her name to me as disgust at the thought.

"Just — the papers." They all say. "You know, there are photos,"

"She's my baby sister's friend, that's all," I'd lie. "We've fucked a few times."

"Oh!" They'd nod like they get it. Like they could ever.

They'd kiss me again after that until — eventually they'd pull back and look up at me.

"What's she like?"

"What's who like?" I'll ask, jaw tight.

They flick their eyes like I'm an idiot. "Magnolia."

"Fine." I shrug. "She's fine."

"Is she funny?"

"Yes." I'll sigh.

"Are her clothes good?"

"They're clothes." I'll breathe out through my nose.

"Is she tall?"

"I don't know—" I'll shrug. "No. Not to me."

"Is she as beautiful as she seems?"

That one, however they word it — and all of them do — every single time it catches me off guard.

"More," I say and then I don't know, maybe it's obvious, like it's leaking out of me that I love her because they all look at me like I'm broken and then we hook up.

There's a knock at my office door and the door opens — Kekoa fills the frame.

There's a girl under the desk, head bobbing away, and I clear my throat to let her know.

Flick my eyes over to my old friend. "I'm busy."

"Yeah, you're always busy these days." He gives me an unimpressed look.

"What do you want?" I shake my head and he gestures behind him.

"Why don't you wrap this up and you and me go have a talk?"

Then he leaves.

Fucking buzzkill. Like I can finish up now.

"Pour yourself a drink, yeah?" I point to my bar in the corner. "I'll be right back."

I step outside my office, close the door behind me and stare up at Kekoa, unimpressed.

"Thanks for that."

"Anytime." He nods. "You good?"

"Oi—" I shake my head. "I swear to God, if you just interrupted me to ask me if I'm okay I'll—"

"You'll what?" he asks, bored, stretching his arms over his head.

"I'm good," I tell him with a look.

He shakes his head. "You're not."

"I am," I tell him, defiantly.

"You fell in love—"

"Who the fuck told you that?" I say loudly.

"You did." He whacks me in the chest. "When you shoved her into my arms that night with the power outage."

I scowl at him. "I dumped her that night."

"Yeah, not like you to overreact to a revelation or anything."

I blink. "Excuse me?"

"Hardly stuck anyway, did it?" He rolls his eyes.

"What is your point?" I ask, exasperated.

"My point is, instead of fucking your way through this—" He grabs me by the shoulder how I reckon a father would. "—massive loss you're going through... You loved her. You fell in love with her — you gave her up to keep her safe, that was an incredible, admirable thing you did." He gives me this look, like he's implying what I'm doing now is less than.

"Reckon with it, Jules. Process it and feel it and—"

"Fuck that." I shake my head. "No."

He pulls back, almost like he's annoyed about it. "No?"

"What's on the other side, Koa?" I ask with a shrug. "I love a girl. I can't be with her. I can't be with anyone—" I point back to my office door with the girl behind it. "That's what I've got, this is it for me— so fuck off with your judgement and your reckoning. I don't want to reconcile shit." I back away from him.

"I'm good," I tell him, even though we both know I'm not.

57

Christian

I didn't get the most overwhelming response from the boys when I told them how it went down with me and Daisy.

Jo and Henry thought she was overreacting a bit, not as much as I did.

BJ said I need to stop listening to the other two because their longest-standing relationships are with their own hands.

Henry didn't like that — said he's had girlfriends, and BJ said, "for more than a month?" And then they started arguing and Henry said "What about Romilly?" and BJ rolled his eyes and said something about it being ten years ago, and then Henry went weird the way Henry always goes weird about Romilly Followill so then I left to go see Daisy because my fuse isn't that good in general, let alone when I'm fighting with her.

When I get to her house, Koa answers the door.

"Hey." I nod my chin at him.

"Hey—" He sort of frowns. Guess he's shitty about the sex tape too.

"Daisy here?" I walk past him.

Kekoa nods slowly. "She know you're coming?"

"No?" I shrug and walk up the stairs to her room.

I don't knock, because why would I knock? Worst thing that could happen is that she's naked and then that's great.

Can't imagine she'll be taking her clothes off for me anytime today so if I burst into her room and she's changing, that's just a softened blow for me, all things considered.

So I swing open her door.

"Dais, listen, I—" I start, but then I stop. Freeze on the spot.

Have you ever seen the person you love in bed with someone else?

I have before, seen it with Parks and Beej. They were in bed all the

374

time, even when they "weren't together" — they'd be in bed together. But she was his so even though I hated it then, this is different.

This is Daisy.

Mine. The girl I love more than anything else on the planet, sitting in bed with her ex boyfriend.

There's space between them. It doesn't look overly romantic. The TV's on. *Ghostbusters* is playing.

And me and Dais, I think we've made some strides. I'm honest; I'm upfront. In my opinion, I think I've been forthcoming with my feelings for her. I think I've communicated to her how much I love her and what she means to me. And some fucker stealing and streaming a sex tape of me and a girl I used to shag that we made while Daisy and I were broken up, that's not a big deal to me.

I had sex with Vanna. I know I did.

Did I want Daisy to see it? No, I'd prefer that she didn't. I'd prefer that it wasn't the most watched adult film in the country at the minute too, but here we are.

It is what it is. I did it. I didn't cheat on her to do it. And I don't really get why she's so upset about it.

It doesn't make sense to me. This kind of upset, all things considered, seems disproportionate.

This upset and running to fucking Rome? She can piss off.

I scoff and her eyes go wide. Launches herself out of bed as I turn to walk away. She's fully clothed, I guess that's something. Sweatpants and a singlet.

"Christian!" She runs after me and I spin back to face her in the hallway, getting up close to her face.

"You're going to have a crack at me about a sex tape I made before we were back together when you're over here in bed with your ex-boyfriend—"

She rolls her eyes. "We're not in bed—"

"You're literally in bed!" I yell at her.

"Not like that!" She yells back. "You know it's not like that."

"How the fuck would I know that, Daisy?" I give her a look. "The last time we had a fight, you ran off and fucked him — why not now?"

"You were in love with Magnolia!" she yells. "He's my oldest friend!"

"Are you telling me that you can't see how fucking hypocritical you are; angry at me for something I did when we were broken up when you're here with him, in your bed, that you used to actually fuck him in—"

"Nothing happened—" Romeo says. Standing behind her.

I give him a steep look. "Oi, I'm trying to have a private conversation with my girlfriend— do you want to go get back into her bed and wait for her to be done out here with me—" I nod my head back towards her room. "That's your thing, right?"

I look between them, eyebrows up, and Daisy scowls at me.

"Fuck you."

I point at Romeo. "Nah, maybe you should fuck him."

And then I turn and leave.

I regret saying that. Immediately I regret it. I feel sick about it, because what if she does it? She could. Girls can be like that. I fucking hate girls. They're monsters, all of them. They don't ever do good, they just fuck you up.

I slam the door as I leave and peel out of their driveway as fast as I can.

My first thought is I want to get even.

I want to do something that's going to make her feel how I feel — and then something kicks in my stomach and I know that's not true. I don't want to make her feel how I feel, even if a bit of me does.

I can't believe she did that. Running to Romeo? It's fucked. As rich as it is fucked.

Of all people, Rome. Probably would have preferred her to run to Tiller, if I'm honest, because I can't beat Romeo. What they have, I can't top it. That ancient history, fabled shit like Parks and Beej, so much trauma in their pockets, too much life between them to properly pull them apart.

Do you know what it's like to love someone who always has a fall-back guy? A tug back towards someone who isn't you? It fucks you up.

It's fucked me up before. It'll fuck me up now.

It already has.

58

Daisy

I haven't spoken to Christian in a day. I don't know whether I should have called? He looked really sad[235] when he saw Rome and I, but I swear — nothing happened. He was just there. He's always just there. And Julian's a fucking head case, he can't help me, he can't even help himself. He's on a bender for the ages and I can't go outside — it's literally everywhere.

I can't turn on the TV, I can't open my phone.

I just wanted someone by me to help navigate all of the insane shit the internet algorithms think is appropriate to show me because I've googled Christian in the past.[236]

As soon as I got home from my fight with him I gave Romeo every device I own that has access to the internet.

My phone, my tablet, my laptop. All I have left is Apple TV and even then, I don't turn it on — just in case.

He should have called me. Instead he just showed up and that made everything worse, because I know what Christian thought we he saw me with Rome.

Rome left not long after that. Said he was sorry, that he should probably go see Tavie anyway and left me there on my own. I kind of hate that. He's never left me when I needed him before.

And then, nothing from Christian.

I feel funny in myself that he was sad, that I made him sad. I hate that, I never want to make him sad— but then, he was mean when he left, telling me to fuck Romeo, how he did. And what about his awful indifference? Why the hell does Christian not give a shit that there's a video of him having sex on the internet with someone who isn't me?

---

[235] Kill me.
[236] Sue me.

Not that I want to be on the internet having sex with him. Or anyone!

I want him to care that he did it, I want him to care that I saw it, I want him to care that other people have — but he doesn't, and I don't understand him at all.

So I'm sitting on my bed — alone! — stewing, reading a magazine[237] angrily, turning the pages so aggressively that I rip every second one.

I get sweaty hands when I think about how I sent him photos of me and Tiller, and Rome and I, because I know it was callous, and if he sent me photos of him with Vanna I'd probably throw myself off a bridge. But then I remember how he apparently has his sex tape with her saved on his computer and I don't feel so bad. Nor do I feel better, but anyway.

Then there's a knock on my door — two light taps.

I know immediately it's neither Christian nor Julian, because neither of them knock, they just waltz on in like they own the place. They're both so shit. Men are shit.

"Knock, knock!" says a familiar voice I'm not at all expecting.

Magnolia Parks pokes her head through my bedroom door.

I frown.

"Hello!" She sing-songs. "That Declan boy let me in, I hope you don't mind.""What are you doing here?" I glare over at her.

She slips inside my bedroom and gives me a curt smile. "I'm going to assume that the hostility in that sentence is less to do with me and more because you've just spent the last 72 hours watching your boyfriend having sex with someone else—" She shifts her skirt, even though it doesn't need shifting; it sits on her perfectly.[238]

"Then you're an idiot," I say, looking over at her, unimpressed and unfazed. She perches on the edge of my bed. Ankles crossed, hands in lap.

"Well." She smiles, brightly. "What a week."

I roll my eyes.

"Firstly, can I just say, congratulations! Truly, mazel tov."

I blink a thousand times. "What?"

"Despite the ever enduring rumours amongst our friends that

---

[237] This month's *New Scientist*.
[238] Annoying.

Christian and I had sex, we truly did not, and it seems as though he's rather spectacular at it, so well done you—" I give her a dark look. "Not the time? Right, okay, well, that's fine." She clears her throat.

She peers over at me, eyes softening.

"Those boys are fuckwits, Daisy." She nods apologetically.

I eye her, suspiciously. "Did he send you here to apologise?"

"He didn't send me — well, he sort of did, but I'm here of my own volition, as a sort of diffuser, you might say." She gives me a delicate smile. "I'm known to have a very calming presence."

"You don't." I shake my head at her.

She shrugs. "Well, lots of people say I do."

"No," I tell her firmly. "Literally no one says that."

"Lots of people—" She nods, resolute.

"Name one."

She gives me a smug smile. "BJ."[239]

"That's called dopamine." I roll my eyes at her. "He's high off of loving you. There's nothing calming about you—"

She flaps her hands to silence me. "Well, let's agree to disagree."

"Why are you here, Magnolia?" I ask her, over-annunciating my question.

"Because," She tucks some hair behind her ears. "I'm somewhat familiar with the feeling of losing the person you love to somebody else—sexually—" She eyes me. "Even if you haven't actually lost them—"

"What—?" I toss her an impatient look. "BJ has a sex tape somewhere out there?"

"Probably." She rolls her eyes. "But not yet that we know of—"

I turn away from her. "Then you don't get it, do you?"

Her face frowns as her mind wanders.

"I've walked in on BJ having sex with someone else at least once. He also had sex with my best friend, in a bathtub. At his house. They've moved house, but I haven't taken a bath since."[240] She flashes me a quick smile. "He slept with a very slutty celebrity who gave a very vivid account of it to Rolling Stone. I've seen him hook up with girls in clubs, in cars, on boats, on planes—" I stare over at her,

---

[239] And Julian, if I'm honest. Never seen him calm down mid-fight except with her.
[240] So I guess we both hate baths.

horrified. "When I asked him, and he did the math, we suspect that the amount of women he's had sex with is in the high hundreds."

My mouth falls open.

"That's people, not times. Which puts the times tally well into the thousands."

Magnolia looks a little shaken up, but she continues. "All that's to say, I do understand that that's not exactly the same as a sex tape being released of your boyfriend and his ex-girlfriend, but I think I'm possibly in the neighbourhood." She gives me a pointed look before it goes soft again. "Daisy, I can't even imagine how horrible that must have been to see." She reaches over and wipes a tear from my face I didn't know was there.

"Here's the thing. All of those boys are undeniably cavalier about sex. Except for when they're in love—" She breathes out her nose and gives me a little shrug. "Somehow, they've managed to distinguish sex with other people from sex with us—"

I swallow heavily and take a breath and stare at my hands. I can't even look at her as I say what I say next. "It looked the same. Him with her. It looked like... us."

She gives me a sad smile and I would have rather died a year ago than have Magnolia Parks look at me like she's sorry for me, but here we are.

"Maybe it did." She shrugs. "But it isn't the same Daisy, because he's never loved her, he just loves you. And to them that's the only part that matters."

I pinch my lip absentmindedly.

"Come on." She nods her head towards the door. "I'll take you to see him."

She pulls me to my feet then stares down at me in my black tracksuit set from Olivia Von Halle,[241] unimpressed.

---

[241] Gia Berlin silk and cashmere-blend hoodie and track pants set, to be precise.

"Let's get you changed first."[242]

---

[242] To further clarify, she tried to make me wear a plunging floor-length gown to see Christian. We had a fight and then I put on the mid-rise cut-off shorts from Denimist ("They're very short," she frowned when I put them on.) with the navy cropped flocked cotton-jersey hoodie from Balmain ("—oh, are you going for a run after? No? Oh. No. Cool! You look…nice."). And then I threw some shoes at her (Bijoux 70mm double-strap sandals; Gianvito Rossi) which she used as a segue into saying those are the shoes I should wear with the following outfit: the Jude printed crepe mini dress (Emilia Wickstead), the black feather-cuff cropped cardigan (Sleeper) and monochromatic black Envelope leather clutch bag (Saint Laurent). And do you know what? I look fucking fantastic. She's so annoying.

59

Christian

How pleased Magnolia looks with herself when she turns up on my doorstep with Daisy is almost enough for me to shut the door in her face, except I can't because she's with the girl I love, and I can't imagine how much pride-swallowing it took for Daisy to come here, with Magnolia of all people.

"Baby Haites!" Jo yells. "What a miracle!"

Beej stares over at Parks — they're semi-back together now, by the way — smiling at her like she's just won a fucking Nobel prize.

I look over at Daisy from the sofa, glaring a bit because I'm still fucking mad.

Say "Oi," though, and nod at her with my chin.

Magnolia shoves Daisy towards me, and Dais snaps her head in her direction, scowling. ("Ooh," Magnolia whispers as she rolls her eyes. "I'm so scared.")

BJ, next to me, elbows me subtly.

"Fucking get up," he whispers, smiling at them as he does.

I stand up, shove my hands in my pockets and Daisy stands there, arms crossed over her chest, glaring at me and Magnolia's standing there between us, literally about to blow her top she's so stressed about it.

"What in the absolute fuck is this? How do you two ever solve issues when I'm not here!"

I toss her an offhanded look. "We normally just don't speak for an undisclosed period of time and then we have sex." I give her a blunt smile.

"Oh," BJ nods, impressed. "That's pretty cutting edge, Parks. We should try that." She gives him a look and Henry and Jo snort a laugh.

I stare over at Daisy — it's shit that she looks so hot when she's cross. That pouty mouth. It's pouty in general, but when she's pissed — I don't stand a fucking chance.

I nod my head up towards my bedroom. "Wanna go have a chat?"

She nods and I take her hand, pulling her up the stairs.

"To talk!" Magnolia calls after us. "Not to have sex!"

"Fuck off and mind your own business?" I call back.

"VERY RICH COMING FROM YOU WHO CALLED ME FOR HELP, YOU UNGRATEFUL PR—" she yells but I slam my door loudly to shut her up.

Once we're in my room, it feels like magic, like all the pride rinses off us and she's staring at me with big, heavy eyes and I'm grabbing her by the waist before I even know I'm doing it — I back her into a wall, pushing her hair behind her ear, stare at her face as I swallow heavy.

"I love you, Dais—" I shake my head. "I'm sorry."

"No, I am—" She buries her face in my neck. "I didn't think — nothing happened."

She sighs and I shake my head.

"I know."

"I promise," she insists.

I nod. "I know."

"I still don't totally get it, but I hated those photos, and I know that you hate this — so I hate it—" I tell her with a shrug.

"I shouldn't have sent them—" She frowns at herself. "I'm sorry. I never delete things from my phone. I still have photos of Rome and I from school on there—"

"Listen—" I hold her face. "I need you to understand, in my mind, sex with you and sex with anyone else, they're not the same." All I can offer her is a shrug. "They're so different. They don't feel like the same thing to me, like at all. But I should have — I don't know — I never thought it would come out."

She nods.

"I didn't want to tell you about it because, like, what good would it have done, you know? But I don't know — I fucked up."

Her eyes start to go soft as I'm talking and she slips her arms around my neck, mouth squashing into a little smile. "Has the undisclosed period of time passed yet?"

I lick my bottom lip and nod once. "I think it has, yeah."

~

"Wow," Henry says, looking at us as we trot back down the stairs half an hour later. "You guys don't look like you've had sex or anything."

Daisy rolls her eyes and I push my hands through my hair. Sit down on the couch and pull Daisy onto my lap.

Balled up on the couch with Beej on the other side of the room, Parks crinkles up her face like fucking little power-hungry bunny rabbit and smiles over at us, clearly proud of herself.

Whether our make-up was due to Magnolia Parks or the double orgasm I just gave Daisy upstairs, who's to say really?

"Now," Magnolia claps her hands together, "what are we going to do about that video?"

"Nothing." I shake my head at her.

Magnolia gives me a look. "We have to figure out who released it and seek retribution."

Daisy elbows me, amused.

Jo thumbs in Magnolia's direction. "Loves a mish, old Parks."

She pulls out a MacBook and flips it open.

"What are you doing?" BJ asks, peering over her shoulder. "What are you — don't watch it!" he yells and Magnolia scowls at him.

"I'm looking for clues!"

"No! Argh—" BJ scowls at the screen but doesn't look away. Actually tilts his head. "Bro, your arms look fit."

I give Daisy a despondent look.

From Magnolia's computer, I can hear myself and Vanna's breathing getting heavy.

"—Can you put it on mute, please?" Daisy sighs.

I hug her tighter and kiss the back of her shoulder.

("Sorry," I whisper. She turns, flashing me a quick smile.)

Magnolia grimaces and mutes it quickly then keeps watching. Doesn't take long before Henry and Jonah stand behind her and lean down to watch. All of them, all my childhood friends, huddled around a laptop, all watching and squinting at me having sex with a girl that isn't my girlfriend.

Jonah looks over at me and Dais. "Is it weird I'm sort of proud of you?"

"Yes," Daisy and I say in unison.

"Oi, but — no wonder this girl had a crack at the club the other night, man—" BJ says, not looking away from the screen. "Look at you go."

I groan, burying my face in Daisy's neck.

"Hey, how'd you do that thing with your back?" Henry nods as he squints at the screen.

Daisy stifles a laugh.

"Why does it stop there?" Magnolia frowns at the screen.

"Where?" I sigh from the safety of Daisy's shoulder.

"Well, you're obviously about to come—"

BJ gives her a look. "Obvious, is it?"

(And I let out a big long groan at the same time Daisy, Henry and Jo start laughing.)

Magnolia flicks Beej an apologetic look, then looks back over to me. "Why does the video cut before you're done?"

I sigh, shaking my head at her. "It doesn't."

Magnolia gives me a look. "Yes, it does."

I shake my head. "It doesn't."

"Yeah," Daisy says, looking at me. "It does."

Magnolia flips her computer around and hits play and before I can cover Daisy's eyes, she sees it all over again — me fucking some girl who isn't her, my back arching and then — black.

I stare at the screen. Holy shit.

"I know who released it."

They all stare over at me.

"What?" Daisy frowns?

"Who?" Jonah and Henry say at the same time.

I stare over at them, sort of in shock. "She did."

Daisy scoffs. "What?"

"She did." I nod. "She did it, Dais."

Beej shakes his head. "Christian, she's all over the news having a cry about her private life being violated..."

"I'm telling you—" I give him a look. "She released it. I know it was her."

"How?" Magnolia asks, eyebrows arched.

I look at Daisy and grimace a little — I might regret this, but then, maybe not.

"Because it's not the full tape."

Daisy sighs like she's beat, covering her face.

"Well, what's on the rest of it?" Henry straightens up.

I jump up from the couch, run upstairs and jog back down a minute later with my laptop.

"Are you fucking kidding me?" Daisy groans as I open it up, opening a folder on my desktop.

"Might have found that a bit quickly, mate," Jonah says under his breath but I ignore him, looking over at Dais.

"Baby, I thought you would have seen all this —" I give her a look then glance at my friends. "This is making a lot more sense—"

Daisy frowns. "What are you talking about?"

"I'm sorry—" I tell her before I hit play. Me and Vanna rear back to life and Magnolia and the boys scramble over to our side of the room.

Daisy hits mute but I give her an apologetic look before I unmute it.

My living room fills with breathy panting and moans and we're back to my back arching again and then where it cuts off online it keeps going...

I'm moving faster and faster, gaining momentum, eyes closed, face turned away from Vans and then, a little moan from my lips:

"Daisy,"

A hand flies to Daisy's mouth and Magnolia gasps.

Beej is whacking Jonah repeatedly, not looking away from the screen, grinning ear-to-ear.

"Oh, fuck!" Henry gasps, face contorted in ultimate amusement.

"What did you just say?" Vanna whispered on the screen, obviously choked. Then she hit me. "What the fuck did you just say to me?"

Me in the porno, I pressed my hand into my gaping mouth, cheeks pink, looking sprung. "I—" I started but she shoved me again.

"Get the fuck off me." She shoved me off her, rolling away. "How the fuck are you still thinking of that bitch?" She moved towards the recorder. You hear me start to say, "Don't call her th—"

And then it cuts to black.

The room is silent.

I turn to Daisy. "I thought you'd seen that."

"I—" She stares over at me, speechless. "No — that would have significantly softened the blow."

"I know." I nod. "I kind of thought you were taking it pretty badly for the only person who sort of comes out on top in all this."

"To be clear, though man—" BJ interjects. "You're definitely, literally on top, mate."

I give him a look.

"You love me!" Daisy grins. "You think about me when you're having casual sex with other women!"

"Yeah." I nod. "Exclusively."

"Aw, so sweet." Magnolia sighs, watching us. "You should stop that though, like let's just stop that now—"

"I agree." Daisy nods.

"Okay." I sniff a laugh. I look over at Daisy. "Are you okay?"

"Yeah—" Daisy shrugs. "Yeah, no, I feel much better about all this now."

"Right, so—" Magnolia points to the computer. "I'm going to need you to send me that—"

"No!" I yell at the same time BJ's head rolls back. "Fuck, Parks — why?"

"BJ, please." She gives him an unimpressed look. "Although it's hardly any of your business as we're temporarily 'just friends'."

"Alright." He nods. "Friend to friend, I don't want you watching videos of Christian having sex with Vanna Ripley."

"I'm not a pervert—" She cross her arms, defensively.

Jo nods his head in her direction. "She's on mish."

Henry grins as her tosses an arm around her. "Fucking love it when Parks is on mish."

"Send it to me," Magnolia tells me again.

"I shake my head."

"Send it!" She frowns.

"No, Parks—"

And then Daisy breathes out and stares over at her. "What are you going to do with it?"

Magnolia gets a defiant look in her eye, her nose in the air. "No one fucks with my friends."

Daisy looks over at me. "Give it to her."

Where are you

Out

With Christian

Come home now

Why?

Now.

What?

I'm not fucking around.

Come home.

Okay?

60

Julian

On the way home from a Liverpool match, an attempt was made on Santino Bambrilla's life.

They were leaving the venue, took a side exit — they rotate exits at the game — and someone shot at them.

He was with Rome, both sustained bullets, Santino's more serious than Romeo's, but neither life-threatening. Santino was hit in the chest, but they missed his heart and his lungs. Got Romeo in the arm.

I think of it and I don't like it, how much I want to call Magnolia. Tell her about this fucking shit thing that happened to someone I love, have her pause uncomfortably, not knowing what to say so she shows me photos of the most important dresses in history and runs her hands through my hair but I can't.

When Daisy busts through our front door I can hear from the way she slams it that she's annoyed I've told her to come home.

She throws open my office door, Christian behind her.

"I was having a really good da—" she starts but then her eyes land on Rome, arm bloody, face a mess, eyes blurry.

"Oh my God—" She rushes to him, one hand on his face, the other on his chest. "Are you okay?"

Christian stands in the doorway, watching on and frowning. "What happened?"

"Dad was shot," Rome says gruffly. "Me too—"

He flashes her his arm.

Daisy doesn't look away from him as she tells anyone who's listening, "Someone get me the kit."

She lifts the bloody sleeve up, peels back the material we've been using to apply pressure, and peers at the wound as best she can.

"Are you okay?" Christian asks, moving towards him.

Rome nods, barely looking at him.

"Santi—" Daisy asks, looking between me and Rome. "Is he okay?"

"He'll live," Rome says, watching her and she touches his face with her hand again.

"I'm so sorry—"

"What the fuck happened?" Christian asks me, hands crossed over his chest.

I gesture over to Rome.

"Sniped at the match." He shrugs. "It happened quickly — and then our boys threw me in one car, Dad in another—"

"Where is he?" Daisy asks.

"I don't know." Rome shrugs. "Hiding."

Declan passes Daisy her kit and she pushes Romeo down on an armchair.

Turns around and sanitises her hands and arms, she and Christian catch eyes and he gives her a sad smile.

"Rome's going to stay here with us—" I tell them, because now feels as good a time as any. "Safe keeping."

Daisy nods, so does Christian. Can't imagine he's stoked, all things considered, but he says nothing.

Walks over to Daisy and looks down at her kneeling by Rome.

"How can I help?"

She grabs some gauze and starts wiping away at the blood.

"I need a bin, I need a lot of sterilised water, or at least bottled water—" She looks over her shoulder. "Can someone try to find me some lidocaine or articaine?"

"Why does he get the drugs?" I eye my sister playfully.

Her eyes pinch at her ex-boyfriend's arm. "He didn't do this to himself."

I shrug and lean back against my desk. "You shot yourself last year, they gave you drugs—"

All four of them, Daisy, Christian, Rome and Miguel, toss me an unimpressed look.

"I'm not ready to joke about that one yet—" Rome says, looking at the other side of the room.

"Yeah." Christian shakes his head. "Me either—"

"Christian—" Daisy grabs him by the wrist, ignoring me. "Shine your phone light in here please."

He nods, does what she tells him to and she gets to work.

Christian stares down at Rome who's looking away.

"Do we know who did it?"

Romeo nods without looking at him. "Got him."

"Who was it?" Daisy asks, looking between us.

Rome glances over at her. "Well, he's dead now—"

"We don't know for sure yet, but it's looking like it was some old connections from Italy."

Daisy nods. "Is your mum okay?"

"Rattled—" He shrugs. "But okay."

"Where's Carmelo?" Christian asks.

"Freshfield, for now," Rome tells him.

"Carms is going to run ops for a while."

"Woah." Christian blinks.

It's a big deal when the seats change hands. James Devlin's dad is still around, but he's stepped back. Danny Jukes and Hughie McCracken came to sit at the table when their respective fathers died. Jukes' was murdered, Hughie's died of cancer. Sad.

Carmelo taking over for the Bambrillas will cause a stir — I'm not worried, but others might be. People have different agendas, things they want to achieve, people have different versions of success in their own mind, and what we do is power hungry, no two ways about it.

Carms isn't like that, it's not what he wants. He'll do it because it's what we do but it's not what he wants. Never has been, just the hand he was dealt.

"Santi'll come back." I shrug, even though I know myself that that's probably not true.

"Yeah, right," Daisy scoffs around the same time Romeo throws me a look like I'm stupid.

Carmelo's best traits aside, he is a man, and men do love power. Historically, it's not often been that someone takes a seat then relinquishes it when asked to.

"Got it." Daisy sighs and then I hear the familiar clang of a bullet in a pan.

Romeo looks down at his arm, then down at her. "Thanks."

"Mmhm." She gives him a tender smile as she tapes it up.

She stands up, looking at his arm with her head tilted, then nods to herself, happy.

"I'm going to go clean up, and then I'll set up your room." She gives Rome a quick smile, then catches Christian's eye, nodding her head for him to go with her.

She pauses at the doorway and looks over at me, her eyes are heavy. She's worried. I hate it when she's worried.

"What does this mean, Jules?"

"For you—?" I stare over. "Triple security—" She opens her mouth to say something but I shake my head and hold up a hand to silence her. "No complaints."

She breathes out loudly.

"Kevlar every time you leave the house—"

"No," she whines.

"Yeah." I nod back, firmly. "Unless you're at my house or his house—" I point to Christian. "It's Kevlar all round."

She sighs and walks away.

Romeo looks over at me, gives me a little shrug.

"Like, to be fair to her though, Kevlar is mad uncomfortable."

61

Daisy

"Do you really want to go out?" I grimace over at Christian in the back my car. Miguel's driving us in. Just to dinner, not out-out.

We're meeting up with his friends.

My friends too these days, maybe.[243]

"No—" he concedes. "But — we're going to have to go out eventually. Might as well be now..."

"Why might it as well be now?" I pout.

He sniffs a smile. "What's the worst that could happen?"

The obvious answer considering everything that's happened recently is that I'm shot, or worse, that he is.

I'm in the Kevlar. He refused.

I sigh. "What if a girl looks at you like she's seen you naked?"

"Baby," he laughs. "The whole world has seen me naked at this point. Fuck, I bet this guy's even seen me naked—" He whacks Miguel on the arm.

"No comment," Miguel says from the front.[244]

Christian nudges me with his elbow. "You nervous, Baby?"

"No," I scowl at him, sitting up straighter. "I'm not scared of anything." He smiles over at me and I sigh. "It's just that if someone looks at you in a way that I hate, I'll have to kill them — and then, that's a mess we don't need right now—" I shrug.

He nods a few times. "That is true."

"So it'd be easier if we just didn't go out."

"Or..." He gives me a look. "You could just not... commit a murder..."

---

[243] Maybe. Depending on the day.

[244] But he did have many comments and one of them was he understood why I was so upset over our break up now.

I give him a look.

"Verona's PR said I just have to show my face for an hour, and then we're out of here." He breathes out his nose. "I thought you'd be happy to get a minute out of the house?"

"I am." I nod quickly, that's true. It's been a lot.

It's a miracle Julian even said yes to this. It was a yes with a thousand caveats.

Kevlar, both Miguel and Kekoa, an armoured car with an escort and no sitting near windows.

He pushes some hair behind my ear. "In and out, Dais."

I breathe out my nose and I stare over at him as we pull up.

It feels extra strange now, everyone's obsession with the sex tape, especially in light of Santino. But no one knows about that. I feel sick every time I think about Romeo being hurt, even though he's okay now.

Okay is subjective. He's losing his mind at the Compound, but he's technically okay. He wanted to come tonight — how desperate he must have been to beg me to let him come out with Christian and I. I said yes, of course, but Julian said no. He said he would have said no about Romeo going out in general, but Rome going out with me? Disaster.

When Christian and I step out of the car it's worse than you could have imagined — the paparazzi and the TMZ cameras everywhere.

"IS IT TRUE YOU LEFT VANNA FOR HER?"

"WHO IS SHE?"

"IS THIS DAISY?"

"DAISY ARE YOU RESPONSIBLE FOR THE BREAK-DOWN OF VASTIAN?"

Miguel shoves the photographers and the reporters out of the way, making a way for us through into the venue.

I spill through the doors and it feels like everyone in the room turns and stares.

Christian squares up his shoulders and hooks his arm around my neck, leading me to the back where I can already see Magnolia and Taura peeking through the crowd staring at us.

"Vastian sounds like ointment for an STD." I squint up at him and he laughs.

"Can't say I was ever a really a fan of it, myself."

Magnolia grabs my hands, pulling me down next to her at the table, hugging me tightly and in what world would we have ever thought that I'd find her embrace a relief, but I do...

"Was that horrible?" she asks, ogling the crowd. "London loves a scandal."

I roll my eyes like it didn't bother me.

"You look great!" Magnolia adds, eyeing my outfit.[245] It sounds like she's complimenting me but she's really just complimenting herself, because she's a fucking psychopath who downloaded an app on my phone and organises my outfits for every day of the week and every event in my calendar.[246]

"Want me to go out there and flash them?" Taura offers. "Divert some attention away from... hard to not acknowledge the elephant in the room—" She gestures to Christian.

"He is the elephant in the room." BJ gives Christian a wink and he rolls his eyes, trying not to laugh.

The night goes on and it's fine.

No one who isn't with us is brave enough to approach, and I reluctantly admit to myself how much I like the friends I've found in these girls I used to hate.

After a little while Magnolia gazes across the restaurant and then whispers[247] to me.

"Isn't that the sexy policeman you used to date?" She asks brightly, peering past me.

Christian, BJ, Henry and Jonah all hear her because she's a terrible whisperer and look over before turning back, each respectively mumbling, "Is he sexy?"[248], "I mean, would you say sexy?"[249], "Yeah, he's pretty sexy"[250] and "Not that sexy."[251]

---

[245] Embellished leather mini dress (Valentino); Intarsia-knit cardigan in black (Burberry); Devon satin heeled mules (The Attico); Four Ring embellished leather pouch (Alexander McQueen); Meryl 18-karat gold hoop earrings (Anita Ko).

[246] "How do you have access to my calendar?" I asked her and she just laughed breezily like it was an insane question.

[247] Loudly.

[248] Christian.

[249] BJ.

[250] Henry.

[251] Jonah.

And Magnolia, Taura and I trade amused glances before I clear my throat and flash her a tiny smile.

"Yes, it is."

He looks good.

Tiller always looks good though, that was never the problem.

Or, conversely, that was always the problem.

He's with Dyson and his ex.

Even from here I can see those eyes of his, always light even in a dark place like this. He's in a plain navy t-shirt and tatty blue Ksubis with Chuck Taylors, and if he didn't have the face he has, no way would he get into a place like this with an outfit like that on, but after all, he is — despite what the boys here might want to admit — The Sexy Policeman.

"You've not seen him since you two ended?" BJ asks me but really he's watching Christian, gauging him.

Christian's eyes are pinched and his breathing's slowed way down. He looks calm on the surface but I get nervous with the look behind his eyes.

All Christian's spikes are up for me the way they go if someone hurts the person you love, but I don't need his spikes up, I just need him.

I dig my chin into his shoulder to pull him out of it and shake my head at BJ.

"No."

"Want to go fuck him up?" Jonah offers merrily.

"Yep," Christian says, pushing back loudly from the table, but I grab his wrist, pulling him back down.

The pushback's loud though, even in here, and Killian Tiller's eyes flicker over to us.

His gaze settles on me, snug in the arm of the person he was always paranoid about.[252] Tiller's face pulls all tight and annoyed, but he tries to force a smile. He nods his head, signalling for me to come talk to him.

"I'm going to go say hey," I tell Christian, who looks at me like I'm crazy.

"What?" He shakes his head. "Why?"

"Because!" I say loudly. "He's my ex-boyfriend, we were together

---

[252] With good reason, I suppose.

for a significant period of my life, for the vast majority of it, he was very good to me, and you and Julian are very likely to run into shit with him in the future, and I don't think being on good terms with him is a terrible idea—"

"No." Christian shakes his head. "I'm never being on good terms with him — don't talk to him."

I stare at him for a few seconds. "You have a sex tape with your ex all over the internet."

"Oh, fuck — fine!" He groans. "That's the only time you can use that for the rest of the week though, okay? I'm not getting you coffee in the morning.[253] If there's only one bagel left tomorrow morning, fuck you, I'm having it and you can't say shit—"

I roll my eyes at him[254] before heading over to Tiller.

He moves towards the edge of the bar, waiting for me.

"Well, hi." I sparkle up at him.

Tiller runs his tongue over his perfect white teeth, eyes a little cinched. He doesn't say anything, not at first. Leaves it for a few seconds, staring straight ahead behind the bar, then he looks down at me.

"Were you ever going to tell me?"

I square my shoulders, arching my brows up at him. "That I got back with my ex-boyfriend?"

He does something with his face that's like an all-over, tacit 'yeah'.

"Oh, shit." I roll my eyes sarcastically. "Did the singing telegram not arrive? That was prepaid."

He gives me an unimpressed look so I poke him in the arm because he's being hypocritical.

"You're one to talk," I tell him.

"How's that now?" he asks, nose in the air, a little pious.

"You're obviously back with Michelle." I nod discretely in her direction.

Tilts his head. "Obvious, is it?"

I stare over at him. "Are you here for me?"

He says nothing for a few seconds. "They don't know we are, but yeah."

---

[253] "Yes, you are." I interrupt him. He rolls his eyes before he concedes.
   "Yes I am."
[254] And make a mental note to hide the bagels.

I nod once. "Okay. Is everything okay?"

He shakes his head. "I don't have anything definitive to tell you, Dais, just that… It feels off?" He shrugs. "Something feels off."

I frown up at him. "Bad chatter?"

He shakes his head, holding my eyes.

"No chatter. None."

I frown a little.

"Everything's quiet. Crime's lulled, robberies are down. It feels like people are bracing for something—"

I cross my arms, like crossing them might keep whatever it is at bay.

"Like what?"

Tiller opens his mouth to say something and then shrugs a bit hopelessly. "I don't know." He sighs out his nose, he's got his stress face. "Are you okay?"

I nod.

"Are you?"

He nods back. "He's being good to you?"

I flash him a quick smile. "Yes."

He gives me a small smile and the edges of it are sad. "Good."

"If you hear anything—" I start.

He nods again. "I'll call you."

"Or drop by?" I offer.

A smile flashes over him, it's quick and sad. "Probably not."

"Fair enough," I take a step away from him and pretend like that didn't sting me a little bit. I give him a tiny, uncomfortable shrug, and gesture toward Christian. "Anyway, I should probably get back."

He nods, measured. "Yeah."

"You know you can call me, Dais. Any time." He stares over at me. "Whatever you need."

I reach over and squeeze his hand, but just for a second. "It was good to see you, Tills."

He cocks a smile. "Liar."

"Yeah." I sigh, playfully. "Always preferred you in a doorway."

He lets out a 'ha' as I walk back over.

"Everything okay?" Christian asks as I sit back down next to him. His brows are furrowed with concern and maybe a hint of jealousy and I kiss his cheek because I love doing jealous with him.

Magnolia clears her throat and leans over the table towards me. "If I might say — far too friendly with your ex."

Christian, BJ, myself, Henry, Jonah and Taura all stare over at her, incredulous.

"Weren't you, dating him—" I point to BJ. "Practically the entire time you were broken up with him?"

She shakes her head, interrupting me. "This isn't about me—"

I cut in again. "—Including times when you were dating other people?"

"Yes, but—"

"And isn't he technically still your ex-boyfriend now?" I clarify.

She rolls her eyes. "Well, technically—"

I toss Christian a look.

"Learn from me Daisy," she says, like she's a sister at a monastery. "Look where that got me — in a real pickle jar."

BJ kisses her cheek in this too cute, too tender way[255] and whispers, "That's not the expression, Parks. It's just 'pickle'. You were in a pickle."

Magnolia gives him a look like he's the problem. "Doesn't make sense."

Christian scratches his neck, amused. "What doesn't?"

"Why would I be in a pickle?" She shrugs, like we're the idiots.

"Why would you be in a pickle jar?" I ask.

Magnolia's eyes pinch together and I think she sees my point because she looks annoyed at me for a split second before she laughs airily and it sounds like bell chimes.

"I'm just saying—" She shrugs, snuggling into BJ in their 'just friends' way. "It wouldn't matter if he was a normal police officer but he's the one on the sexy calendar, yes?"

I look between her and the boys, shaking my head with a cautious confusion. "No?"

"Oh." She grimaces a little. "Well, that's a bit of a missed opportunity then, isn't it? They really should get on that—" BJ gives her a look. "I mean—" She looks at Christian quickly. "No they shouldn't! Eugh!"

Christian flips her off and I kiss his cheek.

---

[255] And I think I'm a bit in love with him too, but just in the way every girl alive is, so whatever, that's neither here nor there.

"Don't worry, man—" BJ grabs his shoulder, shaking it merrily. "I'd buy your calendar a hundred times over."

"Big seller, the Gang Lords of London Calendar—" Henry interjects, grinning.[256] "—Pretty decent spread between Christian, Jonah and Julian—"

"Romeo," Magnolia adds.

"Fuck." Christian rolls his eyes.

She smiles apologetically. "Sorry! Daisy has good taste in men, what can I say?"

"Nothing," BJ tells her, with a look. "Please — just — nothing."

The night moves forward, Christian runs upstairs to his office with the PR guy and I excuse myself to the bathroom.

The night's unfolding less terribly than I'd foreseen, and I'll admit that I'm relieved. It felt good to see Tiller. Like I cracked open a window and let the stale air out. I feel like I'm breathing clearer after it.

I make my way back to our table when—

"Fuck you!" someone yells out at me.

I know it's her before I see her face. I turn on my heel and stare over at Vanna.

"The pair on you—" I shake my head at her. "Unbelievable. Do you know who I am?"

"Nobody." She spits, eyes filling with tear. "You're no one. No one gives a shit about you, no one knows your name."

"Actually—" I grimace. "If you watch to end of that video it would appear that at least Christian knows my name."

Her eyes go to slits.

"Vanna!" Magnolia pops up beside me. "It's so good to see you—"

Vanna frowns, confused.

"You have such an incredible acting range—" Magnolia shakes her head. "I've loved watching you be so sad on the news, you're so convincing." Magnolia gives her a kind smile, except its edges are dull.

"I actually saw the alternative ending to your cheeky film—" She nods over at her. "What a plot twist!"

Vanna's face falters. "What?"

"Christian saying her name at the end—" Magnolia points to me. "Ouch! Hey, tell me, how little self esteem does one need to have to

---

[256] "— Not a gang lord," Christian interrupts.

stay with a boy when he calls you by another name mid-orgasm? I'm guessing, like, none?"

Vanna opens her mouth to say something and Magnolia reaches over and touches her arm gently.

"It's coming out tomorrow."

"What?" Vanna blinks.

"The amended version — the full version, if you will." Magnolia smiles like she's helping her.

"Distributing a sex tape that isn't yours without consent is a sex crime."

"I know!" Magnolia nods, emphatically. "I checked with legal counsel beforehand. Of course I had Christian's express permission to release but not yours, but it's arguable in a court of law that because you were happy to release it initially yourself—"

"Without Christian's consent—" I interject.

Vanna shakes her head. "You can't prove that."

"Oh!" Magnolia winces. "No, but I can — I've obtained proof of a file transfer from your IP address to Martin Wallace's IP address over at the *Daily Mail*, as well as an entire exchange between the two of you laying out the deal, and also a bank transfer into an offshore account of yours the day after the video went live."

Vanna's mouth falls open, and I stare over at Magnolia in[257] awe.

"You should call your PR company," Magnolia tells her with a smug smile. "It's probably going to be a rough couple of weeks, but hey! That's okay, all of Britain already knows that that's just the way you like it." Magnolia flashes her a curt smile and walks away.

Holy fuck.

Even my jaw drops at that one.

---

[257] Reluctant.

62

Christian

Lunch at Mum's today. Always loved a Sunday lunch, my mum. I haven't always been the most obliging, but Daisy loves them. She actually loves them so much it makes me feel sad for her; how much she's craved a family, how shit hers was to her, all things considered.

I don't know, part of me thinks Jonah might have been right about Daisy being magic, because suddenly, Dad's around again.

I don't trust it, really.

He asked me to get lunch last week, I said no. As far as I'm concerned, you can't really fuck off for fifteen years and waltz back in when you feel like it, but Mum's happy.

Jo said he got a drink with him at the pub the other night. I don't know why. He said it was fine. Dad just asked him a bunch of shit about himself, that it sort of felt like a first date.

When Daisy and I pull up to the estate, Uncle Callum's leaving.

I give him a wordless wave and feel a bit relieved he's heading off.

I don't like him around Daisy. Don't like him around me either, but there's something in him that wants to keep him away from her.

Kind of mentioned it to Jonah in passing once and he palmed it off.

"He's not so bad," Jo said, shaking his head. "You're just dirty at him because you were both tuning that same girl from *Love Island* at a party once and she picked him."

That's not entirely true.

Once I realised the girl I was tuning was also being tuned by my uncle, I went off her pretty quick, but yeah — fair assessment. I've liked Callum considerably less since then. I've been known to hold a grudge.

"Where's he going?" Daisy asks as we talk into the foyer.

I shrug. "Who cares?"

I kiss her up against the wall in the hallway.

"Ay!" my brother jeers. "Are we making another video, then?"

Daisy glares over at him and Mum squawks somewhere from in the belly of the house.

"Jonah, we will not be making any sex tape jokes today—"

Jo tosses me a look. "No promises there."

We walk into the dining room and Dad's sitting there, head of the table, a bit like he never left.

Except that he did. Even if he didn't. That office of his down the far end of the house might as well have been in fucking Prague for all we saw of him, for all he didn't do.

I was raised by my mum. That's it.

"Daisy." My dad stands to shake her hand. "Good to see you again — thank you for not leaving Christian after the release of his sex tape."

I toss him an annoyed look and Daisy links her arm with me, resting her head on my arm.

"Oh, Jud — then you've clearly not watched it—" she shakes her head at him. "It's sublimely good work. If you had you'd know why we're still together. He's a talent."

Daisy gives him a bratty smile and my dad sniffs, amused though he doesn't look like he wants to, and me? I love her more than ever.

"Thank you," I say into her ear when no one's looking. Pull her over to the table and hold her hands.

Mum walks into the room, sweeps over to me and Daisy. Kisses the top of my head, kisses the top of Daisy's and squeezes her shoulders.

"Tell me." She sits down across from Dais. "How's Romeo? I spoke to Julian, he said he's with you—"

"He's better." Daisy nods. "He's on some antibiotics to avoid an infection but he's healing fine." She gives my mother an appreciative smile.

"Is it weird?" Jo asks. "Like, him and Christian both sleeping there."

Daisy frowns a bit but glares over at him. "Surely no weirder than you and Henry dating the same girl—"

"Fuck," Jonah says under his breath. "Always at the ready with that in your arsenal."

Daisy pokes her tongue out at him.

"Who is Romeo?" Dad asks.

"Bambrilla," I say at the say time Jo says, "Daisy's ex-boyfriend."

Dad peers over at Daisy.

"Who Daisy saved—" Mum tells him with a look.

"Hardly." Daisy rolls her eyes. "He had a bullet lodged in his brachial. I just fished it out."

I toss my arm around her, proud, and kiss her head.

"Bambrilla," Dad nods. "That's—"

"Santino's son," Mum tells him.

Dad nods along, catching up. "You used to date him."

"Yeah." Daisy leans in to me. "For a very long time."

I stare over at my dad, wondering whether he'll keep picking at the scab that's there — am I happy Daisy's ex-boyfriend is living with her? No, of course. Do I trust him? I don't know. But I trust her.

He stares back at me, then he leaves it.

Dad points to Daisy's glass. "Lifesaver needs wine." And he pushes back from the table.

Mum flaps her hands. "I'll get it, I'll get it!"

She flits away and Daisy looks over at Dad.

"So you grew up in Cawthorpe," she tells him.

He nods, surprised. "I did."

"Christian took me there the other week — it's beautiful."

Dad stares over at me so I look away. Something about Daisy saying that sounds like I was making an effort that I don't really want to be making.

He gives me a look that feels weighted, and then he nods at her. "Yeah, it is."

And then nothing. He says nothing, I say nothing — we just sit there, staring. I don't know what to say to him, don't know how to talk to him. I haven't done it in years.

I don't like that he's making an effort, you know?

I'm twenty fucking five, I don't need a dad now. I needed one when I was twelve and I found Mum crying alone in the pantry, when they shipped us off to boarding school, when I was fifteen and I got my fucking arse handed to me on the rugby pitch and I didn't want to play anymore, when I fell in love with my best friend's girlfriend, when I nearly fucked her last year in New York — I don't need him now. I did it all already without him and I'm fine. So whatever effort he's making, it's too late and I don't want it.

Jo's staring at me and I feel like he's in my thoughts. He's better at this shit than me, forgives quicker and easier, is okay with a grudge — doesn't hold them too easily, unless his ego's bruised, then God help you. Jo's just here for the good times for the most part. We're not the same like that.

"So—" Jo shakes his head. "Any word on Parks' little plan?"

"No." Daisy rolls her eyes. "I'm starting to think she just wanted that video for herself."

I pull a face and drain my glass, then look around.

"Where's Mum with the wine?"

It's been a few minutes.

Jo shrugs with his mouth.

"Barnsey!" Dad calls. "You need a hand?"

Nothing.

"Barnsey!" he calls again. Still nothing, and he pushes back from his chair. "Rebecca?" he calls.

Daisy's eyes go bright with concern and she sits up straighter.

"Rebecca!" Dad proper bellows. The sort of yell you're hearing, like, no matter where you are in this house, you're hearing it.

Still nothing.

That's enough to get me on my feet, Jonah too.

Maybe it's what happened to Rem, maybe it's what happened to Santino the other day, but I feel sick. Immediately.

We all fan out. Jo upstairs, Dad to the living room, me and Daisy to the kitchen.

"I'm sure she's fine," Daisy says, holding my hand, brows low.

I nod but I still feel sick anyway. We check the kitchen, the butler's kitchen, the pantry — the cellar door's open. I nod my chin at it and catch Daisy's eye.

I flash her my gun.

'I don't have one,' she mouths as she shakes her head. She darts to a kitchen drawer and sticks two utility knives up her sleeves — what the fuck life is this?

I pull Daisy behind me as I head down the stairs, push her against the wall so I'm shielding her a bit more. The light's on.

We get to the bottom of the steps and I bring my finger up to my mouth to make sure she stays quiet.

We listen for about ten seconds. Nothing.

"Mum?" I call, and nothing.

Daisy pulls out her phone, pulls up the camera and flips it to selfie mode, then she angles the camera to the ground behind us — it takes me a few seconds to register that it's Mum lying there on the ground. But not Daisy, she swings into action.

Me? I stand there staring down at her, my mum on the floor of our cellar, pool of blood coming from her head like she's been hit over it — and I go blank for a second.

"Christian—" Daisy says but I say nothing.

It's my mum — she came to all my games, dropped us off every Monday, picked us up every Friday, no excuses, always. She still does Easter egg hunts for us now. Christmas Eve she does the Santa footprints from the chimney like we're five. She's the best mum in the world, the only real parent I've had, really. At least for the years that count.

"Christian!" Daisy says loudly, catching my eye and staring at me before she says very clearly, "Call for help."

"Jonah!" I yell. My voice sounds far away though. "Jo!"

"What?" My dad says, appearing at the top of the stairs. "What? What's wrong?"

He runs down them and then sees my mum straight away.

He runs to her. Runs. Falls to his knees, picks up her head—

"No!" Daisy yells. "No, don't touch her head!"

Daisy shifts herself, takes the weight of Mum's head from Dad's hands and lowers it back to the ground.

"She's bleeding so much." Dad stares at her, reaching to touch her face again.

"Please stop touching her," she tells him as Jonah appears at the top of the stairs.

"Christian—?" He darts down. "What's wrong? Is it — fuck," he says when he sees her.

"Give me your shirt," Daisy says to my dad. He just stares at her, blankly.

I take mine off and hand it to her, and Daisy holds it down on Mum's head.

Dad throws Daisy's arms away from Mum. "Stop, you'll hurt her!" he yells savagely and then he hovers over Mum, touching her face.

"Barnsey — can you hear me? I'm sorry — I'm so sorry. I love you, I've always loved you — I just lost you for a while and — I just found you — and—" He pushes some hair behind her ears, then sees blood on his hand and it starts trembling. "Oh my God," he says under his breath.

"Has someone called an ambulance?" Daisy asks.

"We don't do police around here," Jonah tells her with a look.

Daisy shakes her head at him. "You do today."

"Barnsey—" Dad touches Mum's face again, he's crying now — it throws me that he is, that he cares this much in a visceral way after years of fucking nothing — he's starting to get hysterical. Hyperventilating.

"Christian." Daisy stares at me. "Take him away."

"No—" Dad shakes his head. I move towards him and he jumps to his feet, ready to fight me. "No, please — I can help."

"Jud." Daisy stares at him. "You can't help her, I can help her though, I just need you to to go stand over there with Christian—"

I grab him by the shoulders and pull him over, and he's crying, heaving in my arms, and I don't know what to do. I'm just staring at my mum on the floor, bleeding so much, holding my dad who I don't think deserves to cry like that. I don't think he deserves to care like this when he's been so shit for so long.

Daisy checks her pulse.

"Weak—" she says. "But it's there. Give me your phone," she tells Jonah. He hands it to her. She clicks on the flashlight and opens Mum's eyes.

"Fuck," she says under her breath and both Jo and I stare over at her.

Daisy shakes her head. "It's going to be fine—" She nods to herself. "It's going to be fine."

I can hear sirens coming in the background, they seem far away. Everything seems far away.

My mum on the floor, my dad in my arms.

I stare over at Daisy and she stares back.

"It's okay," she tells me.

She's lying.

63

Daisy

There is something about loving a person that makes their agony so much worse than your own.

Watching Christian cry outside his mother's hospital room has been one of the most painful things I've ever seen in my life.

I've never had to comfort someone for a reason like this. I'm usually the one being comforted.

I didn't know what to do, really. I can fix people when they have wounds I can see, but heart wounds, I don't know. I just sit next to him, hold his hand, say nothing because there aren't words anyway. Not right now.

Blunt force trauma to the head, that's the verdict.

Someone hit Barnsey from behind with a wine bottle.

Ignoring the implications of what it means that two different heads of two separate Borough families were targeted in such a short period of time, just someone doing that to her in general is unthinkable.

Everyone loves Rebecca. Her boys[258] aside, and they love her more than anyone, the entire second floor of Weymouth Street Hospital has been inundated with people in our line of work.

My brother was the first to get here.

Rushed straight over, bit down on his bottom lip when he saw her so he wouldn't cry — cried anyway.

Julian loves Rebecca. She's always been patient with him and gracious when he's made rash decisions, good to him through all the shit with our parents — she's just a good woman.

Her room is surrounded with security and thank God because it really is the dog's dinner around here — between Callum Barnes personally vetting every person present and him and Jud being at

---

[258] And I will tentatively include Jud Hemmes under that umbrella.

each other's throats, which they are. Constantly. Callum blaming Jud for not being there, Jud blaming Callum for letting her have this life in the first place — their arguments crest every few hours and it looks like they'll come to blows. My money's on Jud but I also think Callum looks like he probably has a pocket knife hidden somewhere on his body. He'd play dirty to win, I think. Julian and Jonah break up the fights every time they appear, and Jules keeps taking Callum for walks.

Jud isn't leaving Rebecca's side. Christian's finding that difficult to reconcile, I can see it resting on his brow.

Every time his dad touches his mum's face, Christian stares at his hand, shakes his head a bit, jaw tight, nostrils flared.

I went downstairs at one point to buy some flowers to cheer up her room.

I bought bunches and bunches of light colours, blues and purples and whites, and when I carry them in, Christian smiles over at me tiredly. Stands to help me carry them.

I walk over to her bedside table and put some light purple ones next to her.

"No," Jud says, staring over at them. "She hates those."

"What?" I blink, confused.

"She hates peonies—" He picks them up and hands them back to me. "Take them away."

I peer over at Christian, and my cheeks are maybe a bit hot, but I'll be fine — honestly, I wasn't really all that conscious about the types of flowers I was buying in the first place. I don't know the names of flowers, I know the names of different surgical clamps. Want to know all the types of sutures there are in the world? I can tell you that. I can tell you the names of all the surgical needles — but flowers? Daisies, magnolias, roses and tulips and I'm all tapped out.

So I'm staring over at Christian, frowning because I'm confused, not because my feelings are hurt[259] and then he shakes his head.

"How the fuck would you know?" He nods his chin over at his dad.

"Christian—" I shake my head.

"No, actually but— how the fuck would you?" Christian asks, a bit

---

[259] Even if they are a bit hurt.

antagonistically. "You don't know what she likes, you don't know her favourite food, how she has her tea—"

"Black," his dad says.

"White with one," Christian tells him without missing a beat. "You don't know her, at all."

Jud takes a measured breath and points down at Rebecca. "That is my wife."

"On paper, maybe, yeah—" Christian gives him a curt nod. "But she's been a widow the last fifteen years."

His dad stares over at him, jaw tight, eyes dark and then he rushes his son. Grabs him by the collar of his shirt and slams him against the wall.

Julian's on his feet and about to pull them apart when suddenly Christian push-kicks him away. Jud stumbles backwards and then Christian right hooks in him the face.

All those rumours about how good a fighter he is? All true.

With those two moves his dad's knocked to the floor but that doesn't stop Christian from kicking him repeatedly in the stomach. My brother grabs him, tries to pull him back, but he cracks Julian in the face too.

Fight or flight, I can see it in his eyes. A decade and a half of trauma and abandonment issues cracking open on his face, bubbling up under him like magma.

"Christian—" I grab him from behind, trying to pull him back. He swings around and I know to duck because his brain's misfiring, and if I don't, he'll hit me.

I'm right, he makes the swing without even looking me in the eyes and I duck and the whole room sort of freezes and all the sound drops away. Christian catches himself, sees me, sees who he swung at.

He grabs me, grabs my arm, touches my face — pulling me into him.

Julian's staring over at us, eyes wide with worry — but I shake my head.

I'm fine. I've shot myself, had my larynx crushed, been held at knifepoint — ducking a swing from the man I love deep in trauma? Child's play, it's happy days.

"Shit—" He pushes me to the corner of the room, holding my face in his hands. "Daisy, I—"

"You missed. I'm fine." I shake my head. "Knew to duck."

His face pulls in this pained, gut-wrenching way.

His hands are trembling a bit — adrenaline — so I pull him outside. Out into the hallway and then into an empty room, and as soon as we're in there, he wraps his arms around me, holds me tighter than he ever has and cries.

These big, undone sobs and each one of them fastens my heart a little bit tighter to his.

That goes on for about thirty seconds before he pulls away and looks down at me — those hazel eyes all red and teary. I run my finger underneath them and he sniffs.

"You're okay," he tells me, like I'm the one who's crying. He pushes his hand through my hair like he's comforting me.

Some people need to feel like they're in control when they're losing it.

I give him a smile and a quick nod.

"I'm okay," I tell him with a quick smile.

"Baby, you know I'd never—" He cuts himself off, his breathing starts to get ragged.

"I know." I nod quickly. "And once your mum's better we'll work on your swing."

64

Julian

All this shit with Barnsey's fucked me in the head a bit. All that 'she's a good person, she didn't deserve this' shit aside — because she is good and she didn't deserve this — she is a fucking gang lord so then maybe she did. Maybe we all do.

The tensions are high around the hospital. Christian fought his dad — beat the fucking shit out of him. Hit me, nearly hit Dais without meaning to — she's fine. Jud Hemmes and Callum Barnes are at each other's throats, constantly. It's fucked. Jonah's rattled and exhausted, catching up, sitting in the chair now. His mum's been training him well and for a long time. Callum's positioned himself well in Jonah's life to help gird him too.

But it's all just a lot.

Jud there with Barnsey, not letting go of her hand the whole time, like sitting with her now half-dead in a hospital bed will make up for the time he didn't just lose but threw down the fucking sink— that scared me.

He made a choice when Rem died to lock himself up, live in the fear and the hurt and not move past it and he lost years. All that time he could have been happy — you should have seen them before. How in love they were... it was fucking yuck but strangely wholesome. You didn't want to look away. And then one thing happened — and it was a terrible thing, I'm not belittling that, what happened— kids dying, it's fucked.

It'll rip you apart if you let it and they let it.

Jud sank to the bottom of that pool with her.

I head out tonight to one of Jonah's venues. One of his bigger nights, he asked me to stop by, make sure it was going okay.

Fine by me, I wanted to clear my head. My head feels like it's being done in with all the drama.

I hadn't thought about it — being totally honest. I probably should have, but I didn't — that they might be there.

I've thought about her in the context of like, I want to call her, tell her all the shit that's been happening, even though I can't tell her any of it — but I didn't think she'd be here.

But of course she would. She's Jonah's friend as much as I am, both of them are.

It jars me when I see her, standing at the bar with Henry Ballentine.

Thick as thieves, those two.

She swears up and down that they've never naffed — Christian said the same thing when I questioned it. I guess they're more wholesome than I am.

She stands there close to him, they look like they're having a serious conversation — weird that she's not with BJ.

I look around the club, spot him on the side frowning as he watches her and his brother, drink in hand.

I don't want to feel it, but I do. This fucking strange camaraderie between us. He's a little prick in so many ways, but he's sitting there watching her how I'd watch her if I could. This frown that tells me something's amiss.

"Oi." I sit down next to him. Haven't spoken since we had that punch up.

He eyes me a bit suspicious for a couple of seconds but then lifts his eyebrows.

"Hey." Bit unenthusiastic, but I won't take it personally.

We stare over at each other, say nothing about the shit that happened before, what would I say? 'You're a fuck up, I'm a fuck up and we're both in love with the same girl?'

I reckon he already knows.

"You seen the boys?" he asks instead.

"Yeah—" I nod but not at him. Not meaning to, but I'm just staring over at Magnolia. I look back over at him. "I was with them today."

He nods. "They doing okay?"

I pull a face, give him a bit of a shrug.

"Is she?" he asks, frowning. "Barnsey, I mean."

I shake my head. "No, not really—"

Ballentine shakes his head, looking annoyed.

"Fuck." He sighs. "He's being weird, like— I can help, I could—"
His voice trails. Because what could he do? He's not a doctor, he's not
a detective, he's not one of us.

His intentions are good but his hands are tied.

I give him a weak shrug.

"Gang lord shit?" he asks, looking over at me.

I give him a quick nod. "Something like that."

I look over at Magnolia, nod my chin in her direction. "What's
happening there?"

"Oh—" He frowns a bit. "Nothing. We're just friends, for the
minute."

I pull back a bit, staring over at her. "What?"

He shrugs as he watches her. "Figuring shit out."

I stare over at her and it rattles me a bit, makes me swallow heavy
watching her bring up that champagne glass to her lips, toss her hair
over her shoulders, talk too much with her hands — I miss everything about her. I thought I'd be fucking over it by now but I'm not,
I'm so under it I'm sub-fucking-terranean.

Bit pissed about it, really. I glance over at Ballentine. Feels like he
looked a gift horse in the mouth — I handed her back to you on a
silver platter and you're figuring shit out? What shit? She's it.

That's all that matters: her. So fuck him. He's a fucking idiot who
grew up with everything handed to him so all he wants with her is
the chase but I just want her.

I stand up, not taking my eyes off her. "I'll catch you in a bit,
yeah?"

Don't wait for him to respond, don't know whether he's watching
me or not — I don't care.

And then I walk over.

"Hen—" I nod at him first.

Henry reaches past her to smack me in the arm.

"Give us a minute?" I say it like a question but really I'm telling
him.

He flicks his eyes over at her and she gives him a subtle nod and I
wait til he's out of earshot before I duck so I catch her eye.

"Alright — what the fuck is going on with you two?"

She purses her mouth.

"You know what they say — strike while the iron is… tepid."

I roll my eyes.

414

"We're figuring it out." She shrugs.

I give her a look and clock Ballentine over on the couch — he's watching on. Not impressed.

Don't really care. I want her back.

"Figuring it out?" I blink. "He just told me you're just friends—"

That hits her hard, sort of how I hoped it might. She breathes out her nose. "That's a loose term—"

I lean in towards her, close as I can, my mouth right up against her ear.

"Oi, listen, I didn't stop having the best sex of my life so you could go off and be friends with Ballentine—" She rolls her eyes like I'm being annoying, but I give her a look. Want to make sure she knows I'm serious. "You deserve more, Magnolia."

"Julian—" She sighs, looking frustrated. "What are you doing?"

"Nothing—" I shrug.

"You don't like me like that, remember?" She touches her chest. "You never have. 'Relieved to be rid of me', were your exact words." I reckon I see some hurt dance across that face of hers. "I love him... I think I've done a bad job of showing him that."

I know the feeling, Parks. Duck again so I can catch those eyes of hers that keep falling. "And him you."

She looks up at me, eyes all heavy.

I shake my head at her, give her a tight smile. "That stupid face you got — who's not with you if they have the chance?"

She rolls her eyes like I'm just trying to flatter her so I catch her eye again, hold it steady. "I'm serious, Tiges. What's he playing at?"

That looks like it hits her square in the chest because her gaze falls. "I don't know."

Feel angry that he's making her feel like that. "Is he cocking around?"

She glares up at me. "No—"

"How do you know?"

"He's just not—" She takes a staggered breath. "I know he's not."

I sniff a laugh and I lean back in close towards her. "Tiges, I know he makes you go starry-eyed and shit, but honestly, if he loves you how he says he does, why the fuck isn't he with you?" I shrug once.

Licks her bottom lip, looks like she might cry — shit — and then she pushes past me and walks back towards the office.

I'd follow her but BJ's already on his feet, glaring at me as he jogs after her.

I go sit down next to Henry, he peers over at me, eyebrow cocked.

"What are you playing at?"

I shrug. "Not playing at anything—"

"Bullshit you aren't." He shakes his head.

"Do you know who you're talking to?"

"Yeah, I do and I don't give a shit." He looks away, bored. Usually someone saying that would annoy me enough to fuck them up, but from him I don't mind it. Kind of funny, actually.

"How's it going with you and Taura, then?" I ask, happy to change the subject.

"Yeah, fine." He shrugs. "Better, maybe. Or worse?"

That's a bit shit. If things are going better for Henry, they're going worse for Jonah.

"She with him?"

Henry shakes his head. "She's on her way here now — I think she tried to visit, but—" He shrugs.

I frown for him. "Any end in sight?"

He shakes his head, breathes out. "I thought for a minute, yeah — but now with all this shit with Barnsey — I don't know. And that's if it's me, it might not be me." He shrugs.

"I thinks it's you, for what it's worth." I tell him without looking at him. "Reckon Jo knows it too, just hard to admit, you know?"

Henry sighs and then I spot Taura. Nudge him and point and he flashes me a smile, but the smile looks tired. Either way, he gets up and goes to her.

Wonder what Magnolia and BJ are doing in that office. It's been a while. I know what I'd be doing with her in that office, what I've already done with her in that office a hundred times before.

The thought makes me feel like shit so I look around the room, trying to work out who I'll take home instead, and then out of the corner of my eye I see a pink flash moving quickly through the club towards the exit and then I'm on my feet chasing after her.

Catch her halfway down the stairwell.

Grab her by the wrist and spin her around to face me.

"What happened?" I duck so I can see her face.

Crying.

I breathe out of my nose, annoyed. "Want me to fuck him up?"

"No." She shakes her head.

"Where are you going?"

She sniffs, wipes her nose with her sleeve.

"Can I give you a ride?" I offer.

She nods, staring up at me, and I wipe her face with my thumbs.

"What did he say to you?" I ask, tilting her chin up towards me.

"Nothing—" she lies, looks away.

I hook my arm around her and pull her down the stairs, looking back to make sure Koa's following.

"Where am I taking you?" I ask her.

"Home, Julian—" She glares up at me.

"Okay—" I shrug as I open my car door, help her in. She climbs in, I watch her arse as she does. Spectacular arse. Climb in after her.

"You know, you wouldn't be doing anything wrong if you didn't go home—"

She stares over at me from the other side of the car.

"Yes—" she says quietly but gives me a firm nod. "I would."

Tilt my head at her. "Not technically..."

She looks out the window. "Just in all the ways that matter."

"Come on—" I grab her wrist again, pull her over so she's sitting by me. "You're saying you don't want to fuck me as a fuck you?"

She stares up at me, she thinks about it, I can tell she thinks about it. And then she shakes her head.

"Please just take me home."

You good

Yeah

Actually?

No

Want me to come back?

Julian

What

What are you doing

I hate it when you're sad

I'm fine

You're not, but alright

Call me tomorrow?

Maybe.

I'll call you tomorrow.

I will answer you tomorrow.

X

X

65

Christian

Watching my dad unpack decade-and-a-half-old grief with his unconscious wife, not knowing shit about her, not knowing shit about us, all of it written on his face like regret, plain for all to see.

I don't want to be like that. I don't want to be nearly fifty and look back over my life and feel like my dad looks now.

Everything that's happened, these last few days — I'm reconsidering a lot.

I've made a lot of mistakes. I've fucked up, I've hurt people. I've killed people, I can have a temper, I can be petty.

And through it all, I know what I want now.

Mum used to say to me — when you pick who you want to be with, you have to imagine every part of life, every scenario. Good, bad, happy, sad, painful, beautiful — not just the person you want to do road trips with, but the person you want to be stuck in gridlock traffic with. Not just the person you want to have babies with, but the person you want to grieve with, the person you want next to you on the worst day of your life, at the funeral of someone you love, who's next to you? Who do you go home to? You don't need a fair-weather lover, you need the person that's going to stand next to you in their wellies, staring down the barrel of the storm.

It's Daisy.

I know it's Daisy.

If what's happened to Mum has taught me anything, it's that everything's fleeting and nothing's for sure. We have the moments we have in front of us, and then they're gone.

My dad had my mum in front of him for fifteen years, fifteen years she needed him, fifteen years he ignored her to sit in his sadness by himself, and for what? To fall back in love with her three weeks before she falls into a coma?

I stand in the doorway of the hospital room watching Daisy. She's sitting next to my mum, reading to her.

"Hey."

"Hi." She looks up at me from her book. Dog ears the page and rests it on her lap.

I nod my chin over at her. "What are you reading?"

She flashes me the book. *Bradley's Neurology in Clinical Practice.*

I sniff a laugh. "Just some light reading…"

Daisy shrugs. "We're at the part about Sexual Dysfunction in Degenerative and Spinal Cord Disorders, so it's getting spicy…"

I lick my bottom lip and nod once.

I grab a chair, pull it over next to her. "I've been doing some thinking…"

She nods, frowning a little. "Yeah?"

"Um—" I breathe out my nose, shake my head. "You asked me something a year go — about running away with you, do you remember?"

Daisy stares at me a bit nervous but nods again.

"I've regretted it ever since," I tell her. "Literally ever since."

Her face falters.

I give her a small smile. "I'm in."

"What?" She blinks, face confused.

"I'm in, Dais." I shrug. "I want out of this, and I want you, so I'm in — when Mum wakes up and she's good, wherever you want to go, I'm there. Let's do it."

"Really?"

I nod. "Really."

She stares at me for a couple of seconds, like she's thinking it all over, processing everything she's heard, and then she grins, tossing her arms around my neck and kissing me.

I smile down at her, happy she's so happy and then her face pulls in thought.

"How will I leave Julian?"

"We'll visit—" I shrug. "It's not the same as before, we'll be leaving on good terms, living somewhere fun and exciting and—"

"I like Canada."

I give her a look. "I don't think that's fun or exciting…"

She frowns. "You said wherever I want."

"I mean—" I give her a look. "Within reason."

"Nova Scotia's not within reason?"

I shake my head.

"Oh." She frowns. "Vienna's quite beautiful."

"It is." I nod.

"I like Hawaii too."

"Me too," I tell her.

She beams up at me again but picks her nail, absentmindedly.

"What?" I frown.

"I'll be nervous to tell Julian."

I pull her onto my lap.

"Yeah, that's fair." Kiss the top of her head. "We'll tell him together when the time comes."

She nods, taking my hand in hers.

"I don't care where we go, Dais—" Push some hair behind her ear. "It doesn't matter to me. Us together, that's the part that matters from now on."

66

Julian

I sit down in my office chair, kind of feel good I planted the right seeds in Mangolia's head which is all I wanted to do. Just to be on her mind how she's still on mine. I called her like I said I would. Asked her if she wanted to get something to eat and she said she was heading off soon to pick up her sister from somewhere.

Better Bridge than Ballentine.

I think I was overreacting before, just got in my head about it because I love her and I've never loved someone before. Not like that anyway.

And then she was there and fucking Brown was trying to make benign threats against her — I can get rid of him. If he ever looks at Magnolia or my sister sideways again, I'll kill him on the spot. But I think pulling the plug with her was stupid. I think there's something there.

I think she's wading through her own shit with Ballentine, there's enough of it there, it might take a while, but I reckon we could get there, me and her.

It's what I want.

Kekoa wanders in to my office and tosses today's paper down on my desk.

He reclines back on the sofa next to Declan who's playing FIFA on the Xbox.

"You okay after the other night?" Kekoa asks, picking up the other controller and joining him.

I frown over at him. "What other night?"

Koa shrugs. "Reckon I could count on one hand the amount of times you've swung a miss—"

I toss him a dirty look. "I didn't swing a miss."

"Oh, so that's her upstairs in your bed, then?" he shoots and I ignore that comment. Read my paper. But if we're keeping track (and we aren't't), no, it isn't.

"Does she know you've turned into a raging slut?" Declan asks as he shoots a goal.

"Turned into?" Koa repeats. "Always been."

I breathe out my nose, ignoring them.

"She'll come around," I say but not really to either of them. Maybe a bit to myself. "Just needs a minute."

Koa stares over at me. Nods a bit like he doesn't buy it. And maybe he's right, maybe she needs more than a minute but also maybe she's forgotten that we were fucking spectacular together, and we weren't even together. We made sense. I love how I felt when I was with her, I love who she makes me be, how she makes me feel. I hate anyone else in my bed now. That girl upstairs? She can fuck off. There's no post-have infatuation. Not that that's what Magnolia turned out to be in the end, just a slow-motion falling in love. Or maybe it was all at once and I didn't know it. Different feeling, loving a girl to a painting, so it turns out.

I look out over the top of my paper and spot flowers in a vase on the corner of my desk.

"Ey, these are nice—" I nod at them. "Where'd they come from?"

Declan shrugs.

Koa glances over, disinterested. "I don't know."

I pull it over towards me. It's a nice vase, actually. I flick it with my finger. Glass. The Ronsard Opalescent glass vase. White. Double handles. Mid 1920s.

"Is this one of mine?" I ask as I check underneath it.

Koa shrugs again.

"I like Rene Lalique's shit," I tell them as I look over it.

"Gift maybe?" Declan says, then swears at the screen when Koa gets the ball off him.

I lift my eyebrows, thinking about it. "From who?"

He shrugs.

"Daisy?" He offers. "Did your Lalique break?"

I look over at him. I guess it did, yeah. Can't imagine my sister rewarding me for that specific breakage by buying me a different one.

I lean in, take a sniff.

I point to the flowers. "What are those?"

"Don't know." Kekoa looks over at them. "Lilies, I think."

I nod. "Smell good."

Pretty too.

Decks looks over after a couple of seconds, scratches the back of his neck and squints.

"Nah — they're magnolias," Decks says.

"Oh." I nod.

I stare at them for a couple of seconds, thinking it's funny. Fortuitous timing almost, like it's a sign.

It is a sign but it takes me a second for it to land.

Kekoa's head snaps in my direction the same time I jump to my feet.

"Shit—" He drops the controller and runs over. "Is there a note?" He rifles through the flowers and I throw open my computer. Pull up the tracker I hid in her wallet. Size of a pin's head. Don't give me that look — it's obviously necessary. Case in point right now.

"She's by Kennington Park—" I tell them.

I scramble around my desk, grab my keys, Koa running after me.

I run to my car and drop the keys when I get to the door, pick them up again but I'm shaking.

"Give them to me." Kekoa holds his hand out. "I'll drive."

I don't give them to him and he takes them from me anyway.

Opens the car door, shoves me inside and I climb over to the passenger side.

He's pulling out of the driveway before he even closes the door.

"Jules, it could be nothing," he tells me but I know it's a lie because he's driving like a fucking maniac. Weaving in and out of cars like a Formula One racer.

"Call her—" he tells me.

I pull out my phone. Dial her.

Bang my fist a thousand times on the dash as I wait for her to answer but she doesn't.

"Could just be flowers, man—"

I look over at him, my whole face pulled tight. "Someone just sends me some fucking magnolias out of the blue—"

"Maybe?" He shrugs, weakly, grips that wheel tight and accelerates.

I try her again.

"Pick up," I say under my breath. "Pick up, fucking pick up—"

I let out a frustrated sound under my breath and feel sick head to toe. Never felt sick in my toes before but I do now, this sharp feeling, like the edge of pain spreading through me as my mind begins to do the math on how much it really costs to be loved by me.

"Where is she?" Koa asks.

"Heading up Harleyford Road towards Vauxhall."

He nods, accelerates then looks over at me. "Do you have a plan here?"

I shake my head. "Grab her? Take her back to the Compound?"

"How's that going to fly with the boyfriend?"

I shake my head at him. "I don't fucking give a shit!"

We pull on to Vauxhall Bridge.

Call her again and fucking finally — Bridget answers.

"Oh, hello!" she sings. "We were just talking about you!"

"Magnolia—" I say, urgent. "Are you with her? Where are you?"

"What?" Bridget laughs, not sensing the tone.

"Put her on." I tell her.

"She's driving—" Bridget says.

"Where are you — what car are you in?" I ask her, looking around the bridge. It says they're on here somewhere.

"What? Sorry, I can't hear you—" She frowns and it's then I spot them driving the other way. White Aston Martin DBS Superleggera.

Spot them the same time a car slams into her from behind, spinning her onto the other side of the road and Kekoa slams the breaks.

Have you ever seen the person you love be hit by a car just because they love you?

Two cars, actually. Because as I reach for my seatbelt to get out and to her, another car t-bones her.

Love is wild, isn't it? It makes a life so much more valuable... not just to me but to my enemies. No one was trying to kill Magnolia Parks until I loved her.

And I know this is them. They're hit cars.

Black, plain, unnoticeable, no plates.

I barrel out of the car and I'm calling her name — sounds far away, though — I'm yelling for her, running towards her, feels like one of those dream runs. Like your feet are buried in sand and you can't get to where you're trying to go—

Koa grabs me by the shoulders. "We have to go."

I throw him out of the way and keep running to her but he pushes me backwards.

"We have to go now!"

"I have to help her—"

He gestures to the car wreck. "You can't!"

"I have to!" I push past him and he shoves me backwards, plants himself hard on the ground.

"Listen to me—" He grabs me by the shoulders. "You can't."

"I love her!"

"I know," he nods, measured, staring at me. "But Daisy. We have to get to Daisy—"

My chest starts heaving as I try to see past the growing crowd of people who are trying to help her.

"But what if she's—"

I can't see anything. The car's flipped, that's all I can see.

The black cars are gone now — I don't know where they went, I lost them, I should have been paying more attention but I lost them the way I think I'm losing her.

I shove Kekoa off me but he grabs me.

"Julian, we don't know if she's—" He shakes his head and pushes me back towards the car. He opens the door, puts me in the seat.

"I'm sorry—" He shakes his head. "We have to get to Dais."

67

Daisy

Barnsey's still under and we've barely left her side.

Jud literally hasn't left her side. Christian and him still aren't talking, they move around the room, avoiding each other, not meeting one another's eyes.

I go home sometimes, cook things to bring up to him. Make sure my boyfriend sleeps some, but he doesn't go too far.

He finds a spare room on the same floor, sleeps for an hour.

Makes me lie next to him while he does, like he thinks something might go wrong if he's not right by me.

We've been talking about it a lot, where we'll go after this is all over.

He wants somewhere warm, I want somewhere cold.

He's eyeing one of the Hawaiian islands, maybe Bali or Mauritius. I'm really pushing for the Lake District of Marlborough[260] or L'Isle sur la Sorgue[261] or Magdalen Islands or the Thousand Islands in Canada.

Thermostatically, we're envisioning different things, but the part I really care about is that he's envisioning it with me.

I have this nervous feeling about telling my brother.

I won't do it for a while. I'd be worried about leaving him. I think he'd be lonely. Especially now that he's fallen in love and, I mean, you know how loving someone and having them and then losing them — it leaves you different. It leaves you a different kind of empty.

Everything about my brother right now, it feels like he's that kind of empty.

So leaving him here feels selfish.

---

[260] In New Zealand.
[261] In Provence, France.

I wanted so badly to leave all this last year. That normal life I was chasing that I so very briefly had, it wasn't all it was cracked up to be.

Or maybe it was, it was just missing the ingredients that make life truly, properly good. Any life without Christian and my brother was always going to be running at a loss, and I feel this tension start to rise in me about how maybe one day I'll have to choose. Between wanting normalcy and wanting a relationship with my brother.

I squeeze Christian tighter as he sleeps because I feel anxious about it and he opens one eye.

"You good?"

I nod. "Fine, yeah."

My phone rings and I sit up to answer it.

Romeo. He's still staying at our place but because of all this, I haven't seen much of him. We're doing okay though. It's not strange or uncomfortable. Christian's not being weird, though Christian's also been distracted, so.

I answer it. "Hey."

"Hey," he says, voice sounding strained.

"Are you okay?" I straighten up.

"Yeah, yeah — hey, where are you?" Rome asks.

"Weymouth Street." I frown. "Why?"

"Oh — no, I know. I mean — can I meet you there?"

"What?" I frown. He's not really meant to be leaving the house.

"I just have to drop you something?"

"What?"

"Just can you meet me downstairs in ten?"

"Rome—" I shake my head.

"Dais—" he says, impatient. "Just fucking meet me downstairs in ten."

Then he hangs up and I sigh.

"Hey?" Christian pulls me up towards him. "What was that?"

"I don't know—" I shrug. "Romeo needs to drop me something."

"Oh." He shrugs.

I roll in towards him. "What did the doctor say about your mum this morning?"

"Stable." He nods. "But nothing new."

I touch his face. "Are you feeling okay?"

"Yeah, I guess." He flashes me a smile. "Good as I can be, all things considered."

"Good." I lean in to kiss him. It's quick. A mindless brush over the lips. I push back and jump to my feet. "I'm going to go grab this from Rome."

"Want me to come?"

I shake my head. "You rest, I'll just be a minute."

I go stand on the street corner of Weymouth and Beaumont and wait for Rome. It's a nice day. Springtime in London, there's always some charm to it but today the sky's extra blue, perfect fluffy clouds. Conspiratorial, really.

After a few minutes one of our cars pull up, the door swings open and Romeo climbs out.

He looks sort of stressed. Thrown together, disheveled. White t-shirt, baggy jeans, red shirt undone and over it.

Something on his face, it makes me feel nervous.

Romeo Bambrilla and I, we've known each other since day dot. We grew up side by side, we've watched each other fall,[262] we've watched each other grow. I know how he looks when he's angry, I know how he looks when he's happy, when he's feeling himself, when he's feeling me, when he's excited, when he's afraid—

And his face right now, here in front of me — I don't know. I can't place it.

"Hey—" I frown. "Are you okay?"

He nods behind him. "I need you to get in the car, Dais."

I scrunch up my nose, confused. "What?"

"We've got to go—" He reaches for my wrist.

I step back from him. "Where?"

"Daisy — I need you to get in the fucking car—"

"No—" I shake my head.

"Now, Daisy—" He reaches for me.

"Romeo, no—" I smack him off and then what happens next, I'm not expecting.

Miguel comes up from behind me — I didn't realise he'd followed me down — grabs me from behind and lifts me up off the ground, carrying me into the car.

I start bucking and screaming in their arms, kicking and swinging and trying to get free but the two of them are stronger than I am.

---

[262] In more ways than one.

And it's right then that Christian appears at the front door of the hospital. He looks down the street towards me—

"Christian!" I yell for him and he breaks into a run right as Miguel hurls me into the backseat of the car. Rome climbs in after me and they slam the door.

Christian's banging on the glass and I'm banging on the window back and when did my screaming become crying?

I press my nose up against the window and Christian's trying to punch through the glass. I watch him break at least two fingers and probably a knuckle and it doesn't slow him down an inch. His eyes are blurry and red and I watch him as it all falls to some slow kind of motion... The car is pulling out into the busy London street and I keep my eyes on him the whole time and him on me and there's so much I should have told him. So much. But it all boils down to this:

I love him. He's all I want. He's all I think about. Everything I didn't want or believe about love, I want and believe in it with him. And loving him has undone me wide open. But if time has taught me anything it's that loving anyone when my brother is who he is, is a mistake.

Christian gets smaller and smaller and I press my face harder and harder against the glass that separates us, and I've never seen him cry like this before, not even with his mum, but fuck, he's a mess and my heart breaks more seeing him all shattered like this because loving me does this to people.

I lose everyone. Everyone, all the time.

I lose people like a tree loses its leaves in autumn. I'm marred by it. It's the thing that's shaped me most... My distinctive characteristic... Some people have freckles sprinkled on their noses, other people have eyes clear like water, or hair that's the colour of the night, but me?

My unique feature is that I lose everyone, and everyone loses me.

68

Christian

I throw up as soon as I lose sight of the car and then I turn and run as fast as I can back into the hospital.

People are staring but fuck them all because they didn't help the screaming girl before she was grabbed and shoved into a car.

I hit the elevator up button but it takes too long so I run up the stairs.

Just to the third floor and feels like it took me just two steps to get there.

I barrel down the hall, run to my mum's room.

"Jonah—" I lean against the door to steady myself — am I going to throw up again? Holy shit.

"Woah—" Jonah steps towards me, eyes wide. "Whats going on?"

I pull him out into the hallway and Dad sits up straighter, looking over, wondering what's happened.

"They took Daisy," I tell him, shaking my head. "I need your help — they took Daisy."

"Who?" he asks, surprisingly measured.

"Miguel—" I shake my head. It doesn't make sense. "And Romeo — they grabbed her, threw her into a car — and Jo, she didn't want to go—" I shake my head. "She was screaming, trying to get away from them—"

Away from them and back to me and I couldn't get to her.

"Ey—" He pulls me further away from the room, down the hall, a bit away from all the people.

I frown at him — he seems unreasonably calm.

"I need you to listen to me, okay — you're listening, yeah?" He stares at me, face serious in a way I don't think I've ever seen it. He swallows heavy, breathes out his nose.

"Magnolia was in a car accident."

My head pulls back, confused. "When?"

"About an hour ago—"

"What?" I shake my head.

Jonah's face pulls and his eyes go glassy. He blinks it all back. Breathes through his nose twice. "It was a hit, Christian."

I stare over at him in disbelief. "Bullshit."

He wipes his nose. "Julian found a bunch of magnolias delivered to his desk like—"

My heart drops in my chest.

"The daisies." Fuck. "Is Magnolia okay?"

He shakes his head. "Still in surgery."

I rub my hand over my mouth and stare over at my brother, wonder if I'm going to be sick again. What the fuck?

"Daisy—" I shake my head, feel lightheaded, if I'm honest. "I need to get to her—"

I push my hands through my hair, check my watch like the time's going to tell me anything.

I look at my brother. "Where are they taking her?"

Jonah shakes his head. "No, you're not understanding, Christian—"

I give him a look. "Not understanding what?"

Jonah's eyes go heavy and sorry.

"I don't know where they're going—" He shakes his head. "They're fleeing the country."

I stare over at him.

"What?"

"It's not safe for her here—" Jo starts and I shove him hard as I can, point my finger in his face.

"I swear to God, you tell me where they're taking her or I'll kill you right now."

Jonah shoves me off him and I shove him back harder.

"Tell me—" I shove him again.

"Christian, I don't know."

And then I pull my gun out, press it against his chest. "How 'bout now, do you know now?"

"What the fuck are you doing?" my brother yells.

"Tell me where they took her!" I yell and my eyes are white. "Now, Jonah!"

"Why!" he bellows. "What's you knowing going to do — you can't go after her—"

"Yes I can—" I tell him, press the gun deeper into him.

"Yeah, and have the people after her follow you right to her? No — you can't know, man—"

"Christian—" my dad says from the side. "Give me the gun."

I'm crying now. I didn't know I was before — maybe I had been — crying again now, though.

Reluctantly I pull the gun away from my brother's chest and drop it into my dad's hands. He opens the magazine, pockets the bullets, pockets the gun.

Then he grabs me, pulls me in to him, and I lose my fucking shit. Cry like I never have before in my life.

Because I'm afraid of all of it, of what it means, of where she's going, how long she'll be gone, what I'll look like without her — how can I have lost her again when I've just gotten her back?

69

Daisy

I was hysterical for the first part of that drive. Worked myself into a panic attack about half way, and Rome would try to help me, try to get my breathing to go right but I'd just kick him away.[263]

I was shaking from the adrenaline at first and then nothing.

I fell to quiet, stared out the window as we drove further and further up the M11 and I didn't know where we were going, but I had a guess.

There's an old airstrip my dad built in the '80s out by Clavering. No one knows about it. It's on a farm. The boys use it sometimes to smuggle things in and out.

I have a feeling I'm the thing that's being smuggled out.

Romeo stares over at me, tired and wounded like I've hurt him. Like, whatever the fuck is happening to me right now is hard for him.

Gives me a dirty look from the other side of the car.

"You think I'd ever let anyone hurt you?"

His jaw juts out and he looks away like I'm the traitor here.

No word from my brother. That feels strange. I guess all of this is strange, though.

We roll into the farm, lights off, everything's quiet. The car stops and I make a plan in my head. I've been here a few times before. There's another farm about a mile away. They don't do what we do, they're just nice, normal people, uncompromised by crime and my brother — I'll run to them.

Miguel opens the car door, offers me his hand to help me out and I — forgive me, Miguel — front kick him. Catches him off-guard enough that he falls backwards onto the ground and then I fucking leg it.

---

[263] He's a traitor.

Run as fast as I can.

It's dark, I'm in stupid shoes. They're trainers but they're not made for running, those stupid Golden Goose shoes, what are they good for? They arrive tattered, they don't make you faster—

"Daisy!" Romeo calls for me in a whisper, running after me.

He's close.

It's not fair, it's always been like this. He's faster than me, and I'm fast. I'm faster than everyone else except for Romeo. He's always been better than me at running. I used to cry about it when we were kids because no matter how hard I tried, I couldn't win with him and my dad used to sit me on his knee and say, "Faster is faster, Daisy. The only way to beat him is to beat him."

But I never beat him, not then, not now.

He gets out in front of me and shoves me backwards onto the ground, throwing himself down on top of me. We have a full-on physical altercation.[264] I knee him in the groin, wrap my legs around his neck, try to choke him but he just shrugs me off, throws me backwards back on to the ground and then pins me there.

"Fucking stop—" he growls. "We don't have time for this — get up!"

He tries to pull me up off the ground but I kick him again and that's enough for him — he gets angry with me in a way he never does.

"Don't test me, Dais," he says, shoving my shoulders down into the dirt. I stare up at him, eyes wet, face a bit muddy now from the combination of the crying and the fighting, and Romeo throws me over his shoulder and carries me back. Past the car, into a barn where there's a little jet.

As soon as I see the plane I'm crying again, crying and trying to fight him off and he ignores me, carries me on to it anyway. Miguel follows us on, closes the door behind us and then he runs to the cockpit.

Romeo dumps me onto the floor of the plane and then retreats to the back of it like a wounded animal. I jump to my feet, I want to fight him again, get the fuck off this thing — I don't care what I have to do, I have to get off it and get back to Christian.

And then I see him, slumped in a window seat, staring out of it.

---

[264] It's fairly one-sided, if I'm honest.

I watch my brother for a few seconds and I don't know — I've never seen him like this — I don't even know what this is.

"Julian?" I say quietly because I can't help it.

He turns and looks over at me like he's just noticed me.

Blinks twice.

His eyes are red.

I've never seen him cry before, not even with our parents.

And then I don't know, call it instinct, call it family, call him every fucking curse word under the sun, call him my best friend on the planet — I run to him, drop to my knees in front of him. Hold his face with my hand.

"Julian, what happened?"

His breathing is deep and slow. His eyes are blinking slowly.

"They had to give him something," Romeo says as the propellers start up.

"For what?" I look from him back to my brother.

Romeo shrugs. "He was a mess."

I frown at him for that non-answer.

"Julian—" I touch his hand with mine and he stares at it as I do. "What happened?"

"They put a hit out on Magnolia." He blinks.

My face goes slack. "What? No."

"They got her." He breathes out. "They t-boned her on Vauxhall Bridge. I saw it…" His eyes are blurry. "I tried to get to her—" He shakes his head.

"No—" I shake my head. "No, why would they—?"

"Because of me," he says as the plane pulls out of the barn.

I feel winded.[265]

"Did she—" Oh my God. "I mean, is she okay?"

Julian shakes his head and looks out the window. "I don't know."

I sit down next to my brother, rest my head against his arm.

"Where are we going?" I ask, wipe my nose with my hand.

He puts his head on top of mine and stares straight ahead.

"Away, Dais."

---

[265] I hate this life.

Thank Yous

This book has been a blur. I don't even really remember writing it, but it appears I have and here we are.

To my usuals:

Madie Conn and Molly Lee. Thank you for allowing me to pester you constantly about this just because you love me. As always, this book wouldn't be here without you.

Amanda George, thank you for how much you've done and carried for me with the MPU. I'm so grateful for you, thank you for loving these characters (arguably) an insane amount. They love you back.

Avenir Creative House and in particular Luke Hastings and Jay Argaet, my brothers and friends who have helped roll out my vision for this series with such a sweet understanding of me as a person and a creative, and then executing everything with such a vision. So grateful to be doing this with you.

And to Maddi Hewit, you are always my #1 hype girl, and I love getting to do this with you. Thank you.

Benjamin William Hastings, for giving me so much room in our lives to do what I do.

Juniper and Bellamy, for being the most brilliant, exhausting, consistent things in my life.

Ash and Camryn, you are my village here. Thank you.

Emily, for always saying everything I send you is the best thing you've ever read with such fervour that I believe you.

Then to Celia and all the rest of my new Orion family — thank you for working with me on this insane timeline, I know getting here has been a mad dash but I appreciate so much your hard work and your excitement for the series. I cannot wait to do this with you all. It's going to be fun.

And lastly, thank you to you, maybe — if you're one of the people who loved Daisy and Magnolia in such an unbelievable way this last year — my god, you changed my life. You gave me a path when no one else would just by simply liking the imaginary friends who live in my brain.

Thank you.

About the author

Jessa Hastings is an Australian-native who now lives in Southern California with her husband, two children, her cat and a dog that she previously semi-regretted getting after several incidents of said dog intentionally urinating on her son's favourite firehouse toy, but thankfully the regret has dissipated, as has the urine.

She's a chronic over-thinker, an aspiring water-connoisseur and is going through a real soup phase. She finds Twitter and small talk equally terrifying, and still often pines for an Australian breakfast and a sourdough loaf in America that doesn't make her want to impale herself with a rusty fork. *Magnolia Parks* was her debut novel and the launch of the series and she still (obviously) struggles to write a concise or topically relevant author biography. She is sorry for this.